W9-CBJ-755

HOLY
WARRIOR

ALSO BY

ANGUS DONALD

Outlaw

HOLY WARRIOR

Angus Donald

St. Martin's Griffin
New York

HOLY WARRIOR. Copyright © 2010 by Angus Donald. All rights reserved. Printed in the United States of America. For information, address St. Martin's Press, 175 Fifth Avenue, New York, N.Y. 10010.

www.stmartins.com

Book design by Omar Chapa

Library of Congress Cataloging-in-Publication Data

Donald, Angus, 1965–
    Holy warrior: a novel of Robin Hood / Angus Donald.—1st ed.
        p. cm.

ISBN 978-0-312-67837-1 (trade paperback)
ISBN 978-0-312-60436-3 (hardcover)
    1. Robin Hood (Legendary character)—Fiction.   2. Crusades—Third, 1189–1192—Fiction.   3. Great Britain—History—Richard I, 1189–1199—Fiction.

PR6104.O535 H65 2011
823'.92—dc22

2011020534

First published in Great Britain by Sphere, an imprint of
Little, Brown Book Group, an Hachette UK Company.

First U.S. Edition: August 2011

10   9   8   7   6   5   4   3   2   1

For my wonderful parents, Janet and Alan Donald;
thank you for everything

Battle of Arsuf
7th September 1191

Mediterranean Sea

Third Division

Hospitallers

Baggage train

French

Second Division

Flemings

Robin's men

King Richard

Normans & English

First Division

Bretons

Angevins

Poitevins

Templars

0 100 200 yards

Nubians

Light Cavalry

Berber Lancers

Sultan's bodyguard Saladin

Cavalry Reserve

Nubians

Light Cavalry

Marshy ground

1. The Hospitallers and the French knights of the Third Division attack.
2. Robin's men and the Flemings support the Hospitallers' attack. The Templars attack Saladin's left wing.
3. Robin gathers the survivors of the Hospitallers' charge and attacks main body of the enemy on their right.
4. King Richard leads the Norman and English knights to victory with a frontal assault on Saladin's Army.

Town of Arsuf
2 miles

PART ONE

ENGLAND

CHAPTER ONE

I hesitated long before beginning this labor, and had resolutely made up my mind never to set down on parchment this part of my early life, until I heard a man in an alehouse in Nottingham the other day, a professional storyweaver, and a good one, extol the virtues of lionhearted King Richard and his brave warriors who made the Great Pilgrimage to the Holy Land more than forty years ago. The man described the magnificent killing skills of the steel-wrapped Christian knights, and the deathless glory that they won against the Saracens at Acre and Arsuf; he spoke of the certain rewards in Heaven for those who fell in such a noble cause, and the rich rewards on Earth, in plunder and booty, for those who returned . . .

But this eloquent tale-spinner never mentioned the true sights, smells and sounds of a battlefield after a great victory—

the ones that stay with you and plague your dreams. He did not speak of the corpses, thousands of them, chalk-faced and staring, stiffened by death and heaped like cut logs one on top of the other; nor the belly-slashed horses, stepping in their own entrails, eyes rolling, trembling and whinnying with fear; nor the iron-meat stench of fresh blood and spattered shit, an odor that coats the back of your throat and will not easily be washed away; nor the drone of a hundred thousand gore-glutted flies; nor the ceaseless, hopeless shrieking of the badly wounded that makes you yearn to stuff your ears against their pain.

He did not speak of the horror of killing a man close to; the wild kick of his death-writhe against your body, the stench of his onion breath on your cheek; the hot blood washing over your hand as you work the blade deeper into his flesh. And the sick dizziness and relief you feel when the deed is done and the man lies by your boots, suddenly no more than a loose bag of bones and meat.

The storyteller did not lie—and yet he did not tell the truth. And when I saw the eyes of the young men in that tavern shining in the firelight as they listened to his stories of bold Christian heroes carving their way through the ranks of cowardly unbelievers, I knew that I must set down the true events of that great endeavor four decades past, the true courses of those far-off battles, as I saw them with my own youthful eyes.

This is not a tale of bold heroes and everlasting glory, it is a tale of useless slaughter and lakes of innocent blood; a tale of greed, cruelty and hatred—and of love; it is also a tale of loyalty and friendship and forgiveness. Most of all it is the tale of my master Robert Odo, the great Earl of Locksley, the man once known throughout the land as Robin Hood—a cunning thief, an ice-hearted murderer and, God forgive me, for many years my good friend.

As I inscribe this story of my long-ago journeying at a writing stand in the great hall at the manor of Westbury, I feel

4

the crushing weight of my years. My legs ache from standing at my sloped lectern for so long. My hands, which grip penknife and quill, are cramped from hours of work. But our merciful Lord has spared me these past fifty-eight years, through much danger, battle and bloodshed, and I have faith that he will give me the strength to complete this task.

Through the wide-open hall door, a light breeze steals in and stirs the rushes on the floor, wafting the warm scents of early autumn to where I scratch away at this parchment: the sun-baked dust of the courtyard outside, cut grass in my drying barns and a tint of sweetness from the fruit that hangs heavy in my orchard.

It has been a fat year for us here at Westbury: a hot summer ripened the crops, and now they are all gathered in, and the granaries are filled to the rafters with sacks of wheat, oats and barley; daily the cows give up their sweet milk, the pigs are gorging on beech mast in the woods, and Marie, my daughter-in-law, who runs this manor for me, is a contented woman. God be praised for His mercy.

In the spring, her cousin Osric, a portly widower of middle years, came here to occupy the position of bailiff, and he brought with him his two strong sons Edmund and Alfred to toil in my fields as waged farmhands. I cannot say that I like Osric: he may be the most upright, honest, hardworking fellow in Christendom, but he is as dull as unsalted spelt bread. Officious, too, when it comes to his dealings with my villeins. And yet, since his arrival at the manor, he has immeasurably transformed my life for the better. What was once a forlorn, untended estate of weed-choked fields and tumbledown buildings is now a bustling place of industry and plenty. He has collected those rents from my tenants that were long overdue; at harvest time he rose before dawn and chivvied into the fields the villeins of Westbury who owed me weekwork, and arranged a modest daily payment for the franklins of the village who did not, but who were prepared to labor on my demesne. He has brought order and prosperity and happiness to the manor—and yet I still cannot like him.

It may be that I do not care for him because he is such an ugly man—round in the middle like a ball, with short arms and stubby fingers, and his face, under a nearly bald scalp, is pinched like a mole's; his nose is too large, his mouth too small, and an expression of worry permanently haunts his tiny eyes—but I prefer to think it is because he has no music in his soul, no wild untamed joy in his heart.

Nevertheless, Osric's coming has been a good thing. Last year, a melancholy air had pervaded the manor. Marie and I were both struggling to find a reason to carry on living after the death from a sickness of my son, her husband Rob. God be praised we have a living memory of him in my grandson and namesake Alan, who will be eight years old this Christmas—a healthy, raucous little boy.

Alan is in thrall to Osric's younger son Alfred. He looks on the young man as a hero, a kind of demigod, and he copies everything the tall farmhand does. Alfred had taken to wearing a band of linen around his brow, to catch the sweat before it dripped into his eyes as he worked his sickle on the standing wheat. And so, of course, little Alan must fashion a similar cloth headband for himself, too. When Alfred let slip that he was fond of buttermilk, Alan began following him around with a pitcher of the liquor in case he might be thirsty. Harmless boyish foolishness, you will say. Possibly, but I have decided that I will soon send Alan away to be educated in accordance with his rank at another manor far away. There, he will learn to ride and fight like a knight, and dance and sing, and write Latin and French: I do not want him growing up to be a field hand. This infatuation with Alfred may well be harmless but I know that blind admiration of an older man by a younger fellow can cause great anger and hurt when the boy discovers that his idol is not the hero that he seems. I had that very experience myself with Robin of Locksley.

My master first appeared to me as a heroic figure: brave, strong and noble—just as Alfred might appear to young Alan—but I remember well the sickening lurch in my belly when I learned that Robin was not so, that he was as grasping and cruel and selfish as any other mortal man.

I know that I am not being just to Robin when I castigate him for being selfish, cruel and greedy: it was I who misunderstood him, not he who deliberately tricked me. But I still feel rancor, and shame, when I remember the good and noble men who died so that Robin might gain riches. But those who read these parchments shall judge for themselves, and in these pages I shall write as truly as I am able about Robin's adventures beyond the sea, and mine, in that hate-ridden land where men butcher each other by the thousands in the name of God, that country of crushing heat and choking dust, of demon scorpions and giant hairy spiders—the place that men call Outremer.

Ghost, my gray gelding, was exhausted and I, too, was weary beyond belief. We had traveled many hundreds of miles together in the past few weeks—to London, Winchester, Nottingham and back—and, as we rode up the steep slope from the valley of the Locksley River in the county of Yorkshire toward the castle high on the hill, I patted his marbled gray neck and murmured a few words of encouragement. "Nearly home, boy, nearly home, and there's a dish of hot oat mash waiting for you." Ghost pricked up his ears at my words, and even seemed to increase his pace a fraction. As we plodded up the endless grassy hill, scattering ewes and their gawky lambs out of our path, I could make out the square shape of the church of St. Nicholas above me and behind it, on the skyline, the high wooden tower and stoutly palisaded courtyard of Kirkton Castle, the fortress of my master, which overlooks the Vale of Locksley. I wallowed in a great sense of homecoming and the warm glow of a task well done. My head was full of good, fresh intelligence; important, dangerous news, and in my saddlebags, wrapped and well-hidden, was a costly gift. I felt like a hunter, returning after a day in the wild with a fine catch: a satisfying blend of fatigue and joy.

It was early spring, in the year of Our Lord 1190, and, it seemed to me on that beautiful day, all was right in the world: noble King Richard, that most Christian warrior, was on the throne of England, the officials he had placed in positions of power were said to be governing wisely, and he himself would soon be setting off on a great and holy adventure to recover Jerusalem, the navel of the world, from the grip of the Saracen hordes, perhaps bringing about the Second Coming of Our Lord Jesus Christ by his actions. All England prayed that he might be successful. Best of all, I had successfully completed one of my first assignments for my master, Robert Odo, the newly created Earl of Locksley, and Lord of Kirkton, Sheffield, Ecclesfield, Hallam, Grimesthorpe and Greasbrough, and dozens of smaller manors across Yorkshire, Nottinghamshire and Derbyshire.

I was Robin's *trouvère*, or personal musician to his court. *Trouvères* were so called because we "found" or composed songs ourselves, not merely repeating other men's verses like a lowly jongleur. But, for Robin, I also acted as his messenger, envoy and, occasionally, spy. And I was glad to do it. I owed everything I had to him. I was a gutter-born peasant with no family, or even a village or town to call my own, and very young then, only fifteen years old—and Robin had granted me the lordship of the small manor of Westbury. I was Alan of Westbury! I was the lord of a manor; this same manor, where, more than forty years later, I now write these words. After the savage battle at Linden Lea the previous year, in which we had defeated the forces of Sir Ralph Murdac, the corrupt High Sheriff of Nottinghamshire, Robin, a notorious fugitive from the law, had been pardoned by King Richard, married his lovely Marie-Anne and been made Earl of Locksley.

All those who had followed him during the dark years of his outlawry had received a reward for their loyalty—a handful of silver, a sturdy ox, or a fine horse—and, in truth, I had expected a gift of some sort too, but I had not expected to be granted a sizeable piece of land.

I was almost speechless with gratitude when Robin showed me the charter, adorned with the great, heavy red disk of his seal, that made me the custodian of this big old hall and its many outbuildings, five hundred acres of prime farmland, a village of twenty-four cottages occupied by a hundred souls, mostly villeins but with a handful of free men, a water mill, a warren, two pair of oxen, a plow and a fine stone church.

"It's a small manor, Alan, not much more than a big farmstead, really; only half a knight's fee. And it's a bit rundown, I'm afraid, but it is good land, I'm told," Robin said.

"But how will I manage the place?" I asked. "I know nothing of making a living from tilling the earth."

"I don't expect you to be a farm worker, Alan," said Robin laughing. "You must find a good man, a steward or bailiff, to do that for you. All you do is receive the rents, and make sure that nobody cheats you. I require you to serve me. But you need an income and some standing in society if you are to represent me, deliver my messages and what-have-you." He smiled, his strange silver eyes flashing at me: "And I am convinced that England has a great and pressing need for more songs about the bold exploits of handsome Robin Hood and his merry men."

He was teasing me, of course. I had composed a few ditties about our days together beyond the law and they had spread like wildfire across the country, being sung in alehouses from Cockermouth to Canterbury—growing farther from the truth with each drunken rendition. Robin did not mind that he was being turned into a legend; he said it amused him—in fact, I believe he relished it. And he was not in the slightest worried about his past crimes being brought to

9

light. He was a great magnate now, untouchable by any mere sheriff and, to boot, he enjoyed the favor and friendship of King Richard. He had won all this in two days of terrible slaughter last year, but there had been a price—above that paid for in the blood of his loyal men. In order to win that battle, Robin had made an unbreakable pact with the Poor Fellow-Soldiers of Christ and of the Temple of Solomon, the famous Templar Knights: in exchange for their support at a crucial moment in the battle, Robin had sworn that he would lead a force of mercenaries, archers and cavalry to the Holy Land, as part of King Richard's pilgrim army. As Robin's *trouvère*, I would be accompanying the Christian force, and I could not wait to set off on what then seemed to me to be the most noble adventure that it was possible to conceive.

I had a message for Robin from King Richard in my saddlebag and I believed that it contained the date for our departure—it was only by using a great deal of force upon myself that I had refrained from tearing open the sealed parchment and reading this private missive between the King and my lord. But refrain, I did. I wanted more than anything to be his faithful, reliable vassal, utterly trustworthy, utterly loyal: for Robin had done so much more for me than grant me land. In a sense, he had made me what I was. When we first met I had been just a grubby young thief from Nottingham, and he had saved me from mutilation and possibly death at the hands of the law. Then, believing that I had some talent, he had arranged for me to be educated in music, in the Norman-French language, in Latin—the tongue of monks and scholars—and in the art of combat, and I was now as accomplished with a sword and dagger as I was with the vielle, the five-stringed polished apple-wood instrument with which I accompanied my singing.

And so I had spent many hard days and nights in the saddle wearing down the muddy roads of England in the service of my master—and now, laboring up that endless emerald slope, it felt as if I were coming home.

I glanced over to my left, as Ghost put one weary hoof in front of another up that steep hill, to check the height of the sun—it was midafternoon—and noticed to my complete surprise a mass of horsemen not two hundred yards away. At a rough count they numbered about a hundred men, ordered in two lines, helmeted, green-cloaked and clad in mail, all armed with twelve-foot spears, held vertically, and tipped with steel that glinted evilly in the sunlight. My first reaction was fear: they were approaching at a trot and on my exhausted mount there was no way I could outrun them. I must have been daydreaming to let them come up on me without my seeing them. As they approached, the leader, a bareheaded man who was a horse's length ahead of the front line, ripped a long sword from his scabbard and, shouting something over his shoulder, pointed it straight at me in an obvious order to attack. All along the first line of cavalry, the spears were levelled, the ash-wood shafts coming down from their upright positions in a white wave of wood and sparkling metal, the butts couched beneath the riders' armpits, the spearheads pointed directly at me. And then they charged.

From the trot, they moved swiftly to the canter and then, a moment later, they were at full gallop. Behind them the second line followed suit. The thunder of hooves seemed to vibrate the very turf. I could not run; there was no time, and Ghost would not bear me more than a quarter of a mile at a gallop, so I tugged my plain old sword from its battered scabbard, and with a loud cry of "Westbury!" I turned my mount toward them and charged straight at the fast-approaching line of pounding warhorses and implacable mail-clad men.

In no more than three heartbeats they were upon me. The bareheaded leader, a tall youngish man with light brown hair and a mocking grin on his handsome face, raced toward me, sword held high and to his right. As our horses met he cut hard at my head with his long blade. If it had connected with my skull it would have killed me on the spot but I blocked the blow easily with my own sword, and the clash of metal rang out like a church bell. Then, as he swept past me, I twisted my wrist and swung my sword at his mailed back with all my strength. But the leading rider had anticipated this and spurred to his left, away from me, causing my blade to slice through empty air.

Then the second line of horsemen was upon me. I snarled at an onrushing rider, gripping Ghost tight with my knees, and smashed my sword into his kite-shaped shield, kicking out a long splinter of wood; I caught a glimpse of red hair under a badly fitting helmet, a gap-toothed open mouth and a terrified expression on his face as he thundered past me—and then I was through the lines, untouched, and there was empty green grass ahead of me and the diminishing sound of hoof beats behind.

I pulled up Ghost, and wheeled him round to face my opponents. They were half a hundred yards away, still going at the gallop, the two lines of horses merging into one long pack, bulging in the center around the bareheaded leader. Then a trumpet rang out: two notes, bright and clear, a beautiful sound on that perfect sunny afternoon. The riders reined in, sawing at their bits, the horses' forelegs clawing the air and, turning their sweat-streaked mounts, swiftly re-formed the two ranks. It was impressive—or it would have been if all the horses and riders had responded to the trumpet. A handful of men, perhaps a dozen, had lost control of their animals and they were still thundering away from the main body in the opposite direction, heading over the shoulder of a hill and disappearing south down the slope toward the River Locksley. It looked as if nothing would stop them before they were in Nottinghamshire. But there were still eighty or so riders in control of their mounts, re-formed, in line, spears leveled once again. The bareheaded leader's sword came down and, once more, they thundered toward me. I remained still, this time, silently applauding this display of horsemanship, sword resting casually on one shoulder, as the ranks of the enemy cavalry hurled themselves at me. At a distance of fifty paces, the trumpet rang out again one long note, repeated three times, and, miraculously, the reins were hauled back once again, the lances rose to pierce the sky, and with much snorting from the protesting horses, tearing of the turf, and swearing from the riders, the whole huge mass of sweaty horse and armored man-flesh came sliding to a halt about a spear's length from Ghost's soft nose. I stared at the heaving ranks of cavalry, saluted them with my sword and slid the blade back into its battered scabbard.

"Did we give you a good scare then, Alan?" said the bareheaded rider, only slightly out of breath, and grinning at me like a drunken apprentice celebrating a holy day.

"Of course, my lord," I said gravely. "I was so terrified by your fearsome maneuvers that I believe I may have soiled myself." There were a few guffaws from the ranks, which I had intended. Then I grinned back at Robin and said with mock humility: "It was, truly, a very impressive display. But one suggestion, sir," I paused. "I'm no expert on horsemanship, of course, but would it not be even more effective if *all* the horses charged together . . . in the same direction . . . at the same time?"

There was more merriment from the horse soldiers as I pointed behind Robin to the other side of the dale, where a dozen of the Earl of Locksley's newly formed cavalry could be seen tiredly forging up the far slope, the horses lathered in white and still wildly out of control. Robin turned, looked and smiled ruefully.

"We're working on it, Alan," said Robin. "We're working hard on it. And they've still got a little time to learn before we get them to Outremer."

"They are a damned indisciplined rabble, that's what they are. You ought to have the hides off the lot of them!" snapped a man seated on a magnificent bay stallion next to Robin. I looked at him curiously. The ranks of heavily blowing cavalry were filled with familiar faces and I had nodded cheery greetings to half a dozen former outlaws by now, but he was a stranger to me. A tall man of late-middle years, clearly a knight from his dress, weaponry and the quality of his horse, with sandy blonde hair and a battered, much-creased face, the result, I assumed, of a permanent frown.

Robin said: "May I introduce Sir James de Brus, my new captain of horse, the man responsible for knocking these rascals into shape. Sir James, this is Alan Dale, an old comrade, a good friend and my very talented *trouvère*."

"Pleased to know you," said Sir James. I noticed that he had a slight Scottish accent. "Dale, Dale . . ." he said in a puzzled tone. "I don't think I know the name. Where are your family's lands?"

I bridled instinctively. I was ashamed of my humble origins and I hated to be asked about my family, particularly by members of the knightly class, who loved to talk about their Norman lineage as a way of demonstrating their superiority. I glared at the man and said nothing.

Robin spoke for me. "Alan's father came here from France," he said smoothly. "And he was the son of the Seigneur D'Alle, of whom I am sure you will have heard. Alan is the Lord of Westbury in Nottinghamshire."

What Robin said about my father was true. He had been the second son of an obscure French knight, but Robin had not mentioned that he had been a penniless wandering musician, a *trouvère* like me, but without a master. He had made his living, for a time, singing in the halls of the nobility, where he had met Robin, before falling in love with my mother and settling down to raise crops and three children in a small village outside Nottingham. When I was nine, soldiers had burst into our cottage before dawn, ripped my father from his bed and, after falsely accusing him of theft, had hanged him summarily on an oak tree in the center of the village. I have never forgotten the sight of his swollen face as he choked out his life on that makeshift gibbet. And I have never forgiven Sir Ralph Murdac, the Sheriff of Nottinghamshire, who ordered his execution.

Sir James grunted something to me that might have been: "At your service, sir," and I inclined my head at him with the barest civility. Robin said: "Well, that's enough fun for today; shall we adjourn to the castle? I think it is time for a bite of supper."

"I have urgent private news for you, sir," I said to Robin.

"Can it wait till after supper?" he asked. I thought for a moment and then nodded reluctantly. "Come to my chamber after the meal, we'll talk then." He smiled at me. "Good to have you back, Alan," he said, "Kirkton has been dull without your wit and dour without your music." And then: "When you are fully rested, perhaps you'll sing for us. Tomorrow?"

"Of course, sir."

And we turned our horses and began to make our way up the hill to the castle.

The smell of hot soup from the kitchens filled my mouth with water. It is one of the most pleasant experiences that I know: to be physically tired, but washed and clean, and to be hungry, but with the knowledge that good food is just around the corner. I was seated to the left of Robin's place, which was empty, not immediately next to where he would be sitting, but not far away—a position that reflected my standing in Robin's court at Kirkton. In a few moments, Robin would join us and the food would be brought in, and for me it couldn't come soon enough. I gazed around the hall as I waited for the meal to begin. The wooden walls were hung with rich, brightly colored tapestries, and the banners of the notable

15

diners: Robin's device of a snarling black wolf's head on a white background being most prominent, his wife Marie-Anne's badge of a white hawk on a blue field hung beside it, and next to that a strange device, a blue lion on a red and gold background, which I guessed must be Sir James's emblem.

About three dozen of us were waiting to be fed: Robin's *familia*—his closest friends and advisers, top lieutenants and the senior members of his armed troops. Some of the faces about the long table I knew very well—the giant man seated next to Robin's empty place with a thatch of straw-colored hair was my friend and sword teacher John Nailor, who was Robin's right-hand man, and the iron enforcer of his master's will; farther along was a squat muscular shape clad in a raggedy brown robe: Brother Tuck, a Welsh master bowman turned monk, who men said jokingly acted as Robin's conscience; across the table were the gap-toothed grin and red curls of Will Scarlet, a friend of my own age and the nervous horseman I had clashed with that afternoon—but Robin had been recruiting busily in the weeks that I'd been away and at least half the members of the happy throng were unknown to me. Sir James de Brus, I noted with satisfaction, was seated further away from Robin's place than me, his bulldog face creased in to its habitual scowl. He did not seem to fit in that cheery, easy company, where little distinction of rank was made and, saving Robin's superiority over us all, every man believed himself to be equal in worth to his fellow.

But, I noticed as I looked round the hall, things at the castle had changed in my absence. Not just new faces, but a new atmosphere: it was more formal, less like our carefree days as an outlaw band. Of course, that was right: we were no longer a pack of murderers and thieves, with every man's hand against us—we were a company of the soldiers of Christ, blessed by the Church, and sworn to undertake the perilous journey to Outremer to save the Holy Sepulcher in Jerusalem for the True Faith.

Many of the changes to Kirkton were physical, too: indeed, the bailey courtyard had been almost unrecognizable to me when we had cantered in through the high wooden gates that afternoon. It was filled with people, teeming—soldiers, craftsmen, servants, traders, washerwomen, whores—all hurrying about their tasks, and it seemed crammed with new buildings, too, wooden structures thrown up to house the bustling multitudes. The castle courtyard was designed as a vast circle, about a hundred paces across, surrounded by a high oaken palisade, with a wide empty space in the center. Before I had left, there had been a handful of buildings around the edge of the circle: the high hall where we now sat, with Robin and Marie-Anne's solar, or private sleeping chamber, attached to one end; the kitchen, the stables, the stoutly-built counting house that was Robin's treasury, a few storehouses and that was all. Now, the courtyard almost resembled a small town: a new low building had been constructed to house the men-at-arms, a large two-roomed blacksmith's forge had been set up against the palisade, and a burly man and his two assistants were hammering endlessly at bright strips of metal, manufacturing the swords, shields, helmets and spearheads necessary for the troops. A fletcher was at work outside a small half-built hovel, watched closely by his apprentice, painstakingly binding a linen thread around the goose feather flights of an arrow to hold them in place, with a stack of finished missiles beside him.

They would both have plenty of work in the weeks ahead. A good archer could fire twelve arrows a minute in battle and Robin was planning to take nearly two hundred bowmen with him to the Holy Land. If they had to fight only one battle, which lasted for an hour, that would still mean expending a hundred and forty-four *thousand* shafts. Even if the fletcher was busy for months he could not hope to provide enough arrows for the expedition and so, on the march, the men would make their own arrows, and Robin had been buying finished shafts by the thousand from Wales. Many of Robin's hired archers came from that land: tough men, often not particularly tall but thick in the chest and often short in the arms, and with the immense strength necessary to draw the huge deadly war bow that was their weapon of choice. It was easy to tell the archers in the throngs of people about the castle by their low, powerful shapes. The bow, six-foot long and made from yew wood, could sink a steel-tipped ash shaft through a knight's chain mail at two hundred paces. In the time it took a knight to charge an archer, from two hundred yards away, the bowman could sink three or four arrows into the mounted man's chest.

The stables had been extended, too, to almost treble their length, to house the mounts of the hundred or so mounted men-at-arms that Robin planned to take with him on the Great Pilgrimage. And, though the horses would be expected to feed themselves along the way whenever possible, vast amounts of grain must still be carried with us to feed the animals when the grazing was poor, or in the dust-dry deserts of the Levant. As well as fodder, the horses needed blankets, brushes, buckets, feed bags and a dozen other accoutrements, along with saddles, girths, bridles, bits and a host of other straps, buckles and leather gear. Then there was the weaponry: each mounted man would be armed with a shield and a twelve-foot spear as his primary weapons, but each would also carry a sword, and many horsemen preferred to bring with them a mace or axe for close-quarter work in the melee.

So, as we entered the courtyard, which echoed with the shouts of men, the whinnying of horses, the ringing of hammers and the bleating of livestock, I was mildly shocked. I marveled at the castle's transformation from sleepy family home to hive of warlike activity. Even the strong high tower, the motte, which stood on its own hill behind and above the bailey courtyard, was buzzing with activity as a stream of men carrying heavy burdens struggled up the steep earthen ramp to the small iron-bound oak door. The tower was the castle's last line of defense: when an enemy threatened to breach the palisade of the bailey, the occupants of the castle would retreat to the tower. It was always well provisioned and kept stocked with a vast supply of fresh water and ale in giant barrels. Now it was being used as a storehouse for the baggage necessary for the great adventure and it was packed with sheaves of arrows, bundles of swords and bow staves, sacks of grain, barrels of wine, boxes of boots, bales of blankets . . . everything that would be needed to feed, clothe and arm four hundred soldiers on a two thousand-mile journey to the Holy Land.

The food, whose smell had been tantalizing me, finally arrived. Robin was still absent, which concerned me as I was bursting to deliver my news to him and I hoped he had not been called away on some errand before I had the chance to speak to him. However, despite his high-backed chair being empty, the meal was carried in by a train of servants and placed on the long table with little ceremony, and we all fell to eating with a will. The evening repast consisted of vast tureens of hot thick vegetable soup, or pottage, and platters of bread, cheese, butter and fruit—but no meat. It was Lent, and while we at Kirkton ignored the usual religious strictures on cheese and eggs, we did normally forgo meat for form's sake. Robin cared nothing for these matters and always ate whatever he wished.

I filled a wooden bowl with the thick, wonderful smelling soup and with a horn spoon in one hand and a chunk of fresh bread in the other I began to fill my growling belly.

"God's hairy backside," roared a deep familiar voice, "our wandering minstrel has returned!" I looked up to see that

Little John was saluting me with a huge, old-fashioned horn of ale. "And you're sucking up that soup like you haven't eaten for a week! What news, Alan?"

I raised my own cup in reply. "Bad news, I'm afraid, John. Very bad news. The world is about to end, if you believe the learned monks of Canterbury." I took a mouthful of soup. "The Antichrist is loose and is filling the Earth with fire and blood." I paused for dramatic effect. "And I hear the Evil One particularly wants to have a word with *you*." I tried to look grave but kept breaking into a grin. It was an old joke between John and me, to pretend that the end of the world was nigh. But several people around the table glanced at me in fear and crossed themselves.

"Well, if your Antichrist shows his face here in Hallamshire, I'll cut his cock and bollocks off and send him pissing blood all the way back to Hell," said John carelessly, cutting a vast wedge from a round cheese and cramming it into his mouth. "Are you singing tonight?" he added, through a spray of yellow crumbs.

I shook my head. "Too tired. Tomorrow, I promise."

"You mustn't joke about things like that," said Will Scarlet, his nervous face staring at me from across a steaming tureen. "The Antichrist, and all that. Your jests only serve to give the Devil more power."

Will had become noticeably more religious since we had discovered that we were going on this great and holy adventure. "Quite right, Will," said a kind voice with a faint Welsh accent. "Quite right. But young Alan's not afraid of the Devil, are you?" It was Brother Tuck, smiling at me from the far end of the table. "These days, with a sharp blade in each hand, young Alan's not afraid of anything . . . but a couple of years ago, mind, when I first met him, the boy would jump when he caught sight of his own shadow, why he regularly used to burst into tears over a spilled milk pail . . ."

20

Tuck broke off his teasing abruptly as a hurled bread roll crashed into his bulbous red nose, caromed off and skittered away on the hall floor. I was pleased with my accuracy. I had always been a good shot with a rock or stone as a boy, hunting rats in the granary barns with the other children of the village, and I was gratified to see that I had lost none of my skill, even if the missile this time was merely a piece of bread. Tuck roared with outrage, and flung a half-eaten pear back at me, missing and striking a thin man-at-arms next to me on the ear. As if by magic, the whole table suddenly erupted in a hailstorm of thrown food as each diner immediately began to pelt the man opposite with bread, fruit, pieces of cheese rind . . . For a dozen heartbeats it was sheer, joyful chaos, a big lump of cheese whizzed past my cheek, someone flicked a spoonful of soup down the front of my tunic. I prepared to retaliate . . . and then checked myself.

"Enough, enough, by God," Little John was shouting, giving a very good imitation of fury. A thick slice of barley bread, thrown by an unseen hand bounced off the back of his big blond head. "Enough, I say," he bellowed. "The next bastard who throws something, I swear I will batter him into bloody meat."

"For shame, Alan," said Tuck, trying to look solemn, "for shame. Have we not taught you any manners in your time with us? Are you still the uncouth lout we first met two years ago? Just because Robin is away from the table . . ."

I had an apple snug in the palm of my hand and my fist was cocked back and ready to throw; but I managed to still myself; I knew that Little John did not make idle threats.

"Where is Robin, anyway?" I asked. I had caught a glimpse of Sir James's face, his expression was one of total disgust, and I wanted to change the subject. Despite the joyous, silly anarchy of a food battle, my ill news was still looming at the back of my mind like a dark cloud. "Why is he not with us for this fine gathering of noble gentlemen?"

"He's gone to collect the Countess from Locksley village; she's been consulting a wise woman there," said Tuck. "He told me he would be back later this evening, God willing."

Marie-Anne, Countess of Locksley, was heavily pregnant and very near her due time, but the pregnancy had not been an easy one. She had felt sick and out of sorts for much of the early period of her term, and then restless and unhappy more recently as she became very large indeed. Marie-Anne was a beautiful woman, perhaps the most beautiful I had ever seen, with a slim figure, chestnut hair and glorious bright blue eyes, and she hated becoming so fat and lumpy as the baby grew inside her—like a great lumbering sow, as she put it—but there was something else too that was troubling her about the pregnancy. I knew not what, but it was something between her and Robin. I had once come into their solar unannounced to find them shouting at each other. This was very unusual—Robin almost never lost his temper. And Marie-Anne had always appeared to have an almost angelically serene outlook on life. I put the incident down to the trials of pregnancy and forgot about it.

Locksley village was only three miles away and even transporting Marie-Anne in a donkey-cart—she was now too big to ride a horse—it would only take Robin a couple of hours to go there and pick her up and return to Kirkton. I was sure he would return within the hour, and felt a sense of relief. The brief meal was coming to its conclusion and, one by one, the men rose from the long table. Some gathered around the fire in the center of the hall, squatting by its heat, gossiping, throwing dice, and finishing off their cups of wine or ale; a few wandered outside the hall to the farthest building which contained our latrine—a mere plank-covered trench in the earth; some began to make up their beds against the walls on the rush-strewn floor, laying out their blankets and furs and curling up for the night. Robin had still not returned, but he had told me to wait in his chamber, and so after a quick

22

visit to the stables to check that Ghost was comfortable, I collected two goblets of wine, a plate with a large piece of cheese, a loaf of bread, two apples and a small fruit knife and took them on a tray into Robin's and Marie-Anne's solar, which was at the end of the hall. I reasoned that Robin and his lady might be hungry when they returned. Then I settled down to wait in their chamber.

The solar was lit by a single good-quality beeswax candle, in a silver candlestick on a small table of the far side of the big four-poster bed. I came around the bed and placed the food on the night table; then I sat gingerly on the embroidered silk bedcover, and looked around the room as I awaited Robin's return. It was a good-sized chamber, perhaps ten paces long by six paces wide, the walls paneled with dark wood and hung with one or two small tapestries depicting the hunt. It had a polished wooden floor that creaked slightly in the center under a person's weight and was partially covered by a large wolf-skin rug. The great oak bed was at one end of the room against the wall, perhaps three paces in from the door. Beside the bed was a large window with a stout wooden shutter, bolted from the inside, which opened out on to the castle courtyard. At the far end of the room were two clothes chests, one each for Robin and Marie-Anne, and a washbasin on a thin iron stand with a jug of water beside it. A large dresser, on the wall opposite the door, held feminine items such as jewelry, hairpins, face powder, perfume and a large silver mirror. From my seat on the bed, I could just see my reflection in the mirror: a big lad looked back at me, taller than average, and with the broad shoulders and thick arms of a swordsman. My oval face and regular features seemed entirely unremarkable to me, save for the mop of bright blond hair on top. The merest fluff of a beard showed on my cheeks and I remembered that I had not shaved for several days. I ran a hand over my face, and looked away at the rest of the room, noting an antler rack that held cloaks and hats, a crucifix hanging on the wall—which must belong to Marie-Anne—and a large thronelike oak chair.

Considering the power that Robin now wielded in England, his private chamber was rather austere, but then he had never been a man overly concerned with comfort. Years of living wild as an outlaw had given him the ability to travel light, and apparently Marie-Anne was content with only the bare necessities of feminine life.

As I sat on the silk bedcover, I could feel the effects of the long day's travel. I was exhausted; for weeks I had been galloping about England delivering messages for Robin and paying for my board and lodging by entertaining unfamiliar nobles in strange castles with my music and now, warm, well-fed and safe, I could feel my eyelids turning to lead. Surely Robin could not be long. It was perhaps two hours after sunset and he would not like to have Marie-Anne out late at night in her condition. My head was nodding, and I had an overwhelming urge to lie down. I was sure that my master would not mind if I slept for a few minutes, just to be fresh for our discussion. So I kicked off my soft leather shoes and stretched out full length on the comfortable bed. I just managed to lift my head from the soft goose-feather pillow and blow out the candle before I was drowned in sleep.

I came from deep sleep to fully awake very swiftly, like a man rising up fast from a deep pool and breaking the surface to gulp down clean air. But some devious instinct made me remain absolutely still and silent. There was someone coming into the room. I caught a glimpse of his shape, silhouetted by the doorway, back-lit by the dull glow of the banked hall fire. He was short, shorter than Robin, and much broader in the shoulder, too. And in his hand, just glimpsed, was a sword.

The man closed the door behind him, the wooden latch closing with a click, and the room was once again pitch dark.

All the hair on my neck stood to attention, goose bumps rose on my forearms. I lay still for one more moment and then, the knowledge hitting me like a bucket of icy water in the face, I rolled. And only just in time. There was a *whist* of sharp metal passing swiftly through the air, and then a thump as the edge of the man's sword plunged into the bed where I had been lying just a heartbeat before.

I scrambled to my feet, knocking over the night table with a deafening clatter of wood, silver and steel. Like a fool, I bent down to pick up the scattered food and utensils, heard a patter of soft-shod feet running toward me and a hiss above my head as the sword swept over my stooping form in the black of the room. I found the fruit knife in my hand and dived under the bed and squirmed through the dust and cob-webs and out of the other side. But the swordsman anticipated my move, leaping round from the far side of the bed in the same time it took me to crawl under it. As I began cautiously to poke out my nose there was a splintering noise as the in-truder's sword hacked down inches from my head and buried itself in the floorboards. As the man wrestled with his stuck blade, I recoiled under the bed and, turning to my right, fast-crawled out of the end of the four-poster, working forward as silently and swiftly as I could on elbows and knees, scuttling like a crab over to the far wall, and when I reached it I crouched, back to the wooden panels, knees round my ears, trying not to pant, with the little fruit knife held out in front of my body.

The room was silent. The darkness was impenetrable. But my fear was subsiding and, in its place, a cold, hard anger bloomed. I was locked in a room with a sword-wielding ma-niac who was trying to kill me, and who had almost suc-ceeded three times. I tested the edge of the fruit knife. It was very sharp, although the blade was only two inches long. It would serve. After two years of mixing with Robin's outlaws, some of the most efficient cut-throats in England, I knew exactly how to kill a man quickly with a small blade. My heart began to slow, and I remained perfectly still as I waited for my enemy to reveal himself.

Then the man spoke, softly: "My lord earl, why do you not call upon your liegemen to help you?" It was a Welsh voice; I should have guessed by the short powerful body shape that it was an archer—and that was good news. By and large, our archers were not overly proficient as swordsmen, I knew because it was my duty to train them. It was a crumb of comfort, and I felt my courage swelling with the thought. It was also clear that this man thought he had Robin trapped in the room. There was no question of my calling out. It would have brought me help, yes, but if I made the slightest sound, he would be on me with his sword in a heartbeat and, even in that total darkness, I could be cut to pieces. I would be dead or mutilated before any of Robin's men, now snoring in the hall, could come to my rescue, and he would be out of the window and lost in the courtyard. So I remained dumb. And smiled into the blackness. He had revealed his position to me. By the sound of his voice, I knew he was standing by the end of the bed. I heard the swish of his sword as he sliced the air experimentally around his body, trying for a lucky strike. But I was three paces away and crouched low. If I stayed still he was unlikely to catch me with his sword. And, if he was to find me, he must move.

After a long silence, in which all I heard was an indistinct whisper of cloth, the floorboards gave a harsh creak, very loud in the silence, echoing like the cry of a gull. The board creaked once again and then stopped, and I knew he was in the middle of the room, standing still to make no further noise. I could see his position exactly in my mind. But I needed him to come nearer to me, without discovering my own location. Groping around in the dark, my hand alighted on the cool earthenware of the water jug. I put my hand inside to discover that it was half full. Lifting it silently with both hands, knife between my teeth, I hurled the jug away from me and into the corner of the room. It smashed with an unbelievably soul-wringing noise and I heard the floorboards creak again as the man rushed toward the corner and began to flog the air with his sword. On hands and knees I crawled forward to where I believed he stood and, knife in my right hand, grabbed him with my left around the thigh. I was only slightly off the mark and, as I seized his knee, he let out a shriek of surprise and fear. A moment later and I had plunged the knife into the soft inside of his thigh, then ripped the blade out of the flesh in a scooping motion. He screamed horribly in pain and terror and I felt him batter at my shoulders with the hilt of his sword. But I had been rewarded for my strike by a great gush of his blood into my face, a hot fountain that immediately drenched my upper body, and I knew then that he was a dead man.

Dropping the knife, I scrambled out of reach of his flailing sword and scuttled back under the bed. The man's howls filled to room, shrill and heart-rending, and I knew that the alarm had been satisfactorily raised. Scream upon scream echoed about me as his life jetted out of his slashed thigh. Then I heard him slump to the floor like a dropped sack of grain, weak and whimpering now, as he tried to staunch the torrent of spurting lifeblood. I could smell its sour iron odor. Even in the pitch dark I could clearly imagine what was happening as I had seen it once before: as I had intended, I had cut through the great pulsing artery that ran down his inner thigh, and unless he could find a tourniquet to stop the blood flow, in less than thirty heartbeats he would be as dead as last night's dinner.

The door of the solar burst open and a crowd of men-at-arms rushed in bringing torches and rush lights and an excited clamor to the room. The man was seated, legs widespread, in the middle of a lake of blood, his agonized face drained and white. I poked my bloody head out from under the bed and stared at him.

He managed four words before he collapsed, lifeless into the crimson pool: "Not my boy, please . . ." he whispered and then he died.

CHAPTER TWO

The dead man was a nobody—an archer named Lloyd ap Gryffudd, one of scores of men recently hired by Tuck from South Wales. He was an experienced man with a bow and, as far as anyone knew, a trustworthy soldier—so Owain, the captain of Robin's bowmen told me. It was clear that Owain felt somehow responsible that one of his men should have tried to attack Robin; he was visibly upset as we spoke later that night over a cup of wine, which I badly needed.

The household was quiet once again after the uproar, the servants had carried out the body and cleaned up the blood, and the grizzled Welsh bowman and I were chewing over the attack at the long table in the hall.

"He must have been drunk, Alan, or just plain mad," said Owain. "He would never have been able to get away with it. He'd have been ripped apart by the men before he got a hundred yards. They love Robin, you know, absolutely bloody worship him."

"Maybe, maybe not," I said. "It was risky, yes, but everyone in the hall was asleep and he might well have been able to kill Robin and Marie-Anne and get away out of the window before anyone noticed. There was a saddled horse ready in the stables and, in the confusion after an event like that, Robin dead, the whole castle raising a hullabaloo, well, I think he would have had a good chance of escape. And I don't think he was mad. I just think there was great pressure used—money or threats, or both—to force him to make the attempt."

Owain looked even gloomier. "I'll make some inquires in the morning," he said. "What do you think Robin will say when he gets back?"

"He's not going to be happy," I said. And I rose from the table, leaving Owain staring into his wine cup, and took my exhausted body to my blankets by the fire. Although I knew it was ridiculous, and that nobody wanted to kill *me*, I lay for the rest of the night with my unsheathed poniard in my hand. And weary as I was, with the comforting feel of a foot-long razor-sharp Spanish dagger in my fist, I slept like a babe.

Robin returned the next morning, another glorious, sunny spring day, with his pregnant wife Marie-Anne. She was huge, flushed and riding like a queen in a great chair lashed to a donkey cart, surrounded by her ladies in waiting. I waved at one familiar face in her entourage, my little friend Godifa, and received a shy smile in return. Then I turned to greet Robin, and quickly apprised him of the events of last night. My lord seemed genuinely impressed that I had killed the would-be-assassin singlehanded.

"He came at you with a drawn sword, in the dark, while you were fast asleep, and you managed to swiftly dispatch him with, what, a nail-paring knife?" he said as we walked out of the bright sunlight of the courtyard and into the dimness of hall. It was strange to hear him pay me a real compliment without teasing me. It made me feel slightly uneasy.

"It was a fruit knife, actually," I said.

Robin waved my correction away. "I always knew that you could weave a good heroic *chanson*, Alan, I didn't realize that you wanted to *be* the hero in these tales, as well." He grinned at me. The mockery was back in his voice and, somehow, it made me feel a little more comfortable.

"Well, since I was asleep on your bed, and as a result was mistaken for you, my lord, I felt that a little heroic behavior was expected of me."

Robin laughed. "Your flattery is shameless. You know better than anyone how far I am from being a hero."

"All those excellent songs say that you are, my lord, and so it must be true," I said with a grin.

He gave a snort of laughter and then abruptly stopped smiling and drew me over to the long table in the hall, where we both sat down. Playtime was over. "So tell me," he said, all seriousness, "who was he, and why was he trying to chop me into cutlets?"

"There is a very large price on your head," I told him soberly, "very large indeed." I paused. "It is a hundred pounds in pure German silver, and it is being offered by our old friend Sir Ralph Murdac."

There was a long silence at the table while Robin stared at me, his bright gray eyes boring into mine. It was a staggering amount to offer for one life, more than enough to allow a man to live in comfort for his whole span on Earth and still have a large inheritance for his sons and a fat dowry for his daughters. It was more than the whole manor of Westbury was worth.

"So the little viper has come out of his hole," said Robin. "Go and get Little John, Owain, Sir James and Tuck, then you'd better tell us all the whole story." I stood up and handed

Robin the letter from the King, which had been burning a hole in the breast of my tunic all morning. He broke the royal seal on the parchment and began reading while I went to pass the word for his closest lieutenants.

While we waited in silence for Robin's top men to assemble, I noticed Robin looking at me curiously.

"What on earth are you wearing on your head?" he asked. "You look like a procurer of loose women."

I bridled a little; I was wearing a new sky blue hood that I had bought in London. It was made from the finest wool, soft as a baby's cheek; it was embroidered with tiny flakes of gold in the shape of diamonds and red woolen stars and had a long plump tail that dangled over my shoulder like a pet snake. It was the height of city sophistication, the smart London hood-maker had assured me, and I treasured it. I didn't deign to reply to Robin's question and ten minutes later, Little John, Sir James de Brus, Owain the bowman, Robin and I were sitting at the long table, with mugs of ale in our hands.

"Tuck is in the churchyard, burying the dead fellow," John said.

Robin nodded and said nothing. He visited the little church of St. Nicholas, at the southeastern foot of the castle, only when it was absolutely necessary, when *not* to go would be very strange. And I knew why: in his heart, Robin was no Christian. A brutal priest who tormented him while he was growing up had given him a deep hatred for Mother Church, and though he was bound by solemn promises to go on this Great Pilgrimage, he had no room in his soul for Our Lord and Savior Jesus Christ. As shocking, as downright evil as this must seem to you, the reader of this parchment, for some strange reason Robin's men accepted his lack of faith. Or pretended to be ignorant of it. They loved him and followed him despite the fact that he was clearly a damned soul.

"By the Baptist's bleeding bunions, that was good work last night, youngster," said Little John, jerking my thoughts back to the present. "I couldn't have done it better myself." I'm ashamed to say that I blushed at that point and could find nothing to say. May the Lord forgive my pride, but I knew I had behaved well. Unlike Robin, John rarely gave out compliments and, as he was Robin's master-of-arms, and my combat teacher, his praise meant a great deal to me.

"Come on, Alan, enough dramatic silence. You aren't performing a *chanson* now. Tell us about the murderous plots of Sir Ralph Murdac," said Robin, fixing me sternly with his silver gaze. "I thought he was still hiding up in the gloomy wilds of Scotland, no offense, Sir James." The Scotsman scowled but said nothing.

Until a few days before, I had thought Murdac was in Scotland, too. After the battle of Linden Lea, in which Robin had defeated Murdac's forces, the evil little man had fled to the safety of relatives north of the border. As well as escaping from Robin's vengeance, Murdac believed that King Richard was seeking to bring him to account for a large quantity of tax silver that the erstwhile High Sheriff of Nottinghamshire had raised ostensibly for the expedition to Outremer. Instead of passing it on to the royal treasury, Murdac had kept the money he had squeezed from the peasants to himself, and his guilty conscience had caused him to flee from Richard's wrath. Clearly he still had a large amount of silver left, otherwise he could not afford to offer a hundred pounds of the precious metal for Robin's life.

"Well, he's back," I said, "and he's after your heart's blood." And I settled down and began to tell my tale: "I had completed our business in Winchester, Oxford and London," I said. "And all had gone smoothly, so I rode north to Nottingham to deliver your gifts to Prince John . . ."

King Richard's younger brother had prospered since his father's death, being showered with lands and titles by his older sibling—already Lord of Ireland, he had been given the counties of Derby and Nottingham and made master of Lancaster,

Gloucester and Marlborough and wide lands in Wales. The Prince received me in the great hall at the royal castle of Nottingham, but without much royal grace. I was very tired from traveling, soaked through from a cloudburst, and much splashed by road mud, but Prince John insisted on seeing me immediately. And I could do nothing but obey. He had been told that I carried a gift for him and, like a greedy child, he wanted it immediately. So I attended him in the great hall, wet through and chilled to the bone—a sorry sight in front of the dozen or so richly dressed courtiers and royal cronies present—and handed over Robin's gift. It was a magnificent matched pair of hunting falcons that I had bought in London on Robin's instructions. They were exquisite birds, tall with wide mottled wings and creamy breasts speckled with black; their elegant curved beaks were of a light blue hue turning to black at the cruel tip and the two proud birds were hooded in soft red Spanish leather, adorned with silver bells. I was particularly pleased to have persuaded the falconer in London to part with them, although it had taken a large quantity of my master's silver to strike the deal. I also gave Prince John Robin's letter, which I knew wished him well and contained the usual platitudes from a fellow magnate and powerful neighbor—Robin's main castle of Kirkton was, of course, less than forty miles north of Nottingham, and some of the other manors he held were even closer.

Prince John, a young man of less than medium height, with dark red curly hair and a thick-built body, adored the falcons. He was very fond of hunting and he crooned over the birds like a mother over a newborn baby. The letter he merely glanced at, and then handed to the man standing next to him: a tall, well-built knight, poorly dressed for royal company but wearing a fine sword, and with a distinctive lock of white hair sprouting over the center of his forehead from a russet thatch. He stared at me and I noticed another curious feature of the man: he had the eyes of a fox—hazel, but starred and splintered and with a feral gleam that I did not like at all. "What am I supposed to do with this?" the fox-knight said in Norman French, his voice deep and slow. He looked down at the letter in his big hands.

"Oh, of course, that's no good to you," said the Prince, with a trace of a sneer, in the same language. The Prince snatched the letter back. "Mally, you really must learn to read one of these days." Prince John turned to his right and passed the letter to a short, dark-haired man dressed entirely in black who was standing on his other side, and slightly behind, with his face buried in a small jewel-encrusted prayer book. "It's from your old sparring partner, the so-called Earl of Locksley," the Prince said, handing over the parchment. He had a harsh, high voice that always seemed to contain a full measure of contempt for the world. The dark man put down the book, took the letter, stared directly at me with his icy blue eyes for a few moments—his face quite expressionless—then he began to read.

It took me a couple of heartbeats to recognize him but then, with a shock, I realized that I was looking at Sir Ralph Murdac, the former High Sheriff of Nottinghamshire: the man who had ordered the death of my father; the man who had, in a stinking dungeon in Winchester last summer, tortured me in the most humiliating way; and the man whose death I craved more than any other. My hand was on the handle of my poniard and, for a moment, I considered simply stepping over to him and plunging the blade hilt-deep into his belly. But reason reasserted itself, thank God. I was a guest at the court of a royal prince. There were dozens of witnesses in the room. If I slaughtered Murdac in front of all these people, as deeply satisfying as that would be, I'd be hanging from a gibbet by nightfall.

Murdac lifted his eyes from the letter. He gave me another long, long look. "Make him sing something," he said to the Prince in the soft, lisping French voice that I knew so well. Prince John was oblivious of me: making little clucking noises and stroking the soft, leopard-patterned breast feathers of one of the falcons. "It says here that this muddy wretch is Robert of Locksley's personal *trouvère*," continued Murdac in a louder tone. "Get him to sing us something, sire, to entertain us all." He looked around the gathering of courtiers and there was a ripple of sycophantic agreement. The big man with the lock of white hair smiled gleefully, sensing my discomfort at the suggestion and showing big, pointed yellow teeth.

"What?" said Prince John. "Oh. Good idea. Yes, sing us something, boy."

I stood before them, dripping, cold, exhausted, without my vielle or any instrument, secretly contemplating bloody murder, and this royal idiot wanted me to sing?

"My lord prince, I am rather wet, if I might have leave to retire and change . . ."

"Don't make excuses, boy," interrupted Murdac, his pale eyes glinting with malice. "His Highness has commanded you to sing. So sing up, boy, sing up!" He clapped his hands together once, and gave me a thin, venomous smile.

I stared at him, my brain almost exploding with blood-curdling hatred. He was thinner than he had been the last time I saw him, with more lines on his face, but more richly dressed, too, in thick black silk trimmed with sable, and around his neck hung a gold chain at the end of which dangled an enormous ruby. I knew that jewel well. My knuckles were white, my clenched fist just inches from the hilt of my dagger, and I don't believe I have ever been closer to throwing my life away. But then I realized that I didn't just want his death, I didn't want to strike down now, here, at the cost of my own neck, I wanted to humiliate him first, as he was humiliating me, as he had humiliated me before in that stinking dungeon. I wanted him to beg my pardon for killing my father, beseech forgiveness for torturing me and murdering my friends . . . So I unclenched my fists and folded my twitching hands behind my back. And I began to sing.

I don't remember what I sang, truly I do not, perhaps one of the dozen or so *cansos* that I had written by then and knew by heart. My tired old brain has rubbed out the memory; shame can sometimes do that. After the first song, they made me sing another, although my teeth were chattering so hard that I'm sure nobody could make out the words; and then another. Finally, Prince John seemed to tire of this cruel game and he dismissed me. I bowed low, my cheeks flushed with rage and mortification, and the Prince reached into his purse, groped about for a moment, and then tossed a couple of silver pennies on the floor in front of me. The foxy man laughed out loud. It was a calculated insult. *Trouvères* might well expect to receive discreet gifts from satisfied lords, but to throw the money on the floor, as if rewarding a tumbler for turning somersaults, or some beggarly street musician, was worse than a slap in the face.

I bowed a second time and, ignoring the money glinting in the dirty rushes at my feet, amid the discarded animal bones, the dog hair and ancient grime of the hall floor, I turned my back on my three tormentors and walked out of the hall.

"What an extraordinary fellow!" I heard Prince John croaking loudly in his harsh voice as I approached the great oak doors. "Did you see that? He turned his back on me. I ought to have him flogged."

"He's from serf stock, you know," said Murdac loudly. "No breeding, no manners." I stumbled slightly over the threshold, longing to be out of earshot. "An outlaw, too," the little shit-weasel continued. "That was before he was pardoned by your royal brother. I had him in the cells once for his misdeeds but the slippery villain wriggled out of there somehow. Escaped . . ."

And I was through the door, and out into the huge courtyard of Nottingham castle. My legs were faltering beneath
me and I found a stone mounting block to sit upon and, under scowling leaden skies, I slumped down and closed my
eyes hoping to wipe the shame and embarrassment from my
mind. I concentrated on images of Sir Ralph Murdac begging for his life, tied to the rack, bloody and screaming for
mercy, and was just beginning to feel slightly better when I
heard the patter of running feet and opened my eyes to see a
poorly dressed servant boy standing before me, panting and
holding out one hand with the palm flat. On his palm were
three greasy-looking silver pennies.

"Sir, be-be-begging your pardon, sir, but this is your
silver," said the boy.

For a moment I wondered if this was some fresh humiliation, dreamed up by Murdac and his new royal master.
Then I looked again at the servant boy, at his earnest face and
shabby clothes, his outstretched hand trembling slightly, and
I knew it could not be. He was a fairly good-looking lad,
about eleven or so, well-made and tall for his age, with light
brown hair and brown eyes. I stared at him for a few moments
and then said brusquely: "You keep it, boy."

He looked distressed. "But, sir, it is your money. The
prince gave it to you. A roy-roy-royal gift."

"I do not care to receive it," I said shortly. And then, real-
izing that my public shaming had not been his fault, and that
there was no reason to be unkind to him, I smiled: "Buy
yourself something in the market, a pie or two, or get yourself
a good new knife . . ." He looked doubtful and I wondered if
he was perhaps slow in the head, but suddenly I did not have
the patience for him any longer and so I sat back on my stone
block, closed my eyes and returned to my dark thoughts.

"Please excuse my im-impertinence, sir," said the boy,
breaking in on a delightful reverie in which Murdac was

dangling by his thumbs over a pit filled with snakes. I opened my eyes; the boy was still there, but his hands were by his sides and the silver, I noticed, had disappeared. "If you will forgive me asking, sir, but did His Royal Highness say that you served the Earl of Locksley? The one the people call Robin Hood?" His face was glowing with a strange excitement and he seemed to have wrested control over his stammer.

"It is true, I do serve the Earl; I have that honor," I said, smiling again. I knew the boy's type, and had met youngsters like him all over the country. He had heard the songs and legends about Robin Hood and his band of desperadoes and was entranced by the romance of the stories: a happy band of brothers, dining in woodland glades, sleeping under the stars, and running rings around the officers of the law. I could have told him a few tales of my own that would have changed his opinion of Robin, about bloody human sacrifice, and bold-faced theft and extortion, and the mutilation of enemies but, as usual, I refrained.

"I would beg for the honor . . ." the boy said and swallowed, ". . . of serving him. And I have news that con-con-concerns him."

"What news?" I said.

"Sir Ralph Murdac means to see your master dead."

"There is nothing new in that, boy—Sir Ralph and Robin of Sherwood have been enemies since before you were born," I said dismissively, and I closed my eyes again.

"But Sir Ralph has made it known that he will give a hundred pounds of fine German silver for any man who kills him, and brings in his head," the boy said.

My eyes flashed open. I was stunned, speechless: I had no idea that Murdac had that amount of money to give away for one man's death. "Where did you hear this?" I asked.

"I over-overheard Sir Ralph tell the captain of the castle guard to pass the message of the reward to his men." The boy looked at me anxiously. "If you give this information to the Earl, perhaps he will look favorably upon me and take me into his service," he said. His eyes were pleading.

I looked at him again, perhaps he wasn't so slack-witted after all; and a bold idea began to grow in my head, a way to test the mettle of this boy, give myself some satisfaction, right a wrong, and strike at Ralph Murdac's pride in the bargain.

"What is your name, boy?" I asked.

"William, sir," he replied.

"And you are employed here as a servant," I said.

"Yes, sir. I work in the kitchens—but on feast days sometimes I am allowed to serve in the great hall."

"Do you truly wish to serve Robert of Locksley?" I asked.

"Yes, sir, I will serve him right well; I will serve him as a man of his kind deserves to be served. I swear by Our Lady Mary the Mother of God."

"If you wish to serve Robin, first you must serve me. Will you do that? And later, in a few months, you may be allowed to join my master on the Great Pilgrimage to the Holy Land. That privilege carries with it the promise of Salvation, and exemption from all your sins. Would you like that?" The boy nodded so fast and furiously, I feared he might break his neck.

"But, William, and this is very important, you must not tell a soul that you are serving my lord Locksley until it is time to leave the castle to join your master. Can you do that?"

"Yes, sir, I am new here at Nottingham, and all alone in the world, I have no friends or family to talk to." He looked down at his shoes. "My father was fou–foully murdered, sir, by thieves, and my mother died of grief soon afterward." He was sniveling slightly and I felt sorry for the poor lad. I knew what it was to have no one.

"Nevertheless, you may feel the urge to tell someone that you secretly serve the famous Robin Hood. It's a natural urge. But, just remember, if you tell anyone about your service, you will never be allowed to join him. Is that clear?"

"Yes, sir."

"There is one more thing; you might think of it as a test of your loyalty to Robin. A proof that you truly wish to serve him faithfully."

"Tell me what it is, sir, I will do anything."

"There is an object, a jewel of great price that rightfully belongs to Robin's lady Marie-Anne. But Sir Ralph Murdac has stolen it. He wears this jewel around his neck every day— have you seen it? It is a great red ruby—I want you to help me reclaim it for its rightful owner."

He didn't even blink at the thought of daylight robbery, but agreed immediately, working his head as vigorously as before; and I knew he was going to fit in fine with Robin's men. So I put my arm around William's shoulder and quietly explained to him what we were going to do and how it would be done.

I stayed in Nottingham for two more days, but not at the castle. I could not bear to remain there, where I might be called back into the presence of Prince John for another round of musical humiliation. I stayed instead at the house of an old friend, Albert, a crony from my days as a snot-nosed street-thief, when I would cut away the purses of rich merchants and rely on the thickness of the market crowds to hide me as I made my escape. Albert was an honest man now, and married; he lived in a one-room hovel in the poorest part of the old English borough of Nottingham. So he knew better than to ask about the job I was planning; he knew I was up to no good but he was content to tolerate my presence in his home for the friendship we had enjoyed in the past—and for the silver penny that I had promised him when my business was over.

On the morning of the second day, William came to

Albert's house and told me that Sir Ralph Murdac was look-ing at rings in the street of the goldsmiths in the northern part of the town.

"But he is not alone, sir," said William, looking worried. "He has two men-at-arms with him."

"I'm not concerned about that," I said, and I wasn't. "Is he wearing the ruby?"

"Yes, sir, on the gold chain, as always."

I grinned at him: "Then let us go to him!"

William and I pushed through the thick market crowds none too gently and soon found ourselves at the southern end of Goldsmith's Street. As we wanted to avoid being recog-nized by Murdac or his men, William had smeared his face with mud and wore a hood pulled far forward over his brow. I was dressed like an off-duty soldier, in a distinctive blue cloak, hauberk, and sword, with a bloody bandage covering one eye and a good deal of my cheek. I had also pasted some short clippings of Albert's black hair on my upper lip and chin and covered up my blond locks with a floppy-brimmed hat. To be honest, I felt slightly ridiculous, but Albert assured me that no one would recognize me; the black artificial stubble, though it was crudely stuck on, made me look older, and a much rougher customer; they might realize later that I had been a person in disguise but, as everyone in the castle believed that the gifted *trouvère* Alan Dale had left Nottingham two days before with his serf-born tail between his legs, I would not be immediately suspected as the thief.

Our plan was very simple, as the best plans always are. And it was a maneuver I had made several times before, though not for a couple of years or more. It depended on surprise, timing and the natural human reaction to a hard, winding blow to the stomach.

Sir Ralph Murdac was standing beside a shop counter that opened on to the street; inside the shop, I could just see two young goldsmiths hard at work, tapping away at delicate work with their tiny hammers. I felt the usual thrill of pleasure in my gut at the thought of imminent larceny. On the street, standing next to Murdac, was the master goldsmith, who was showing him a fine gold broach. He had clearly made the effort to come out of his shop to wait upon such a distinguished customer. Two men-at-arms, in Murdac's personal colors of black and red, were standing about ten yards away, leaning against a wall and looking bored.

I walked toward the shop where Murdac was haggling with the goldsmith and stopped at the one before it, keeping my face hidden from the former sheriff and pretending to examine some rather fine gold-chased spurs. William had been following me at a discreet distance. I was about twenty feet from Murdac and half-facing away from him. Out of the corner of my eye I could see William, coming toward me stealthily. He was a natural, moving like a predator, stopping now on this side of the street, now on the other, browsing, never touching the bright metal that was laid out on public display, never drawing attention to himself. But anyone watching him, if they cared to notice his movements, would think he was stalking me, like a house cat sidling up to an unsuspecting starling. Then he was next to me, on my right-hand side, between Murdac and myself.

He didn't look at me, the obedient boy, just tapped his finger against my thigh. I whispered: "Now!" and then immediately shouted, "Hoy! Stop, thief!" and quick as a cornered rat William darted away from me directly toward Ralph Murdac. I shouted: "My purse!" and pelted after him. We were only twenty feet from Murdac and, in two heartbeats, William had charged straight into the little black-clad knight, butting him hard in the belly, just below the rib cage with his head as he charged forward. I was right on his heels bellowing: "Thief! Thief!" As William's brown head smashed into Murdac's midriff, I was less than a yard behind him. All the breath came out of the evil little bastard in a short, agonized

43

"Whoomf!" His body doubled over, and, as William bounced back and dodged away around Murdac's bent-over form, I pointed and shouted at William to stop. While the world watched William take to his toes, I pretended to steady Sir Ralph Murdac with an arm round his shoulders and neatly whipped the gold chain and ruby over his lowered neck, and thrust the jewel into a sleeve of my tunic. Then I was past the winded knight and the gaping, flat-footed men-at-arms and with a great cry of "Forgive me, sir, I must catch him!" I was away and around the corner hot on William's heels.

William was quick, I have to give him that, quicker than me, and I believed that I was as fit as I have ever been. In ten heartbeats we were a hundred paces away and at a crossroads where three roads converged. I had stopped shouting by this time—I hadn't the breath—but also I wanted no one to intercept William. At the crossroads, William came to an abrupt halt, and ducked into the porch of a church. I followed him in, swiftly handed him the ruby, and walked away to the center of the crossroads. The mid-afternoon crowds were fairly thick and the streets were crammed with ox-carts, horsemen, pedlars with big packs, housewives with their baskets and even a drover herding a great passel of sheep. William blended into the throng and began to walk swiftly but without appearing to hurry down the street to the left.

I looked behind me: the two men-at-arms were approaching at speed, and I pointed up the right-hand street and shouted: "There he is! Stop him somebody!" indicating an imaginary William some distance ahead. Then I ran. I bolted up the wrong street, shouting and halloo-ing and causing quite a stir. People stopped and left their businesses and began to run with me. By sheer luck, for this was no part of the plan, I saw a boy about William's age walking up the street ahead. I shouted: "That's him, that's the thief," and urged my fellow pursuers to lay hands on him as I lent against a wall and pretended to catch my breath. The unfortunate lad saw a crowd of enraged townsmen racing toward him shouting "Thief!" and took off like a frightened rabbit. Once the pack had passed me, I was down the first alley I saw; the distinctive blue cloak, eye bandage and hat buried in a mound of wet straw, and I was doing my best to scrub off the fake stubble with a spit-wetted palm as I walked south to rejoin William at Albert's house.

"That was bravely done," said Robin. He was chuckling at my tale, but his mirth was nothing to Little John's reaction: his big man's laugh boomed out across the hall, drawing attention from scores of Robin's men, and the tears were pouring down his cheeks as he slapped sturdy Owain on the back with glee. Even Sir James de Brus gave me a wintry smile.

"And you have the ruby with you?" asked Robin.

"I have it," I said. And unbuckling my saddlebag, I pulled a cloth-wrapped lump from inside. Robin sent a servant for Marie-Anne and while my lord's good lady waddled over to the table, bringing her lady-in-waiting Godifa with her, I unwrapped the parcel and pulled out the fruits of my larceny.

"We must reward William with employment in your household," I reminded Robin.

"Certainly, certainly, I can always use talent for mischief like his," he said but his eyes were fixed on the great jewel. It seemed to sparkle with a demonic light in the dim hall, glistening and malevolent, like a congealed drop of the Devil's blood.

"This belongs to you, my lady," I said and, lifting the jewel on its bright gold chain, I presented it to Marie-Anne, holding it in outstretched hands. She took it, but reluctantly. And then she turned to Godifa, a slim girl of about twelve years on the very lip of womanhood, who had grown up with Robin Hood's outlaws, and who now served Marie-Anne as maid, companion and friend.

"This is yours, Goody, surely you remember it?" said Marie-Anne, placing the gold chain around the girl's neck. "It was your mother's, and you kindly lent it to me, and then I foolishly lost it when I was held captive by Sir Ralph last year." She was smiling at the girl. "I think you are old enough for it to look well on you now."

Goody gazed down at the bright gold around her neck and at the great red jewel nestling between the buds of her breasts. She looked up at me, shining with happiness: "What do you think, Alan, does this stone become me?"

"You look beautiful," I said. And it was true. Her face had changed shape since I last saw her, only several weeks ago, it had become longer, less round and the cheekbones more prominent. Her hair was long and fine, its color the exact same shade as the gold around her neck. I could clearly see the beauty that she would become in a few years. And so I said again: "You truly look wonderful." And then strangely, her face became flushed bright pink, and she slipped off the bench she had been sitting on, came over to me, kissed me on the cheek, muttering, "Thank you, Alan" before pelting off to the solar, shouting rudely behind her to her mistress, as she ran from the table without a by-your-leave, that she must look directly into Marie-Anne's silver mirror.

"She's still not quite tamed, that one," said Robin, with a rueful smile at me. "Still wild deep in her soul."

I knew Robin was right: the year before, after a catastrophe of fire and blood in which Goody's parents had perished violently, she and I had been hunted like beasts by Ralph Murdac's men through the remote places of Sherwood. We had survived the swords of mounted men-at-arms, attack by wild wolves and a madman who wanted to eat our flesh—and it had been Goody who had dispatched the lunatic with a brave dagger thrust through the eye. She had a strong, savage flame in her soul, which I knew would never be extinguished.

"She'll need a husband soon, Alan. Perhaps you are the man lusty enough to tame that wildcat," said Little John, and gave one of his great, hearty big-man guffaws.

I glared at him. "Goody is a child," I snapped. "I think of her as my sister, under my protection, and I will not hear talk like that about her. From anyone!"

Little John looked astounded by my outburst but he said nothing in reply. Marie-Anne spoke then, as always, her tact in a difficult situation smoothing the rough waters: "We all thank you for returning the jewel, Alan," she said. "But can I prevail upon you to tell the tale again of its recovery? I have not heard it. Could you bear to tell it again?"

And so, mollified, I told my beautiful friend Marie-Anne how brave and clever I had been, and how foolish and sore Sir Ralph Murdac must now feel, while others who had heard the story drifted away from the table and still others joined the throng about me. Wine was fetched, and then food for the mid-day meal. Marie-Anne told me how she and Robin had visited the wise woman in Locksley village, and been forced to spend the night because of the lateness of the hour, and how the woman had said that the baby would be a boy, and that he would grow into a powerful man, a great warrior. "He kicks like a warrior, at least," said my lady, wincing as a ripple shuddered across her great belly.

It was a Sunday, and no work was to be done, and so the day passed in eating and drinking, storytelling and riddles and laughter, and other gentle amusements. As the light began to fade, and the candles were lit, I brought out my apple-wood veille and played and sang for my master's wife and the men of our bold company, until it was time for sleep. But that night I dreamed of a huge mound of German silver coins, half as high as a man, standing, glinting, in a pool of Robin's blood.

We trained hard at Kirkton; each morning I was out in the fields giving basic lessons in swordcraft to the archers. If an archer has run out of arrows, he is more or less defenseless, so each of our bowmen had been issued with a short sword, and it was my task to teach them the rudiments of its use. It is not easy to train two hundred men, but they were broken down into groups of twenty under the command of a junior officer called a vintenar, who was paid double wages. The vintenars answered to Owain for the conduct and discipline of their men and they also received extra training from me and from Little John in the sword. Usually I would gather the ten vintenars together an hour or so before a training session and explain what we would be practicing that day, perhaps a simple block and thrust routine, and work with them until they understood it. Then the vintenars were expected to demonstrate it to the men. I would wander about the flat-ish piece of worn field where we practiced, watching groups of twenty men hacking and lunging at each other, giving advice, and correcting technique where necessary. I was treated with a great deal of respect after my midnight encounter with the would-be murderer and, despite my tender years, on the subject of swordplay I was listened to as if my words were The Gospel itself. After a couple of hours with the archers, I would dismiss them and have a one-on-one sword practice session with Little John; often a crowd of bowmen lingered to watch.

John had been master-at-arms for Robin's father and he was the finest man with any weapon that I ever saw, perhaps save Robin himself, and one other. The big man preferred, in battle, to wield a great double-bladed war axe but, when we practiced, he usually fought with an ordinary sword and shield, and I with my old sword and my Spanish poniard. Sword and shield was a foot soldier's normal combination, perhaps with a long spear, too. Two fields over from where my archers were banging away at each other with their short blades, Little John would be putting our hundred or so spearmen through their paces. At his bellowed commands, the spearmen would perform intricate evolutions with locked shields, creating a number of massed formations—"the hedgehog," a defensive circle of spears, "the boar's snout," an attacking arrow-shaped configuration, and "the shield wall," the standard lineup against a similarly arranged enemy.

Little John and I had a long-running argument about my choice of weapons: he strongly believed that I needed to use a shield; I preferred the freedom and speed gained by fighting without one. I also argued that my role in battle was not primarily as a fighting man but as Robin's aide-de-camp and messenger: I would be galloping to the various parts of his army, scattered wherever they might be, and delivering his orders. The kite-shaped shields that we used were heavy and cumbersome items, and I needed to be swift and light on the field. Of course, I did know in theory how to use a shield. Its uses had been knocked into me since my first days with Robin's outlaw band, but I preferred, if I had to fight, the elegant dance of poniard and sword. Little John muttered that I was being far too fancy. "Battle is about killing the most men as fast as you can, and keeping as many of our men as safe as possible. It's not a dance; it's not a game. It's about killing him quickly, and saving your own neck from his blade. And for that you need a shield." I shook my head. In battle my Spanish dagger was sturdy enough at its hilt to block a sword strike, my body was usually armored with a knee-length hauberk and heavy boots, my head defended with a stout helmet and, in a melee, I liked to be able to give out deadly blows with both hands.

When John and I made our battle practices, the main difficulty I had was overcoming his brawn. I was a mere youth then, still slim of hip and, although very fit, not yet in my full bodily strength. John was a seasoned warrior of more than thirty summers, nearly seven feet in height and with a chest that was nearly two-feet thick. When he struck at me with the sword, I had to avoid the blow altogether as its power would have smashed straight through the sword-and-dagger blocks I might have tried with another man. Instead, I always waited for him to launch his brutal attack, evaded it and then counterattacked against his sword arm. I knew that a powerful blow from a sword on the upper arm could break bone, even if it could not penetrate a chain mail hauberk. And a man before me with a broken sword arm is a dead man.

One fine morning not long after my return from Nottingham, John and I were circling each other on the scrubby grass. I was taunting him, suggesting that, as he was so long unmarried, his preference for bed partners must be handsome boys, and making damn sure that I stayed out of his long sword's reach. He was suggesting that I come a little closer and find out what he really liked to do to insolent children like me. It was all good ribald fun and raised many a laugh from the watching circle of archers and spearmen. But I thought I had genuinely managed to anger him this time, and when I was reciting a little rhyme that went, if I remember rightly, "Little John, he's not pretty, but he loves to get his member shitty . . ." he gave a great snarl like a maddened bear and lunged at me, slicing down hard at my head. I thought I saw my chance and, dodging outside the massive blow, swung my blade hard, backhanded at his outreached arm. And missed. He was feinting, of course, and my blade never came within an inch of his arm. I was off balance and the next thing I knew, John's shield had crashed with stunning force into my sword-arm and side, I was lifted high in the air—I saw the faces of the watching men whirling around me—and then God deposited me softly on the turf before the hard world came hurtling up and smashed into my back. There was a noise like the roaring of the sea and I found, panicking, that I could not breathe. My lungs had ceased to function, I was drowning on dry land.

"You all right, youngster?" said a huge head with a thatch of straw-colored hair directly above me. It was almost blocking out the sun. I could not breathe and I only made the merest of nods. "That," the giant head continued, "is another use of the shield. Take note." An enormous hand came toward me and, taking a bunch of my chain mail hauberk in its fist, raised me to my feet. "Had enough?" said John, as I stumbled around on legs of jelly trying to collect my dropped sword and poniard.

"'Course not," I said, but I was weaving on my feet, trying to find my balance and walking in circles. "Do your worst, John, you big bug bigger . . . Come on, come on, I'll have you this time . . ." Suddenly I vomited; a heave and a gush of half-digested food splashed out on to the green grass.

"If that is your weapon of choice," said John indicating the pool of stinking vomit, "I surrender to you, O noble knight. You have bested me." And he bowed low, to ironic cheers from the crowd.

A tall figure with sandy blond hair and a crumpled face pushed through the throng and made his way over to me. "Dale," said Sir James de Brus, "Lord Locksley wants to see you in his counting house. If you are at liberty . . ." He looked down his nose at me, as I stood there swaying: sweaty, winded, with strands of yellow spit-vomit hanging from my mouth. Then he sniffed once and turned away.

I recovered my wind on the way back up to the castle, but my right forearm and ribs ached from the mighty blow that John had dealt me. But, by the time I was entering the courtyard of the castle, my head had cleared and I was thinking about my next bout with John. And I knew exactly how to get him . . .

Robin's counting house, the treasury where he kept his silver, was a low, strongly built structure next to the hall. I knocked on the door and was called in and I found Robin, seated in front of a large table covered with a checkered cloth of black and white squares on which he used to reckon his accounts. Colored pebbles were placed on various squares of the cloth, tokens that represented different amounts of money. The room was dim, the narrow windows not permitting much light, and Robin had a candle on the table in front of him. He looked half-furious, half-puzzled and was alternately peering at a sheaf of parchments gripped in one fist and glaring at the pebbles on the checkered cloth.

"I don't understand it," he said. "This can't be right . . . I wish Hugh was here to deal with this . . ." and then he stopped abruptly as if he had bitten his tongue.

I knew why: Hugh, his older brother, had at one time been his chief lieutenant, chancellor, spy master and had controlled the money for Robin's band when they had been outlaws. But Hugh had betrayed Robin to Sir Ralph Murdac and when his treachery had been exposed he had been messily executed in front of us all by Little John.

Robin threw down the parchments on the table in disgust. "I can't make head nor tail of this," he said, "but I can show you in a much more simple way why we have a big problem. Go to the big coffer yonder and open it."

On the far side of the room was a huge iron-bound chest. In more carefree days, it had contained Robin's hoard of silver; the river of money that flowed from robbing wealthy travelers in Sherwood, or which had been paid to Robin by villages seeking his protection, or offered as tribute by friends, rivals, even enemies, seeking his justice—the silver river had flowed into that huge, oak-and-iron bound box, filling it to the brim.

I hesitated—in our outlaw days, to touch the coffer was an offense punishable by death. "Go on," said Robin with a touch of irritation, as he saw me pausing, "just open it. You have my full permission."

I turned the key in the lock, with some difficulty, and slid back the locking bar. Then I pushed up the heavy oak lid of the box. I looked inside: the coffer was empty, apart from a handful of silver pennies that winked at me from the bottom of the wooden space. The money was gone.

CHAPTER THREE

I looked at Robin aghast. "It's been stolen," I blurted. "Who would dare? And how could they . . ."

"It hasn't been stolen, Alan, at least I don't think so," interrupted Robin. "It has been spent. By me. I handed over an earl's ransom—quite literally—to arrange our pardons, and outfitting this company for war in Outremer has not been cheap. The Locksley rents are mostly paid in kind, and with an army to feed . . . No, Alan, I have simply spent more than I should have. So, we have a problem. The King bids us join him in Lyons with all our forces in July—that's what his letter said—and I have to transport four hundred men-at-arms, and two hundred horses, as well as a mountain of equipment, food, weapons and forage to France. And though the King has promised to recompense me for providing battle-ready men, I have yet to see any of his silver, and if I know royalty, I won't

see any before we parade inside the broken gates of Jerusalem."
He paused, thinking for a moment. Then he said: "We need
the Jews, Alan; we need Reuben."

An hour later, Robin and myself were on the road, our
horses' noses pointing north toward York. We rode fast, just
the two of us, unaccompanied by any of Robin's men. This
was unusual behavior for a great man, and not a little dangerous, too: Robin had plenty of enemies between Sheffield
and York who would be pleased to have him fall into their
hands. Although he was no longer an outlaw, with the King
abroad he could have been held for ransom by any avaricious
baron; and then there was the matter of Murdac's price on
his head.

"I don't want to be bothered with a long train of servants
and men-at-arms," said Robin when I raised my concerns
about him traveling without protection. "And, besides, I'm
taking you along to look after me," he grinned. "Are you not
up to the job?" I frowned at him. I knew why he wanted to
travel light; he didn't want anyone to know that he was short
of money. He planned to visit Reuben, an old and trusted
friend, arrange to borrow a large quantity of cash from the Jews
of York, and be back in Kirkton in a couple of days. "Come
on, Alan. We'll travel in plain, ordinary clothes, a couple of
pilgrims, but well armed and moving fast—no pomp, no fan-
fare, it'll be just like the old days, we'll have some fun . . ."

And it was fun. I rarely got to spend time alone with
Robin these days, and while I was still very slightly afraid of
him—I never forgot that among other heinous crimes he had
condoned the murder of his own brother—I always relished
his company. And we were well armed: both of us in mail
coats, Robin with his war bow and arrow bag, and a fine
sword, myself with my old sword and poniard. I also wore
my new sky blue embroidered hood, but that was only to
annoy Robin and show him that, while I'd always be his

loyal man, I cared not a fig for his hidebound ideas about headwear.

We pushed our horses hard for several hours and then, as night began to fall, we bivouacked in a small wood not far from Pontefract Castle. That great castle was held by Roger de Lacy, the new Sheriff of Nottinghamshire, and we could have received a welcome worthy of an Earl in his stone hall, had we chosen; but Robin wanted to keep his journey secret; and I was happy for as few people as possible to know that Robin was roaming the countryside with only one armed retainer. I think, too, in hindsight, that Robin occasionally found the trappings of his earldom a heavy burden and he longed for a return to the simple life of an outlaw; although he had never yet actually voiced this feeling to me.

Robin had brought cold roast beef, typically ignoring the fact that it was Lent, in fact, only five days away from Easter Sunday, and according to Church law we were supposed to be eschewing meat of any kind. He also brought bread, onions and a skin of wine and we made a cheerful camp with a small fire under a great spreading oak. And after we'd eaten, as the sparks danced above the fire, we wrapped ourselves in our warm green cloaks and sat cross-legged around the cheerful blaze, with our weapons close at hand. Robin took a long pull from the half-full wine skin before passing it to me. I drank deeply and passed it back.

"Do you think Murdac actually has a hundred pounds of German silver?" I asked him, wiping my mouth.

"It doesn't matter," he said. "Every man within a hundred miles will have heard of the offer by now; and half of them will be thinking of how they can claim it. It was a very good move on his part. I salute the slimy little bastard." Robin lifted the wine skin toward the fire and took another long drink.

"I had him once, you know," he said. "I had his life in the palm of my hand, and I let him go. Foolish of me; I should have killed him there and then. And I wouldn't have this problem now. I could have avoided a lot of trouble if I had just snuffed him out there and then." He brought his forefinger and thumb together with a soft snap. "But I felt pity for him. I say pity, but it was merely weakness, in truth. He begged for his life on his knees and I couldn't kill him. Sheer bloody weakness—arrogance, too. But then no man can see the future." He sighed and drank again.

"When was this?" I asked.

"Here, take this; I've had enough," said Robin passing me the wine skin. He never drank to excess but I sensed that, that night, he might have wanted to. I took a small drink myself and kept quiet.

"It was about seven, eight years ago, long before you joined us. We were just a handful of men then: John, Much the miller's son, Owain and a dozen or so others. Waylaying rich travelers, mainly. I used to invite them to dinner in the forest, and then make they pay for the privilege. It was just a childish game, really. We were on the move all the time in Sherwood, dodging the sheriff's men, fearful that a decent-sized company of soldiers would find us. No more than a piti-ful band of wandering footpads. I realized that I needed some real money to build the organization I wanted; I needed, well . . . respect from the villages. I wanted to do something big. I needed to do something spectacular. So John and I cooked up a plan."

He shrugged off his cloak, went over to the woodpile and threw another branch on the fire. Sitting down again, and extending his hands to the blaze, he continued: "We de-cided to rob the High Sheriff of Nottinghamshire, Derbyshire and the Royal Forests himself, in his own castle." Through the leaping flames I could see his face clearly: he was smiling with pleasure at the thought, his silver eyes shining in the darkness.

"There was to be a swordplay competition at the

Nottingham Fair, open to all, and we decided that John should enter, calling himself . . . What was it? . . . something preposterous, something woody . . . Greenleaf, I think. That's it. Reynald Greenleaf was to be his name. He was to try and get himself noticed by Sir Ralph Murdac and get himself taken on as sergeant-at-arms in the castle. Well, you know John, he won the contest easily, even killing his opponent in the final round. And Murdac swiftly took John on as a sergeant in the castle."

I was fascinated. I had never heard this tale before. Robin rummaged in the food sack and brought out the remains of the beef joint. He cut off a thin, delicate slice, and popped it in his mouth. I took another drink from the wine skin. "It wasn't a subtle plan, the robbery," said Robin, chewing slowly. "We were after Murdac's dining silver; the best goblets, cups and plates, mazers, bowls and platters that he used on feast days in his hall. And we heard that they were kept in a locked room off the kitchen.

"John waited three days, playing the part of a loyal man-at-arms, and after midnight on the third day he went down to the kitchen, broke open the door of the store and filled a sack with the silver plates. Halfway through, he was discovered by the head cook, a huge man, and almost as strong as John himself. Apparently, they had an almighty set-to in the kitchen, pots and pans flying everywhere, and they beat each other to bloody steak. Must have made a hell of a racket. Eventually, John managed to knock him out and get away with the sack of clanking metal. But it wasn't a smooth escape; the disturbance made by the fight in the kitchen had roused the castle and when John galloped out of Nottingham on a stolen horse, he was followed by Sir Ralph Murdac and a score of his men-at-arms, buzzing like angry wasps, hastily dressed and only half-armed." Robin poked the fire with a thin stick, setting his makeshift poker alight. He waved it in the air to extinguish the blue flames.

"Of course, we were waiting for John in the forest, and when Murdac's half-dressed soldiers turned up, we shot them to pieces with our bows from dense cover. They didn't stand a chance. The soldiers charged into a hail of arrows and, without proper armor, in three heartbeats there were a dozen empty saddles and a trail of men bleeding, cursing and dying on the forest floor. The rest had to run for it."

He stopped for a moment. "But they left Ralph Murdac behind."

"So you captured the sheriff himself?"

"Yes, we had him, and he was wounded, not badly, just an arrow in the flesh of his left arm. But his horse had been pierced by a couple of shafts and had thrown him. He was terrified: surrounded by a pack of bloodthirsty outlaws, men he would have hanged on sight if he had caught them in Nottingham; his own men wounded and dying around him, the rest fled. He was on his knees, pleading for his life, tears absolutely running down his face. I'll never forget the sight of someone so . . . lost.

"The men thought it was funny, of course—the high and mighty sheriff, begging for our mercy. I had my sword drawn and I was preparing to dispatch him, when Tuck intervened. And in my youthful weakness, I listened to him. 'Make him swear, on the Cross, that he will not molest us in the future,' said Tuck. 'Make him swear, by all that is holy that he will pay a ransom,' he insisted, 'and spare your soul another black stain.'

"I was soft then, a fool, and I listened to Tuck's plea. So Murdac swore a great oath that he would not pursue us in the forest, that we outlaws might do as we chose in Sherwood. He promised to deliver a ransom to the very spot he was kneeling on in three days' time, I forget how much now, but a decent sum; twenty marks, I think. And, being the idiot that I was then, I let him go."

Robin stabbed at the fire again with the stick. "He

never paid up, of course. Perhaps he had intended to do so when he was begging for his life but, once he was snug at home in Nottingham Castle, there was no chance he was going to part with his silver to an outlaw. But, strangely, he did leave us alone, for a year or more, and it gave me more than enough time to build up my strength. All manner of people came to join me. I was made, then, with the common people. The robbery was a success, in that aspect. I had their attention, and their respect."

"If you had killed Murdac, it would have brought the wrath of the King down upon you," I said. "Henry would have come north with all his might and crushed you like an insect."

"Yes, there is that," conceded Robin, "but I wish I had slit the little poison-toad's throat nonetheless."

The next day, by the early afternoon, we were walking our horses through the low arch of Micklegate Bar—with its gruesome array of the severed heads of criminals set on spikes on top—and into York. It was my first visit to this great northern town, and I was most curious to see the place. As we rode down the center of the wide street to the old bridge over the River Ouse, I took in the closely packed workshops and houses, the milling citizens, the noise and smells of the streets; there seemed to be a great number of people out of doors, far more than would be abroad in Nottingham at this hour, and many seemed to be agitated about something. There were also, I noticed, many more men-at-arms among the throng than would be usual in a town this size.

Robin seemed to be reading my thoughts: "Sir John Marshal, the sheriff of Yorkshire, is assembling local contingents here to go on the Great Pilgrimage," he noted. "You need to mind your manners, Alan, with so many soldiers about. Don't get into any trouble; don't provoke anyone to violence." As so often when he spoke to me, Robin was half-serious and half-joking.

Crossing the old bridge over the river, Robin and I moved into single file, and I covered my nose at the stench of the public latrines, wooden shacks that had been set up, their backs extending out over the slow-moving brown water so that the townsmen could relieve themselves directly into the Ouse. To my right, a couple of hundred yards away, was the mound and high wooden walls of the King's Tower, the great keep of York Castle, that glowered over the town as a reminder of the King's power in the North. On my left, a quarter of a mile away, was the magnificent soaring bulk of the Minster, a huge monument to God's glory on Earth; and next to it, slightly closer to the river, was the Abbey of St. Mary's, one of the holiest institutions in Yorkshire. Robin, I knew, had had problems with the Abbot in the past—he had mocked him publicly for his wealth, and robbed his servants as they traveled through Sherwood—and I knew he wanted to avoid the place, if at all possible.

We headed neither right to the castle nor left to the Minster, but straight up the hill through ranks of squeezed in houses, some of them two or even three stories high. It was an impressive town. And yet, even though I had never been in York before, I could sense that something was wrong in the place: fellows would scurry about shouting half-heard messages to their fellows; a gang of apprentices crossed our path heading north, drunkenly singing a song that ended in the chorus . . . "Ah-ha, ah-ha, ah-ha, another pint of ale, my boys, ah-ha, ah-ah, ah-ha, and then the Jew shall die, my boys, ah-ha, ah-ha, ah-ha . . ." It seemed that a great many people were walking up the road with us and toward the market; a tide of humanity all moving in the same direction.

I felt uneasy and glanced at Robin; he, too, was frowning but we pushed on up the hill until a space opened up to our left and, by the ripe smell of rotting meat, I knew we were passing the town's shambles. Robin put a hand on my arm and we reined in at the entrance to the meat market. In a wide space, lined with rough stalls selling bloody cuts of pork and beef, and with row upon row of dead chickens hanging by their feet, a huge crowd had formed. Standing on a box at the back of the market, a short, middle-aged man dressed in a robe like that of a monk—except that it was a grubby off-white color, instead of the usual brown—was haranguing the multitude. As Robin and I stopped to listen, more and more townspeople joined the throng in front of the monk, straining to hear his message: it soon became clear that his theme was the Great Pilgrimage, and the urgent need to free the Holy Land.

". . . and yet their beasts continue to defile our holy places; the unbelievers' cattle shitting on the very floors of the Church of the Holy Sepulcher itself; their Satan-black slaves pissing in the font where many a devout Christian babe has been baptized. How long, O Lord, how long will you suffer these Saracen desecrators to live? Where is the strong right arm of the Christian faith? Where is the army of the righteous who will scrub the Holy Land clean of these filthy, Christ-denying wretches?

"I tell you, brothers: the great men of the land are doing their part; even our good King Richard has made his solemn vow to recapture Jerusalem and rid it of these unbelieving lice that swarm on the very stones where Christ preached his blessed ministry. And all the great lords of England and France, too, are doing their part to rid the world of the foul corruption of the paynim: our noble sheriff, Sir John Marshal, brother to Christendom's greatest knight, William the Marshal, is summoning his men, brave knights from across the county of Yorkshire, to cross the seas and vanquish these stinking hordes of the Devil."

The crowd was cheering by now; wrapped up in the white priest's words. "But what can I do, you ask; how can I play my part in this great endeavor to rid the world of sin and faithlessness? What can I do?" The white monk paused, searching the crowd with his eyes. "I am no great knight, nor lord nor king, you say. I am but a humble man, a good Christian but no sword-wielding horse-warrior, with wide lands and great estates. And to you I say this: the Devil is among you! Here! Today! In this very town!" There was a collective hiss from the crowd. The white monk held out his arm, index finger extended and he moved it slowly over the crowd. For some strange reason, it was difficult not to follow the pointing finger with your eyes.

"The Devil is here, I say, among you, at this moment. You do not need to go to far Outremer to fight the good fight. You do not need to risk life and limb on the long road eastward. There are evil heretics, unbelievers, demons shaped like men who dare to reject Christ, to spit in the face of Holy Mary Mother of God . . . and they are right here in York; living among good Christian folk like human rats. You know of whom I speak; you know this form of mankind; they are the ones who steal the bread out of honest men's mouths; who with their God-cursed debt payments ruin the lives of honest men; they are the race who defy Christ, who murdered our Blessed Savior on the Cross; who even today kidnap little Christian children and slaughter them for their foul Satanic rituals . . ."

The growls from the crowd had been growing and then somebody shouted: "The Jews! The Jews!" and the crowd took up the chant, drawing out the long syllable into a deep booming "Oooooooh." It was a sound to freeze the blood, the deep roaring of the crowd chanting: "Jooooooos; kill the Jooooooos; kill the Jooooooos," low and reverberating, like the base howling of a crazed beast.

"It is God who wills it; God wills it, I say; it is God Almighty who demands that the Jews, that race of degenerate fiends be wiped from the face of the Earth . . ."

Robin was watching the monk's performance with a grim face, the white-robed man had flecks of spittle at either side of his mouth and he exhorted the crowd to hatred. "Someone should cut down that madman before he drowns the world in blood," Robin said quietly, almost to himself.

I looked at him, worried by his tone. He meant it; and yet to kill a monk or a priest, it was sacrilege of the worst sort. As a youth Robin had been outlawed for killing a holy man; surely he could not be contemplating another gross mortal sin of that magnitude. "I've heard more than enough here," said Robin. "Let's ride on. We need to warn Reuben."

There was no need to warn Reuben: when we approached the Jewish quarter, which was just outside the town's earth and wood ramparts, we could clearly see that the area had already been attacked. The street was filled with burned and broken chattels. What had been the large stone building of a wealthy man was now a smoldering ruin; Christian looters scurried in and out of the building with armfuls of smoke-blackened goods; pots and pans, blankets and chairs, small items of low value mostly but I saw a man making off with a small iron-bound chest that looked as if it had been used for storing jewels.

"That is Benedict's house; or rather, that was his house," said Robin grimly. "He is the leader of the Jews in York, if he still lives. But Reuben's place seems untouched—so far." He led us to a stout two-story wooden structure a hundred paces from the burned-out shell, set in a large garden filled with strange exotic shrubs and huge beds of herbs, for Reuben was a healer as well as a money-lender. We stopped and dismounted at the gate. The smell of the herbs was intoxicating: I could detect fine whiffs of sage and borage, rosemary and marjoram . . .

I was just stepping through the gate in the garden, and looking up at the tightly shuttered windows and studded oak door, when suddenly I felt a great shove in my back and I sprawled on the brick paving of the garden path. There was a thud behind me and I turned to see the neat black handle of a throwing knife vibrating in the gatepost.

"Reuben, it is me, Robert of Locksley, and young Alan Dale. We are your friends. We mean you no harm," called Robin, who was crouched behind a small bush behind me. "Reuben, you know us! Let us enter!"

A window shutter opened a fraction on the first floor, and I saw a brown face peering out suspiciously, curly brown hair and oak-tough brown eyes. "What do you want with me, Christian?" said a hard voice.

"Actually, I want to borrow some money," said Robin and his face creased into one of his finest smiles.

Reuben's daughter Ruth brought us bread, cheese and wine. She was a comely girl about my own age; tall, slender but full-breasted, veiled, of course, but with huge liquid brown eyes, and I sensed that she was smiling at me behind the thin white curtain of fine cloth that covered her face. I smiled back at her, then dropped my eyes uncertainly, as she continued to gaze at me boldly over her veil.

"That will be all, Ruth," snapped Reuben, and his daughter turned away and dutifully left us to our meal.

"I should beat the sauciness out of her, I know," said Reuben, "but as she is my only child, and she reminds me so much of her mother—may her soul rest in the bosom of Abraham—who died bringing Ruth into this world, I cannot bring myself to chastise her." He ushered the three of us over to a great table in his hall, and invited us to sit. For a townhouse, it was huge, and I wondered whether the decision by the people of York to exclude Jews from living inside their walls had not, in some way, been beneficial to Reuben and his tribe: compared with the cramped rows of houses in town, the Jews had the space to build themselves large, stout houses with spacious gardens between the wall and the river Foss, and yet they were still only a quarter of an hour's walk from the center of York.

"These are bad times to be a Jew in a Christian land, my young friend," said Reuben, half-apologizing with a smile as I handed his throwing knife back to him. It had been stuck nearly an inch deep into the oak gatepost, and it had taken a considerable amount of force to remove it from the grip of the wood. For such a thin man, Reuben was extremely strong, and I knew this, but his ability to throw a knife so far and so hard still amazed me. He tucked the blade away into a fold in his robe and poured Robin and myself a cup of wine.

"You heard what happened to us in London?" he asked Robin. My master nodded: "A terrible business," he replied gravely. At Richard's coronation in September of the previous year, a delegation of Jews had attempted to make a gift of gold to the new King. Due to some confusion at the entrance of the palace of Westminster, a riot had broken out and the Jewish delegation had been cut down by Richard's men-at-arms. Worse, the rioting spread through the whole city like a plague of hatred and many Jews had been hunted like animals through the streets of London and mercilessly slaughtered.

"But the King has since decreed that your people are under his personal protection," said Robin. "Does that not reassure you?"

"The King is in France," said Reuben darkly. "And soon he will be on the road to Outremer. He does not care for us; we are merely his sheep, to be shorn whenever it is his royal whim. Last night the mob came out of the city and burned down my friend Benedict's house. He's dead, you know, he died on the way back from London after being wounded in Westminster in the riot, but now, so too are his wife and

66

family, dragged from the house and hacked apart in the street like animals. His treasure has been stolen; the records of his debts have been destroyed. I fear that when night falls, we—Ruth and myself—will be next. But I will kill her myself before I let her fall into the hands of a Christian mob." He spoke with very little emotion in his voice but a little muscle jumped in his cheek, betraying his true feelings.

"But what of Sir John Marshal?" I asked. "As sheriff, surely it is his duty to keep the King's peace in Yorkshire."

"He is a weak man and he too owes money to Jews," said Reuben. "I do not think he would be too tormented if we were all murdered and his debts were wiped clean. But perhaps I am being unfair. These days I cannot tell friend from foe; these days, all Christians seem alike to me," he smiled at Robin to make it clear that he was speaking, at least partly, in jest. "But you came here to discuss money," he continued, "let us talk of gold and silver, not of death. How can I and my friends be of service to you?"

Robin nodded at me and I excused myself from the table—Robin preferred his financial conversations to be private—so I went over to the far side of the hall to examine a particularly beautiful tapestry that was hanging there: it showed the Holy City of Jerusalem, high on a hill, with depictions of the angels, archangels and ancient prophets, and I pondered how much, in matters of faith and tradition, the Jews and Christians had in common. Tuck had told me that much of the Bible was sacred to the Jews, too. Of course, I believed then, as I still do to this day, that all Jews are eternally damned because they have not accepted Our Lord Jesus Christ into their hearts. But I also knew in my heart that Reuben was a good man, a kind man, and a loyal friend to Robin, and I could not see any reason for him or his people to be hunted down and murdered. I turned to look at Robin and Reuben, their heads bent close together, talking quietly out of earshot at the other end of the hall. I knew what

Robin's opinion would be about the murder of Jews: he had little time for religious dogma, and he would not care a jot if a thousand Jews—or Christians—were to die, if he did not have a personal connection to them; but Reuben was his friend and erstwhile partner, and he would defend him to the death against all comers, Christian, Jew, pagan or Saracen.

Looking over at Robin and Reuben, I noticed a curious thing. Reuben was showing Robin a small packet of whitish crystals. Robin picked one up and sniffed it before handing it back to Reuben. Reuben took the small yellow-white lump in a pair of silver tongs and held it to the flame of a candle on the table. There was a crackle and a burst of white smoke, a small cloud formed over the table and a few moments later the scent reached me—it was a rich, sweet fragrance, like burning flowers, familiar—I knew I had smelled it before in a totally different context. But where? I could not think.

Robin saw me looking at them and the fast-disappearing cloud of smoke, and he frowned at me. I turned away again and resumed my study of the beautiful tapestry. What was this mysterious fragrant white substance, and why would Reuben and Robin be so interested in it?

Perhaps a quarter of an hour later, Robin called me over. The package of white crystals had disappeared, I guessed into one of the folds of Reuben's voluminous robe, and Robin and Reuben were clasping hands solemnly.

"So, it is settled then," said Robin. "Alan, we have a little errand to do before we go home, we are going to escort Reuben and Ruth to the castle. They will be safe there until this religious foolishness is over."

While Reuben gathered his rolls of parchment, his account books and valuables, and Ruth packed food and clothing, I stared out of a window on the second floor. I had a fine view of the broad street outside and the gatehouse down by the bridge over the Foss. Far beyond the city wall to my right,

I could see the Minster glowing in the evening sunlight; as I gazed on it in wonder, the great bells of the cathedral began to ring out for Vespers, and they were immediately followed by the chimes of every other belfry in York. The golden evening rang with the music of God, calling all to evening prayers, and the sound filled my heart. How could one think of hatred and death with that glorious din in your ears?

"Come on, Alan, stop daydreaming or they'll close the gatehouse," shouted Robin from below. He had the horses' reins in his hands, including a packhorse for Reuben's possessions, and I scrambled down and joined my friends.

We got to the gatehouse just as the man-at-arms was beginning to swing the great wooden doors shut. He let us through with a grumble and a dark look at Reuben and Ruth, who even though they were well swathed in cloaks, were somehow almost instantly recognizable as Jews. As we entered the town and made our way southwest toward the castle, I noticed with growing alarm that there were still far more folk in the streets than was natural at this hour. Some passersby shouted insults at Reuben and his daughter, but more worryingly, some began to follow us as we walked our horses down the narrow streets toward the castle. In the darkening streets, we began to attract an ugly train. I put my hand on my sword hilt, but Robin caught my eye and shook his head. One angry youth in a red-brown peasant's tunic lifted his garment and made an obscene gesture, jerking his hips toward Ruth.

"Jew-lovers," he yelled at us, and the rest of the gathering crowd repeated the call: "Jew-lovers, Jew-lovers." A passing man spat a great gobbet of phlegm at us, which splattered on the rump of the packhorse. I wanted to break into a trot, but again Robin signaled that we would continue to proceed at walking pace. Then, out of the corner of my eye, I saw another man pick up a loose cobblestone, and, with a shout of "Death to the Christ-killers," hurled it at our party. It hit

Ruth square in the middle of her back and she gasped in pain. Immediately, I dug my toes into Ghost's shoulder, turned him toward Ruth's assailant and spurring back, I charged my horse straight into the wretch. Ghost's chest smashed into his shoulder and he spun round and went down and under the hooves of my mount. I heard clearly the crisp snap of bone, and a muffled scream, and then drawing my sword and pausing above his groaning body, I tried, for a moment or so, to catch the eyes of anyone in the growing crowd who would match my stare—nobody would. So I turned Ghost again and trotted back to my place in our little cavalcade.

I was feeling pleased with myself but, by riding down the stone-thrower, I had unleashed something even worse. The shouting from the crowd changed from individual taunts to massed yells, growing louder and louder. Another cobblestone whistled past Ghost's neck, and another, then one hit Robin on the thigh with a meaty smack. He made no sound, merely drew his sword and signaled to me that now we should pick up the pace. We began to trot, the horses' steel shoes making a sharp rattle on the cobbles, forcing angry folk out of our path. A few more stones flew, splintering on the road ahead of us, but although we swiftly outdistanced the angry mob behind us, there were more folk appearing in front. One misshapen fellow, his back unnaturally twisted, who was supporting himself on a large wooden crutch, was capering directly in our path, pointing a finger at our party and shouting: "Jews . . . Jews . . . Jews . . ." As we approached at the trot, he swung his crutch up at Robin who was nearest to him in a vicious scything blow that would have crushed his skull if it had landed. But Robin front-blocked the blow easily with his sword, and then chopped down in a classic move that Little John had made me practice hundreds of times. The blade sliced into the twisted man's scalp, there was a spray of bright blood and he dropped as if boneless to the cobbles.

There was a roar of rage from the crowd behind, a deep,

animal sound that lifted the hairs on the back of my neck, and they surged forward in a pack. "Close up," said Robin, raising his voice above the tumult. He sounded calm, icy, as he always did in battle. "Close up, Alan, and feel free to take out anyone, anyone who stands in our path." I grinned at him nervously.

As he spoke a man suddenly leaped from the open window in the house we were passing. He launched himself from a position almost level with me and nearly knocked me from the saddle; he grabbed me around the waist and, before I had time to react, he had straddled Ghost's hindquarters and was punching a short knife into my back, trying for my kidneys. Praise God, my chain mail hauberk under my cloak kept the blade from my flesh. Without thinking, I swiveled fast and elbowed him hard in the side of the head. I felt his grasp loosen, so then reversing my grip on my drawn sword, pointing it toward my own body, I drove it backward, through the gap between my own left arm and my left side, and deep into the flesh of his side. He fell away, screeching and spurting blood. We spurred back and shot out from the press of folk, and suddenly we were clear and moving fast, bloody swords in our fists, galloping toward the castle, the gates of which were only two hundred yards away. Behind us the mob howled like a wolf pack and broke into a run.

I saw a big, dark-haired man, directly in our path, cradling a great Dane axe and swaying his weight gently from foot to foot. He smiled broadly, madly, and waited for us to thunder down on him; no doubt planning to dodge at the last moment and slash the legs of one of the horses as they passed, bringing one of us tumbling to earth. Suddenly his expression changed, the smile drained away and his face sagged like a candle put too close to the fire. I noticed in the same instant that the black handle of a throwing knife had sprouted from his broad chest; he sank to his knees, the axe clattered to the ground, and then we were past. A spearman appeared on my left and stabbed a rusty point at me, but I swept his spearhead out of my way, and slashed back at him with my poniard; Robin effortlessly cut down a man wielding a huge ancient two-handed sword and then we were through the gates and safely into the bailey of York Castle.

Panting, we hauled our beasts to a halt in the center of the broad space—and immediately noticed that something was wrong. There were no mounted men-at-arms to greet us, to ask us our business, there were almost no people in sight at all, and those we could see were in the garb of servants. Where was Sir John Marshal? We had expected to have the gate shut behind us by trained soldiers, determined to hold the castle in the face of the deranged mob. But the place seemed almost deserted. I turned to look at the gate. It was still wide open, and a column of furious, shouting citizens, filling the street, hundreds of them, was rapidly approaching. Torches had been lit to counter the gloom, and in the flickering light I caught a glimpse of a dirty white robe in the leading ranks of the throng. Then I ducked instinctively as a hail of sticks, stones, even a few arrows came showering toward us.

"To the Tower, to the King's Tower," said Reuben breathlessly. "All the others are in the Tower."

I looked to my right, at the grim, brooding height of the King's Tower, the strong, square wooden keep of York Castle. And we all instinctively spurred toward it. It was built on a great mound of earth nearly thirty feet high, and the high, stout walls added another twenty feet to its grandeur. It looked strong enough to stand until Judgment Day, and as we cantered over the narrow rammed-earth causeway that linked the Tower to the bailey, I began to feel a little safer. Leading our horses up the steep set of wooden steps that was the final approach to the keep, and through the narrow, thick iron-studded door at the top, we were welcomed by a tall balding man, wearing a black skullcap, with a kindly lined face and gray beard.

"*Shalom aleichem,*" the old man said. "I am Josce of York, and you are most welcome here." The thick oak door slammed behind us, closing out the buzz of the angry world, and the locking bar slid home with a reassuring thump.

CHAPTER FOUR

The King's Tower was packed with Jews—from doddery old crones to strapping young men, and suckling babes in their mother's arms—there must have been at least a hundred and fifty souls squashed into the three stories of the keep like salted fish in a barrel. And two good Christians. Well, one Christian and Robin. I had never seen so many Jews in one place before, and it was a strange experience for me. They spoke English or French to each other but occasionally dropped briefly into another guttural language that I could not understand; very few of them had brought arms with them when they had come to the Tower, which seemed strange to me for people under threat of violence, but it was no matter as the keep was already well stocked with weapons. And they argued constantly about everything. But the strange thing was that, although they could be shouting at their fellows or family members one minute, the next, they had hugged and kissed and all was calm again; and they never came to blows with each other no matter what insults had been exchanged. I was astounded. In a Christian community, the aggressive tone of their disputations alone would have been enough to start the fists flying.

They were a sober, orderly lot, too, courteous and kind to me; and so I liked them. They had all brought food, too, and it was comforting to know that while we had to shelter in the Tower, there would be plenty to eat.

There was precious little room in the lower part of the Tower for equine accommodation but we managed to make our horses reasonably comfortable with food bags and water within reach of their noses. Then Robin and I climbed three stories to the roof of the Tower by a narrow staircase in one corner of the building. As we surveyed the area around the castle keep, it dawned on me that we were surrounded. The King's Tower had been built for defense, it was undeniably a secure fortress, but for us it was also a trap from which we could not easily escape. To the southwest ran the river Ouse, deep and slow; a fit man could swim it easily but what about a horde of Jewish grandmothers and suckling babies? There was no escape for us there. To the east ran the river Foss, once again unpassable except by one small bridge. To the north there was a line of campfires burning in the evening gloom around which moved scores of men-at-arms and towns-folk, clearly beginning to prepare their suppers. To the south was the bailey of the castle, now filling with the very people, the maddened Jew-haters, we had had to run from in the streets. It was full dark by now, but the bailey was so well lit with torches and fires that the scene was easy to make out. Hundreds of folk were milling around in confusion in the open space at the center of the bailey, but a knot had gathered around a short speaker in a light-colored robe by the chapel on the western side who was holding a large wooden staff with a cross piece tied to it to make the holy symbol.

He was haranguing the crowd and thumping the earth with his cross to emphasize his points, and I recognized the white-robed monk from that afternoon. His message seemed to be the same vile spew of poison as then, for every now and then he would fling out his arm and indicate the Tower. Beside him stood a tall knight in chain mail, a long sword at his waist, carrying a shield with the device of a scarlet clenched fist on a pale blue field. He looked familiar, but it was only when two men-at-arms approached with lit torches and stood beside him that I caught sight of his face. He had a shock of white hair in the center of his forehead, standing out clearly from the russet mass of the rest, and I recognized the illiterate, feral-eyed foxy knight from my encounter with Prince John.

Just then Josce of York appeared beside us, his gray beard awry and out of breath from climbing the Tower's stairs too fast, and the three of us stood at the battlements and stared out over the bailey. I was straining my ears to make out the white monk's hate-filled words when Robin spoke: "Who is that ill-looking knight?" he asked Josce.

"He is Sir Richard Malbête, sometimes called the Evil Beast," the tall Jew replied. "Some say he is part demon, for it is whispered that he loves the pain of other men more than he loves meat and drink. My friend Joseph of Lincoln holds his note for twenty thousand marks. He is a ferocious one, Malbête, and he hates all mankind, but especially he hates Jews. More than just for his great debts to us, I believe; he hates us with a passion that surpasses all earthly reason. Perhaps he really is a demon."

"He is a close friend of Prince John," I added. And both Josce and Robin looked at me in surprise. "He was at Nottingham two weeks ago."

Robin nodded and then said to Josce: "And the other man, the white monk. Who is he?"

"He is Brother Ademar, a wandering lunatic who formerly belonged to a Premonstratensian canonry; he escaped the cloister walls and has been preaching hatred against the Jews for more than a month now, since your Christian season of Lent began. But the people listen to him for all his lunacy. They say he has been touched by God."

Robin said nothing. But I remembered his comment earlier in the day: *Someone should cut down that madman before he drowns the world in blood.*

"Can we hold out here until things become calmer—or the King sends help?" asked Josce; he sounded more weary than worried. Robin looked around the small square of the Tower's ramparts. About a score of angry-looking young Jewish men were watching the bailey from behind the crenellations, occasionally replying in kind to the insults from below. And every five yards or so along the parapet there was a pile of a dozen stones, each one about the size of a man's head, which could be hurled down on any attacker with devastating effect. Robin always said that the main weapon in any castle's armory was its height, and we were a good fifty feet above any attackers. Stones that had been laboriously hauled up to the top by members of the former garrison could be sent back down again at great cost in blood to the enemy.

"I believe so," said Robin. "We have enough men to see them off until help arrives or they come to their senses. It would be better if this place were stone-built. But I think we may hold them. As long as that rabble doesn't get hold of any artillery." He looked at me. And I remembered with a shudder how, at the battle of Linden Lea, Sir Ralph Murdac had brought up a machine for throwing great boulders and how, once he had the range, the massive missiles had smashed through our wooden walls as if they were made of straw.

Josce seemed satisfied. "Will you come down and speak to everybody?" he asked. "I think it would help."

Robin stared at him for a second. His eyes were blank and metallic and the silence went on for an uncomfortably long time. "I will be down in a few moments. I must speak to Alan, first," he said finally. Josce bowed his balding head. "Thank you. I will call everyone together," he said and he gathered up his robe to free his feet and moved away to the stairs.

When the old man had gone, Robin took me by the arm. "You must go, Alan. You can get out, you know." I merely stared at him in disbelief. He continued: "Wait until midnight, and take a rope from the stores. You just have to shin down the walls and swim the Ouse; even if you're caught, as a Christian, you will be safe."

"We could both go," I said, testing him, although I knew what his answer would be.

"I can't leave." Robin looked me full in the face. "I need Reuben. Reuben is the money and the connection; I need to keep Reuben alive, or . . . well, I must keep him alive," he said simply, then: "I think this is going to be very bad, very bad indeed, and so I must urge you to leave—tonight. This is not your fight."

I squared my shoulders, and looked back into his pale, grey eyes. "When I first entered your service," I said stiffly, "I swore that I would be loyal to you until death. I will not break that oath. If you will stay here and face battle against these madmen, then I will remain with you."

"You really are an idiot, Alan," said Robin but in a kindly voice, "a sentimental idiot. But thank you." And he smiled and slapped me on the shoulder. "So be it, then. We fight. Now I suppose I'd better go and rally the troops."

With that, he was gone. I remained at the battlements staring out into the darkness and wondering whether I had made an enormous, possibly fatal mistake. The bailey seemed to be settling down for the night and I saw in the light of the few remaining torches hundreds of people making up beds under the eaves of the castle buildings while others, armed any-old-how with rusty spears and axes, rakes and scythes, were standing guard, almost like regular soldiers. The white monk had ceased his shouting and gone, and of Sir Richard Malbête there was nothing to be seen. I looked down to my right, at the black Ouse, and saw that dozens of campfires had now been built between the bottom of the Tower mound and the river. The Jew-hating rabble had not dispersed, not at all. They appeared to have grown in number, and someone was organizing them, almost certainly a soldier—for they surrounded us like a besieging army. Whatever Robin had said, it would not have been easy for me to escape. The blood-hungry mob had not gone away, back to their homes, calmed by the falling of night. They were there to stay. And, come morning, they would try to get into the Tower. We were in for a hard fight. My hands went to my waist, to the hilts of my poniard and sword on either side of my body. If I were to die the next day, I would take a few of these damned lunatics with me, I said bravely to myself, but the ice-snake in my belly gave a little slither of fear.

Just then a small hand touched my arm and I jumped like a startled rabbit, jerking the poniard half out of its scabbard. Ruth was at my side, and she was proffering a steaming wooden bowl. "Don't do that," I said crossly, "don't sneak up on people. I could easily have killed you."

She frowned. "I am sorry for frightening you like that," she said.

"You did not frighten me," I said, still annoyed. "I was merely regarding the enemy and considering our best stratagems for tomorrow." I was being pompous and I regretted it as soon as the words were out of my mouth.

She said nothing, but handed me the bowl of fish stew, gesturing that I should eat. I sank down on to the floor of the parapet, back against the thick wooden wall and began to spoon the mixture into my mouth. She crouched down beside me, watching. The food was absolutely delicious, and

I was surprised that somebody had bothered to make a proper hot meal in these difficult circumstances. I flashed a smile at her, and she smiled back. Friends again.

"I never thanked you for escorting us here," she said. Her brown eyes above her veil filled with warmth and gratitude. "I was so scared and you were so brave, like a hero, like Jonathan fighting the Philistines . . ."

I seemed to be losing my appetite as I stared into those deep twin pools. Gruffly, I said: "I'm no Jonathan, I was merely doing my duty . . ." I couldn't think of anything more to say, there was a lump in my throat and my cheeks were glowing. I was secretly very glad that she thought me a hero. But I hoped she could not see my blushes in the darkness.

"Will you stay and protect us against . . ." she made a sideways jerk of her head, indicating the bailey of the castle, ". . . them?" I put down the nearly empty bowl and took her hand. "My lady," I said awkwardly, too loud for the quiet of the night, "I shall protect you from these evil men, even at cost of my own life. They shall never harm you." Ruth lifted her free hand to my cheek and softly stroked the downy skin. "Thank you, Alan," she said.

I shudder now, looking back after more than forty years, to hear my young self making such rash promises. And I can scarcely bear to remember what happened afterward—but recall it I shall, as I swore to do so. And perhaps by remembering the past unflinchingly, I shall be granted forgiveness by Our Lord for my sins in those dark days.

I followed Ruth down the spiral staircase in the corner of the Tower, watching with great interest the narrow waist and the way she swayed her hips as she walked, and on the ground floor, we came across a gathering of all the Jewish men of fighting age. They did not look a very formidable force. There were about forty of them, ranging in years from fourteen to fifty, mostly dark or gray haired and with a beaten, hangdog look. They looked ashamed, frightened; no one man wanting to meet another's eye. Ruth slipped away and I watched as Robin, confidence personified, strode into the center of the square space and stood on an old wooden box so that everyone could see him. He had an unloaded crossbow held casually over his shoulder, and began, as he had put it "to rally the troops."

"My friends, be quiet and listen to me for a moment," he said loudly. "Give me your ears, my friends, and I will give you the good news, the excellent news about our situation." The Jews looked at him curiously, as if they had another madman in their midst. "We are fortunate," Robin began again, even more loudly, and there was a stirring and muttering in the crowd. "I say we are fortunate because we are here . . ."

One man stepped out from the loose circle that had formed around Robin; a big, sturdy man in a dark blue robe with a magnificent bushy red beard. His angry voice cut straight across Robin's speech. "Fortunate, how? Fortunate to be hunted like wild pigs through our own city? Fortunate to be driven from our homes, our friends and family butchered, our silver stolen?"

"You are fortunate that you are not dead," interrupted Robin coolly. "Would you not agree?" He paused for a beat or two, but the red-haired man said nothing. "Fortunate that that pack of murderous lunatics"—Robin flung out an arm and pointed to the door that led outside and down to the bailey—"did not tear you apart." There were growls of anger from the crowd. "But that aside," said Robin continuing calmly, "at this moment you are fortunate in other matters, too. Firstly, in this Tower; this is a stronghold designed to be held by a handful of warriors against a much bigger army. And we have those warriors. Before me I see men of courage; men who are willing to fight as hard as any knight and, if necessary, to die, in defense of their families, in defense of their pride, and their honor as men." I saw a few of the younger Jews nodding.

"I see men of courage before me, men ready for battle, and in that we are most fortunate," Robin went on. "With good men such as you, we can hold this Tower until the heavens fall. We have food, we have water and ale, and we have brave men. So, I say, we are fortunate." I saw then that the mood had changed subtly; it was something that I had noticed before when Robin spoke. He could command men's feelings; he had a trick of making them feel that they were better than they truly were. The Jews were standing more erect now, shoulders more square, stomachs pulled in, heads high. They saw themselves as warriors, not sheep to be driven by a hate-filled mob, but hard fighters, men of blood and iron.

"The second piece of good fortune is that we have these," said Robin, lifting the crossbow off his shoulder and holding it up in the air. "We have more than three dozen of these weapons, and enough quarrels to send more than a thousand souls to Hell." He took the crossbow and cradled it in his arms. "With this weapon, and the others we have here, we can easily hold fast until this evil sickness which has seized the towns-people releases them. We can keep the Devil at bay until they return to their senses or until help comes. So I say again that we are fortunate. We have the men, we have the weapons, and we have the guts to use them. God smiles on us. We . . . are . . . fortunate."

The crowd of Jews actually cheered him. It was an astonishing turnaround. A few moments ago they had been a sullen, frightened herd of persecuted sheep; now they saw themselves as a band of noble warriors ready to do or die.

"Now listen closely to me, my friends," said Robin. "These weapons are very simple to use but quite deadly." As I watched him demonstrate how to load the crossbow, I caught his eye and he shot me a surreptitious grin and a wink.

It was indeed a simple weapon to use. The stiff crossbow cord is pulled back using the power of the whole of a man's body. You put your right foot in the stirrup at the end of the machine and haul back the cord with both hands while extending the right leg until the cord is locked into place with a pair of iron teeth near the stock. Then you place a quarrel in the groove on the top of the weapon, put the weapon to your shoulder, aim and pull up the trigger, or tickle as it is known, below the stock. The iron teeth are pulled down by the tickle, releasing the bow cord, which springs forward and shoots the quarrel away at man-killing speed. It was quite accurate at close range, and packed enough power to penetrate chain mail at fifty paces.

"Take off your hood, Alan, and hold it out to the side," Robin suddenly addressed me as I lounged against a stack of boxes by the wall, trying to look confident—and I felt my heart sink. I knew what he had in mind. I sighed but, loyal as ever, I took my headgear off and held it out as far as possible from my body, close to the rough wooden planks of the wall.

There was a *twang,* and my beautiful hood was snatched from my grasp and pinned to the wood by a foot of steel-tipped oak. "Everybody see that?" said Robin. "Right, form a line, everyone gets one shot at the hood," he gave me a grin of pure mischief, "and then Alan will issue each one of you with a crossbow and a dozen quarrels."

I passed an uneasy but largely uneventful night, curled up below the battlements and sleeping only fitfully. Without my hood my head was cold. The one excitement during the night was that one of Robin's bold new warriors had managed to shoot himself in the foot with a crossbow bolt and had to be carried down the stairs, weeping with pain, while his fellows jeered at his ineptitude.

Dawn broke on a dismal scene. More townspeople seemed to have arrived during the night to swell the ranks of the besiegers—there were now perhaps five or six hundred people milling around below the Tower, occasionally shouting up insults and making threatening gestures but largely ignoring us.

There was no sign of the garrison of the castle, or Sir John Marshal, the sheriff of Yorkshire. One of the young Jewish men had told me that there had been a handful of soldiers when the first refugees arrived at the Tower, but they had departed as soon as the place began to fill with Jews. That made me uneasy. It sounded as if they had orders to leave the Tower to the Jews. Why else would they abandon their posts? Had it been somebody's plan to lure all the Jews into one place where they could more easily be killed? No, surely that was madness.

The sun was high in the sky, about halfway to its zenith, and the bells of York were ringing out for the office of Terce when Brother Ademar, the mad white monk, began to preach again. As had been the case the night before, the foxy knight Malbête stood beside him, towering over the short monk as he ranted about God and the Devil, the Holy Pilgrimage and the deaths of Jews. I could not actually make out the full sense of the monk's words, but small snatches caught on the breeze and wafted his hatred to my ears like the smell of rotting filth. His audience, however, seemed to appreciate his speech. At one point, he bade everyone kneel and he blessed them before leading the crowd in the *Pater Noster*. Then he resumed his hate-filled ranting, thumping the ground with his cross-staff.

Robin had divided his fighting men into three groups, or companies, of about fifteen men, a mix of ages and abilities. At all times, one company would be resting on the ground floor and two would be on duty defending the castle. There were enough crossbows for each man on duty to have one, and several men had found swords and even a spear or two with which to defend themselves.

"When they come," said Robin to the thirty-odd Jewish men, the two companies who were to take first turn at the Tower's defense, "they will be confident. We let them come close, closer than is comfortable and then we smash them. Utterly. With luck we can make them regret they ever challenged us. Does everybody understand?" There were murmurs of assent.

"I'm going to repeat it anyway. When they come, we let them get close. Nobody is to shoot until I give the order. Is that clear? If anybody shoots before I give the order, I will personally throw him off the walls and feed him to the Christians. Is that clear?"

The man who had interrupted Robin's speech the night before muttered something inaudible into his big, red bushy beard. But when Robin looked hard at him, he said nothing. I caught Reuben's eye in the throng of Jewish warriors and we exchanged wry smiles. He looked tired, but he held the crossbow casually as if he had been born with it in his hands.

"Now it's just a question of waiting," said Robin and he sat down in the shade of the battlements. Stretching out his long legs and pulling his hood over his eyes, he appeared to be readying himself for sleep. He had his long war bow, unstrung beside him, and he put one hand on it, lifted up a corner of his hood with the other hand and glanced at me. "Keep an eye on things, will you Alan," he said, and yawned. "Wake me in two hours if nothing has happened." And then he fell asleep.

The Jews were mystified by his nonchalance. But they too began to find comfortable places to sit with their backs to the battlements. Food was passed around, and wineskins, and some men even began to sing quietly to themselves, a weird and wonderful tune of the like I had never heard before. Their eerie music did not seem to obey the golden rules of that art that I had so painstakingly learned from my former music master, the French *trouvère* Bernard de Sezanne, who now served Queen Eleanor of Aquitaine, the mother of King Richard—and yet it was truly beautiful.

As ancient Jewish music drifted around me, I looked out over the bailey at the crowd of misguided Christian fools listening to the hate-blasted preaching of Brother Ademar, and loosened my blades in their scabbards. My own loaded crossbow was propped against the battlement, and I had a dozen quarrels stuffed in my belt. There were times when I could almost understand Robin's mistrust of the Christian faith—times like these, when a holy representative of God on earth was exhorting Christians to slaughter their fellow countrymen—but I knew in my heart that it could not be Jesus's teachings that were at fault. The evil did not come from Him, it must come from the Devil, or from Man's original sinfulness. Only Christ held the answer, only Christ could rid the world of evil, I was sure. Or almost sure.

The attack came not long after noon. I had been half listening to the sounds of the crowd as Ademar whipped them with his words, while Robin snored gently at my feet. The crowd sounded like the roar and crash of the sea breaking on a shingle beach; in a strange, horrible way, it was soothing; just a big ceaseless sound, seemingly unconnected with any evil. Then suddenly there was movement in the bailey; Brother Ademar had ended a long harangue with a great shout, there was a louder than usual roar from the masses and he plunged into the crowd of listeners, and forced his way through the bodies like a man swimming in a sea of humanity. He was followed by Malbête, surging forward through the populace in the wake of the monk, and surrounded by a knot of half a dozen men-at arms wearing surcoats in scarlet and sky blue, the colors of the Evil Beast himself.

Ademar emerged from the press at the gate of the bailey and entrance of the rammed-earth causeway leading up to the Tower. He turned to the packed masses behind him and shouted a last exhortation, at this distance I could hear him clearly, and I swear he bellowed: "These Christ-killing lice must be swept from the earth! The earth must be cleansed! God wills it! God wills it!" And his words were answered by another great roar from the crowd. He raised his six-foot wooden cross and, alone, he charged up the earth ramp and on to the wooden steps that led the last few yards up to the Tower. And with a crazed howl that froze my heart, the crowd of screaming Christians, the good citizens of York, rushed after him like a river in spate.

I had long since woken Robin and he was passing along the file of Jews lining the parapet giving encouragement. Each Jew was clutching a crossbow, but many looked terrified. "Do not shoot, do *not* shoot," Robin was shouting, his freshly strung war bow in one hand, and it was hard to hear him over the deep booming hatred of the crowd below. "When I give the signal, we will crush these vermin, not before, hold your peace until I give the order. Do. Not. Shoot."

Miraculously, not a Jew fired his crossbow, not a javelin or stone was hurled. "Wait for it, wait for it," Robin was shouting, and then I noticed him doing a strange thing. He put down his bow and reached for a boulder, one of hundreds that had been piled in heaps around the battlements. He took it in both hands, holding it to his chest. It was about the same size as a man's head. Then he looked out over the parapet and down at the surging mob below. The white monk was at the iron-bound gate of the Tower; he was hammering at the oak door with the butt end of his cross, ordering the Jews to open it in the name of Christ, and making no discernable impact at all. Robin leaned out over the battlements, lifted the great boulder out over the edge, paused for a second to take aim and then hurled the great lump of stone almost straight downward on to the head of the white monk.

The monk's head exploded like a smashed egg, splashing glistening blood and brain over the dull wood of the steps. His body collapsed, the feet jerked once and then he was still.

I swear, I swear by Mary the Mother of God, that for just an instant the whole blood-crazed mob stopped, stock still, frozen in shock at the holy man's death. And then, Richard Malbête, who was in the middle ranks of the mob, raised his sword and bellowed "Kill them, kill them all," and the crowd screamed as if in terrible pain and surged forward again.

"Now shoot," yelled Robin. "Shoot. Reload, and shoot again." And with a leathery ripple of noise, the defenders fired as one man, and a hail of black quarrels sliced down and smacked into the crowd below. Dozens of Christians dropped out of the press before the Tower door, staggering back, punctured by hideous wounds in the neck, shoulders and head. One man in a red hood snarling up at the Jews on the battlements received a quarrel through the eye. He fell to his knees and was trampled by the mob. Some of our men followed Robin's example and, after firing their crossbows, picked up stones from the piles by the battlements and hurled them down on the attackers with terrible force. Others methodically reloaded, hauling back the powerful cords with their leg and back muscles, loading a quarrel into the groove, leaning over the parapet and shooting into the mass of folk below again and again.

The slope was now littered with wounded and dying townsmen, and a few women, too, caught up in the fire of zealotry. More Christians surged over the earth and log causeway from the bailey, taking the places of their fallen neighbors, boiling around the little iron door and battering at it with axes, swords, even plain wooden staves. They had no chance. The black quarrels flew thick and fast, a swarm of death, punching into the unarmored bodies of the people below and doing appalling slaughter. Robin, beside me, had regained his bow. He had an arrow nocked and was searching the crowd for a particular target. And I knew who it was. Richard Malbête, surrounded by men-at-arms, was urging the mob forward from the back of the press around the door with oaths and loud cries of "God wills it!" I saw Robin mark him, pull back his bow cord the final couple of inches to his ear, and loose. It flew straight and true but, at the last minute, the man-at-arms next to Malbête threw up his kite-shaped shield and caught the arrow with a flat thump, an inch or two below the curved top edge. Robin cursed and pulled another arrow from his bag. I saw Malbête staring directly at us, his feral eyes glittering madly, and then he began to move away, squirming backward through the crowd like an eel, keeping low. He gave us one parting glance of sheer hatred, before he turned and disappeared back across the bridge into the bailey courtyard.

The fight below us was not over, but there were signs that the people's ardour was fading under the terrible onslaught of quarrels and stones. A young man, thin and agile, his face burning with religious fervor, in desperation tried to climb the rough wooden exterior of the Tower using two thick knives, driving them into the wood to give him handholds. I leaned over the parapet and shot him in the throat with a bolt from my crossbow. It was the first shot I had loosed, and I watched with a numb feeling of vague regret as he tumbled away, rolling down the slope, choking on his own blood, dying and scrabbling at the thick black shaft that protruded from his neck.

And then suddenly it was over. The townspeople were streaming back over the causeway to the bailey, helping their wounded friends to limp along, but leaving more than two score of bodies scattered on the bloody grass of the mound below us. A few of the Jews loosed bolts at their retreating backs, but they missed, and Robin shouted: "Cease shooting, stop! Save your quarrels." And suddenly we were a gang of grinning, cheering men, panting and sweating, slapping each other on the back, shaking but alive and, for the moment, victorious.

The sound of hammering was relentless, a ceaseless pounding that seemed to attack directly a spot at the base of my skull. It began almost as soon as the last citizen had retreated into the bailey and continued for hours. Worse than the noise was the knowledge of what they were building: ladders. We had not defeated them in the bloody skirmish by the Tower's gate; they would return, and in a much more businesslike fashion.

The Jews were jubilant, however, and as one company was sent down to the ground floor to rest, replaced by a fresh group of warriors, there was much singing and joking, and men exaggerating the numbers they had personally slain. I went down with them, out of the sunlight, and took bread and cheese and a mug of ale from Ruth in the dim ground-floor hall. She was glowing with happiness, eyes sparkling as she passed around food to the hungry men.

I had an uncomfortable feeling that she thought the battle was over. But I could not bring myself to disillusion her: I knew we were in for a much harder fight before we could count ourselves the victors. And every Christian we killed would harden opinion against us when Sir John Marshal and his troops finally returned from wherever they had been.

Robin found me dozing against the wall of the hall; he had brought Reuben with him and three other Jews. They were all armed with swords, and two of the men I didn't know carried shields. Reuben's sword was unlike any I had ever seen before: it was slim, delicate even, and slightly curved. I stared at it wondering how a man could wield such a girlish weapon.

"They will attack again soon," Robin said without any preamble. "And they will attack from all sides, with ladders." He stopped and looked speculatively at the three men with Reuben. "We may be able to hold them, but if they do get over the parapet, you Alan, with the help of Reuben and these good men, must repel them. Stay back from the fight, the five of you, and watch for breaches. Your job is to be a stopper, Alan, like a cork in a bottle, to fill any gap that may open in our defenses. Clear?"

I nodded. Robin grinned at me. "Good. Alan, you are

in command, and—remember—we're all relying on you," he said with a grin and then he was gone. We clumped up the stairs again to the roof and took up a position in the center of the open space. It was midafternoon, and even in the weak March sunlight it was pleasantly warm up there. We were fifteen paces from each of the four sides of the battlements; and I could see the logic of Robin's decision to deploy us as he had. If the enemy got over the wall, we five could charge them in a few heartbeats and should be able to push them back. I pulled out my old battered sword and began to run a whetstone along the long blade. The shriek of stone on metal made a counterpoint to the hammering from the bailey, a sort of unearthly martial music. I found I was timing my strokes of the stone to fit in with the sound of the hammers. And then, all of a sudden, the hammering stopped.

I got up and walked over to the parapet, telling my little troop of "Stoppers" to stay where they were. The courtyard of the bailey was once again filled with men, but this time there seemed to be many more men-at-arms in scarlet and sky blue in the throng and fewer townsmen. I could see ladders being passed hand to hand over the tops of people's heads and then suddenly there was the blast of a trumpet and the whole mass of humanity began to move toward the Tower.

"Here they come again," shouted somebody and, glancing to my left and right, I saw the grim faces of the Jewish defenders, knuckles white on the stocks of their crossbows, bracing their legs on the wooden floor as if to resist a physical impact. Once again Robin insisted that they did not shoot. "Wait till they begin the attack," he was yelling. "Wait till I give the signal. Wait."

The attackers split into two groups and, ignoring the steep wooden steps up to the iron-bound gate that had defeated them before, two streams of men flowed around the base of the huge earth mound on which the Tower was built. They were just out of effective crossbow range and, anyway, Robin insisted that we should save our quarrels for a proper attack. But they were well within earshot. Some shouted curses at us as they passed by at the foot of the mound, others waved swords and spears and jeered, others grimly ignored us. They formed up in two loose bodies, to the west on the banks of the Ouse, and to the north on the flat piece of ground before the beginning of the town itself. Then a figure stepped out from the mass of men to the north, accompanied by a man-at-arms holding a white flag. It was Sir Richard Malbête. I saw Robin with his war bow in his left hand reaching for an arrow from the linen bag at his waist and Josce putting a hand on his arm to restrain him. "Let us hear what he has to say," said the old Jew in a low, reasonable tone. Robin frowned but let the arrow fall back into his bag.

"Jews of York," shouted Malbête; his words were faint but quite audible. "Jews of York," he repeated. "Release the Christian children you hold captive, come down from the King's Tower and we shall be merciful."

There was a murmur of astonishment on the roof of the Tower. "What children?" somebody shouted. "What are you talking about? Are you mad?"

"Release the Christian children: give us back the two boys you have kidnapped; our two little blond Christian angels. Restore them to their mother unharmed and we shall be merciful," boomed Sir Richard.

Josce stepped up to the parapet. He cupped his hands around his mouth and shouted. "We have no Christian children here. Whoever says that lies. There are no Christian children in this place. Why do you make war on us?"

Malbête turned his back on the Tower to face the crowd. A man-at-arms stepped forward protectively, raising his shield to cover the knight's back. "They have murdered them," he shouted. "They have murdered our little angels. Shall we leave them in peace? Shall we walk away and leave these baby-killers, these unbelievers to work their foul sorcery?"

92

In unison, the crowd yelled back the negative. A trumpet blew, two blasts, and both enemy forces, to the east and the north, lumbered forward toward the Tower, ladders held high.

I saw little of the attack as I stood back to back with my Stoppers, our swords drawn, in the center of the roof. But the noise was nearly deafening: the shouts of rage from the attackers, the screams of the wounded, the snap and hiss of a crossbow bolt being fired down on to the enemy, the occasional crash of sword on shield. All three companies of Jewish crossbowmen had been called to the roof to defend the Tower, but my Stoppers and I were aloof from the fray. A pair of parallel poles with perhaps one or two crossbars would appear at the top of the battlements, and immediately a mob of Jews would rush over to it and shoot, reload and shoot again down the length of the ladder, clearing it of attackers. Then someone would grasp the ladder and hurl it away from the walls. Another one would appear and the rush would begin again. Robin was shooting his war bow, but sparingly. I knew he had only brought two dozen arrows with him and, by the look of it, his arrow bag was already half empty.

Despite the mad energy of our crossbowmen, there were many hundreds of enemy and they had dozens of ladders. The time gap between the appearance of a ladder-top and its rejection by the Jews began to grow and sometimes we could even see a head appear at the top of the ladder before it was transfixed by a hasty quarrel. And then, suddenly, as if in a dream, there were enemy spilling over the parapet to the west and in three heartbeats there were half a dozen Christians on to the roof; and more men were tumbling over the wall, picking themselves up, lifting their weapons . . .

The Stoppers rushed forward as a tight group, myself in the lead, unsheathed sword in my right hand and poniard in my left. I cut hard at a man just as he was rising from the floor of the roof, hacking into his neck with my sword, and then whirled and plunged the poniard underhand into another man's belly. I felt the hot spray of blood on my fist, twisted the foot-long blade and pulled it free. I blocked a cut at my head with my sword and punched forward again with my poniard, hearing a scream close to my ear as the blade licked into the flesh of a man's upper leg. I was moving automatically, blocking and cutting, hacking and slashing, never still, always trying, as I had been taught, to think not about the move I was making at the time but about the counterstroke, the natural follow-on from a strike, and even sometimes the third and fourth plays as well.

I felt as if another man was controlling my body; the thousands of hours of training making my body move and react like some mechanical device. I had no thoughts in my head; I just cut, and parried and stabbed and dodged in the midst of my enemies. Blood spurted, men screamed, faces loomed before me and I smashed them away with my sword. I was aware that there were several enemy men-at-arms around me, behind me, but I left them for Reuben and the other Stoppers and cut my way forward, ever forward, hacking, grunting, heaving mail-clad men aside, heading straight for the ladder top which was still disgorging enemy men-at-arms. I nearly slipped on a slick of fresh blood, but recovered and pounded my sword hilt into a bearded face at the top of the ladder. He disappeared and I leaned out over the edge and cut down into the forearm of another man standing lower down clutching a rung. He screamed and fell away. An arrow whizzed past my face from the mound below and I jerked my head back from the ladder top. The blood was singing in my veins, I felt as if I was in the grip of a powerful apothecary's drug; I could hear Reuben and the men behind me grunting and screaming as they fought enemies I had already wounded. But I ignored their struggles, trying to dislodge the ladder with my weapons still in my hands.

A man-at-arms already on the roof lunged suddenly

toward me from the left, an axe in his bloodied hands, and I drove him away with two feints and then a flick-fast sword-lunge that opened his throat. As he dropped to his knees, gurgling and spewing blood, another head had appeared over the parapet, and I desperately turned and stabbed at his eyes with my dagger. He pulled back from the poniard thrust and swinging round I thumped my sword into the side of his helmeted head. I must have half-stunned him for he released his grip on the rung and dropped straight backward like a stone, knocking the man below him off his precarious perch. As I peered over the battlements, I saw that the ladder was almost clear, save for a nervous man near the bottom who was in no hurry to climb up to his death, and so I dropped my weapons at my feet and grabbing the wood, twisted the rungs at the top of the ladder, to the left and then right, until he jumped clear; then I hurled the wooden frame away from the walls with as much force as I could muster.

I gathered up my bloody blades and turned to see what had happened to my men. The roof was now thick with enemy dead. Townsmen and men-at-arms, perhaps a dozen, lay entwined and still in their own gore, while few more men were twitching and groaning, flopping about in agony. One man-at-arms was on his knees, disarmed, badly wounded and being gradually hacked apart by two of the Jews, who were screaming in rage and holding their swords two-handed as they battered at his ripped chain mail, slicing into his naked hands as he tried to ward off their blows. The third Jew from my little troop of Stoppers was standing upright, swaying slightly, unbloodied sword by his side, a huge crimson stain at his waist where an enemy sword had pierced him. He was dying on his feet, his eyes wide with fear as the dark, wet patch widened and grew until it soaked the whole side of his tunic. He dropped to his knees, then tipped over, face forward to the wooden roof and lay still.

And then there was Reuben. Reuben was dueling with

a mail-clad man-at-arms, no mere angry townsman with a rusty rake but a professional soldier. Reuben's slim, girlish blade was everywhere, feinting high and cutting at his ankles, lunging for the eyes and then suddenly turning the blow into a sweep at the neck. He was masterful; I should have gone to his aid but it was clear that he did not need my help. The soldier had no chance, his clumsy swings with his heavy, straight-edged sword came nowhere near Reuben's body. And then, in a flash, it was over: Reuben took two small steps forward, knocked the man's weapon out of the way with a steely snap of his wrist and almost delicately passed his curved sword through his throat. The man dropped to one knee, white hands clasped at his neck, his life pissing away in great, spurting red arcs.

The attack was over, too. I could see defeated men—townsmen and men-at-arms—streaming back into the bailey, and looking over the parapet I saw the mounds of dead—scores and scores, some sprouting black quarrels like hedge pigs—and a host of wounded who were unable to walk. Many had broken legs from falling from the ladders. The Jews were unmerciful and Robin did not try to stop them. They loaded crossbows, leaned out over the parapet and shot bolt after bolt into the injured men below. And then they hurled the enemy dead, and the wounded, too, over the parapet to crash and roll down the grassy slope of the mound twenty feet below.

We had taken casualties as well. Apart from my Stopper, who was being tended to by his comrades, we had two dead men killed by thrown spears, one with a bad arrow wound and several men slashed by the swords of our attackers as they pushed the ladders away from the wall. But, all things considered, the damage done to us was slight; and we had held them off once again.

As the sun set on our battlefield, the mood in the Tower was fiercely defiant. The men had been attacked twice and had fought off their enemies with great courage. As always for me after battle, I felt a great wash of sadness, and was almost close to tears. And when the excitement was over, and my heart returned to its normal state, I felt a great weight on my soul; a sorrow for all those Christians who would never see another sunrise. I fell to my knees on that rooftop and prayed to Almighty God to receive the souls of the slain into His Grace, and to forgive them for their sins. I also offered up a small prayer of thanks for keeping me safe through the blood and carnage of that day. Then I began to clean and oil my weapons. I knew I would need them again before long.

CHAPTER FIVE

We kept watch that night, by companies, two companies on watch, one resting, but they did not come again. The enemy picket lines around the Tower remained, we could glimpse bodies moving about in the light of small campfires, but there was no attack. Instead, in the center of the bailey courtyard, they built a great bonfire and by means of a tripod, they suspended a great cauldron over the blaze and filled it with river water. It took several hours for the water in the huge iron bowl to come to the boil, but by the time it was merrily bubbling away, a crowd had formed in the darkness around the fire and the great cooking pot. I had assumed that the Christians were making some great pottage to feed the hundreds that had gathered to watch the Jews in the Tower being murdered, but I was wrong. Horribly wrong.

In the crowd around the cauldron I saw two men in the dark vestments of priests and the tall figure of Sir Richard Malbête; one of the priests seemed to be holding a service of some sort, he was chanting psalms and leading the crowd in the recitation of prayers; then there was a ripple from the crowd and a large oddly shaped parcel was ejected from the mass and plumped down on the ground beside the bonfire. Then it moved and I saw that it was a girl, thin, terrified, badly beaten and tightly bound.

Someone gave a sharp cry of pain beside me on the parapet and I turned to see a portly Jew in a good quality robe, mouth hanging open in anguish, pointing out at the bailey and the girl bound on the ground. He was soon surrounded by his fellows who comforted him, and tried to pull him away from the battlements. "It's his daughter," said a voice beside me and I turned to see Robin, looking grim, and leaning on his bow staff. "Whatever they do to her, it's not going to be good for him to see it," he said. His voice was icy and flat.

A young man leaned out over the wall and shouted into the darkness below in the direction of the nearest picket fire. "Hey, Christian! Hey, you."

No reply. So the man leaned out even further, his comrades holding his legs. "Hey Christian, talk to me."

There was a short silence and then a voice shouted back from the darkness. "What do you want, you damned Jew? Stop making so much noise and let us sleep."

"What's going on in there, in the castle? They've got Mordecai the silversmith's daughter; what are they going to do with her? Tell me, Christian, for the love of God, tell me. She is only ten years old, and has never hurt a soul."

There was a muttered conference in the darkness below. Then there was raucous laughter and a new voice spoke. "She's a dirty Jew and they are going to thoroughly wash her, you pig. They are going to baptize her, and send her soul to

Jesus, who will no doubt take one look and send her to Hell where she belongs!" There was more laughter, not a pleasant sound, a ragged cackling like the mirth of devils.

Robin and I stared over at the far side of the bailey, where the religious service seemed to be coming to an end. "How far would you say that distance was, Alan," Robin murmured to me, "here to the cauldron, two hundred and twenty-five yards?" He might have been asking a question about the weather for all the emotion in his voice.

"Nearer to two thirty, I'd say," I replied, trying to emulate his lack of concern. But then I was held in rapt horror by the unfolding scene before me.

As the two men-at-arms picked up the bound girl, her head fell back and I caught a flash of her white, terrified face as her dark hair tumbled behind her. The men-at-arms lifted her high, the priest made the sign of the cross, there were scattered shouts from the crowd—and with a heave they plunged her into the boiling water. I can hear her bloodcurdling scream of utter torment even now after more than forty years. It shriveled my soul, my ball sack contracted violently and every muscle in my body became taut as iron. But beside me Robin was moving. As the awful howls of that scalded girl echoed round the Tower like a banshee riding the wind, Robin had pulled an arrow from his bag, nocked it to the bow and loosed it in one swift fluid movement. The arrow flew in a shallow arc, the white ash wood flashing as it passed through pools of light in the darkness and smacked home right on target into the chest of the unfortunate girl. The screaming ended as abruptly as if her head had been cut off with an axe. It was a staggering bowshot, impossibly accurate at that distance and in that light, miraculous, and yet Robin had made it. The figures around the cauldron were frozen in shock; one minute they had been watching a Jewish girl scream her lungs out in excruciating agony, the next she was a corpse floating in the bubbling water, bobbing in the roil like a loose white dumpling in a pan of stew.

Robin loosed again, and again his shot was almost supernatural. The arrow thumped home into the belly of the priest who had conducted the service; his horrified expression as a white shaft appeared in his fat stomach was truly comical, but as he stared down at his midriff in disbelief, the crowd realized the danger and split into fragments, finding cover where they could. There was no sign of Richard Malbête. Once again, at the first signs of trouble he had disappeared.

I heard Robin curse softly beside me, and turned to look at him. He was looking into his empty arrow bag and muttering to himself a stream of utterly foul obscenity. I saw then that he had only one arrow left, the one in his hand. He caught my eye and shrugged as he nocked it and loosed at a man-at-arms who was running across the bailey to the shelter of the chapel. The arrow took the man full in the back, even at two hundred yards piercing his chain mail hauberk, and hurled him to the ground. He was still moving feebly but Robin ignored him and turned to me.

"I should have brought more shafts, Alan. That was a mistake."

"We didn't plan to fight a full-scale battle," I said.

"True; but mistakes like that that can get a man quite badly killed." And then, with a wry smile, he turned away and made his way toward the staircase and the hall below.

I stayed at the wall, standing that whole night, as a mad, pointless, utterly foolish tribute to that little girl; thinking about her and the swift, merciful death that Robin had given her; and thinking of Sir Richard Malbête, too.

In the first gray light, Ruth came to me, bringing ale and bread, and I finally eased my stiff legs down, lowered my rump to the floor and began to eat. But I was startled from my breakfast by the sound of trumpets. With my fellow warriors, I gathered at the parapet to watch a cavalcade of fifty knights and a hundred or so foot soldiers, followed by a great train of ox-wagons carrying what seemed to be huge squared lengths of timber, ride into the bailey through the eastern gate. Sir John Marshal had returned to his castle.

Feelings were mixed among the besieged Jews of the Tower: some men assumed that they were saved now that the King's representative had returned; others of a darker cast of mind saw only reinforcements for our enemies.

"At the least now we should be able to negotiate," said Reuben to me as we stood side-by-side, leaning on the battlements and looking over the bailey. He had brought his own breakfast and was munching on a crust as we surveyed the soldiers spilling into the courtyard. Directly below us the bodies of the dead lay undisturbed, except by the ravens who had gathered in their scores and who pecked at Christian flesh with a glassy avian disregard for human dignity.

"May I see your sword," I asked Reuben presently. And he obligingly pulled the slim curved blade from its ornate scabbard and passed it hilt first to me. It felt light, too light, in my hand. I made a few experimental passes in the air. It was like waving an ash wand; it had none of the brute power of my own weapon. But, by God, a man could strike fast with this blade. Then Reuben took a flimsy silk scarf from around his neck and asked me to hold out the sword at arm's length. He held the scarf over the weapon and dropped it. The silk was cut in two, merely by its own weight. I was astounded. I had never seen a blade as keen in my life; I tested the edge of the sword and immediately cut deep into the ball of my thumb. Sucking the injured digit ruefully, I asked Reuben where he had obtained such a fine weapon.

"It is a scimitar, in the Arabian pattern," he replied, not quite answering my question. "If we live through this siege and you travel with the King to Outremer, you will see many more swords of this type—and perhaps you may wish you had not. It is a common weapon in the great army of the warlord you Christians call Saladin."

I asked him again, looking directly at him: "But where did *you* get it?"

He sighed. "Where do you think I am from, Alan?"

"Why, York, of course. Although I have heard it said that you also have a dwelling in Nottingham."

"Look at my skin, my eyes, my hair—do I look as if I come from the north of England?" he said.

"Well, you are a Jew," I said, acknowledging the hazelnut hue of his face and his midnight eyes, "so I suppose that at one time your family must have come from the Holy Land."

"Do I resemble these others?" He indicated the Jews at the battlements beside us.

"Of course, well, a little . . . actually, not very much." I could not believe that I had not noticed it before but Reuben was much darker than all the other Jews; some of the crossbowmen at the battlements had red-gold hair, some even had blue eyes.

"We are all equally the children of Israel," Reuben said, "but these good Jews are from northern France and their families lived there for many generations before they came to try their luck in England."

"So you *are* from Outremer?" I asked. I was fascinated. I had never really thought about Reuben's antecedents before. He had just been Robin's friend, the Jew, the merchant and moneylender from York. To hail from Outremer, where Christ's blessed feet had walked, the sacred land of John the Baptist, and Moses, and King David, and Samson and Delilah, and all those other figures from the Bible . . . it seemed impossibly exotic and mysterious.

"I am of the Temanim, a Jew from the far south. I come from a land far beyond Outremer, which the Arabs call al-Yaman—it was once known as the land of the Queen of Sheba," he said, a note of pride in his voice.

This seemed even more fabulous. Beyond Outremer? He might have said that he came from the moon. Tuck had told me the story of King Solomon and the Queen of Sheba, but it had all seemed so long ago, so far away. A legend. It was as if I had just come face to face with a unicorn.

"What is it like—al-Yaman?" I asked, stumbling over the unfamiliar name, but imagining a perfumed land flowing with rivers of wine, where jewels grew in the earth like flowers, and sweet cakes grew on trees.

"It's a desert, mostly, sand and rock and merciless sun. But it is home, I suppose, in a way. Or it would be home if any of my family still lived."

I said nothing at this point, and just stared at him willing him to tell me the story; listening with my eyes. He smiled at me again, indicated that we should sit with a graceful wave of his hand, and then, settling himself down, with his back to the battlements, his beautiful sword across his knees, he began.

"My father, may his soul rest with God, was a sword-maker. He made this very weapon," he said laying a hand reverently on the ornate silver-chased scabbard. "We were a wealthy family, business was very good, and for the most part there was harmony between the Jews of our town and the Arabs. I was trained in the use of arms by the best teachers my father's money could buy; and taught languages—Greek and Latin—as well as history, philosophy, a little medicine and courtly manners. I was happy. It was my father's dream that I should be a gentleman, a poet perhaps, or a musician like you Alan, not an artisan, not a sword-smith such as himself, sweating over a forge fire all day in a leather apron. And I was content with that ambition; I attended the best parties, mixed with the sons of other rich men, and there was talk of a marriage between myself and the daughter of a wealthy merchant from a neighboring town. Life was very good." He paused here and closed his eyes, savoring that youthful happiness for a moment or so. Then he continued. "When I was

104

sixteen, a wandering Muslim cleric came to our town. He dressed almost in rags, but his eyes burned with passion and he preached with great eloquence to the faithful in the local mosque. His preaching was considered sublime; people came from far and wide to hear his words. He was inspired by the Prophet himself, praise be upon him, the people said. But what he preached was purity. Only by keeping himself pure, he said, could a Muslim reach paradise at the end of his life. Only by living a saintly life and eschewing all defilement, could a true Muslim honor God in the proper way. All impurity was to be shunned; it must be swept away, banished, and if it could not be banished then it must be destroyed. And we Jews, said this so-called holy man, were impure."

I was beginning to see where this story was going. There was a note of deep bitterness in Reuben's voice, and I thought of the evening when Robin and I had arrived at his house to be greeted with a thrown knife. But I held my peace, and waited for Reuben to continue.

"At first, the cleric merely preached avoidance of Jews, but in our town we had been living together peacefully for many hundreds of years. Jew lived next door to Muslim, we ate in each other's houses; we respected each other, our children played together in the streets. And so, seeing that the majority of his flock was not heeding his message of separation, the cleric began preaching to the young Muslim men of the town. He met them at night, preaching almost in secret, and telling them that they had a holy mission to cleanse the town of Jews. He called it *jihad*." Reuben spat out the word as if it were poison on his tongue.

"Most of the young men ignored this mullah, and drifted away; despite being so eloquent, he was clearly mad: how could the town be cleansed of a quarter of its population? Jews were part of its life, part of its very fabric, and always had been. But some of the young men, the wild ones, the unhappy ones, the lost souls, they listened. And they began to hate.

"One night a gang of them, perhaps fifteen or twenty young men, came to our house; they were drugged on hashish and maybe a little drunk, too, and they burned our house down and killed my father and mother when they came out to protest. My younger brother fought them, and killed two before he was overcome and killed himself. They burned other Jewish houses, too, and many families lost beloved ones that terrible night. I happened to be away, by chance, visiting friends in a town fifty miles away, and I suppose that saved my life. The very next day the mullah was driven from the town with stones and curses, both Jews and Muslims wanted him gone, and the young men who had committed the outrage submitted themselves for punishment to the elders of the town and were severely punished; two were executed, the ringleaders, and the others had one eye put out, as punishment and a mark of their shame. But despite this restitution, the town was never the same again. The seed of hatred had been planted, and it grew, watered by the tears of the families destroyed by the violence. Those whose sons had been half-blinded, began to hate the Jews; the Jews whose friends had been killed by the young men, began to hate and fear their Muslim neighbors.

"I could not live in the town anymore after the deaths of my family. I was afflicted with a great guilt; if I had been there I could have protected them, I told myself. It was not true, of course, and a part of me knew this, too; I would have died with them but for my absence. But I felt the guilt of one who survives a catastrophe. I could not stay in that town, and I gathered the money, the horses and camels that my father had left to me and took to the open road. For three years I traveled Arabia and the lands around. I visited Alexandria and Baghdad, Jerusalem and Mecca; I lived like the young prince my father had wanted me to be, traveling in great splendor, staying only at the best houses, spending a fortune on food and wine, perfumes and jewels—and then, one day, inevitably, the money ran out. And I found myself in Acre, a Christian city on the coast of Palestine, penniless and with no idea what I should do with the rest of my life."

Reuben closed his eyes for a moment, remembering.

"So what did you do?" I prompted. He sighed.

"You must understand that I am ashamed of this, Alan, and while this is no excuse, it might help to explain: I was still in despair over the deaths of my parents, and I had no clear direction in which to travel, no goals, and no money and so for a while I became a brigand, a thief, robbing the rich camel-trains on the roads of Outremer. I took many innocent lives that year, and I got to know the secret ways of the desert. After a season, though, I was thoroughly sickened by my profession and I hired myself out as a guard on the caravans that plied the dusty roads all the way south to al-Yaman. I was, you might say, a poacher turned gamekeeper, an outlaw who became a forester. I felt that if I could protect the merchants that I had previously robbed I would somehow, in God's eyes, be making amends for my sins.

"After two years of eating caravan dust, and seeing off would-be predators—many of them calling themselves Christians, I might add—after two years of saddle blisters and thirst, and half-healed wounds, I tired of that, too. I happened to be in Acre once again, unemployed, and I was resting out of the hot sun in a beautiful garden, with neatly clipped grass, and trimmed orange trees that perfumed the air. It was so green, so soothing. A fountain was bubbling nearby and I felt a deep sense of calm. I could hear Christian monks chanting, a beautiful sound, pure and Godly; although, believe me, Alan, I have never been tempted to abandon the faith of my fathers. But I admit I felt close to God in that Christian garden. I looked down at my feet—they were dirty, scratched, distorted with callouses and scars and one sandal had a broken strap—and I came to a realization. I wanted two things from this life. I wanted to live somewhere where it was not always so hot; and I wanted to be rich."

"So you came to England?" I suggested, with a note of incredulity in my voice.

"As you say, young Alan," Reuben replied. "I came here. It took me two years to get here, and I was penniless when I arrived, and reviled by almost everyone as a wandering Jew, but I have prospered since then."

I knew what he was going to say next before he said it. "It was Robin who first helped me, actually. And I will never forget his kindness. It was Robin who advanced me the initial money to set up my business, and I honor him for it. For what it is worth, he will always have my loyalty and my friendship, no matter what he may do."

"Usury," I said, with a touch of asperity. It was a mortal sin, and I did not like the fact that Robin was mixed up in it.

"You disapprove? What else could I do? As a Jew, I am barred from almost every other profession. I have a good deal medical training, but I cannot treat Christians as a doctor; I have been trained to fight, but I would not be welcome in the ranks of Christian men-at-arms. So, yes, usury." He looked at me directly, brown head tilted on one side. "Think of it as a service," he said. "People need to borrow money from time to time and I provide that service."

I was not disposed to argue with him after he had so generously shared his life story with me—and I was saved from making a comment by the blast of a trumpet. As we scrambled to our feet and looked out over the parapet, I saw that a delegation of mounted knights and men-at-arms was coming across the bridge, under a white banner of truce. In front of the cavalcade was a richly dressed knight, in the full shining panoply of war. It was Sir John Marshal. And beside him, on a raw-boned piebald destrier, was the tall form of Sir Richard Malbête.

The sheriff of Yorkshire halted his horse a few yards from the door of the Tower, well within range of a crossbow bolt but confident that his white flag would protect him, and he stared up at the ramparts.

"Jews of York," he shouted. "You must release the Christian children that you hold and come down from the Tower. We will spare your lives if you accept baptism into the True Faith of Our Lord Jesus Christ."

Beside him Malbête looked up at us and gave a little smirk. And I shuddered and remembered the "baptism" in boiling water that the little Jewish girl had suffered the night before.

"Why do they keep talking about children?" I asked Reuben. He looked at me hard. "Evidently, someone has been libeling us. It is not unusual. They are no doubt saying that we have kidnapped a couple of children to eat as a light snack before supper, and these Christian fools believe it."

I saw that Josce was standing in the center of the battlements, looking down on Sir John Marshal. Robin was nowhere to be seen. I assumed he was deliberately staying out of Sir John's sight.

"As I told your henchman, Sir Richard Malbête, we have no Christian children here," the old Jew shouted. "And we will not abandon our faith. What guarantees can you give us for our safety if we come out? Can you protect us against them?" He gestured beyond Sir John and his troops, to where the townspeople of York had been gathering in a mass at the far side of the causeway. The crowd looked ugly, many were sporting bloody bandages or walked with crutches. Most were armed. There were some angry shouts, and fists shaken, in reply to Josce's words.

"This is the King's Tower, I order you in the name of the King to come down and hand over your weapons. Or I will expel you from royal property by force of arms. I say for the last time: surrender and hand over your weapons."

109

"Come and take them," muttered Reuben and then he said something in a strange tongue that I didn't understand: "*Molon labe*," he said, "*Molon labe*, you bastards."

Josce was conferring with an elderly rabbi, as the priests of the Jews are called. He leaned over the parapet and said: "We cannot surrender our weapons unless we receive guarantees for the safety of our families."

"You have until noon to come out, unarmed, under a flag of truce; after that I will expel you by force," shouted Sir John angrily, and he turned his horse and rode back over the causeway. Sir Richard Malbête vouchsafed us one last smirk and followed him back into the bailey.

I looked at the sky; it was midmorning. And once again, in the bailey courtyard, the hammers began to ring out.

In the permanent gloom of the ground floor of the Tower, a furious argument was in progress. Half a dozen Jews were shouting at the tops of their voices, none listening to the other, some wringing their hands in despair, other gesticulating with raised hands. Robin and I sat apart from the tumult, sharing a loaf of bread on a bench in a corner and feeling alien in this chaos of shouting Jewry. Finally Josce managed to establish some sort of order, after bellowing for silence and hammering on a table with a pewter mug.

"Brothers," he said, when he had at last managed to achieve some quiet. "Pray be quiet and listen to what our revered Rabbi Yomtob has to say."

The old Jewish holy man, who had been sitting quietly at the table, rose with difficulty. He was an aged man, gray and full bearded and venerable, with red-rimmed eyes that seemed even older than his bent body.

"My friends," he said quietly, and the noise ceased immediately as people strained to hear his words. "I was born a Jew. I have lived all my life according to the Commandments of Moses and the laws of the Torah; I will never give up the faith of my fathers. This talk of baptism, of the Christians' forgiveness, is a lie; if we leave this place, today, tomorrow, we will die, our wives will die, our children will die. We may not all suffer unspeakable torture before we die, but die we will. And I would rather die as what I have always been, a devout Jew, than suffer the indignity of death at the hands of these blood-crazed maniacs. Remember our forefathers at Masada, the followers of Elazar ben Ya'ir; when they were surrounded by the forces of the mighty Roman Empire they chose to take their own lives, as free Jews, rather than accept slavery or a degrading death at the hands of their oppressors. I plan to follow their example." I noticed Reuben, on the other side of the room, staring at the rabbi intently, his dark face strangely pale. The whole Tower now seemed as silent as a tomb.

"Tonight, as we all know, is Pesach," the old man continued, "the holy night when, through the protection of the Almighty, the Angel of Death took the first-born sons of Egypt, but passed over the sons of Israel, and gave us our freedom from slavery. Tonight, after we have eaten our matzo bread, and drunk a glass of wine, I will take a knife and take the life of my own firstborn son, Isaac there"—a frightened-looking young man in the throng took an involuntary step backward—"and I will take the life of my beloved wife of fifty years, and my daughter. I invite all of you to do the same. And then we will draw lots as to who should kill whom, among the surviving men. Tonight we shall all be Angels of Death, and give freedom to our families, and I pray that the Lord God of Moses and Isaac will forgive us. I have spoken." And he sat down.

For a few heartbeats the silence was held, and then there was bedlam. Half the Jews were wailing, lamenting Rabbi Yomtob's extraordinary words, some were weeping, others were angrily shouting about fighting to the death, taking Christian dogs with them. Robin took me by the arm and said: "Let us go up to the roof."

I was dazed by Rabbi Yomtob's speech; it seemed to rob me of breath as I climbed the stairs. It was an extraordinary, and grossly sinful attitude to take, I felt. I had been in hopeless situations before—well, one at least, at Linden Lea—but it would never occur to me to take my own life.

On the roof, I took up my familiar position overlooking the bailey, and my heart sank even further.

"Do you know what that is?" asked Robin, pointing out into the bailey, where a huge wooden structure was being erected by many busy craftsmen from the town. It was not a question that required a reply. The hammering once again was giving me the most colossal headache. The workmen had finished the frame, a square of foot-thick beams, nailed and lashed together and set on solid wooden wheels. The upright bars were in place, too, topped by a cross piece looking for all the world like a gibbet. In the center of the structure, in a spider's web of thick ropes and pulleys, was a great wooden arm, with what looked like a giant spoon attached to the far end. I knew what it was, all right. And I shuddered. It was a mangonel, a siege weapon capable of hurling huge boulders at the Tower, a sort of catapult that I had seen reduce the stout palisade of a fortified manor house to kindling.

"Once they start with that," said Robin, "we have only hours before this place is falling around our ears." He sounded completely detached, almost relaxed, as if just idly remarking on an interesting phenomenon.

"What are we going to do?" I asked him, trying to keep my voice firm and practical, though a sick feeling had lodged in my stomach.

"If I had a dozen arrows, I could slow them down a bit," mused Robin. Then he shrugged. "I tell you one thing, Alan. We are *not* going to kill ourselves." And he gave me a grin, which I managed to return as bravely as I could.

★　★　★

112

There was no more parlaying with Sir John Marshal, which I admit I had been secretly hoping for. It seems he intended to stay true to his word for, as the sun was at its height, the first missile sailed up from the mangonel, almost slowly, and came smashing into the lower part of the wall of the Tower with a shrieking crash that rocked the whole building. I had watched the townsmen, supervised by a squad of men-at-arms, hauling back the great spoonlike arm, loading a massive rock into the cup, and releasing the ropes that held it captive.

There was just one ray of hope; they seemed to be slow at loading the machine, perhaps because, as civilians, they were unused to it, and there seemed to be a shortage of missiles, too. But the boulders that they hurled were having a devastating effect on the Tower. By midafternoon, they had managed to strike the Tower five times. One corner of the building was sagging slightly, huge splinters of wood hanging free; a narrow window on the second floor had been smashed into a much wider space, which we hastily covered with nailed planks. And a high shot had smashed through a section of the battlements on the left facing the bailey, killing two men instantly and plunging through the floor of the roof and two stories below to maim a woman preparing food on the ground floor. Then, thank the Lord, the bombardment stopped. The men tending the great killing machine sat about idly, drinking from a great barrel of ale that had appeared in their midst and, after a while, when the ale had cheered them, capering around and baring their arses at the Jews in the Tower. I perceived then that they had run out of missiles. And hope blossomed in my breast—perhaps there would be no more damage done today—only to be dashed when a great cart rumbled through the open gates of the bailey filled with huge stones. The men stirred themselves, the arm was once again pulled back with stout ropes, the cup was filled with a block of gray stone, the ropes were loosed and another chunk of hate-sent masonry crashed into our defenses. And another. And another. Fat jagged planks of wood were falling free with each strike by now, and another hole had been smashed in the wall to the right and slightly above the iron-bound door. We blocked it as best we could with a large oak table and a couple of benches, but I knew as I sweated and heaved the heavy furniture into place that a single strike on our makeshift patching would blow the hole wide open in less than a heartbeat. As Robin had predicted, the place was falling around our ears. As another boulder boomed against the walls, I felt black despair clawing at my heart. When this mighty Tower was reduced to a splintered woodpile, the men-at-arms would come again and, with swinging axe and stabbing spear, they would swallow us in a huge red wave of priest-whipped hatred.

On the roof again, averting my eyes from the great hole in the floor, I felt the battlements rock unsteadily under the light touch of my hands. The ground floor I had just left was by now filled with wounded, most with splinter wounds; as the boulders crashed into the walls with demonic force, spears of wood, sharp as a barber-surgeon's knife, would burst free from the inside wall lancing through unarmored bodies like a hot needle through butter. The stench of blood filled the dank air inside the Tower, and the cries of wounded and bereaved, the frightened women and children, aye, and a few men, echoed around like the moaning of lost souls. We were in Hell. And there was no escape.

And then there was a miracle. I heard the great bells of the Minster ring out, their cheerful peal, a hideous joke in the blood and carnage of the Tower. It was Vespers. The bells rang out endlessly and as I listened, and offered up a prayer to the Virgin to keep me safe, I noticed that the bombardment had stopped. It must have been a quarter of an hour since the last shattering strike. The sun was very low in the sky, and I saw that the mangonel had been all but abandoned by the men who served it. A lonely man-at-arms sat on the front bar of the machine, looking up at the ramshackle remains of the Tower, hunched, battered and bleeding, wooden planks hanging off in crazy shapes. My prayer to the Mother of God had been answered—but as the Vespers' bells continued to ring out, I realized that there might be another explanation for our miraculous respite. It suddenly occurred to me that it was Good Friday, and our Christian tormentors were observing a Truce of God on this holy evening. The bailey was less full than before, though the circle of steel-clad men-at-arms around the Tower was still intact; all who could be excused from the task of keeping us penned-in were attending Mass.

CHAPTER SIX

By full dark it was clear that we were indeed being spared any further attack by the mangonel. And I guessed that we would be free from its depredations for the night, but that it would begin again in the morning; followed, when we were battered unrecognizable, by an assault on the ruins by the blood-lusting frustrated citizenry, backed by the trained soldiers of Sir Richard and Sir John. Robin agreed with me.

I suggested to my master that we might go below to help with the interior wall repairs, but he shook his head. "They are not going to repair anything," he said in a strange chilling voice. "They have decided to die. At this moment they are praying, and following the rituals of their faith on this holy day; we must leave them in peace for the moment."

I stared at him in horror. "All of them?" I asked.

"All but a very few," he replied. "Tomorrow you and I,

with Reuben and Ruth, will lead a handful of Jews out of here, and we will surrender to the mercies of Sir John Marshal. Don't worry, Alan, he will not harm us—you and me. At least, I don't think he will. There would be . . . certain repercussions, and I am worth more to him in ransom than as a corpse. As for Reuben and Ruth, I have persuaded them to undergo baptism, and promised to protect them. It's better than certain death . . ."

"Let's hope Sir John has not heard of Ralph Murdac's munificent offer of German silver for your head," I said grimly.

"Well, if you have a better plan, let me hear it," snapped Robin. I realized that he must have been feeling the strain just as much as I—but still it was an uncharacteristically sharp answer for my master. I had nothing practical to suggest, and so I held my peace.

We passed the hours sitting together in the lee of the rickety battlements looking up at the stars. I was thinking of Ruth, the touch of her hand against my face, the way her body moved as she walked, and my idiotic promise to her to keep her safe. Below in the Tower, I could hear the sound of solemn singing as the Jews celebrated their Passover and prepared for the appalling, unthinkable bloodletting to come. Just imagining that kindly faced, venerable Rabbi cutting the throats of his family, the knife gripped in his trembling, purple-veined hands, the innocent blood spurting red and soaking his dark sleeve, the loved one slumping in his cradling arms . . . I couldn't bear it. Then the singing from below stopped. For a long, long time there was silence; only the distant sounds of the men-at-arms down in the bailey and in the encircling picket lines, joking, cursing, ignorant of the tragedy taking place beneath only fifty yards away, that faint raucous soldierly chorus and the hooting of a distant owl. My scalp prickled and I heard the first cries of anguish. It was a long, sharp, anguished howl, from one throat, and then moments later the cry was taken up by many more: a chorus of the damned wallowing in unbearable torment.

I couldn't stand it. I scrambled to my feet and made my way across the ruined space, littered with abandoned weapons, unneeded clothing and splinters of wood, to the staircase. "Alan," cried Robin behind me, sharply, "Alan, don't go down there . . ." But I ignored my master and began, with heavy unwilling feet, the leaden tread of a condemned man, to step downward into the human slaughterhouse.

I have seen some sights, perhaps I have viewed more horror than I have a right to in one soul's passage across this Earth, but this was one of the most heart-wrenching. Even these days, mind-scarred, jaded and ancient as I am, and tucked-up safe in Westbury, I can barely bring myself to revisit that ground floor room in my mind.

But I will try: I owe it to Ruth. It is a debt I must pay.

After the noise, the animal howling of unimaginable grief, the first sensation to strike me was smell: long before I had turned the last corner of the staircase I could scent the blood, clogging in my throat, steely, warm and disgustingly sweet. Gazing in on the square hall, I saw that the earth floor was awash, a shimmering crimson lake. And on this slick of human gore, bodies, dozens of bodies, scores; curled like babies, hands and fingers most often crooked to their gashed throats, as if in an attempt to force back in the life-sustaining fluid that soaked their hair and lay in pools about their white faces and staring empty eyes. Some of the men were still standing, some looking dazed, appalled at what they had done, others on their knees, eyes raw with weeping, stroking the red-spattered face of a beloved wife or child. And there in the middle of the room was Reuben, eyes wild but focused in his madness, his left arm curled about his daughter, my sweet Ruth, a bright sliver of steel in his right fist.

I shouted "No!" and launched myself across the room, slipping and sliding on the blood-greased floor. Reuben saw me and hesitated and I reached him and grabbed his right arm in my two hands. He was fearfully strong, but Ruth fixed her huge terrified eyes on mine and I managed to pull his arm away. She fell toward me and I wrapped her in my arms and held her sobbing face to my chest, crushing her against my chain mail hauberk, glaring with infinite hatred at Reuben's exhausted, half-grateful, gray-white face. Then Robin was there, his hands on Reuben's shoulders, his blazing silver eyes boring into the Jew's face. "We agreed," he snarled. "We had an agreement. You come out with me. Your life is in my hands; I will save you, you have my solemn word." He slapped Reuben hard around the face, a ringing blow that snapped the Jew's head around. Once again Robin's customary coolness appeared to have deserted him. Reuben shook his head to clear it from the blow but said nothing. I do not think, at that moment, he was capable of speech. He had just come back from the brink of some hellish pit, a mental state I do not even wish to contemplate. And Robin sensing this, and once more in command of himself, began to bundle his friend's long, un-resisting body away from that charnel house and back up the stairs. I followed with Ruth, weeping and shaking uncontrollably in my arms.

We made our camp in a store room on the second floor; Ruth wrapped in my warm green cloak, Reuben sitting with his head in his hands, weeping quietly. Robin and I stood guard, I don't know why, as there was nobody in the Tower who might attack us, and if the Christians who surrounded us had known what was happening inside, they could have taken the Tower any time they cared to. But perhaps we were guarding against more than human foes. The Devil stalked the Tower that night, I am sure of it. The wailing cries from that stinking hall of blood below continued, sporadically through-out the night. And then finally there was silence.

Long past midnight a great storm brewed up, and light-ning lashed the sky, while the great crash of thunder overhead was nearly deafening. The rain fell like a curtain of spears descending from Heaven. I knew then that this was the judgment of God. He was angry that his Christian servants had caused so many Jews to die, and die so horribly. I shivered in an old blanket, being dripped on from holes in the roof, and watched the vengeful wrath of the Almighty through a narrow window slit.

We fired the Tower in the morning light, setting sparks to tinder and wood shavings in five different places to make a funeral pyre for the Jewish dead, and rode out of the battered iron-bound gate under a billow of smoke and grubby once-white chemise tied to a spear. Robin, myself, Reuben and Ruth, accompanied by a very young Jewish couple with a baby we had found hiding in the pantry. I was glad to leave that place of blood and horror, even though we were riding out to surrender to our enemies. I was the last to pass through the iron gate and, as I gave a final glance back upon that scene of hideous carnage, I saw through the gathering smoke, Josce sitting slumped on a stool in a dark corner, his kind, doleful eyes seemingly fixed on mine. I checked Ghost and was about to call to Robin to wait, when I saw that the old man's stillness was unnatural and his beard and the whole front of his robe was drenched in black blood. I stared into his unseeing Jewish eyes for just a moment, and then turned back and guided Ghost down the steep wooden steps toward my fellow Christians.

Our appearance caused the alarm to be sounded in the bailey and men-at-arms came running as we thudded quickly over the earthen causeway and down into the courtyard. Robin led our pathetic group with his chin lifted and, with his light brown hair, silver eyes and fine-wrought hauberk, he looked the very opposite of a besieged and beaten Jew, which was, I expect, his intention. I was at the rear of our group, watching the gathering troops and trying to show no fear. We were all armed, in direct contravention of Sir John's orders, but Robin had told us that, if things got ugly, we all were to cut and run for the open gate of the bailey that led out toward the bridge over the Foss, and beyond to Walmgate. And there was no way on this sinful earth that I was going to leave that Tower without my weapons. I was fully determined to fight and die, if necessary, to protect Ruth, who had still not spoken a word since her near-death last night at the hands of her father. I could not even look at Reuben.

"I am the Earl of Locksley, and I wish to speak to your commander, Sir John Marshal," said Robin in his most haughty voice to the awed circle of men-at-arms on foot that had gathered around us in the center of the bailey. The soldiery appeared to be unsure of what to do. Behind us the Tower was now visibly burning: flames licking greedily at the shattered wooden defenses; black smoke pouring upward to the heavens. We represented no serious threat to the men-at-arms, and we should surely be taken prisoner at the least, but Robin's demeanor and noble bearing kept them at a respectful distance. Beyond the soldiers I could see townsmen, in russet tunics and hoods, appearing from the buildings around the perimeter of the bailey, rubbing sleep from their eyes, and then my heart sank. There was no sign of Sir John Marshal, the sheriff of Yorkshire, charged with keeping the King's peace in this county, but another knightly figure, tall and with a shock of white hair in the center of his forehead, could be seen mounting a horse, drawing a sword and trotting over toward the knot of men around us. The townsmen followed him, in growing numbers, swarming out from their holes like the vicious latrine rats they truly were.

Sir Richard Malbête wasted no time: "What are you waiting for?" he shouted to the men-at-arms while still twenty paces away. "Seize the Jews!"

A man-at-arms tentatively put out a hand to take hold

121

of Robin's bridle, but my master pulled his horse's head away. Someone in the crowd shouted: "Kill the Jews!" and the cry was taken up by many voices. And suddenly we were in the midst of a full-blown battle.

"Make for the gate!" yelled Robin, hauling out his sword and cutting savagely at the man-at-arms who was still trying to grab his horse's reins. A man clutched at my leg and I shook the limb free and booted him in the face. I had my blades out by now as well; poniard in my left hand, sword in my right, tied reins over the pommel of my saddle. I slapped the flat of my blade on the rump of Ruth's horse, it reared and dislodged a man-at-arms who was grappling around Ruth's waist and trying to pull her down. The horse started forward, mercifully toward the gate, I plunged forward after her, cracking my sword into the man's mail-clad arm as Ghost shouldered past. There were soldiers running at me, left and right, and I hacked and kicked, and slashed at faces and limbs until momentarily I had a circle of space around me; but there were too many men-at-arms rushing in for that to last. A soldier unwisely came at me from behind. I gave Ghost the battle signal I had so patiently taught him and he lashed out behind him with both back hooves; with a terrific crack of bone the man went flying, his chest caved in. I cut down another man with sword and sank my poniard into another's back, the fine strong Spanish steel easily punching through the links on his hauberk, as it had been designed to do. There was no sign of the Jewish couple and their baby, the only evidence that they had once lived was a knot of men-at-arms stabbing down again and again with their swords into a half-glimpsed mound of wriggling blood-soaked cloth. I looked away. Reuben, still horsed, was laying about him with his deadly scimitar, men staggering back from his blows with terrible gashes to face and head. Robin had already cut his way clear of the mêlée. He was halfway to the gate and I saw him look back.

We had agreed that, if these circumstances arose, it was every man for himself, but he reined in, looking at Reuben who was still surrounded by soldiers and a group of townsmen flailing at him with scythes and rakes, screaming for his Jewish blood. Then Robin looked to his left, and I, too, saw what he was seeing. My lovely friend Ruth was being dragged from her horse by many grasping hands. I exchanged sword cuts with a man-at-arms who had run up to me and sent him tumbling away then looked back at Robin. He was nearer to Ruth than to Reuben, both of whom now desperately needed his help but—and I will remember these few moments for the rest of my life—he pulled hard at his reins, and wheeling his horse, he lifted his sword and charged back into the fray . . . to Reuben's rescue. I gave a great shout of rage, batted a townsman out of my way and put spurs to Ghost, forcing a way through the crush toward Ruth, chopping desperately about me as I urged my mount forward. But Ruth had disappeared into the press of the mob. I saw hands raised and the glint of steel in them and imagined I heard the dreadful chopping noise as the blades sliced into her sweet flesh.

Suddenly I was in free space again, the nearest soldier ten paces away. I turned and saw that Reuben and Robin too had broken free of the crowd and were heading toward the open gate. I made to follow, but a man on horseback was coming at me from my right—it was Sir Richard Malbête. He smirked as he swung his sword at my head, and I blocked instinctively and twisting my wrist, turned the block into a blow, crashing the edge of the blade hard into his face. It was not a killing strike, but it contained the manic strength of a rage I had never felt before. There was a great gout of blood, a muffled cry and Sir Richard almost slipped from the saddle. But I had no time to turn Ghost and finish him. A score of men-at-arms in Malbête's scarlet and sky blue surcoats was rushing toward me. With one last despairing glance at Ruth's horse, which was standing alone with its head lowered, as if in mourning, I put my heels to Ghost's ribs and galloped for the gate and freedom.

I swear that if I had caught up with Robin by the gate to the bailey of York Castle, I would have killed him—or, at least, tried to. I was sobbing like a baby as I rode hell-for-leather through the gate, the image of Ruth slipping down into that sea of grasping hands and hate-filled faces. But I cuffed my tears away—this was not the time for weakness—and made it over the bridge on the River Foss, before turning right down the straight road toward Walmgate. Ahead of me, and far out of reach, Robin and Reuben galloped down the road, not bothering to pause at Walmgate but surging straight through, past a startled pair of men-at-arms and into the open countyside beyond.

How could he have done it? I asked myself, again and again, how Robin could have made that decision? How could he have decided, when he came to that crossroads in the bailey, to save the life of a man, a very competent and deadly warrior at that, and choose to sacrifice the life of a young, sweet innocent girl? I knew why, of course. I knew in my heart why Robin had done it. Robin needed Reuben for whatever his money-grubbing scheme was; Reuben was his route to riches; the girl was valueless to him. But even though I knew the reason, I still could not believe it. I had seen Robin do some terrible things in my time with him. He had condoned the ritual death of a human being to celebrate a rite for a foul pagan god, he had cut off a man's arms and legs to inspire terror in a community, but this . . . This was the deliberate sacrifice, murder, you might say, of a young girl, whose only crime had been to be a Jewess.

When I caught up with Robin and Reuben, and we all slowed to a canter, I did not want to speak to either man. It seemed that neither of them was in much mood for conversation either. Reuben wept silently as we rode, and Robin, after checking that we were all unharmed—I had a shallow cut on my hand but no recollection as to who had inflicted it on me, Reuben had been stabbed in the calf muscle but seemed not to notice it—we rode back toward Kirkton in silence, our heads hanging in shame and grief, each sunk in his own melancholic thoughts.

The next morning, after a cold, silent night under the stars, as we trotted along the road to Kirkton, which runs to the north and above the beautiful valley of Locksley, I heard the bells of our little church of St. Nicholas ringing out, echoing across the peaceful rolling dale. And I realized it was Easter Sunday: the holiest day in the year.

PART TWO

SICILY AND CYPRUS

CHAPTER SEVEN

My daughter-in-law Marie is in love. She sings as she feeds the chickens outside in the courtyard, she gave me an extra spoonful of honey on my porridge this morning, and she smoothed the thin gray hair off my forehead in a gesture of rare tenderness when she brought me my mug of warmed ale this evening before bed. Her eyes are bright, merry even, her cheeks slightly flushed, and she laughs for no reason; and occasionally she dances a few steps, swinging her skirts gaily, when she thinks nobody is looking.

The object of her affections? Osric. Her distant cousin, my rotund bailiff, has brought joy to her heart after several fumbling weeks of a courtship, which was often almost too painful for an old man to watch. Finally, she consented to his ponderous advances, and now she has moved into the small guest hall on the far side of the courtyard, where he and his sons reside, and talks of a marriage in the spring. I am glad for her but I cannot say I understand why she loves him: he is an ugly plodder, a painstaking dullard, in whom the last ember of youth has long been extinguished. He is one of the last people on earth I would choose to spend my remaining years with; while she, only five years younger than him, still has the waist and wits of a saucy young maiden. But love him she does. What can it be that has aroused her ardour?

"He is a good man, Alan, and that is why I have chosen to wed him. He is steady, honest and caring, and he will never leave me," Marie told me with a smug smile, "and I want you to love him, too. He has saved Westbury with his hard work; you must try to think of him as another son."

That, I think, is unlikely. But, for Marie's sake, I will try to behave a little more warmly toward him.

Christmas is approaching: the season of feasts and frivolity. We have slaughtered most of the pigs and great round hams, sides of bacon and long strings of plump sausages hang from an iron ring, drying and smoking above the fire in the center of the hall. We have more than enough firewood for the winter; Osric and his sons spent a week clearing dead timber from the copse by the stream and hauling it with ox teams to the hall. The buttery is stacked with barrels of good wine from Aquitaine, and Marie has been baking huge game pies and fat pastries out in the big oven in the courtyard. We had the first snowfall last week and more is coming: perhaps strangely, I am looking forward to a really good snowstorm, to being snug in my hall with a roaring fire and plenty to eat and drink.

There is one dark cloud on my horizon: Osric has reported to me that Dickon, my elderly swineherd, has been stealing from me. Apparently, a few weeks after the sows have farrowed, he quite often takes one of the piglets away from its mother and either sells it for meat or, if it is old enough, fattens it himself for his pot. He always claims that the mother pig has rolled on her offspring while asleep and that the piglet has died, and as my sows can have anywhere between eight and sixteen piglets in a litter, nobody has noticed the crime until now. Dickon, that one-armed old fool, was drunkenly boasting of it in the ale house, and Osric overheard him. Now Osric wants to raise a jury of twelve men from the village and have Dickon tried for his crimes at the next manor court, just before Christmas. I am troubled about this: is a piglet here or there so much to worry about? I have not missed them in the past and I still have many breeding pigs, and as much pork meat as I require, and more. Marie says there is a principle at stake here, that I am too soft with the villeins, and it is my fault that I let Westbury decline so much in the years before Osric arrived. As lord of the manor, she says, the villeins should fear and respect me, how else will they refrain from robbing me blind me and laughing up their sleeves? Osric says that, as Dickon has over the years laid his one good hand on chattels of mine worth more than a shilling, I could have him prosecuted for a felony: if found guilty, the penalty for old Dickon would then be death by hanging. I sometimes wonder to myself what Robin would do in these circumstances. Would he have a man hanged for a piglet? In the old Sherwood days, to even touch Robin's money chest was a death sentence. The manor court is to be held two weeks from now: I must think on this some more before then.

I do find it touching, if utterly bewildering, to watch Marie and Osric together: she so happy and girlish; he a great blundering mole-faced booby. Under my brows, I observe their tender glances, the way they fondle each other's hands and arms, discreetly, whenever possible. It reminds me of my own first true love, of the first time I felt that breathtaking, swooping feeling, the hollowness in my chest in the presence of my beloved, the soaring happiness at her smile, and the physical ache at her absence. I think, foolish old man that I am, that I'm in truth a little jealous of their happiness.

When I talk of my own first love, I do not, of course, mean with Reuben's daughter Ruth, God rest her soul. I knew her only for a few days, in extraordinary, appalling circumstances, and if I felt any long-lasting emotions over her death, the uppermost one was guilt. I had liked her, admired her beauty and, wanting to play-act the chivalrous knight, promised to guard her life with my own. I broke my promise. In the months that followed I felt a huge pressing sense of guilt at her death, like a lead cope around my shoulders—and a wheeling flock of unanswerable questions circled inside my head: what if I had been quicker with my sword? Should I have fled the bailey of York Castle when I did? Would it have been more honorable to have stayed and died with her? I felt a little spike of hatred, too—for Robin. I fully believed that he could have saved her had he chosen to, though it would probably have meant abandoning Reuben to his doom.

I spoke to my solid friend Tuck, on our return to Kirkton, at length and in private. Or as private as one can be in a castle packed with four hundred men all busily preparing for a long campaign.

"He's a deeply practical man," Tuck said to me after I had told him the story and revealed my feelings of shame, guilt and anger. We were sitting side by side on a great wooden coffer in the gloomy northeast corner of St. Nicholas's church. "And there is not much room in his heart for sentimentality. He sees that something needs to be done and he does it, regardless of the cost to himself or anyone else. As we both know well, he can be utterly, utterly ruthless."

There were a handful of archers standing near the font while the priest, an innocuous but slightly silly man named Simon, blessed their bows with holy water before our departure for war, but the men were out of earshot. "And you must ask yourself, Alan—honestly—what would have been achieved by saving the girl?" the monk said. I looked at Tuck, in confusion. Surely saving the girl, or any human life, was a noble end in itself?

"I mean, if you take the longer view," he said. He had the good grace to drop his eyes, but he struggled on despite his evident feelings of shame: "By saving Reuben, Robin preserved this army. Without Reuben's Jewish friends in Lincoln, who have since lent us a dragon's hoard of silver, we would not be able to leave for France next month to join in the Great Pilgrimage to save the Holy Land. If he had saved the girl, but lost Reuben, well, without wages our soldiers here would slip away back to their homes, or take to the forests as footpads, and the army would have disintegrated; Robin would have disappointed King Richard, disobeyed him in truth. He would be out of favor; he might even have been outlawed again for dereliction of duty. No, as you have described it, with so many enemies about him, and so little time, he was bound to save Reuben . . ."

I glared stonily at the floor. Tuck remained quiet for a while and then he said: "Remember that, even when we can't see it or understand it, Almighty God always has a plan, Alan. Perhaps, this poor girl had to die so that Robin might lead his men to recapture holy Jerusalem for the True Faith."

I could see the point Tuck was making, although I did not want to acknowledge it; and I still felt a knot of anger in my gut at the seemingly easy way Robin had made up his mind to sacrifice the girl.

"Tell me honestly, Tuck," I said at last, "will Ruth be received by Our Lord Jesus Christ in Heaven? Surely she was an innocent soul?"

Tuck sighed, a long low exhalation like the last breath of a dying man; then he looked up at me, his kindly, nut-brown gaze meeting mine. "I fear not," he said finally. "She was a Jew and, as Our Lord has taught us, the only way to find a place in

Heaven is through His grace." I looked away from Tuck, tears pricking my eyes, and found I was staring at a great painting of Christ on the Cross on the church wall, a beautiful image of the Savior suffering and dying for our sins. I was grateful that Tuck had not lied to me. Then, to my surprise, he went on: "But God is ineffable and all merciful, Alan, and his forgiveness is boundless. In His wisdom, He may perhaps see fit to take her to His bosom."

I was comforted by his words. Christ preached love— and how could he fail to show His love to one who was so clearly an innocent, slaughtered by fiends possessed by the Devil.

We rode out of Kirkton on the last day of April, heading for Southampton to take ship to Normandy. Robin rode at the front of a long double line of horsemen, a hundred and two men strong, each clad in newly burnished chain mail and a square-topped, rivetted steel helmet, and armed with a big kite-shaped shield, a sword and a twelve-foot lance. Beside Robin rode Sir James de Brus, the cavalry commander, scowling as usual and grumbling to himself as he twisted in the saddle and surveyed the ranks of our mounted men-at-arms. Behind the cavalry came the archers, one hundred and eighty-five men carrying long bow staves, full arrow bags and short swords, laughing and joking but walking briskly in the spring sunshine. They were Owain's pride and joy, men selected by him for their strength and skill with a war bow, which as the grizzled Welsh captain boasted, "could put a bodkin point between a man's eyes at a hundred paces, and another in his belly before he fell to the ground."

Next came the baggage train, ten big wagons pulled by huge, slow-moving oxen, and loaded impossibly high with food, wine, ale, tents, clothing, horse gear and extra weapons. Four of the ox wagons carried only arrow shafts, in bundles of a dozen, piled high and lashed tight to each lumbering wooden vehicle. Last of all came the rear-guard, ninety-three leather-jacketed spearmen, commanded by Little John, with sixteen-foot broad-headed weapons, sharp hand axes in their belts and their old-fashioned round shields slung on their backs. They were responsible for the safety of the baggage train, and for driving the herd of sheep that would feed us *en route*, and they had orders to move at their own pace rather than try to keep up with the main body of Robin's men.

Our mood was high as a hunting falcon: we were setting off on a noble task, doing God's work and with the prospect of adventure, glory, loot and loose women ahead of us, and the promise of Heaven for any who died in battle. There wasn't a soldier among us who did not feel proud to be part of our company. Swept up in the excitement of our leave-taking, I had temporarily forgotten that I was angry with Robin, the shade of Ruth grew fainter and I rode behind him and Sir James with the glorious sense of a great and exciting journey begun.

Joy, though, was not universal. Beside me rode Reuben. He seemed to have aged ten years since the terrible days at York Castle, and if I am honest, though he was only in his middle thirties, he was beginning to look like an old man, his lean brown face cut with fresh deep lines of grief. Robin had persuaded him to join us on this great mission to the Holy Land as our treasurer and Robin's personal physician, and Reuben, perhaps because he was too dispirited to argue, had consented to accompany us and look after the financial matters of Robin's army, and to tend to my master's health. He told me in a dull voice that now that his daughter was dead, he had nothing in England to hold him here, and he longed to see his desert homeland once more before he grew too old. He rarely spoke now, and when I looked over into his red-eyed face as we rode along that spring morning, I realized that once again he had been weeping, and I felt a twinge of my old guilt.

At Kirkton, we left behind us Goody, Marie-Anne and

Robin's newly born son and heir, Hugh. With excellent timing, the Countess of Locksley had given birth two weeks before our departure; the labor had been long, a full day closeted in her chamber with Goody, a serving maid and the wise crone from the village, with only the odd stifled moan and request for more hot water making its way through to the hall. Robin, as was his habit when his raw emotions might expect to be engaged, had remained icily calm throughout the experience, waiting hour after hour in the hall, reading a scroll of romances in a large ornately carved chair, almost a throne, and occasionally summoning me to sing to him or talk of inconsequential things. He ate and drank very little and did not move from his position in the chair until Goody threw open the door of the chamber and came running out, eyes sparkling, face clay-red, shouting: "It's a boy, Robin, a healthy boy. Oh, come and see. Come and meet him. He is so beautiful."

Robin's son was a lusty child with light blue eyes and jet black hair and the squashed face of a monkey. To me, little Hugh did not look in the slightest bit beautiful and I was puzzled at first that the child should have this coloring: Robin had light brown hair and Marie had chestnut locks. But Goody explained the facts of nature to me, as we stood together over the cradle in Robin and Marie-Anne's chamber a day or so later.

"Oh, Alan, you men know nothing about babies"—this from a twelve-year-old maiden—"some babies are just born with black hair. I was myself, or so my mother told me. And look at me now." She twirled in front of me, her Saxon-blonde hair, which had been tied in two braids on either side of her pink cheeks, swinging as she moved.

I reached out and took a braid in my hand as it swung past me; it was the color of spun gold but soft as feathers. Goody snatched it back. "I said 'look' not 'touch.'" Suddenly she was all busyness. "Now Alan, I need you out of the way, we have to make the place properly clean for the baby," and she shooed me briskly out of the chamber like a middle-aged good wife dealing with an unruly schoolboy.

Traveling as part of an army is obviously a very different experience to journeying as a lone man, or as part of a small group, as I had been used to. We carried with us a sense of sprawling menace that nothing could dispel even in our own land. Shepherds would flee before us on the peaceful downs, and villagers would bar their doors and shutter their windows at our approach, even in the tranquil southern counties of England. It was not so long ago—grandfathers could clearly recall it— that, during the Anarchy of Stephen and Maud, gangs of armed men would roam the land and pillage at will. And country folk have long memories.

But we did not despoil our own people; we had plenty of supplies, thanks to the loans of silver from Reuben's friends, and each night when we made camp in a fallow field or common wood, we killed an animal or two and roasted the mutton and made merry. My music was in great demand. Almost every night I would be called upon to sing and play for my supper, and I was glad to do so. I sang the old country songs, for the most part. Amusing peasant ditties about unfaithful husbands and angry wives, songs of the farmer and his beasts, or tales of great battles fought long ago by King Arthur and his knights. The *cansos* and *sirvantes*, the songs of courtly love and satirical poems that I used to sing in the halls of the nobility, were less popular with the rough soldiery. Occasionally, Robin would call his officers together and we would dine and make plans for the next few days or weeks, and at the end of our gatherings I would indulge my audience in a more sophisticated musical offering: there was one I was particularly proud of which I composed at that time. The song tells of a beautiful golden brooch, with a pin in the shape of a sword, worn by a noble lady. The brooch is in love with the *domina* whose breast he adorns—and guards from the touch of another lover—but of course there can never be true love between a jewel, however beautiful, and a great lady. The brooch can only ever serve his mistress, he can never possess her, but he is content with this role. Tragically, at the end of the *canso*, the brooch is cast away by the lady, who says she has grown tired of it, and the bright jewel rests in a deep, muddy ditch, remembering its love until Judgment Day.

You might think that my mood was particularly black when I wrote that song of talking jewelry and tragic love, but in truth, I was feeling very optimistic. My relations with Robin were more or less back to normal. I had decided to forgive him—I told myself that I must strive to be a loyal vassal and support all of his decisions, whether I agreed with them or not—and I was happy in the company of the other captains and vintenars, with the exception of James de Brus. But that was no problem: I was merely courteous and distant with the Scotsman, and he with me. And I had a new body servant, which made me feel very grand. William—the boy who had helped me steal the ruby from Sir Ralph Murdac—had been summoned from Nottingham Castle. The loyal fellow had been regularly sending verbal reports on the activities of Murdac through some mysterious network of Robin's spies and as a reward, as we marched past Nottingham on our way south, young William had joined us as my manservant. He was a diligent lad, quick-moving and eager to please, very intelligent, though with a slight stammer, and good at anticipating my requirements. He kept my applewood vielle and its horsehair bow, a much prized gift from my old musical mentor Bernard, in a highly polished state and he was always on hand to fetch and carry. He was a grave boy, though, only smiling rarely and never up to the high jinks that I indulged in when I was his age. But I liked him, and I was glad of his service.

The one cloud in my sky was that Tuck was not accompanying us on this great adventure. Partly as a result of

William's reports—Murdac had apparently repeated his offer of a hundred pounds of silver for Robin's head—Robin had asked Tuck to remain at Kirkton Castle to watch over Marie-Anne and the baby with his two enormous, battle-trained wolfhounds Gog and Magog. These great beasts could tear the arm off a man as easily as I could tear the leg off a boiled capon, but they were as mild as the Baby Jesus around Tuck's friends. Robin had also left a score of bowmen, ten cavalrymen and ten veteran spearmen as a garrison. It was not enough to hold the bailey of the castle but, if attacked, as I well knew from my experiences in York, they were a big enough force to hold the strong keep.

Instead of my friend, the jolly fighting monk, we were accompanied by Father Simon, the priest of St. Nicholas's Church in Kirkton, a man I did not particularly care for, who seemed to have been born without a chin; his mouth merged seamlessly into his neck, almost as if somebody had removed his lower jaw. Father Simon held brief prayers every morning before we marched, mumbled in bad Latin and incomprehensible to the men, and on Sundays he sang Holy Mass, out of tune, I may say, for the whole army. I got the distinct feeling that he did not like Robin much; in fact, I could sometimes imagine that he hated him, although like any sensible mortal who wished to remain on this earth a while longer, he feared my master and treated him with respect.

I believe I knew why the priest disliked him: as many of the men knew, Robin had been involved in the old pagan worship of the Mother Goddess during his time as an outlaw, and although he now paid the proper homage to the True Religion of the Living Christ, his devilish past allegiances had not been forgotten. Whatever Robin felt about Father Simon in return, or privately believed, we were on a holy pilgrimage to the birthplace of Our Lord and it would have been unthinkable to travel without at least one priest. So the chinless cleric came with us.

I have this to say in Father Simon's favor. He did not set himself above the men, as some priests are wont to do. He just got on with his allotted tasks. Before we embarked on to three great cargo ships at Southampton, Father Simon insisted on blessing the vessels to protect us from the dangers of the deep; and his prayers seemed to work. The crossing was smooth and uneventful, and it took only a day and a night before we were trooping out at the quay at Honfleur, King Richard's port at the mouth of the great river Seine in Normandy.

I had never been out of England before, and was astounded to find that Normandy looked almost exactly the same as my homeland. Perhaps I had expected the grass to be blue and the sky green, I don't know. But the sensation of familiarity was extraordinary. The fields looked the same, the houses were similar and, until they opened their mouths to speak French, the people could have been easily mistaken for good honest English folk.

During the march through the Norman countryside, as we made our way southward, there were certain elements of our army—mainly the folk who had previously been outlaws—who held the opinion that the French peasants existed solely to provide us with free food and drink. Robin had other ideas and was determined to maintain strict discipline. This land was the patrimony of our King, he said, and we were not to ravage it. Little John caught and summarily hanged two cavalrymen for stealing a chicken on the first day on Norman soil, and Robin gathered the men together and made a quiet, determined speech directly under the swinging heels of the looters.

"You think I'm being harsh?" he asked the four hundred angry men who were assembled before him. He used his loud, carrying battle voice. "Do you think I'm being unjust? I don't give a damn. No man under my command steals so much as a penny, desecrates a Church, or beds any woman without her consent—unless I have given them permission. I will hang any bastard who does so from the nearest tree. No trial, no mercy, just a final dance at the end of a rope. Is that clear?"

There were a few sullen murmurs from the men, but they knew that there had to be discipline, and the former outlaws among them also knew that Robin could be a great deal more brutal if he chose to.

But Robin had not finished: "And that goes for the officers, too. Any captain who robs or rapes will be whipped in front of the men as a lesson to all, and then demoted." This was most unusual. Shocking, too. By common custom the officers were disciplined under different rules to the men, and their chastisements never included corporal punishment. Perhaps Robin had said this because we were, unusually, an almost entirely base-born contingent of King Richard's army. Although led by an Earl, we were mercenaries—or we would be when Richard paid Robin the money he had promised. I saw Sir James de Brus glowering at Robin and fingering his sword hilt. He was the only man among us, apart from Robin, who had been born noble, and I could almost hear him thinking: *I will die with my sword in your belly before I submit to a whipping like an errant serf.* But he said nothing. He was, after all, a good, professional soldier and he knew when to hold his tongue.

There was little need for rape: as we marched through Normandy, women seemed to appear from nowhere and attach themselves to our column, like bees attracted to a honeypot. Some were whores looking for rich pickings, and some were fairly virtuous women who were looking for adventure and who believed that by attaching themselves to a strapping young man-at-arms they would see the world. And, as they made no complaints to Robin, he did not need to enforce his discipline. One extraordinary creature caught my eye, though not for the reasons you might expect a young man to find a woman interesting. She was a very tall woman of about thirty or more years, extremely thin with long hands and feet. She dressed in a long, dirty green robe that covered her from shoulder to ankle and she seemed to have no breasts or womanly curves at all. Her hair, though, was a magnificent explosion of tangled, white locks, which stood out straight from her scalp. She resembled nothing so much as a dandelion about to shed its seeds. And her name was Elise.

"Read your fortune, master?" she called to me in camp one evening as I was replacing a broken strap on Ghost's saddle-rig. Amused, I allowed her to look at my right palm.

"I see great love in your future," Elise said peering up into my face. I nodded indulgently: it was a fairly standard, almost obligatory prediction for a young man. She went on: "And I see great pain. You will think you are strong in your love; that your love is a castle that cannot be broken, but you are not as strong as you believe. And you will betray your love with the sight of your eyes. Love comes in by the eyes—and leaves the same way. On that day; you will wish you were blind, for your sight will have killed all the love in your heart."

I snatched my hand away. It was all nonsense, of course, but it sounded suspiciously like a curse. And, to be truthful, these women who claim to have second sight make me uneasy; some of them have real power given to them by the Devil, so it does not do to cross them.

"You do not like my prophecy," she said, looking at me curiously. "Very well, I will give you another: you will die an old man, in your own bed, at your own hearth." It was a standard piece of nonsense, given out to many a fighting man to gain favor, I assumed, and thought no more about it. I merely smiled, gave her a farthing and told her to be off.

But Elise stayed with our column; she rarely spoke to me, and I avoided her, but she became, I noticed, the leader and spokeswoman of the women who had joined our pilgrimage. Robin saw that she kept the peace between the women, who before she had joined us often argued like cats and dogs, and he did not care that she made a few coppers here and there telling stories and reading palms; he reckoned her harmless and tolerated her presence, and the presence of the other women, on the march.

But two weeks into our journey across France, Robin was forced to show his steel. Will Scarlet was exposed by Sir James de Brus as a thief. And worse he had stolen from a church. It was sheer weakness of character: Will had always been an accomplished pickpocket and lock-breaker; as a boy outlaw he had been known as "Scoff-lock" because of the contempt with which he treated the big iron devices that rich men used to secure their money chests. With the right tools he could have any lock opened as fast as a whore's legs. But he was not an outlaw anymore, he was a holy soldier of Christ, a pilgrim, and Robin was ready to make this point clear with brutal force.

Will had been in charge of a patrol of twenty mounted men-at-arms, a *conroi* as these squadrons are called, but I knew he had been having trouble getting the men to obey him. He was younger than most of the troopers, and if the truth be told, while he was a gifted thief, he was not a gifted soldier. He did not even ride very well. It seems that the men had come across an empty church while on forward patrol and they had egged Will on to pick the lock of the coffer where the church's silver was kept. It was a foolish thing to do a mere week after Robin's edict, particularly since his own men had later turned traitor and informed on him to Sir James. But I imagine that Will wanted to show the men under his command that there was something he could do well.

Actually, I blamed Robin. Will Scarlet was not the man to lead a *conroi* of twenty tough, salty cavalrymen and Robin should have known that. The young redhead—he was my age, fifteen summers—had been given the command as a reward for serving Robin loyally during the outlaw years. But Will was a fool, too: firstly, he had trusted his men to stay

143

silent about their crime; and he had thought that by playing the good fellow with them he would gain their respect; lastly, he had relied on his long relationship with Robin to protect him. He was wrong on all three counts.

He was roughly stripped to his *braies* and hose and lashed to a tree in a peaceful woodland clearing and, while Sir James, Robin and Will's *conroi* looked on, Little John cut his naked back to ribbons with a horsewhip. Although they were old friends, Little John laid it on with fury—he was not overly concerned about a theft from the church, but he did not like Robin's orders to be flouted.

Will screamed from the first blow, which echoed like a meaty slap around the clearing, and by the time Little John had reached the allotted number of twenty lashes, and the blood was running thickly down his ripped white back and soaking into his *braies*, Will was mercifully unconscious.

The boy was cut down and tended to by the strange woman Elise, who gently washed his back free of blood, then smeared it with a goose fat salve and bandaged it with clean linen, and the whole column was given a day of rest. Before Will's *conroi* were allowed to disperse, Robin spoke to them: "You are disgraced," he said coldly, his eyes glinting like cold metal in the morning sunshine. "Not only did you steal from a church, against my express orders, but you also betrayed your captain—which is a far worse crime, to my mind. I should hang every man jack of you." The men-at-arms were looking at the ground, fiddling with their bridles and the manes of their horses, their shame written clear on their faces. "But I will not do that." There was a collective exhalation of breath, audible where I was sitting on Ghost across the clearing. "Instead," Robin continued, "I have decided that, as a *conroi*, you are disbanded. This unit is no longer part of my force. Any man who wishes to leave may return his horse, saddle and weapons to John Nailor and depart this company, immediately, on foot, never to return. The men who wish to stay, Sir James will allocate to a new *conroi*; if the officer will take traitorous curs such as you. You are dismissed."

And he turned his back on them and rode away.

The men of the disgraced *conroi*, some of whom looked mightily relieved, were divided between the other squadrons; but I was interested to see that not a man elected to leave the army. I was glad, too, that Robin had shown mercy—but a part of me suspected that my master realized that he could not afford to sacrifice so many men over what was, in truth, a fairly trivial affair.

Will recovered swiftly and within two days he was back in the saddle, as an ordinary trooper, of course. He bore his hurts without complaint, but seemed strangely quiet, never speaking unless it was absolutely necessary. The episode left a slightly bad taste in all our mouths, but it was soon forgotten in a fresh crisis—a week later somebody tried to murder the Earl of Locksley.

On the march through France and Burgundy to Lyon, we avoided castles and towns, partly to keep the men away from temptation, and partly because, as we had found in England, a large group of heavily armed men is seldom given a warm welcome in any settlement. So every afternoon, our scouts guided us into the camping ground for the night, usually a large field near a stream, or a piece of common ground. Occasionally we would descend on an isolated farm, where Reuben would silence the protests of the farmer with a gift of silver, and we would pack ourselves into the outbuildings where we were guaranteed a dry night. But most of the time we pitched tents, twenty men to each one, and cooked on great communal fires. Robin had his own tent, which a couple of the archers would set up for him every night. Robin had the tent to himself but, until he retired, it was the hub around which the whole camp revolved. His officers, and even some of the men, those who had known him since their outlaw days, felt free to come in and out of the tent almost at will. It was only when he retired for the night, usually long past midnight, that he had the space to himself.

One night, we were somewhere near the great city of Tours, after I had been trying out a new *canso* on my master, I saw that he was tired and, picking up my vielle and bow, I left him to his rest. I laced the tent flaps shut behind me and had taken no more than two steps away toward my own tent when I heard a sharp cry of pain, followed by a series of crashes and metallic bangs, exactly as if someone was sword fighting inside the tent. Not bothering with the tent flap, I plunged my poniard through the canvas and ripped a great hole in it and then I ducked into the tent, blades in both fists.

The candle was still lit and I could see Robin, shirtless, sitting on the edge of his sleeping pallet, drawn sword on the floor below him, clutching his bare lower arm and cursing quietly under his breath. The tent's meager furniture looked as if it had been hacked apart and in the center of the floor was a thin jet-black snake, originally more than two or three foot long, an adder, I assumed, that had been hacked into three bloody pieces.

"Get Reuben," Robin croaked. His right arm was turning an angry red color and it was beginning to swell.

"Are you all right?" I asked stupidly.

"No, I'm not . . . go . . . get Reuben . . . fast," Robin could hardly speak for the pain, and I cursed myself for hesitating and rushed out of the tent. In less than thirty heartbeats I had Reuben, hair tousled from sleep, eyes gummy, kneeling beside Robin and examining two swollen puncture wounds on the outside of Robin's right forearm. Then Reuben had a knife in his hands, as usual I didn't see where it came from, and he was cutting a strip from Robin's shirt and tying it around the Earl's upper arm above the elbow. Then he gently

146

pushed Robin down on to the pallet and tied his wounded arm loosely to one of the struts that supported his bed. Now, with Robin lying, white-faced on the pallet, his right arm tied below him, Reuben began very gently to sponge the puncture wounds with diluted wine.

"Are you going to cut the wound and suck out the poison?" I asked Reuben, perhaps just a little ghoulishly. An old outlaw had told me once that this was the only way to prevent death after a snakebite. He joked that the only problem with this infallible cure was that if you got bitten on the arse, nobody would volunteer to save you.

"Of course not," snapped Reuben. "What a ridiculous idea! He's already been wounded, should I make the wound larger and spread the poison around in a bigger cut? And I certainly don't want any of that venom in my mouth. Just bring me some bandages, Alan, and hold your silly tongue."

At that moment, Robin rolled over on to his side and vomited copiously over the edge of the bed only narrowly missing the arm that Reuben was so tenderly washing. I retreated to fetch clean bandages, and some Holy Water, hurriedly blessed by Father Simon, for Robin to drink.

When I returned, Robin was unconscious. His face was white, but sweating heavily, his arm purple-red and hugely swollen below the tourniquet. Reuben was sitting beside him on a stool calmly drinking a beaker of wine.

"Will he live?" I asked Reuben, trying hard to keep the tremor out of my voice.

"I expect so," said Reuben. "Although he will doubtless be ill for some days. He's young and strong and, while adders do kill people, it is usually the old, the very young and the weak who die from their bite. A more interesting question is: How did the adder get into his bed?"

"Could it have crawled there to hide from people, or perhaps to sleep?" I suggested, and I already knew the answer before Reuben supplied it.

"No wild serpent is going to voluntarily enter a camp full of hundreds of men, dodge all those pairs of booted feet and decide to take a nap in a bed two feet off the floor," Reuben said scathingly. "Someone put it there. The question is who?"

It was a question we pondered fruitlessly over the next few days. Clearly it had been an assassination attempt, if a clumsy one, but who could have been responsible? Was it another archer trying to claim Ralph Murdac's hundred pounds of silver? Almost everyone in the camp had access to Robin's tent, and people were in and out every day. It would have been relatively easy to slip a sleepy adder from a bag into Robin's blankets with nobody the wiser.

I posted two men-at-arms outside his tent every night from then onward. And kept an eye on them to make sure that they didn't sleep. I also told them that Little John would have them flayed alive if another assassin got past them, which was quite unnecessary as the whole camp was outraged by the cowardly attempt on Robin's life, and a murderer, once unmasked, would have been hacked to death in moments by a mob.

Little John had taken command, and we didn't let Robin's unconscious state affect the march. He was merely strapped to his pallet each morning with stout leather belts and carried by four strong archers in the center of our column. For the first day, when he merely lay there, whey-faced, wounded arm bandaged, I had the powerful illusion that he was dead, and we were carrying his bier in a ceremonial procession. I felt an unexpectedly powerful stab of grief, a physical ache in my chest, before I told myself sternly to pull myself together. Gradually Robin improved, and after two days the swelling in his arm began to subside.

When we reached the outskirts of Lyon, Robin had regained his senses but was still as weak as a kitten. He insisted on mounting a horse, though, and looking like a three-day-old corpse he rode up and down the length of the column to show the men that he was fit and well. They cheered him, God bless them, and Robin just managed to lift his sword with his bandaged arm to return the salute.

As we marched down the Saône Valley toward the city of Lyon, just inside the borders of the Holy Roman Empire, it became clear that we were not the first large force to have passed that way in recent weeks. King Richard and King Philip had joined their vast forces at Vézelay, a hundred and twenty miles to the north in Burgundy a few weeks ago and had marched the grand army down to Lyon in a magnificent parade of their joint strength. The road was dusty, worn down and the grass verges had been stamped flat and were littered with the detritus of a passing multitude, broken clay cups, bones and scraps of food, abandoned boots, hoods, old rags, even a few good blankets had been tossed aside as the mighty host had flowed past.

And then, one day, we came over a rise and I looked down at the largest assembly of souls I had ever seen. I stood breathless, stunned that there could be so many people in the whole world, and all crammed into such a small area of land. Between the arms of the rivers Saône and the mighty Rhône was massed the chivalry of Western Europe, more than twenty thousand souls, the population of a large city, encamped there in a gigantic heaving sprawl of gaudy tents, glinting steel, mud and humming humanity that stretched almost as far as the eye could see. Horse lines, fluttering pennants, burnished shields, rough buildings of turf and wood, bright striped pavilions for the knights, blacksmiths in canvas tents beating out helmets, barbers pulling teeth, squires bustling about their duties, heralds in parti-colored tunics announcing their lords with a brave squeal of brass. At the edge of the field a horse race was in progress, watched by ladies and gentlemen in their finest clothes. Knights in full armor practiced combat with each other, men-at-arms sat drinking outside makeshift taverns in the summer sunshine, whores paraded about in their finery seeking trade, priests preached to gatherings of the faithful, mendicant friars in brown robes begged alms for the poor, dogs barked, beggars whined, children played tag around wigwams of stacked lances . . .

We were in the presence of the greatest, most powerful army the world had ever seen. Surely, with this vast assembled might, Saladin and his Saracen army of infidels was doomed and Jerusalem, the blessed site of Christ's Passion, would soon once again be safe in Christian hands.

CHAPTER EIGHT

The Messina strait was a sheet of pure dark blue water, only wrinkled by a few petulant white-capped waves. I had been told by the sailors that in ancient times it was home to two monsters called Scylla and Charybdis, but they were full of such ridiculous tales, as I had discovered over the past few weeks, and it seemed altogether too harmless a stretch of water for such an evil reputation. The late September sun smiled down on us with a friendly warmth, the sky was untroubled by a single cloud, and a fair wind pushed our massive fleet of ships swiftly across the channel between the scuffed toe of Italy and the golden island of Sicily—the rich land of oranges, lemons and grain, and sugarcane, of Norman kings and Greek merchants, of Saracen traders and Jewish money-lenders, of Latin priests and Orthodox monks living side by side in a colorful mix of creeds and races. Sicily was where the fabulous East began, and it had been chosen by our sovereign lords as the launching off point of our great and noble expedition.

King Richard's mighty force—more than ten thousand soldiers and seamen, with more men expected to join him in the coming weeks—was packed into an armada of more than a hundred and thirty great sea-going ships. There were scores of big, lumbering busses, great fat-bellied crafts used for transporting bulky stores, some fitted with special berths for the war horses; dozens of smaller cogs that carried men-at-arms and their mountains of equipment; swift galleys packed with knights, with ranks of chained Muslim slaves at the oars; there were flat-bottomed boats that could be used for landing men and horses directly on to beaches, and snacks, or snake boats, as they were sometimes called, the slim, elegant descendants of the Viking longships; and a host of smaller fry, fast with low, triangular sails, which zipped between the large craft and communicated the King's commands to the fleet. The whole sea-borne pack of us, perhaps the greatest force ever assembled, was advancing in one great colorful, cacophonous swarm toward the ancient harbor of Messina. Pennants were flying from every masthead, trumpets and clarions blared, and drums beat out the time for the slaves at the galley's oars. It must have been a daunting sight for the thousands of local people who lined the Sicilian shore to watch our approach.

The city of Messina was laid out on the coast roughly on a north-south axis and we approached it from the sea to the east. The famous harbor, the source of Messina's wealth, lay snug inside a curled peninsula at the southern end of the city where it gave precious protection to the shipping from the winter storms. As we turned south to begin our approach toward the harbor's narrow mouth, I looked west and saw the great stone palace of Messina, one of the residences of Tancred, the Norman King of Sicily, where Philip of France and a handful of his knights, at Tancred's gracious request,

152

had set up their headquarters a week before. My heart gave a little skip of excitement as I saw the royal lilies of France on the banners fluttering over its battlements. The palace lay on the edge of the city, slightly to the north of the great Latin cathedral of Messina, blessed by the Virgin herself in a famous letter, with its tall square stone tower and long, high nave.

Beyond the palace and the cathedral, higher up the slope and slightly to the south, was the Greek monastery of San Salvatore, low but stoutly walled and with a fine reputation for producing illuminated copies of great and rare books. The old walled town of Messina, the kernel from which the city had grown, lay to the south of the palace, the cathedral and the monastery. Curved around the harbor but set slightly back from the water's edge, it was surrounded by strong stone ramparts, pierced by several gates and defended by many towers—but it looked prosperous rather than formidable. It contained many large houses, some two or even three stories high, and at least half a dozen well-maintained churches in both the Greek and Latin styles. Its merchants had a reputation for being rich but frugal and its women were said to be both beautiful and lecherous—but woe betide any man who dishonored them, for their fathers and husbands were as vengeful as scorpions. Three stout wooden gates opened out from the town wall on to jetties that ran out into the harbor so that rich, exotic goods could be unloaded and easily transported into the safety of the warehouses in the old town itself. Beyond the sprawl of the city of Messina, high in the west, soared the gray mountains of Sicily, brooding like a gathering of huge, disapproving churchmen over our triumphant arrival.

As we swept through the narrow mouth of the bay and into the harbor, I was standing at the prow of the *Santa Maria*, an ancient sixty-foot cog with a single square sail that had been my home for the past six weeks. It was also home to forty-seven tired, wet, seasick archers, a dozen crew, and a scattering of the soldiers' women—all of us crammed as tight as an egg into the little ship so that there was no space anywhere to lie down at full stretch.

I knew every inch of the old *Santa Maria*—from her sharp beaky prow and leaky clinker-built wooden sides to the round stern with its long, scarred steering oar tended by her craggy master Joachim—and I was thoroughly sick of her. I could not wait to disembark in Messina and end this stage of a seemingly interminable, tedious and uncomfortable journey.

After a week of feasting and jesting and resting our tired bodies in Lyon, and many conferences between Robin and King Richard, to which I had not, of course, been privy, Robin's force had set off again southward with the rest of the King's army. King Philip and the French host, which was less than one third the size of Richard's force, had marched east to take ship with the Genoese merchants in their fine city. The two armies were to rendezvous in Sicily and proceed from there to the Holy Land. Under King Richard's personal command, his huge force—Englishmen, Welshmen, Normans, as well as Angevins, Poitevins, Gascons and men from Maine and Limoges—had marched south along the valley of the Rhône to Marseilles. We sang as we marched and were cheered by Provençal villagers, who lined the roads to throw flowers at us and watch our great, slow-moving procession. We waited another week at Marseilles for the King's ships and yet more knights and men-at-arms to arrive, as a goodly number had traveled via the long route from England by sea. But on the eighth day news reached us, carried by local fishermen, that the grand fleet had been delayed in Portugal. The men-at-arms had run riot in Lisbon, killing Jews, Muslims and Christians and had sacked the city in a three-day orgy of destruction. The word "York" leaped into my mind.

King Richard was furious. The shouting from his royal apartments in Marseilles, the commandeered inn of a local nobleman, could be clearly heard fifty paces down the street. And ever the impatient man, Richard immediately hired, borrowed or bought every ship he could lay his hands on in Marseilles and the neighboring ports, and dispatched one half of his force, under the command of Baldwin, the Arch-bishop of Canterbury and Ranulf Glanville, the former Justi-ciar of England, directly to the Holy Land. Their task was to relieve the Christian forces there, which, we had heard, were engaged in a desperate struggle against the Saracens at the great, fortified port of Acre.

The rest of his army, with myself and forty-eight archers berthed in the *Santa Maria,* began a leisurely crawl eastward along the coast, round the gulf of Genoa and down the Italian seaboard. We were deliberately traveling slowly, stopping each evening to weigh anchor in a convenient bay and scare up sup-plies and fresh water, dawdling and waiting for the main fleet to come round the Spanish peninsula and catch up. I had suf-fered terribly at first from seasickness, as had almost all the archers, and the beginning of the voyage had been accompa-nied by the sound of dozens of big men taking turns to retch over the side, when they were not lying, moaning and praying in the bottom of the ship. When it rained, we were soaked to the skin, when the sun shone, which was most days, we burned in the strong unfamiliar Mediterranean light. The food was execrable: casks of salted pork, most of which had already gone rotten, moldy cheese, makeshift bread of flour and water cooked like pancakes on a griddle, sour ale, and wine that tasted salty. And the smell was appalling: the con-stant stink of unwashed men, of damp salt-rotted clothes, of black and evil bilge water, wafts of rotting fish from the store-rooms in the stern, and the occasional whiff from the feces that streaked the outer sides of the cog where the archers did their latrine business. I soon began to long for the sun to sink, just for the chance to get off the damned ship and stretch my legs on God's good, clean, dry unmoving land.

Going ashore was dangerous, though. One of our men was murdered by villagers near Livorno: they caught him alone near a farmstead and, being suspicious peasant folk, they accused him of being a thief and beat him to death with sticks and stones. The King would not allow us to take revenge and Robin, unfairly, I thought, rebuked me for allowing one of his men to wander off alone.

At Salerno, where we tarried for several days, we finally had good news. The main fleet had reached Marseilles. It had refitted for one week and was now fast approaching Messina. We set out from Salerno with our hearts high, and as the fast spy boats reported sighting the main fleet, cheering burst spontaneously from all our lips. We were united with all our strength, and I assumed, after a quick stop at Messina for fresh food and water we would be heading on to the Holy Land. I hugged myself. I might even, I thought, with God's good grace, celebrate this Christmas in Jerusalem. As it turned out, I could not have been more wrong.

It took the best part of two days for the whole fleet to disembark at Messina and for King Richard's quartermasters to allocate accommodation for fifteen thousand men. King Richard was determined to make his presence felt on the island and almost immediately after landing he occupied the monastery of San Salvatore, claiming it as his main headquarters and as the store dump for his vast army. The bewildered Greek monks were removed, kindly but firmly by the King's household knights, and the place began to fill with bundles and boxes and stacks of weapons and the cries of large confident men.

Robin's troops were allocated a large field to the north of the palace as a campsite, close to the rocky shoreline where there was a convenient stream for drinking water and washing. We pitched our tents and dried our salt-wet clothes as best we could, spreading them out on bushes and scrubby olive trees;

we oiled our weapons, shaved for the first time in weeks, and washed the salt from our long hair. Some of the men wandered down to the old town to buy bread and cheese and olives and fruit, some went in search of women, some killed the time gambling, drinking and sleeping while we all waited for orders. It was the last week in September and a disconcerting rumor had begun to circulate among the men: we had missed the sailing season; there was no way our fleet could safely make it across the stormy Mediterranean this side of spring. So there would be no Christmas in Jerusalem this year.

Our camping field began to change overnight, timber was cut and hauled in and the men began throwing up more permanent shelters than our thin canvas tents: huts with walls of woven branches, plastered with mud, roofed with turf or double layers of canvas which had been smeared with oil and wax; lean-to shelters and even small cottages with straw-thatched roofs and wooden plank walls. In less than a week our field began to look like a village, and the same was happening all over the area to the north of Messina, where along the shoreline other contingents of the army were making their temporary homes more weatherproof. Firewood was in short supply and the men soon had to travel miles up the steep slopes of the mountains to find even a small bundle of sticks to cook their pottage. As the first autumn rain lashed down, the mood in the camp began to change: the shopkeepers in the old town had doubled the price of bread and wine, much to the anger of the men; dried fish now sold for a shilling a pound, an outrageous price; even fresh fish became scarce as so many men were trying their luck with baited lines from the ships in the harbor. There was little to do, although John did organize battle practice at least once a day for his spearmen, the archers set up butts to shoot at and Sir James took his cavalry out each morning for a couple of hours of exercise in the mountains. But most of the time the men were idle and spent the days foraging for food or firewood or gambling in the old town.

Three men were flogged on Little John's orders for brawling in the old town. There were two fatal fights between Robin's soldiers and local men over dice before the beginning of October. Reports of men being insulted or even robbed by the locals were common.

I was lucky: Robin had taken over one part of the monastery of San Salvatore, and William and I were soon snug in a monk's cell, myself sleeping on a stone ledge padded with cloaks and a wool-filled palliasse, William on a pile of straw on the floor. Little John, Owain and Sir James de Brus had similar accommodation in the cells next to mine, and each had been allocated a soldier-servant to look after them. Reuben had taken up residence in the old town. He knew of some Jews who lived there, merchants of some sort, and he had wangled an invitation to stay with them. I believe he had the most comfortable lodgings of all of us. Although, Robin had a proper chamber to himself in the monastery, with a fire to warm the cold stone, a small bed and a big table where his officers would meet to eat and discuss our plans. And I saw to it that he always had a guard of at least two men-at-arms keeping an eye on him at all times. Whoever had tried to kill him with the adder in Burgundy might well try again.

To be honest, like most of the men, I was very bored. I practiced weapons skills with Little John every day—he was teaching me the finer points of the flanged mace—and attended as many services in Messina's beautiful cathedral as I could. I was bitterly disappointed that we were to stay in Sicily all winter. And I had a nagging feeling that I was not worthy to set foot on the holy soil where Jesus Christ had walked, that I was too mired in sin, and that God was delaying my arrival in Outremer until I had fully repented of my transgressions and cleansed my soul. The weight of the souls of the Christians I had killed at York hung heavily upon me. But I could also sometimes hear my empty promise of salvation to Ruth echoing in my ears at night, mocking my failure to keep my word. So every morning before dawn I would rise and attend Matins in the cathedral and every evening before I slept I attended Compline, and I went to as many services in between as I could. But, despite the ethereal beauty of the cathedral, its glorious colored-glass windows, and its exquisite golden paintings of the Christ child and his mother on the walls, which I gazed at in humble devotion, nothing seemed to shift my deep feelings of guilt. I prayed for long, uncomfortable hours on my knees in front of the great altar, asking the Virgin for forgiveness, but still I could not shake the bad thoughts from my head. I wished Tuck were with us; he would have eased my conscience, of that I was certain.

"God's great fat oozing hemorrhoids! What you need is a good fight," said Little John, when I complained about my mood to him one afternoon. "Or a good fuck. Sort you out in no time." But the prospect of either seemed very remote.

And then, in the midst of all this gloom and guilt, King Richard decreed that he would host a day of joy and music in honor of his royal cousin Philip of France—they were not getting on at all well, so the scuttlebutt went, and this was an attempt to mend fences—and, Robin told me, I was to perform in front of two kings in the fragrant herb garden at the back of the monastery, if the weather was kind. He took me to one side one drizzly morning under a covered walkway where the monks had once met for chapter and told me about the musical event and my part in it. "Stick to the lovey-dovey stuff, and maybe something traditional; nothing at all political, we are supposed to be smoothing Philip's feathers not ruffling them," said Robin. Before I could protest at his calling my beautiful, finely wrought *cansos* "lovey-dovey stuff," he shocked me into silence with his next words. "And, by the way, Sir Richard Malbête is here, with our lord King Richard. He arrived last night from Marseilles."

I goggled at him. The Evil Beast was here, in Messina, with the King? "He was in dire disgrace after the bloodbath in

York," continued Robin. "The King did not take kindly to his Jews being killed. I'm told he was really quite upset; he relies on them to lend him money for his military adventures." He smiled at me in a lopsided way. This was Robin's financial position, too, in a nutshell. "So Malbête lost his lands in the North and has come on this Great Pilgrimage as a penance." Robin grinned at me, and then said jokingly, "Under your Christian logic, to cleanse his soul from the foul sin of killing Jews, Malbête must kill an equal number of Saracens."

I frowned. I did not like it when Robin was disrespectful about the True Religion or our great mission to save the Holy Land. Robin ignored my sour look and went on: "Our story is that you and I were never in York, never in the Tower, and we never cut our way through a crowd of men-at-arms to get free and clear. That, if it ever happened—and it does sound far-fetched, doesn't it?—it was done by some other men. Not us. Understand?"

"You declared your name and rank to the men-at-arms," I pointed out.

"An impostor," said Robin briskly. "A wily Jew who wanted to save his skin by pretending to be the famous Earl of Locksley. Tell me that you understand?"

I understood. Robin did not want himself to be associated with this catastrophe; he did not wish to explain why he was there, or to admit that he had killed Christian townsmen in defense of Jews. Mostly, I felt he was embarrassed; it was not a glorious episode for anyone. But that was fine with me. I would be perfectly content never to think or speak of that bloody few days again. "What about Reuben?" I asked. "When Reuben finds out Malbête is here, he will cut his living heart out."

"Yes, I thought of that. So I told Reuben myself that Malbête was now with the King and I promised him that, if he let the evil bastard live until we got to the Holy Land, I'd help him quietly kill him myself. I said you'd probably want to pitch in, too."

I nodded; I'd gladly help send Malbête's soul to join his master the Devil. "But why wait?" I asked. "Why not just kill him now?"

He looked for a moment as if he wasn't going to answer me, and then he seemed to come to a decision. "Two reasons, Alan. And this is not to be repeated. I am in deadly earnest, you are not to breathe a word of this, all right? Firstly, I don't want to disturb calm waters just now. If the King's knights start killing each other, even if we managed a discreet, tidy little murder, it could tear this expedition apart—it's bad enough that Richard's hardly speaking to Philip—and while I couldn't care less which bunch of religious fanatics flies their flag above Jerusalem, I do want this campaign to succeed for reasons of my own. Which leads me to the second point. If it went wrong, I wouldn't want Reuben hanged for murder in Sicily—King Richard has vowed that he will speedily ex-ecute any man who takes the life of another pilgrim; and Mal-bête, curse him, is a pilgrim. I need . . . I need Reuben to help me do something in Outremer, and only he can help me do it. No, Alan, I'm not going to tell you what it is yet, and please don't ask me. I'll tell you more about it nearer the time."

I was not the only *trouvère* to accompany the army to the Holy Land. In fact, there were quite a few of us and we had begun to gather in the evenings for wine and conviviality in a tavern in the old town of Messina where we would tell stories and play each other bits of our new compositions. I was especially fond of Ambroise, a jolly little soul, almost as wide as he was tall, with great beaming cheeks, sparkling black eyes like a bird's and, when he chose to exercise it, a ferocious wit. He was a Norman from Evrecy, near Caen, a minor vassal of King Richard's and as well as composing music for his lord's enter-tainment, he told me he was writing a history of the holy war. I first came across him at the edge of the crowded harbor, bent

161

over a slate that he was scratching at with a piece of chalk. "What rhymes with 'full dock?'" he asked me suddenly, twisting his fat neck round to look at me. I had not realized he knew I was there. I replied without thinking: "Bull's cock." He laughed, his whole little round body shaking with mirth, and he wheezed: "I admire the way your dirty mind works, but I don't think that's an appropriate phrase for a poem in praise of our King's glorious arrival in Messina. You're Alan, the Earl of Locksley's *trouvère*, aren't you? I've heard people say you are pretty good, for a youngster. I am Ambroise, the King's man. Part-poet, part-singer, part-historian—but all gourmand," and he slapped his ample belly and laughed again.

We were firm friends from that day onward.

In fact, our arrival in Messina had not been as uniformly glorious as Ambroise or the King might have hoped. The local population was a mixed crew: mainly Greeks, with a sprinkling of Italians, a few Jews and even some Arabs—and they all hated us. When we had arrived at the harbor there had been some booing and jeering from the crowd, audible even over the blare of the trumpets, even a few pieces of rotten fruit thrown. Fists were shaken, and King Richard had been extremely angry, white-faced, his blue eyes seeming to spark with fury. He had wanted to put on a show of his power and majesty and had assumed that his Sicilian audience—quickly dubbed the Messy Nessies by Little John—would be suitably awed. They were not. They seemed to regard us as something between an army of occupation and a crowd of foreign bumpkins who could be robbed and insulted at will. The feelings of dislike, I have to say, were entirely mutual: we referred to the Greeks dismissively as "Griffons," and the Italians as "Lombards"; the Arabs, many of them slaves, we ignored as beneath our Christian contempt.

Ambroise had the honor of beginning the musical festivities on a bright October morning in the herb garden of the mon-

162

astery of San Salvatore. The weather had cleared and it was a half-warm sunny day, the sky a pale blue but streaked with woolly clouds. He opened with a simple and supposedly melancholic song of a knight who is bemoaning the departure of his mistress. It was hardly an original theme. Actually, as my friend is long dead now, I can admit to myself that Ambroise was not an enormously gifted *trouvère*. God rest his jolly soul. He had a fine voice, it is true, but his musical compositions were rarely inspiring. And, occasionally, I even suspected him of appropriating other men's ideas. He admitted to me once that he found all the conventions of troubadour-style music-making, with its focus on unrequited love, a tremendous bore. What interested him most was poetry, specifically epic poetry that recorded dramatic events. He was talking once again about his history of the Great Pilgrimage, something he would bang on and on about when he was in his cups in the Lamb, our favorite watering hole in the old town.

If I remember correctly, Ambroise's song began:

Farewell my joy,
And welcome pain,
Till I see my lady again . . .

Grim, I think you'll agree. And it was quite difficult to imagine rotund little Ambroise as a heartsick swain, as he described himself later in the piece, unable to eat or drink for love of his departed lady. But perhaps I am wrong: I'm ashamed to say that I paid scant attention to my friend's turgid verses and spent the time studying his audience instead. King Richard sat in the place of most honor, next to his royal French guest. Richard was a tall man, well-muscled and strong, although with a slight quiver to his hands when he was nervous or excited. At the age of thirty-three he was in his prime. His red-gold hair was truly regal, it glinted and sparkled in the brisk morning light; his complexion was fair and slightly sunburned, and his honest blue gaze was unflinching. His reputation as a warrior was second to none, and it was said that he loved nothing more than a good, bloody fight. Richard was what Tuck would have called a "hot" man, whose anger was always near the surface, and who, when riled, was a fearsome sight. Beside him, the French King, Philip Augustus, was as different as chalk from cheese. He was a sallow, dark fellow; thin, even frail looking with large luminous eyes and, at twenty-five, the bowed back of a much older man. Tuck would have called him a "cold" man, hiding his true feelings behind a wall of ice. Richard and Philip had been great friends in their youth, some even said that the young Richard had been infatuated with Philip, but it was clear in the way that they held their bodies, seated on cushioned chairs in the sweet-smelling herb garden, that there was very little love now between the two kings. Also present were Robin and several of King Richard's other senior commanders, including Robert of Thurnham, a knight I had met last year at Winchester and who had helped me then to escape the clutches of Ralph Murdac. He was now a very important man, Richard's high admiral no less, and I had not had time to renew our acquaintance beyond a brief smile and nod.

Seated next to Sir Robert was Sir Richard Malbête. The Evil Beast had a fresh pink scar down the right side of his face, I noticed with great satisfaction, but other than that he seemed regrettably unchanged. His white forelock and splintered feral eyes were exactly as I remembered them, but it seemed that he did not remember me at all as, when our eyes met briefly, his blank animal gaze showed no flicker of recognition. I felt it would be unwise to stare so I looked away quickly.

There were also a handful of French knights present at the gathering, a gaggle of local prelates, and the governors of Messina, appointed by King Tancred, two creatures who called themselves Margarit and Jordan del Pin, a pair of nervous, shifty-looking knights, richly dressed but who said little and watched the two kings unceasingly with dark, worried little eyes.

The governors had good reason to be nervous; Richard and Tancred were involved in a vicious dispute over money. I never completely understood the complexities of it, but it seemed that Tancred's predecessor had promised Richard's predecessor a large sum of money to support the great expedition to the Holy Land. Both were now dead, but Richard was insisting that Tancred make good on the old King William's promise. Then there was the matter of Richard's sister Joanna: she had been married to William and when he died, and Tancred became king, she should have been given a large sum of money, a dower, and allowed to live as she chose. Instead, Tancred had withheld the money and kept her in close confinement, virtually a prisoner. When Richard and his huge army arrived in Sicily, Tancred took fright, released Joanna, and sent her with a smaller sum of money to Richard. She was now lodged securely in great comfort across the Messina straits at the monastery of Bagnara on the mainland. Richard was still demanding the rest of the cash from Tancred and, with fifteen thousand men at his back, and yet more on the way, he made a very compelling argument. Some people have suggested—Robin for one, but that was how his mind always worked—that Richard's bloody actions in the next few hours were merely a move in the chess game between himself and Tancred, with an eye to forcing the King of Sicily to pay up.

As the notes of Ambroise's song faded away, and the courtiers smattered their applause, a small cloud covered the sun, and I could feel the true chill of October in the air. I got to my feet, picked up my instrument, and bowed low to the two kings—it had been arranged that I should perform next. As Robin had suggested, I stuck to the traditional: rendering the tragic poem of Tristan and Isolde quite exquisitely, I

165

think, accompanying myself on the vielle with a simple but elegant tune I had devised that morning. You will think it merely the boasting of an old man, but I swear to you that I saw genuine tears in King Richard's eyes as I bowed the last haunting chord.

The next performer was an old friend of King Richard's: a grizzled warrior of fifty years, much-hated by the other courtiers, and known as Bertran de Born, viscount of Hautefort, who had a reputation for raping his female servants and stirring up trouble between the great princes of Europe whenever he got the chance. He got up and launched into a long unaccompanied song in praise of warfare, all axes clashing and shields splintering, broken heads and pierced bodies, which ended . . . "Go speedily to Yea-and-nay, and tell him there is too much peace about." In fact, the poem was rather good, a bit old-fashioned but darkly funny and very stirring; and much as I disapproved of the old man's troublemaking reputation, I could not fault his music.

"Yea-and-nay" was Bertran's nickname for King Richard, something to do with his supposed indecisiveness as a youth, which our sovereign lord seemed not to mind at all— but then they had known each other for a very long time. Afterward, I did wonder if Richard and Bertran had secretly been in collusion because the moment his poem was done, a knight burst into the garden and, without the slightest ceremony, blurted: "The Griffons are rioting; and they are attacking Hugh de Lusignan!"

Hugh was one of the barons of Aquitaine, a vassal of King Richard's and a member of a powerful family that included one of the claimants to the throne of Jerusalem. Hugh had, perhaps unwisely, taken up a comfortable residence in the old town of Messina despite the fact that tension between the pilgrims and the locals was running so high.

"What!" roared the King, leaping to his feet. To give him due credit, he did sound quite genuine in his anger.

"Sire," said the messenger, "there has been trouble all morning, great insolence from the Sicilians, our men-at-arms pelted with stones. Then fighting broke out and now a large force of armed Griffons has surrounded Lusignan's house and seems determined to break in and do murder."

"By God's legs, that is enough," said the King. "To arms, gentlemen, to arms! We will teach these riotous dogs some respect for Christ's holy pilgrims."

He beckoned Robin, Robert of Thurnham, Richard Malbête and the other knights. "There is no time to waste," he said. "Arm yourselves and gather what men you can. We will take this town in the time it takes for a priest to say Matins. Do not tarry: to arms! And may God preserve us all."

The King then strode over to where Philip was still sitting, surrounded by his French knights. "Cousin, will you join me in subduing these insolent curs?" Philip's expression was blank. I could tell he was furious from his clenched jaw muscles—perhaps he, too, suspected that Richard was stage-managing the events—but he merely shook his head but said nothing. Richard stared at him for a moment, then nodded, turned on his heel and strode from the garden.

The speed and fury of Richard's attack was truly astonishing. It might have appeared reckless, to attack a town of more than fifty thousand souls with no more than a handful of knights, but it proved an extraordinarily effective strategy. I was later to discover that King Richard was quite capable of subtlety in warfare, and subterfuge, finesse, and fine generalship, when it was appropriate, but what he loved most was a mad, all-out rage-fueled charge, with himself in the lead, wading into the enemy his great sword swinging, and slaughtering his foes by the dozen.

We gathered outside the monastery, some thirty armored horsemen, ready to fight and die beside our King. I had struggled into a chain mail hauberk, crammed a plain steel cap on my head and strapped on sword and poniard, grabbing my mace as an afterthought, before mounting Ghost in the monastery forecourt—but I noticed that the King had dressed himself for war even more quickly. He was outside the big gates of the monastery, literally bouncing up and down in the saddle, urging his knights to "hurry, hurry for God's sake!"

We had sent off Owain with messages for the rest of the army to come and join us but King Richard was like a man possessed: he could not wait another moment for battle to begin. And, bizarrely, his haste made the task of capturing Messina far easier than it would have been if we had waited for the army to get organized and come up.

The King ran an eye over the handful of assembled knights, nodded, and said: "Right, let's go and teach these scum some manners." And with that we were off, galloping down the hill in a mad scramble toward the old town, the King in the vanguard, Robin just behind him and myself somewhere in the middle of the pack, with Little John beside me on a giant white horse, grinning with pleasure at the thought of imminent slaughter. I, too, was filled with a euphoric sense of excitement. For some reason, I felt that I could not die if I followed King Richard into battle, that somehow the sacred aura of kingly power that radiated from him would protect me. Absolute nonsense, of course: being in the King's company was no safer than being anywhere else in a battle, quite the opposite given his reckless streak, if the truth be told.

Outside the main gate of the old town a mob of about four hundred Sicilians had formed up in what I can only assume they thought was a military manner on a small knoll. The Griffons were armed with a random assortment of weapons and armor, some with swords and spears, some with crossbows and round shields, some helmeted with leather caps, a few with large wood axes, some even carrying fishing tridents. They pushed and shoved at each other, and a dozen men, their leaders, I suppose, seemed to be shouting at the tops of their voices at each other and at their men and trying to squeeze the loose, unruly crowd into some semblance of order. I learned later that they had planned to march on the monastery and hold the King to ransom. They would never have succeeded; they couldn't even form up properly without jostling and shoving each other.

When Richard saw them he did not slacken his mount's pace for an instant. He just shouted: "For God and Holy Mary!" and charged straight up the hill and into the mass of Sicilians, whirling his sword in a near-berserk fury, hacking and stabbing, cutting down men and forcing his way yard by yard into that huge sea of confused humanity. And we all piled in right after him; thirty steel-clad knights at full gallop in a tight wedge, with Richard as the point. It was like an axe blade chopping into a rotten cabbage.

God forgive me, but I enjoyed that fight. Ghost leaped into the ranks of the enemy knocking two men down with sheer momentum, and I skewered a third through the gullet on the point of my sword as we followed our battle-mad King into the fray. Little John was wielding a giant axe with terrifying skill to my left, cutting down foes with short controlled sweeps of the double-edged blade. I had my reins looped over the pommel and with sword in one hand and mace in the other, I lashed out left and right slicing into unprotected bodies and crushing skulls, controlling Ghost with my legs alone. The mace was a vicious weapon: a two-foot steel-shafted club with a ring of eight sharp, flat triangles of metal welded to the heavy head; it had the power to punch through iron helmets and breach the skulls beneath. Swung at full strength against chain mail, it could easily break an arm or leg. I crushed the jaw of one man with an upward blow, then scythed the mace laterally at another man-at-arms, cracking into his temple. A great jet of blood sprayed in my eyes and I was momentarily blinded. I half sensed half saw someone lunging at me with a spear from my right-hand side and knocked away the point on pure instinct with my sword, then reversed the direction of the blow and chopped the blade down into his skull.

The noise was deafening: the battle cries of our warriors, the clash of steel, the neighing and squealing of horses and the shouts of rage and agony from wounded men. I spurred Ghost forward, felt a hard blow against my left boot, hacked at a retreating back, and suddenly the mass of Griffon soldiers had broken, like a smashed cage of doves, all the birds set free at the same time, and hundreds of men were streaming back toward the gate of the town—which I noticed with disbelief was slowly opening to receive the fugitives. It was a terrible, fatal mistake on their part.

"After them," shouted Richard, waving his huge sword in the air; the long blade and his sword arm completely drenched in gore. "After them while the gate is open." And we barrelled down the hill mingling with the running Sicilians, spurring past a victim and then hacking back into face and neck with our swords as we rode past, slicing open cheeks, cracking skulls and dropping bodies in our wake. Whoever was in command of the gate must have realized his error in letting the terrified fugitives in, for as we approached I saw men on either side of the portal struggling to shut the heavy wooden barrier in the face of a blood-splashed tide of terrified men. They would have had more chance trying to hold back the sea. Our knights were in and among the crowd, cutting and stabbing down into the mass, churning up the horror. I saw Robin spur back, level his sword like a spear and charge at the knot of men trying to shut the left-hand gate. He half blinded one man with a lunge that smashed into his eye socket, the ripped eyeball popping free and dangling on a bloody thread of tissue, then Robin chopped down hard with his sharp blade into another man's bare arm, half severing it from his body, and the other fellows pushing at the gate turned and ran, back into the muddy streets of old Messina. All resis-

170

tance at the town gate ceased in a few short moments; any living Griffons took to their heels, disappearing into the warrenlike streets of the town as fast as their legs would carry them.

The gates were ours, and the King finally called for a pause for breath. As the horsemen milled in the entrance to the old town, stroking the flanks of their sweat-streaked mounts and puffing and blowing from the exertion of slaughter, I looked for my friends. Robin appeared to be unhurt but Little John had a bloody cut on the side of his thigh, which he was in the process of roughly bandaging with an old shirt. I called out to him but he merely said: "A scratch, Alan, just a scratch. God's hairy bollocks, I must be getting old." He gave me a huge lunatic grin that warmed my heart.

I looked down at my boot and there was a long deep cut in the thick leather but whatever blade had caused it had not penetrated through to my flesh. I'd need a new pair of boots when the day was over, though. Not all of us had been so lucky. There were four riderless horses in our company and two more, heads down cropping the grass, by the blood-drenched knoll where we had made our first madcap attack. The site of our first charge was marked by mounds of Griffon dead and wounded, some crawling, others lying crying and cursing in fear and pain. One horse, disembowled, with purple innards bulging and glistening on the grass, screamed incessantly until a passing knight dismounted and gave it its final ease with his dagger. Several men in the King's company had deep cuts or stab wounds to show for our battle with the Sicilians. One knight's arm dangled limply from a dislocated shoulder. Robert of Thurnham had a bad cut across his cheekbone, but he appeared cheerful, joking with the King, Bertran de Born and Mercardier, Richard's grim-faced mercenary captain, as he mopped at his wounded face with a silk scarf. *That will leave a bad scar,* I thought to myself, and unconsciously looked for Malbête in the crowd of horsemen.

I caught his flat gaze, noted that his own scar seemed to have become a deeper red; I quickly looked away. From what I could see the evil bastard was completely unhurt. Despite what Robin had said about waiting till we reached the Holy Land, I knew that if I had the chance, and I could be sure nobody would witness it, I would cut down Malbête and feel no more guilt than I would killing a rabid dog.

My thoughts turned unbidden to Reuben. Presumably he was at his lodging inside the old town. Was he safe? Through the open gate, I could see our reinforcements streaming down the hill, making for the knot of our horsemen at the entrance to the town. A crowd of archers on foot, lead by Owain, was hurrying toward us, and mounted men-at-arms, sergeants and spearmen, knights and their squires, all were converging on the King with savage grins of delight. With the gate in our hands, the capture of the old town was a foregone conclusion, and then would come the sack, a night of fire and blood, of women raped, men slaughtered, and valuable goods stolen or smashed for pure pleasure.

The Griffons seemed to realize their peril, as they had regrouped while we tended our horses and our wounds, and a wall of men had been formed across the main street leading into the heart of the town. The wall thickened with every passing moment, as townsmen, terrified of what our victorious troops would do if set loose in their homes, swelled the wall. Those with armor were pushed to the front, and there was a fairly credible barrier of linked shields and spears to stop our advance. The shield wall might have been almost formidable— a difficult obstacle to overcome—but for two things. We had plenty of archers, who were now grinning with pleasure at the chance of loot and mayhem and hastily stringing their bows, and King Richard was our commander.

Robin and Owain formed up our bowmen in no time at all and at a nod from the King, they began to loose volley after volley into the wall of Griffons. Waves of gray shafts fell like sheets of winter rain on the townsmen's shield wall. The slaughter was appalling, relentless; and the Griffons had no reply. They stood bravely, bleeding and dying in defense of their homes and families. As the needle-tipped arrows slashed down again into their ranks; men screamed and dropped to the floor by the dozen at each volley, clutching at yard-long ash shafts that sprouted from their bodies before they were dragged in a gore-slicked trail to the back of the wall and nervous, unhurt men took their places. The wall began to thin, to waver under the bowmen's onslaught, the back ranks began to fade away in ones and twos, family men slipping away into the back alleys of the town, shunning the fight to protect their children, and King Richard, seizing the moment perfectly, hauled out his blood-encrusted sword, and shouted "For God and the Virgin! Havoc! I say havoc!" and he and every able-bodied man on horseback—there must have been sixty or seventy of us gathered by this time—raked our horses sides with our spurs and thundered forward in a great galloping steel-clad mass and crashed through the enfeebled shield wall like a birch broom through a pile of dry leaves. We charged into them, swords raised, punched easily through the wavering curtain of frightened men—and unleashed hell on the ancient, once-peaceful town of Messina.

CHAPTER NINE

The sack of a town is never a pretty sight. But this was one of the worst I have ever seen. King Richard had cried "Havoc!" and this meant that his men were set free to plunder and rape and kill to their hearts' content. No quarter would be given, everything in the town now belonged to the victorious troops. Richard was deliberately punishing the town for its insolence, for the rotten fruit thrown and the jeers when he made his magnificent entry into the harbor. As the cavalry careered through the last defenses of the town, the archers and footmen came roaring after them, racing into the streets beyond, kicking down doors and charging inside private houses, killing anyone who opposed them and ransacking the interior and more often than not setting fire to the buildings for sheer spite. They were looking for wine and coin and women—but not necessarily in that order. It was as if they had all run mad, like the Christians of York, crazed with lust and cruelty and the urge to shed human blood.

As the sun dipped behind the hills to the west, much of the town was ablaze, blood and wine flowed in the gutters and bodies littered the streets. Drunken men-at-arms blundered through the burning town, naked steel in hand, tripping over their own feet and snarling at shadows, looking for unmolested houses to pillage, women to rape, another barrel of wine to broach. More often than not, the drunken man-at-arms or archer would collapse unconscious in a doorway, all his lusts slaked—and a good few had their throats cut by morning by locals seeking revenge for daughters deflowered, sons cut down before their own hearths and property destroyed or stolen. Fear and death stalked the fire-splashed darkness, as the citizens cowered in their cellars, or hid behind barred, even nailed-shut doors and prayed for the nightmare to end. But dawn was a long way off, and the desires of Richard's victorious men were far from satisfied.

King Richard and his household knights, including my master Robin, had ridden to Hugh de Lusignan's house. He was quite safe, firmly barricaded in a strong two-story stone building with a score of well-armed men to protect him, and the bodies of a dozen Griffons at his door. After ceremonially embracing Hugh—the King had, after all, ostensibly attacked Messina to come to his defense—Richard withdrew back to the monastery on the hill with his household knights to bandage their scrapes and enjoy a victory feast together. Robin, rather reluctantly I believe, accompanied his liege lord; he was obliged to, in truth. But I had the strong feeling that he would have preferred to do a little lucrative plundering in the burning town. Little John had long disappeared, presumably in search of merriment and valuables, and I was left alone, walking Ghost up a narrow street, stepping around the bodies, heading toward the Jewish quarter. I wanted to be sure that Reuben was unharmed. Although I knew he

175

could take care of himself, I was uneasy with memories of the last blood-crazed mob of fanatics I had encountered in York.

I rode slowly past a dark side street, and glancing into it, I saw a knot of men-at-arms, perhaps a dozen or so, shoving and squabbling excitedly. There was a woman on the floor and some ruffian was covering her, while the others waited to take their turn. I paused, and half of my mind wanted me to go to her, save her, and drive off those drunken beasts. But I was alone, and they were a dozen violent men. I hesitated, like a craven coward. Was it my duty to save that poor woman? She was a legitimate prize of war, an enemy. My own King wanted her punished. I remembered something that Robin had said to me the year before. I had not understood it at the time, although I thought about it often since then. He had said: "Right and wrong is rarely simple. The world is full of evil folk. But if I were to rush about the earth punishing all the bad men that I found, I would have no rest. And, if I spent my entire life punishing evil deeds, I would not increase the amount of happiness in this world in the slightest. The world has an endless supply of evil. All I can do is to try to provide protection for those who ask it from me, for those whom I love and who serve me."

He had told me this only a few hours before he had ordered that a captive brigand, an evil fellow called Sir John Peveril, be strapped to the earth of a woodland glade and have three of his limbs chopped off in cold blood in front of his ten-year-old son. The man Peveril lived, I was told, if you can call him a man after that: he was just a trunk, a head and one good arm. My master let the boy live, too; not out of kindness or mercy but to spread the tale of this horror.

I now understood what Robin meant by his little speech about right and wrong: that woman was nothing to me, so why should I risk my neck to save her? But I also knew what the right thing to do would have been. I knew what a truly chivalrous knight would have done. Sadly, the coward in me was too strong and, as I argued right and wrong with myself, Ghost sensibly walked on past the alley, and I surrendered to my weaker side and rode on by, cursing my own cowardice.

When I reached the house where Reuben had taken lodgings, I saw that there was nobody at home. The place was heavily boarded up and not a chink of light escaped from the shutters into the dark street. Reuben, probably sensing trouble, had evidently abandoned the town for some other safer place. While I was worrying about him, I thought bitterly, and braving the streets of a blood-drunk town, he was probably playing dice in some snug shelter north of Messina with Robin's men—and no doubt winning.

I turned Ghost back toward the main gate of the town. As so often after a battle, I felt a sense of melancholy. I was tired, my foot, where the boot had taken a sword blow, was aching, and I couldn't stop thinking about the girl being repeatedly raped by a dozen lust-crazed men. Then, just as I was passing a wide wooden two-story house with the door smashed to kindling and hanging from its hinges, I heard a long, drawn-out scream of fear. It was a woman's voice, a young woman, I believed, and she was in mortal terror. I stopped Ghost this time, and she screamed again, a long rising howl of utter dread. Then I heard a man laugh, an evil gloating sound, and a jest shouted to someone else.

Without allowing myself to think this time, I got down from Ghost's back, tied him to a post, drew my battered old sword and entered the house.

It was the dwelling of a rich man, clearly. The large front room with its high ceiling, which had once been a fine chamber, had been completely ransacked. By the moonlight that spilled through the open shutters in front of the window, I could see that ornate furniture, smashed, was scattered about the place, priceless hangings had been torn down from the walls. There was a strong smell of wine and excrement, someone had recently relieved themselves in that plush chamber and I guessed that it was not the owner. In the dim light, I could just make out the corpse of a very fat man, richly dressed and lying in a black puddle at one side of the room. I ignored the body and threaded my way through the detritus of his house, toward the rear of the building. I heard the scream again, but this time it ended abruptly in a hideous bubbling gurgle. It sounded exactly like a woman having her throat cut.

I stepped through a doorway into an open-air courtyard that was brightly lit by a pair of torches fixed to beckets on the wall. And I saw that I had walked into a slaughter yard. The stone floor was literally running with blood, trickles of the liquid oozing between the cobbles, and the naked forms of two young women were lying curled together on the floor, their plump white lifeless bodies resembling the carcasses of butchered pigs in the flickering torchlight. A third girl was hanging limply from an upright wooden frame in the shape of an X. It was a whipping frame, I realized, and I knew I was in the slave quarters of a merchant's house. The girl was obviously dead. Though her back was toward me I could see that her throat had been cut to the bone. And the man who killed her was standing by the whipping frame gaping at me in surprise. The girl had been whipped, and stabbed through the buttocks and no doubt raped before the man had ended her life. He wore a scarlet and sky blue surcoat, spattered with her blood and the blood of her dead sisters. And he carried a long, smeared knife in his right hand.

I said no words of challenge but simply took two steps toward him and swung my sword at his head in a fast roundhouse cut. He desperately tried to block my strike with his gore-smirched dagger, and it saved my blade from burying itself in his skull, but then I stepped in toward him and smashed the iron pommel of my weapon into his mouth, shattering teeth, smearing lips and dropping the man to the floor. He stared up at me, as I stood over him, and he just had time to scream through his broken mouth, "My lord, help me!" in English before I plunged the sword point down hard into his throat and silenced his voice forever.

I stood away from him. In my black fury, I could have hacked his dead body into morsels—but I managed to control myself. I had done murder, although I did not regret it for a moment, and I knew I must leave this place as quickly as possible. King Richard had vowed that he would execute anyone who killed a fellow pilgrim: on the voyage from Marseilles, he had had a murderer tied to his dead victim and thrown into the sea to perish. I cocked my head to one side: could I hear singing coming from somewhere? It must be my imagination. As I looked around the courtyard before making my departure, I noticed a fourth girl, bound and gagged and crouching naked in the corner of the space by a shadow-dappled whitewashed wall. She was so still and white, she almost seemed part of the wall. But when I went to her, I saw that her eyes were huge and dark with horror, and her hair was a slick of shining black down her naked back almost to her tiny waist. Even terrified as she was, and in that place of blood and pain and death, I saw that she was beautiful; extraordinarily beautiful. But she had seen me kill the man-at-arms. She was a witness. A thought flashed across my mind: I knew what Robin would do in these circumstances; she was a witness to a capital crime, she would have to die. In our outlaw days in Sherwood, Much the miller's son had once killed an innocent page boy because he was a witness to a murder Little John had committed. Much even boasted about it until I told him I would shut his mouth for him, if he did not. So I knew what Robin, in his ruthlessness, would advise me to do. But I was not Robin.

I went back into the front room and seized a silk wall hanging that was lying on the floor, but which was mostly clean, and brought it back into the slave quarters. The girl had not moved. I cut through the ropes that bound her and wrapped her snugly in the silk cloth. And all the while she

179

stared at me with her huge, beautiful eyes. I thought I could hear boots moving about on the floor above and I tried to hurry the girl along as gently as I could. But she did not seem to understand my words. With gestures and pointing I finally managed to communicate the urgency to her, and get her to understand that we must leave that house—now! And in a dozen heartbeats I had her outside in the street. I could definitely hear the sound of drunken singing: soldiers, no doubt, who were looking for another victim to rape, another house to plunder, and the sound was coming closer. I wanted to get the girl on the horse and lead her away from that place of death as quickly as possible—I could feel my skin crawling in anticipation of deadly danger—but she seemed very worried about her silk wall hanging coming open and was refusing to mount up on Ghost until she had fixed her dress. So I cut a hole in the hanging for her head, and cut a strip off the end to make a belt, and with her head poking through the priceless silk and the material tied to her waist, she at last consented to climb into the saddle.

I had just settled her in her seat when a voice behind me spoke; a slow, deep voice I had heard before: "You killed my man, singing boy; you murdered my sergeant!" The voice sounded mildly annoyed rather than madly enraged. I spun as fast as I could, my sword in my hand, and there in the doorway of the house loomed the tall form of Sir Richard Malbête, with four men-at-arms holding torches and peering out from behind his bulk. "And I have not forgotten that you gave me this," the Beast said, running a finger down the red scar on the side of his face. "I have not forgiven you, singing boy, and I remember well your Jew-loving master's tomfoolery at York," he rumbled, his feral eyes glittering madly in the torchlight. "You, and your so-called Earl, will pay a pretty price for standing in the way of my pleasures."

★   ★   ★

I don't believe I felt fear when I saw Malbête standing there with his four men—more swords than I could expect to fight and survive—and it wasn't hatred either, although I had long dreamed of killing him. Instead, I felt a strange calmness, a clearheaded detachment. I was very conscious of my body, how I was standing, sword in my right hand, my left foot slightly in front of the other, and I was beginning to think about the exact moves I would make when the fighting began. The first thing would be to get the girl away. She was well seated on Ghost, bare feet in the stirrups, and looked as if she knew how to ride, and so a hard slap on my animal's rump should set him off at the gallop. I was confident that Ghost could carry her to safety. It is strange that my first thoughts should have been of her. I had not formed any attachment to her, I was not in love with her; I saw that she was beautiful, yes, but she was nothing to me and yet my first instinct was to see her safe, at the risk of my own life. Truly, God moves in mysterious ways.

My next thought was that, in fact, there were too many of them to fight only one man efficiently, they would get in each other's way, and they were standing, crowded in a doorway behind Malbête. Therefore, I realized, I had to go forward, toward them, to take the fight into that doorway. If I stood there in that narrow opening, only one or possibly two men could come at me at a time, until one or two of them took it into his head to climb out the window, and come at me from behind. Then I was probably dead. But for several precious moments, if I could hold the doorway, the girl would have the time to get away.

So. Now. Time to move, Alan: I'd slap the horse with my left hand, make a lunge at Richard Malbête's head to make him move back, and then get into the door to hold that space as long as I could. The singing was growing louder, the singers were in this very street, and just before I launched myself into my doomed attack, a wonderful thought struck me. God was surely with me: I knew that song! I had heard it sung, many, many times over the long miles between England and the Mediterranean Sea. It was a song in the Welsh language! And the men singing it . . .

"Ho there, it's young Alan; joy to you on this fine night," said Owain, his voice thickened with wine. "How's about you give the boys a tune?" I turned my head slowly, my neck muscles seeming to be stiff and unyielding, and there was Owain standing like a Visitation of Christ, at the head of about thirty red-faced archers—bows unstrung, it was true, and all drunk as lords, but each with a short sword in his belt, which I had personally trained them to use. God be thanked for his mercy.

"Look, he's found himself a woman; and, by Jesu, she's a tasty piece," shouted one of the archers. He was quickly shushed into silence by his drunken fellow bowmen. Sober, on the whole, they showed great respect for me.

"Are you all right, Alan?" asked Owain. "Only you look a little pale. Have a drink." He held out a flask.

I turned back to look at the doorway. Sir Richard Malbête was gone. And halfway up the street, walking away from us at a brisk pace was a knot of men-at-arms in surcoats of scarlet and sky blue. I was content for now to let them go.

I sheathed my sword. "I am well, thank you, Owain," I said. "But I would be grateful if you could provide me with an escort to take this lady back to headquarters. There are a lot of drunken, disreputable types on the streets tonight." I looked down my nose like a schoolmaster at the gang of tough, wine-flushed men who had undoubtedly just saved my life. And the Welshmen all cackled merrily at my feeble jest.

Love is perhaps the strangest of all human experiences; the moments of happiness it offers are truly sublime, but I'm not sure you could describe it as pleasant, and often it is a source of great torment; yet we seem to seek it out all our lives like moths drawn to a deadly flame. In a matter of days, I was deeply in love with Nur, for that was the name of the slave girl that I rescued from the grand house in the old town that night. It started for me with a terrible kind of lust; when I looked at her slim body, her great dark eyes, her perfect skin, and plump, almost bruised looking mouth, I wanted to possess her, to wrap her in my arms and kiss her, to encompass her with my body so that we were joined, made one. I don't mean in the crude physical way that ordinary men and women couple—I refused to allow myself to touch her, which was foolish of me. I know now that when you find love, you should grab it with both hands and enjoy it while it lasts. But then I was young, on a holy pilgrimage, and I was filled with a deep sense of boyish morality.

There were practical reasons, too. For a start, I could find no language to communicate with her—she spoke no English, French, Latin—I even tried her in the Langue d'oc, the southern tongue that many of the troubadours spoke and which was King Richard's native language. But she could not understand a word of any of them. Only by hand gestures and eye contact did we establish that I was Alan and she was Nur, and that I was her protector in the camp and she should stay close to me and my servant William and not wander off on her own. She told me that she was "Filistini," and I took that to mean that she was an Arab from Outremer, one of the Philistines of the Bible, though how she had become a slave in a household in Sicily I had no idea.

On the first night, when we had returned to the monastery, William and I scoured around and found her some clean female clothes, a little food and wine, and some water and a cloth for washing. She seemed terrified of both of us, which was understandable. But William was kind to her and, by mimicry, showed her what was expected, and that we meant her no harm. He was a good boy, deeply kind and loyal to me. Then we both stood guard outside the door of the cell, feeling noble and, for my part, wondering what on earth I was going to do with her and desperately trying not to think of her perfect thrusting young breasts beneath that thin silk wall hanging. After an age of listening to her splashing and singing inside the cell, and trying to suppress my imagination, I had a brilliant idea and sent William off to find Reuben. He had grown up in the Arab lands and would surely know how to speak to her in her own tongue.

William returned shortly with the Jew—he had indeed been playing dice while I was searching for him in Messina, but he was touched by the fact that I had tried to seek him out. He knocked on the door of the cell and entered. A quarter of an hour later he emerged.

"I have told her that, although young, you are a great Christian warrior from the north and that you are traveling with this army to seek battle in Outremer. I have said to her that, if she serves you faithfully, you will allow her to accompany you as a servant, that you will feed and clothe her and protect her until you reach the Holy Land and then you will return her to her father's village unharmed. All of this she has agreed to, and she is waiting inside to show her undying loyalty to such a noble knight." He said all this with a perfectly straight face, but I scowled at him anyway.

"But where will she sleep?" I asked. "What am I going to do about clothes and—you know—women's things . . ."

"As to where she will sleep, I believe she expects to sleep with you. That is her trade, she is a pleasure girl . . ."

"Certainly not," I snapped, straightening my shoulders and glaring at Reuben. "I rescued her from rapists and took her away from a life of degradation, and now that she is safe, I will not use her for my own sinful purposes."

By God, I was a pompous little tyke in those days. Reuben was already laughing, his brown eyes creased shut with pleasure, tears dripping down his cheeks. He howled with glee, clutching his stomach and doubling himself over in his merriment. I put my hand on my sword, and took a step toward him, and he just managed to smother his mirth and avoid bloodshed. "Of course, young Alan, of course," he finally managed to say, covering his laughter with a coughing fit. "She can stay with the other women, if you wish. I will arrange it with Elise." And giggling, shaking his head ruefully and snuffling wetly he walked away, with my furious eyes boring into his back.

By staying with the other women, Reuben meant the collection of tents that had been set up at the back of the monastery, and which housed the two dozen or so women that followed the officers of the headquarters staff. They were cooks and cleaners, washerwomen and seamstresses, mistresses and prostitutes, and Elise, the strange Norman fortune-teller, was their leader; but they were hardly acknowledged to exist by the knights of King Richard's household. We were after all supposed to be keeping ourselves pure, as befits holy pilgrims on a sacred journey.

When I entered the cell, Nur was kneeling on the floor, with her eyes lowered submissively. She was clean, her wet hair tied in a thick braid at the back of her head, and dressed in a clean but threadbare old chemise that fell past her knees. Then she looked up at me and I felt a shock like a bolt of lightning. Her deep tar-pit eyes stared into mine and sucked me into her soul. I tried to break our locked gaze and yet I could not look completely away; I took in her gorgeous dark red lips, high cheekbones, tiny upturned nose, the long elegant neck, the swell of her generous bosoms beneath the thin chemise. I was stiffening in my undergarments just looking at her kneeling there, and I was sure that behind those doelike eyes she could tell that my prick was filling up with pure lust. Behind me William coughed. And I realized I had been staring at her for too long. I looked away guiltily and noticed that the food and wine had disappeared, and that the plate and goblet had been washed and dried. Then I took a step closer and came to stand in front of her—I was painfully aware that my fully erect member was just inches from her face—and I put out an arm to raise her up but she grasped my hand, turned it over and softly kissed my palm. My member gave a visible twitch below the cloth of my tunic. It was an extraordinary erotic act. I felt her soft lips barely touch the skin of my calloused paw but it was like the touch of a hot iron and I jerked involuntarily.

I lifted her to her feet and William wrapped her in his cloak—she could not wander the halls of the monastery in that flimsy chemise, it would have started a full-scale battle—and I gruffly ordered William to escort her to the women's quarters and see that she was well received by Elise. Then I went to the lavatorium, stripped my body naked and poured bucket after bucket of cold water over my body to try to expunge the sinful thoughts that were careening crazily around my head.

Within three days, I was completely, utterly, insanely in love with Nur. I found that I missed her face, her proximity and I wanted more than anything else to be in her company. I constantly thought about touching her, stroking her face. In my dreams we made love endlessly, our bodies entwined in a wonderful array of shapes and patterns. And I would awake, covered in sweat, with my member as hard as a sword hilt . . .

Nur would come to me every morning and bring me bread and cheese and ale and a pitcher of water and a basin to wash in. Sometimes, if I awoke early from an erotic dream, the long gray early morning hours seemed an eternity, I could hardly wait to hear her timid knock and see her beautiful face at the door. And then she would come in, and smile a greeting, and pick up my clothes to wash and mend. I was lost in love—and yet we never touched. Since that kiss on my palm the first night, I had not touched her again. I didn't trust myself. I was miserable and elated; I was so happy just to gaze upon her beauty, and cast down when she left me to go about her womanly chores. And then there was the guilt; and the totally unwarranted shame. Father Simon came to see me and preached a homily on young men's lusts and how God would turn his face away from youthful sinners who took advantage of poor serving women, even if they were infidels. If only he knew, the chinless old fool. He told me that I was the talk of headquarters, that Little John was making crude jests about Nur and myself—and I blushed hotly in rage at the injustice of it all. But I could not really complain—I had Nur in my life and every morning when she greeted me, my soul was full of joy. I went about my duties that autumn and winter like a sleepwalker. When I practiced swordplay with Little John, he beat me easily and scolded me for lacking attention. I did not care. I thought of nothing but Nur and her body: her deep black eyes; her creamy breasts; her tiny waist, and how it would feel to put my hands around it; how her lips would feel against mine; how her buttocks would feel nestled in the curve of my pelvis. What it would be like to enter her . . .

But enough of this nonsense. I am sure that you, my patient reader, have experienced love and know full well its pleasures and pains. Let it suffice to say that I was a young man, and I was truly in love for the first time.

I tried to expunge Nur from my fevered thoughts with healthy outdoor exercise. Robin had suggested that I work on my skills with a lance, which were surely lacking, and he had also asked our captain of cavalry Sir James de Brus to teach me.

Sir James started me off on the quintain, which he had set up beyond the army camp on a fairly level piece of ground north of the city. Above us on a high hill that overlooked the whole of Messina, King Richard was constructing a great wooden castle. It was a curious building, formed of already fabricated parts, which Richard had brought with him from France. It was strange to see a pack of foot soldiers toiling up the hill and carrying with them a long section of ready-made rampart complete with toothlike crenellations, or to watch a group of cavalrymen using their horses to haul a great wooden door up the steep side of the hill. But I could see the logic: timber was scarce and it was much more sensible of Richard to have brought his own materials to construct a defensible position than to rely on God to provide the appropriate materials locally. The castle was to be called "Mategriffon"—literally "Kill the Griffons"—as a grim reminder that Richard, from his new stronghold high above the town, could take Messina and punish its citizens whenever he chose.

The sacking of the town had two interesting consequences: firstly, King Philip had been furious when he saw Richard's royal standard flying above the walls of the town—I think he had expected Richard's insane attack with a tiny band of knights to fail—and he had threatened to take his men back to France if he was not given half the spoils of the captured town. The second consequence was that King Tancred of Sicily was completely intimidated by the swift capture of his most lucrative port, and had paid Richard a mountain of gold and silver to end the trouble between them. The money, chest upon chest of it, was supposed to be the full and final payment of Queen Joanna's dower, but it was also in actual fact a bribe to gain Richard's goodwill and support in the future. Tancred had his own enemies in Italy and an alliance with the most powerful prince in Christendom was more valuable than mere money.

Some quiet diplomacy on the part of Robert of Thurnham did a great deal toward smoothing things over between the English King and the French. Richard took down his own banners from the ramparts of Messina, and replaced them with the flags of the Knights Templar and the Knights Hospitaller. And these two great orders of fighting monks henceforth assumed charge of the town. Richard then decreed that all the plunder taken from Messina must be returned. Of course, nobody in our army was foolish enough to admit that they had any ill-gotten goods or silver, so this was a meaningless gesture; and certainly Richard did not press this point. But, in an effort to keep relations between the townsmen and our soldiers sweet, Richard did outlaw gambling, under pain of ferocious punishment. And he fixed the price of bread at a penny a loaf and wine at so-and-so-much a pint and decreed that these essentials of life could not be sold by the Griffons any dearer.

As the final gesture of his desire to keep the peace, and most generously in my view, Richard gave one third of the gold he had received from Tancred to King Philip. Thus mollified, the French King went back to his lair at the palace, no doubt to begin searching for a fresh grievance against our generous monarch. My friend Ambroise said to me, over a cup of wine and a haunch of crisp roasted pork one night, that the French King's great and holy expedition was not so much aimed against the Saracens as against King Richard—and although it was meant only as a sly witticism, there was a great deal of truth in his boozy jest.

The quintain was a horizontal pole with a circular wooden target at one end and a counterweight in the shape of a leather bag of grain, or sometimes water, at the other. The pole was mounted on a vertical post and when the shield was struck from horseback by the lance, the contraption would rotate at high speed and the counterweight bag of grain could sweep an unwary horseman off his seat as he rode past.

I had used one before a couple of times, when I lived deep in Sherwood Forest at the home of an old Saxon warrior called Thangbrand, but I had never mastered it. I did know, however, that the answer was speed. So the first time Sir James told me to ride at it, I put my heels to Ghost and cantered at the target, going at a fair lick, with an unfamiliar kite-shaped shield strapped to my left arm and a long blunted spear couched under my right.

I found that trying to control the heavy lance was much more difficult than I had thought. The padded tip wavered all over the place as I moved with the gait of the horse and as a result, I missed the target completely. Ghost faltered but carried on charging forward, impelled by his own momentum. At the last minute he shied slightly to the side to avoid the target, which crashed into my shield a heartbeat later with surprising force and nearly unseated me. The swinging sack of grain whistled past my back, missing me by a whisker.

As I trotted back to Sir James de Brus, I was expecting a stream of ridicule to spew from his scowling face. I had heard him upbraiding his troopers and the man's language, when he was angry, would have disgraced a whoremaster. But he merely said: "Nobody gets it right to begin with. Watch me again." And he cantered off toward the target, his lance straight out in front of his body, the long heavy wooden pole as unmoving as if it were held in a vice. He charged up to the target, going up to the gallop for the last few yards, hit the circle of wood dead center and was riding easily past before the swinging bag of corn was a quarter way round its circular path.

I tried again, missed again, and had to fend off the target with my shield once more. Then I made a mistake and slowed right down, to make sure I could hit the target foursquare. But Ghost and I were moving too slowly and the swinging sack caught me hard in the ribs and tumbled me out of the saddle. Bruised and breathless, I remounted Ghost and returned once again to Sir James. "I think we'll start with something a wee bit simpler," he said, but not altogether unkindly.

Sir James set up a pole at about head height, with a fork cut into the wood, into which was stuck a ring of plaited straw about the size of an apple. With a real lance, not a padded one this time, I had to put the spear point through the ring as I rode past and lift the straw circle off the pole. It was extremely difficult. I missed time and again, even only going at the trot, and found I was growing frustrated, angry even, with myself and with Sir James de Brus for making me feel so small and incompetent.

"Now try it at the gallop," my teacher suggested after I had missed the ring for the twentieth time. I bit back an angry retort and dug my spurs into Ghost. He responded and we thundered toward the ring on the pole. Strangely, the galloping horse gave me a more stable platform and as we approached the ring I lunged forward with the lance, as if it had been a sword, and to my amazement, I pierced the straw ring and lifted it clean off the pole. I was elated. Triumph at last! Sir James even offered me a twisted grimace, which I took to be his scrumpled version of a congratulatory smile. "Now do it again," he said gruffly. So I did.

Within the week I had mastered the straw ring. I could lift it off the pole nineteen times out of twenty. And so we went back to the quintain. Two weeks later and I had mastered that, too. And made a friend.

After a long day tilting at the quintain, Sir James invited me to share a flask of wine with him. It was late November and the days were growing short. On that gray afternoon we sat in the monk's refectory alone apart from a pair of knights sitting at the far end of the room playing tables, or as some call it, backgammon.

We had been discussing the tactics of the Saracen cavalry; Sir James had already made a pilgrimage to Jerusalem, before it was lost to Saladin, and he had been told much about the fighting style of Turkish cavalry—apparently they were superb horsemen, whose practice it was to ride up close to their enemies, shoot arrows at them from horseback and then ride away swiftly—when Nur appeared at our table bringing bread and cold meat to go with the rather fine wine that Sir James had provided.

Brus scowled at her, but then he scowled at everybody, it was just his habitual expression. But Nur seemed afraid of him and stepped closer to me. Then she noticed a loose thread on my tunic, and with a classically feminine gesture, she tugged it away from the cloth and then smoothed the material down again over my shoulder.

I wasn't paying attention to Nur, for once. I was watching Sir James and thinking about how one could defeat Saracen cavalry, and I saw his mouth fall open in surprise. When Nur had left, he leaned forward. And said to me in a low voice: "I beg your pardon, Alan, if I am being impertinent, but is that lovely lassie your bed-partner?"

I blushed, and said, "Of course not. She is not a common whore. She is a good girl, a young servant who I am helping to return to her family in the Holy Land."

"But you do ken that she's in head over heels love with you?" Sir James continued, "I mean, it stands out a mile."

I was struck speechless. It had genuinely not occurred to me that my feelings for Nur might be reciprocated.

Sir James seemed to realize that he had stepped into marshy ground and he began to talk at random to give me time to recover myself.

"I knew a beautiful lass like that once, well not as beautiful as her, and she loved me, too, but I had a rival for her affections," he said. "It was back in Scotland, oh years ago, but I remember her face well. Dorothea, or Dotty, was her name . . ."

I wasn't really listening. I wanted to run after Nur and grab her by the arms and demand to know if she loved me or not. Instead, I managed to control myself and said distractedly: "Is that why you left Scotland? For love?"

"Ach no, nothing so fine. It was just a killing. I killed a Douglas, and if you kill a Douglas you need to watch yourself because they'll all be coming after you, the whole boiling pot of them looking for revenge. They are as bad as the Murdacs for vengeance, but then, of course, the Murdacs would be on our own side."

"What happened?" I asked, my curiosity aroused in spite of myself.

"It was just a grubby squabble in an ale-house in Annandale but tempers flew and swords were drawn, and before I knew it young Archie Douglas was dead at my feet. I went to the castle to see the chief of the Brus himself, my uncle Robert, to find out what could be done about the matter, and he was sympathetic, right enough. He was no stranger to an accidental killing himself. And so he gave the Douglases a blood price, wee Archie wasn't worth all that much, he was a wastrel and a drunkard, and the Brus was a rich man, but as part of the agreement to save a feud breaking out between our two clans, he had to send me away. The Earl of Huntingdon, who was staying at the castle at the time and who is kin to the Countess of Locksley, suggested that I join Robin's cavalry and help whip them into shape. And, I'll tell you this, Alan, I'm glad I did. I've never been happier since I joined this crew of scruffy layabouts." He gave me one of his horrible screwed-up smiles again—and I realized that I believed him. He *was* happy; the scowling and the ferocious demeanor was just his way of disguising his feelings, of protecting himself and his dignity from overfamiliarity.

"What was that you said earlier about the Murdacs?" I asked.

"Oh, they're worse than the very Devil himself for vengeance," said Sir James. "Cross a Murdac and there'll be murder for sure, as we say at home."

"You said something about them being on your side?"

"Oh aye, my mother was a Murdac; she was the daughter of Sir William Murdac of Dumfries and Mary Scott of Liddesdale. But, of course, *her* father, Mary's that is, was a damned Douglas from Lanarkshire . . ."

I was only listening to him with half an ear as I had other, more urgent things on my mind: I needed to know how Nur felt about me, and for that I needed to be able to speak to her.

I found Reuben in the old town, back at his comfortable lodgings at the Jewish merchant's home. After a good deal of cajoling, he agreed to teach me the rudiments of Arabic; we would have a lesson every day, and we would start the next day. I could have asked Reuben to act as an interpreter but was determined that I would be able to speak to Nur myself, and divine for myself her true feelings for me. At a moment of tender love, I did not want another man coming between us.

I rode back from the old town and my meeting with Reuben in high spirits: but when I reached the monastery I found the place stricken with terror. The Devil was abroad, one old soldier who guarded the gate whispered to me; and he had laid his red hand on the Earl of Locksley.

It was true that Robin was gravely ill, near death, and had been laid out in his bed, pale and streaked with his own vomit—but I did not believe it was the Devil's work. Somebody in the monastery had tried to poison my master; the same person, no doubt, who had tried to kill him in Burgundy.

CHAPTER TEN

The whole of Robin's force—just under four hundred archers, cavalry and spearmen—was drawn up at the harbor side to witness the punishment. It was a gloomy day, the fat gray clouds lightly spitting rain from time to time, a weak sun only rarely peeping through. The prisoner, a sailor called Jehan from my own hated ship the *Santa Maria*, had been gambling with a local fisherman. He had lost his dice game and owed the Griffon five shillings; more than he could afford. And so he had refused to pay the man claiming that, as a pilgrim heading for the Holy Land, his debts should be frozen until he returned from his sacred journey. It was a cheeky way to avoid his debt, for it was true, the Holy Father, the Pope himself, had ruled that the debts of anyone on this Great Pilgrimage should be suspended until the debtor returned home. But that was a move designed to encourage knightly landowners with great mortgages to go off to fight for Jerusalem. His Holiness clearly did not intend his words to allow shifty gamblers to welsh on their agreements. The Griffon fisherman had complained to the Knights Hospitaller, who controlled his part of Messina, and they had reported the matter to the King; and Richard was determined to make an example of the poor man. Jehan should have paid up or, better still, heeded King Richard's decree that outlawed gambling with the Griffons.

He was to be keelhauled—a harsh punishment that involved dragging the prisoner's living body under the keel of a ship from one end to the other. And it is much worse than it sounds: after months at sea the keel of any ship is covered with tiny barnacles, sharp rock-like structures less than a quarter of an inch in height but rough and spiky enough to cut through skin and muscle if a naked body is dragged against them. The second danger, of course, is drowning. The man must hold his breath under water while undergoing the agony of being dragged over the keel-barnacles. Many drowned during this punishment; and those who did not were left appallingly lacerated. King Richard had ordered that this man must undergo keelhauling three times on three successive days. It was, in effect, a death sentence.

The man was stripped down to a pair of linen breeches, his hands and feet tied and attached to long ropes. He lay forlornly, eyes closed, skin puckered with cold, at the prow of the *Santa Maria*, which was moored about twenty yards from the quay, while a priest recited prayers over his thin, shivering frame. The rain began to fall harder.

Our men stood there in silence. Nobody had complained too much about the punishment: Jehan had been stupid and the consensus was that the punishment, while brutal, was not unfair. We had all been warned about gambling; Jehan had ignored that warning and then, much worse, had tried to welsh. The men hated a welsher. Besides, although we knew him, he was not truly one of us; just a Provencal sailor, hired in Marseilles to crew the ship.

I was standing on the harbor wall, chewing on a chicken leg, with William beside me, and thinking about Nur. At my feet was a yellow cur, a foul limping street dog from the stews of Messina; half its fur had been eaten away by mange exposing scabbed pink skin; its ears were no more than ragged tatters after many a ferocious canine battle and it had but one yellow eye. But the hideous dog seemed to be strangely attracted to me. It had followed me all the way from the monastery as I walked down to the harbor and I could not seem to shake it no matter how many times I kicked at it or shooed it away. It was a bitch, I noticed, and she just stared up at me from her position at my feet on the rough stone of the harbor with her pathetic yellow eye, quietly loving me. It occurred to me that she looked at me in exactly the same way that I looked at Nur.

"Gi-gi-give her your chicken bone," said William. "That's a-a-all she wants, give her the bone and perhaps she will go-go-go away." William was always a kindly fellow, and I thought that his plan might work, so I tossed the chicken bone to the smelly yellow mongrel at my feet. The dog snatched the bone out of the air with an amazing swiftness and darted away through our legs. *Well,* I thought to myself with a smile, *so much for love!*

On the *Santa Maria,* Jehan had been picked up, head and feet, by two of his fellow sailors, with two more holding the ropes. With very little ceremony, they threw the man over the prow and with one man holding the rope attached to his feet and another on the rope attached to his arms they began to walk quickly along the two gunwales of the ship, dragging their ropes behind them.

"Stop!" a deep voice boomed from the stern of the ship. "Stop, you vermin, in the name of the King!" It was Sir Richard Malbête. He had been given a new role by Richard—he was now the knight responsible for discipline and punishment in the whole army. It was an office that fitted his black soul like a glove. But it troubled me to see the Beast getting close to King Richard and being given responsibilities by him.

At Malbête's command, the two sailors pulling their unfortunate fellow under the ship stopped dead. I could only imagine what the poor victim was feeling, unmoving, bleeding from a hundred cuts and slowly drowning under the keel of the *Santa Maria*. "You go too fast," rumbled Malbête. And summoning two of his men-at-arms, he had them draw swords and stand in front of the rope-bearing sailors, walking backward along either side of the deck, only allowing the men dragging the victim to advance at a very slow walking pace unless they wished to impale themselves on the swords. Finally they reached the stern and, sheathing his sword, Sir Richard Malbête indicated, at last, that the sailors might pull up their colleague.

The victim was a mass of oozing cuts from his forehead to his shins; he had lost one eye, his nose was split and squashed against his face, and there were deep cuts across his belly and chest where the barnacles had sliced deeply. He looked as if he had been scraped repeatedly and deeply across his body with a particularly sharp rake. But he lived. He vomited what seemed like a gallon of seawater on to the deck, and while his friends among the crew swabbed gently at his wounds and tried to bind them, he coughed and flopped on the wooden deck, leaking gore like a gutted mackerel.

"Tomorrow at noon he goes again," said Malbête. One of the sailors looked fearfully up at the Beast.

"Begging your pardon, sir, but he'll not survive another hauling," he said in a respectful tone.

The tall knight shrugged. "Tomorrow at noon," he said again and easily swung himself down into a skiff to be rowed the few yards ashore.

★ ★ ★

The sailor was right. The poor man did not survive the second keelhauling, but was dragged, bloody but quite dead, from the water at a little past noon the next day. I did not see it, for I was tending to my master. And feeding the yellow dog, who because of her skinned and battered appearance had been nicknamed Keelhaul, or Keelie, for short.

Keelie had not deserted me, as I had assumed. She reappeared as William and I were leaving the harbor after watching the punishment, and she followed us all the way back to the monastery. She had a pleading look in her eye, clearly wishing for another chicken bone, and though I shouted at her and even threw a half-hearted stone, she would not abandon me. So I decided to poison her. Well, not quite poison her but to feed her a small portion of everything that Robin ate. She would become his canine food-taster.

It was a plan that proved popular with Keelie. We tethered her with a rope around her skinny neck in a corner of Robin's chamber and fed her choice portions from Robin's bowl. It was William's duty to take her, on her rope leash, out into the monastery garden morning and night and, after a few mistakes, when she soiled the floor of Robin's chamber, she soon learned where she was to go about her natural functions.

Regular feeding did wonders for Keelie. She quickly put on flesh and her fur began to grow back over the awful, naked pink skin. Her pathetic eye began to look brighter and, after a week or so, she developed a spring in her step that resembled that of a normal, healthy young dog. She looked well.

The same could not be said of Robin. Three days before the keelhauling he had eaten a piece of candied fruit peel from a bowl on the table in his chamber and he had become very ill immediately. No one could remember when the bowl had appeared on the table. The cooks and servants of the monastery had denied all knowledge of it, and there were dozens of

199

candied-fruit sellers in the old town of Messina. The fruit could have been bought by almost anyone and, when Robin was not in his chamber, the room was not guarded and so any man or woman in the monastery could have slipped in and placed the bowl of poisoned fruit there.

Immediately after eating the sugar-coated slivers of fruit peel, Robin experienced a tingling feeling, and then numbness on his mouth and tongue. He managed to tell Reuben, who had been summoned once again in his role as Robin's physician. The numbness of the mouth was followed, Robin whispered to his Jewish friend, by nausea, vomiting and the flux, and a burning pain in his stomach. When Reuben had examined him he found that his pulse was dangerously slow, the heart struggling to beat. And Robin lay, gray, eyes closed and unmoving as his body valiantly struggled to rid him of the evil humors in his system.

Reuben could not immediately identify the poison, but he also seemed distracted as if his mind lay elsewhere; the King sent Robin a golden drinking cup which was set with four emeralds, and a message that he had been informed by the finest doctors in Sicily that the emeralds would serve to purify any poisons in wine. "A unicorn's horn works just as well," muttered Reuben when he saw the cup. I did not know if he was being serious or not but he allowed Robin to use the cup to take large quantities of well-watered wine, brought to him by William. Father Simon came and filled the room with the sound of his mumbled Latin prayers and the smoke of costly incense to purify it of any harmful airs, and once again I smelled the pungent fragrance I had smelled in Reuben's house so long ago in York.

"What is that churchy smell?" I asked Reuben when Father Simon had finished his endless beseeching of God for Robin's deliverance from the Devil's grip.

"It is frankincense," said Reuben, not quite meeting my eye. "Do you not know it? It is burned in every great church in Christendom. I would have thought you Christians would be entirely familiar with it."

"I know its scent, I was just not familiar with the name," I said with a touch of hauteur. I hated it when my low-born ignorance was unearthed. "So, frankincense, then," I said, tasting the word as if it were a fine wine. "Does it come then from France?"

Once again Reuben gave me a slightly strange look. "Have you been talking to him about this?" he asked, nodding at the sleeping form of my master on the bed—who but for the very slight movement of his chest, looked as if he were dead.

"No, we've never mentioned it. So does it come from France; is it the incense of the Franks?"

"No." Reuben said nothing more. I stayed silent, too, and just stared at my friend willing him to go on.

"Oh, well, if you must know everything," said Reuben grumpily, "it is called frankincense because it is the 'true' or 'pure' incense. It is worth more than its weight in gold, far more, and it comes from my homeland Al-Yaman, in the far south, beyond the great deserts of Arabia." Then he turned back to his patient and ignored me. I sat down on a stool and thought for a while about frankincense. Was it truly worth more than its weight in gold? And every great church in the whole of Christendom was burning it at every holy service? Somebody was making a lot of money from this "pure" incense. I realized that I had been staring at Robin's battle standard, which was hanging on the wall of his chamber for some time: the image of a snarling wolf's head in black on a white background that always seemed to be leaping out of the cloth toward me.

An idea suddenly struck me, like a bolt of lightning. "Reuben," I said, "could . . . could it possibly be wolfsbane that is poisoning him?"

Reuben jerked his head round and stared at me. "Oh,

my God, I've been a fool," he said. "An utter fool. I was thinking of more exotic Sicilian poisons. Or something subtle and Persian . . ."

Suddenly he seemed to come to a decision, he turned back to Robin and very gently began slapping his face.

"Robert, Robert, wake up; I need to see your eyes," said the Jew. As Robin struggled up from the depths of sleep, Reuben peered into his eyes. He seemed satisfied by what he saw and turned to me.

"He has been poisoned with aconite; as you correctly guessed, what we would ordinarily call wolfsbane. So I need you to find some foxglove," he said. "It's the only thing that I know can cure him. And don't let him have any more wine. Just boiled water from now on."

I looked at Reuben doubtfully. Foxglove was a known poison, why would he want to give a man who had already been poisoned, more poison? And where on earth was I to find an English flower in Sicily?

Reuben must have seen my indecision. "Go to the herbalist in the old town, the shop next to the butcher's in the main street. Mention my name, he is a good fellow and we have met several times to discuss medicinal matters; tell him that I need an ounce of powdered *digitalis* leaves. You will remember the Latin name? *Digitalis*—like fingers. Hurry boy, your master is dying." And so I went.

I found the herbalist easily, and procured the powder. But it was with some misgivings that I gave the little packet to Reuben, and watched him brew up a concoction of boiling water, honey, sage and the *digitalis* powder. He saw me watching suspiciously and gave me a hard stare. "Leave us, boy," he said. "Let your master have some peace to get well."

I left, but I could not shake the dark thoughts that were gathering in my mind about Reuben. Could he be the one who was trying to kill Robin? It was impossible, surely. Robin had saved Reuben at York. But then, the dark side of my mind argued, Robin had also been indirectly responsible for the death of his beloved daughter Ruth.

Until that moment, I'd half assumed that the poisoning had been accomplished by some wretch in the pay of Malbête. He had directly threatened Robin, and me, on the night Messina was sacked and I found Nur. I could easily imagine the Beast suborning a man-at-arms with money and the promise of a good position in his service, slipping him a box of poisoned candied fruit, and laughing into his wine at the reports that Robin was at death's door. But a dark maggot was eating away at my trust; could it have been Reuben? No, never, Reuben was loyal to Robin. He would never stoop to poisoning his friend. If he had a problem with Robin he would either leave him or, if it was a serious matter of honor, challenge him to fight. But poison? Never.

But, argued my distrustful maggot, he knew about poisons and medicine—did he not just admit that he discussed such matters with the herbalist in Messina—and he didn't recognize that the poison was common wolfsbane, which was odd . . . unless he *did* know that it was wolfsbane because he had given it to Robin himself, and now he was giving him another poison—foxglove! I was on the point of rushing back into Robin's chamber and confronting Reuben with an open accusation when reason was restored to its throne and the maggot banished to its fetid hole. Reuben was loyal; Reuben was a true friend. Besides, there was nothing I could do. I had no proof. If I accused Reuben, he might take offense and stop treating Robin, who might then die. For all I knew, foxglove might well be a miracle cure . . .

In the end, I did nothing but prayed hard for Robin's speedy recovery in the cathedral and vowed to visit my master regularly to check his health. If he sank any lower, perhaps I would consult the King's personal physician. If he died, I would take bloody revenge on the Jew.

In the event, Robin began to recover. Slowly, at first,

his pulse became stronger and more regular. His color improved and within three days he was able to sit up in bed and sip the hot concoctions that Reuben prepared for him. I was terribly relieved and happy: Reuben was not the poisoner and, thanks to his care, Robin would live. But I had another reason to be filled with great soul-filling joy: Nur and I had become one.

One evening I came late to my cell, after sitting with Robin for several hours, to find William looking worried. He was waiting for me outside the door of the little chamber.

"I, I, I think there is so-something wr-wrong with Nur," he said as he saw me walking up the corridor toward him. "She's cr-crying her eyes out but I can't understand what the pe-pe-problem is."

I walked into the monk's cell and saw Nur sitting on the padded stone shelf that served as my bed wrapped in my warm green cloak. He eyes were red and the black kohl that she used around them was streaked down her cheeks. She looked like a little lost girl and my heart melted inside my body. When she saw me she burst into a fit of uncontrollable sobbing and in two steps she was in my arms. "You . . . have . . . no . . . love . . . for . . . me . . ." she said between gasping sobs. She said it like a phrase that she had learned by heart, parrot-fashion. And I believed I knew who had taught it to her: a certain meddling Jew, who was also a wonderful, miraculous life-giving friend. I held Nur tenderly and stroked her silky black hair, smoothing it over her head and down her long back. My hands discovered that she was naked under the cloak, and I just had time to gruffly dismiss William, who was gawping at us from the doorway, and watch him leave and gently shut the door, before I surrendered to the searing passion that had been raging inside me for so many weeks and crushed her soft mouth against mine.

★ ★ ★

What can an old man write about lovemaking? Each new generation believes that it has discovered it for the first time and that its elders are utterly grotesque in their coupling. But even though I am old now, I was not then, and I remember the first time that I made love with Nur as perhaps the most. beautiful, moving, deeply wonderful night of my life.

After the initial kiss, which was like a long draft of sweet wine, we tore at each other like wild beasts in our passion. She ripped my clothes from me and I mounted her without hesitation and felt the exquisite plunge as I slid deep inside her, the heat roaring in my loins, her legs wrapping around my waist, her soft breasts crushed against my chest. I was swiftly swept away in a whirlwind of pleasure; I bucked and plowed and kissed her, teeth clashing, whenever I could find her mouth, the unbearable pressure building beneath my balls as I teetered on the brink of explosion, each stroke more exquisite than the last, until at last I erupted in a series of gasping shudders deep inside her.

That night lasted for the blink of an eye, and will stay forever in my memory. Time had no meaning when I was with her, inside her, beside her and, in the breaks between each bout of lovemaking, we kissed long and deep, as if we were sucking life itself from each other's sweet lips. After we had made love twice, Nur began to show me a little of the arts she had learned in the big house in Messina. With her tongue and fingers, kissing and licking and stroking in every secret place, she brought me to the point of ecstasy, and then let me subside before it was too late. Again and again, I was made breathless by her wanton, silky carnality, her suppleness, and her willingness to bring me pleasure by every means possible, including some delightful practices of which I had never even dreamed, and which I was fairly sure would have been thoroughly condemned by any priest or monk. Near dawn, we lay in each other's arms, spent, and I stared in wonder into her fathomless dark eyes, her slim, infinitely precious body in the circle of my arms. We did not speak, for my Arabic had not progressed much beyond the formal greetings, and Nur had only that phrase of French that Reuben had taught her, but in that moment we needed no words. We lay together in a bubble of love, wrapped safe in each other's tender gaze.

I believe I reached a pitch of happiness in those early morning hours, after our first night together, with the monastery silent around us and that dark head sleeping on my shoulder, the like of which I have never reached again. My body felt empty and yet so full of joy; light of soul and yet weary beyond belief.

After that wondrous, magical night she came to me again the next evening, and the next. William was banished to the monastery dormitory, which he told me was occupied by a lot of snoring, farting men-at-arms, but the boy bore his exile with fortitude and I caught him smiling at me on several occasions, happy for my happiness.

Sir James de Brus made no comment about my new situation, but I knew that he knew, and he seemed to show me a greater respect as I honed my technique at the quintain and on the practice field. One day, as we were just finishing our routines, I noticed that Sir Robert of Thurnham had been watching, with an entourage of knights. We rode over to him, and he greeted us both with a cheery salute.

"Your skills are coming along very nicely, Alan," said Sir Robert in a friendly tone. "You are almost as good with a lance as a well-seasoned knight."

"Thank you, Sir Robert," I said, bowing from the waist. "But I think the skill resides mainly in my horse Ghost."

Sir Robert laughed. "Nonsense; I've had my eye on you for some time now and I see the makings of a first-class chevalier. If you can impress the King on the field of battle in the Holy Land, who knows, maybe God willing, he will one day grant you the honor of knighthood, of serving him as one of his household knights, the elite of the army. Your father was from a noble family, I believe, and you hold some land of the Earl of Locksley?"

I nodded, surprised that he knew all this, and very pleased. It had never crossed my mind that I would ever make it into the ranks of the knighthood, to be Sir Alan of Westbury. In my own head, I was still a ragged cutpurse from the stews of Nottingham, an orphaned thief and outlaw. It was a wonderful thought and I beamed happily at Sir Robert.

"The King is already impressed with your courtly talents," he went on. "He likes you; he much admired your rendering of *Tristan and Isolde*, a month or so ago. In fact, I come directly from Him, bearing an invitation to dine with him on Christmas Eve. The King wishes you to sing for his party. How about that?"

I was a great honor, but as often happens to me in the presence of great men, I was unable to think of a suitable reply. So I muttered something about how grateful I was and bowed once again.

"The day after tomorrow at noon, then. In the new castle," he said nodding up at the dark bulk of Mategriffon, which loomed over us. Then he smiled, turned his horse and, followed by his knights, he rode away.

"That is a rare privilege," said Sir James. "To dine with the King. You'd best make sure you don't disgrace yourself."

He was right, and I had to perform, too. I bid him a swift farewell and hurried back to the monastery to begin working on the music; I needed to create something really special, I said to myself. But inside my head the words Sir Alan Dale, Sir Alan of Westbury, and Alan, the Knight of Westbury, were darting about like a flock of sparrows trapped in a hall.

Robin was pleased for me when I told him I would be playing for the King. He was out of bed and feeding Keelie with scraps from a plate of boiled mutton. He had lost a lot of weight but seemed cheerful considering how close to death he had been. "I've decided that I should have more fun," he declared. "Life is short and death awaits us all, and as I am doubtless damned for all eternity for my many sins, I have decided that I will have some pleasure before I face the fires of Hell. So come on, Alan, let us drink a flask of wine together and you can play something for me."

And so I indulged my master. And we passed a very pleasant evening, singing, drinking, making merry. At midnight, when my head was swimming and my hands were stiff and cramped from the vielle, I laid down my instrument and made to leave. Nur would be waiting for me in my cell and I longed to be naked with her under the blankets.

"Alan," said Robin, as I had risen and was making unsteadily for the door. "Sit down again for a moment. I want to talk to you." I duly sat down again on a stool by the big table. "I want you to do something for me," Robin said, and he seemed entirely sober, his eyes shining in the candlelight. "I want you to find out who is trying to kill me. Discreetly and quickly, find out who it is, and report back to me. There have been three attempts in the past year, and by sheer luck, I have survived them all. But I will not always be so lucky. If you wish to serve me well, find the man responsible."

I had been half expecting something like this. Robin was right; the situation could not go on with a killer running loose, undetected in Robin's *familia*.

I nodded my acceptance at Robin. And he said: "Tell me what we know so far of the three attempts . . ."

"Well," I said, "the first attempt, in your chamber at Kirkton, was made by that archer Lloyd ap Gruffudd—Owain has discovered from his inquiries in Wales that Lloyd was promised the hundred pounds of German silver by Murdac's man, and also that his only son's life had been threatened if he did not kill you. Obviously, he's dead but his wife back in Wales was quick to tell Owain's man everything she knew; she wanted to be sure there would be no reprisals from us. Owain sent her a handful of coins for her honesty and has brought her and her son to live at Kirkton Castle where they will be safe. So Lloyd is dead, but the lure of Murdac's blood money could be inducing anyone, any archer, man-at-arms, or even knight to try to claim it."

"I wish I could claim it myself," said Robin gloomily. I knew that he was growing very short of money; the King had yet to pay him a single penny piece, and the money he had borrowed in England was nearly gone—but I did not wish to be distracted from the discussion of the assassin and so I ig-nored his comment and said: "We also know that, whoever it is, it is someone close to you because both times, with the snake and the poisoned fruit, the killer had easy access to your private chamber or pavilion, therefore it is someone whose presence there would not be commented on. But that still doesn't narrow the field. Almost anyone who serves you could find an excuse to come in here; they could say, if asked, that they were delivering a message from Owain, or Little John, or Sir James, for example. So that doesn't help us much."

"Well, that stops now," said Robin decisively. "From now on, the only way to get in touch with me, to speak to me, to see me is through you . . . and through John, I suppose. I can't believe John Nailor would want me dead after all these years. In fact, if he did want me dead, I'd already be dead.

"So," my master continued, "all contact with me must go through you and John. You bring me my food, tasted by Keelie, of course," and he smiled at the yellow bundle that was curled up peacefully in the corner of the chamber. "You bring me my wine, any orders for the men go through you, any one who wants to speak to me talks to you or John and you relay that to me. If I leave this place, either you or John accompanies me at all times. Is that clear?"

"Yes," I said, "but is all this really necessary? It's going to look very odd—and the men won't like it. They will feel you don't trust them."

"Can't be helped," said Robin. "The more quickly you find out who the assassin is, the more quickly we can stop this charade. Have you any ideas?"

"I have a feeling the assassin may be a woman," I said. "And I'm not truly convinced the motive is Murdac's money. It may well be Sir Richard Malbête. When I ran into him in Messina, the night after the battle, he promised me that he would have his revenge on you—and me."

"It could be Malbête," he said, musingly. "But that would mean the attempt in France was still made by somebody else, as the Beast did not join us until Messina. Could there really be three assassins—one in Yorkshire, one in France and one here? I can't see it. It must be one person." He rested his chin in his left palm and stared into space for a while.

"Why do you think it might be a woman?" Robin asked after a while.

"Because of the nature of the attacks," I said. "They are underhand, silent, sneaky: a snake in the bed, poisoned food; that's not the work of a man, a soldier."

"I think you may have an exaggerated idea of the honor of our fighting men," said Robin with a laugh. "And while I hesitate to boast of my prowess, the odds against killing me, man to man, face to face, each of us armed are reasonably long. And even if he could do it, it might take time to dispatch me, and, who knows, the renowned swordsman Alan of Westbury might come to my aide." He was teasing me. "No, if you have to kill someone, poison is as good a way as any."

I said nothing; I couldn't explain it, but I felt sure that the assassin was not a warrior. I could not think how to express it properly to Robin, so I held my tongue on the matter. Instead, we discussed the practicalities of Robin's plan to isolate himself, and how it would work on a daily basis.

As I was leaving, Robin grasped my arm. He said: "I know that we have not always seen things the same way; I know that sometimes, for whatever reasons, you are angry with me; but I want you to know that I appreciate your undertaking this task, and I'm aware that, if you succeed, I will owe you my life."

As I stared into his eyes, I thought of Ruth, and a man whose life was sacrificed to appease a false woodland god in our outlaw days, and a dozen other cruelties that Robin had practiced in pursuit of his personal goals—but in that moment I could not find any of the anger I had felt in the past.

And then I thought of all he had done for me, of the number of times he had saved me, in battle and by altering the course of my life; of the lordship of Westbury, of the friendship he had shown me, of my position of honor among the ranks of his tough men-at-arms.

"I am doing nothing but my duty as a loyal vassal, and nothing I do not owe you a hundred times over," I said with genuine feeling in my voice. And gripped his forearm and left before my emotions undid me.

The King was in a festive mood as we gathered in the great hall of Mategriffon Castle for his revels. A great fire roared on two giant flagstones in the center of the hall, the sparks flying upward to disappear in the dark bank of smoke in the ceiling which only slowly dissipated through the openings, high up at the sides of the hall roof. Tables were set out in a horseshoe shape around the great fire, which gave the meal a cozy family feeling that was seldom seen at a royal feast. At the center of the head table sat the King, who was calling out toasts and greetings to his guests—there were no more than two dozen of us—and urging them to taste the choicest cuts of meat on the silver platters scattered about the table. Beside the King, to his right in the place of honor, sat Tancred,

King of Sicily, a wizened little monkey of a man with a ribbon of dark hair scraped over the top of his bald head in an attempt to hide his dearth of locks.

I sat at one of the tables at the side, next to Sir Robert of Thurnham, whom I greeted with happiness, and a surly French knight that I did not know. We addressed each other politely, the Frenchman and I, but with a lack of genuine interest; anyway, in the presence of kings, it is more rewarding to pay attention to the greatest man in the room. Richard joked and laughed and devoured great quantities of suckling pig, ripping the meat from the ribs with his strong white teeth, and after an hour or so of gorging, he wiped the grease from his chin with a crisp linen napkin and after toasting me with a goblet of wine, he invited me to perform for his guests.

I had written something especially for that evening, which was infused with my love for Nur; although of course I could not proclaim that I was in love with a slave girl who had been a rich man's plaything. So I made up a standard tale of love for a great lady, far above my station, whom I could only adore from afar. If I remember rightly, it began:

> "My joy summons me
> To sing in this sweet season
> And my generous heart replies
> That it is right to feel this way . . ."

It was accompanied with a straightforward but pretty tune on the vielle, the music never overpowering the lyrics, but adding to their beauty and twisting a melody around the lines of poetry.

Richard adored the song. He loved it so much that he wanted to be part of it, to own it, even to claim it for himself. A second vielle was fetched, I think it belonged to that old troublemaker Bertran de Born, and while a servant was tuning it, Richard paced up and down the hall muttering to himself, and scowling. Then he swung around on me and, giving me a beatific smile, said: "I have it, Blondel. Verse and verse, yes? Turn and turn about?"

I believe he had forgotten my given name at this point, caught up as he was in the act of composing, and that was why he gave me a nickname that referred to my blond hair, but I was not going to complain. I was to swap verses with my King. Was there any greater honor for a young *trouvère*?

Richard made me begin again, and once more I sang the first verse:

> "*My joy summons me*
> *To sing in this sweet season*
> *And my generous heart replies*
> *That it is right to feel this way . . .*"

When I had finished the line and the accompanying musical chords, the King took over. Bowing his vielle a little stiffly, he repeated the refrain and then he subtly altered the phrasing and sang, to the same timing as my verse:

> "*My heart commands me*
> *To love my sweet mistress*
> *And my joy in doing so*
> *Is a generous reward in itself . . .*"

It was very witty, the use of my own words—joy, sweet, generous and heart—but in a different order to convey a similar message, and I'll confess that I was slightly taken aback at my sovereign's skill as a poet. It had taken me all day to write the song, but Richard's response had taken less time than it takes to put on a pair of boots. But I rallied quickly and when he had finished I replied to his verse with one of my own, with a little

213

twist in the tail. It was a cheeky thing to do, nearly insolent, and I knew it, but I sang:

> *"A lord has one obligation*
> *Greater than love itself*
> *Which is to reward most generously*
> *The knight who serves him well . . ."*

I was not looking for gain myself, truly I was not, but I dearly wished the King would pay Robin the money he had promised him. So while using a common *trouvère*'s theme—the duty of a good lord to be generous—I also wanted to get a subtle message across that would benefit my master Robin and help him out of his financial difficulties.

King Richard was not troubled in the slightest by my verse, and after a line or two of vielle music, improvising on my theme, he returned with:

> *"A knight who sings so sweetly*
> *Of obligation, to his noble lord*
> *Should consider the great virtue*
> *Of courtly manners, not discord."*

And with a great flourish of his horsehair bow, Richard played the final notes and set down his vielle. The applause was deafening. It was a brilliant rebuttal of my verse, and Richard was rightfully pleased with himself. He grinned at me across the tables laden with half-eaten food. And then, he turned to his left and forced an elderly English knight out of his place so that I might sit beside him. When I was ensconced in a huge oak chair next to my sovereign, he filled a jeweled cup with his own hand and gave it to me, and as I drank he said: "Bravo, young Blondel, one day we will make more music together, you and I, perhaps a duet beautiful enough to tame the Saracens, even Saladin himself, eh? And he grinned at me, blue eyes

214

twinkling, white teeth gleaming in the candlelight. I could think of nothing to say but merely nodded, murmured, "Yes, sire, as you wish," and sat back in the great chair basking in his good favor.

Then he leaned in close to my ear and said: "And you may tell your master, the cunning Earl of Locksley, that I have not forgotten my debt to him—and he shall have his precious silver in the morning."

CHAPTER ELEVEN

The King was as good as his word and several heavily laden chests were brought to Robin's chamber the next day. It was Christmas morning and the bells of the Cathedral were ringing out across the whole of Messina, summoning us to Matins with their joyful peals. A small pouch of gold was also delivered to my cell by a servant, a nervous boy who was admitted by William too early, while Nur and I were still abed. The youth, who was much plagued by pimples, said in a high squeaky voice: "There is a message, sir, that comes from the King with this gift." I nodded and said nothing, waiting. The boy cleared his throat and gabbled: "To Blondel, who, I trust, will never lack either good manners or generous lords. God be with you this Christmas Day." And with that the boy spun on his heel and was gone.

I gladly risked damnation that Christmas morning, and

a severe penance from Father Simon if he found out, by ignoring the summoning of the bells to Matins and remaining entwined with Nur in our snug bed. She was delighted that the King should so honor me with gold, and began talking excitedly about the fine clothes we could buy with the money—my Arabic had improved, and she was picking up some words of Norman French, and I could now understand about one word in three of her happy multilingual chatter. I was more than a little pleased with the King's gift myself. Robin was a less worried man, too, now that he had silver with which to pay his troops and to repay the loans that Reuben had had to arrange with the local Jewish community in Sicily to tide us over. "It's not nearly everything that he promised me in England," admitted Robin to me one morning a handful of days after Christmas, as we rode out into the mountains for a day's hunting. "But it's a start; and much better than nothing. 'A lord has one obligation, greater than love itself, which is to reward most generously . . .' I like it, and I thank you for that, Alan, I truly do."

I was pleased that my cheeky verse had had such a beneficial effect, but a tiny maggot's voice inside me suggested that, when my master and I were discussing who might be the would-be murderer in our ranks, Robin had artfully planted the idea in my head that I should ask my King for his money. On the trail of the assassin, I had made little further progress, except to make inquiries at the herbalist's in the old town and discover that he did sell wolfsbane—said he sold dozens of ounces a week but he claimed that he had never sold any to Reuben. This knowledge neither cleared nor incriminated Robin's physician—even if the man were telling the truth, Reuben could easily have asked someone else to purchase the poison for him.

We were heading up into the mountains of Sicily that day in search of wild boar. Will Scarlet had found a local man who knew of a place where there was a great pig apparently ravaging the land, tearing up the crops and terrorizing the local peasants. He had brought this intelligence to Little John and he had passed it on to Robin and now we were all riding in the hope of an exciting day's sport. Robin and myself rode in front, followed by John and Will Scarlet, with my servant William and the local guide, a thin-faced, dark-haired untrustworthy-looking man called Carlo, who spoke barbarous French, bringing up the rear. William and the guide were leading the packhorses, which were laden with the nets and long boar spears necessary to kill these powerful brutes. Around our horses' hooves trotted three alaunts, great shaggy hunting dogs, owned by Carlo, and Keelie, frisky as a puppy, bright as a golden coin with canine joy.

I had never hunted boar before and I was excited to be included in the chase. Sicilian boars are fierce great animals with enormous strength and long tusks capable of gutting a man from crotch to throat if they can get close to you, and to kill them we planned to use special heavy boar spears—sixteen-foot-long lengths of ash, two-inches thick at the butt, with steel cross-pieces a foot below the spear head. The cross-piece was to stop the animal, once impaled, from charging up the length of the spear in his fury, with the wooden shaft running through his body, to get at the man on the other end.

Will Scarlet was a changed man since his whipping, more somber, silent and God-fearing, much less the happy-go-lucky chattering boy-thief I had known in Sherwood. But, in a way, the punishment seemed to have steadied him: and he seemed much more comfortable now that he was just an ordinary trooper, no different than any other in Robin's force. He performed his duties seriously and stayed out of trouble and never flaunted his long acquaintance with Robin.

William too seemed very excited about the prospect of the hunt, and quizzed Carlo incessantly about the techniques of killing the boar, its behavior when harassed and how it would respond to the dogs and the nets. Carlo, for all his ill-favored looks, was a patient man and he answered William's endless questions in good grace as best he could in his halting French. The plan was to spread the nets—they were about three-foot high when erected and fine enough to be almost invisible, but they were made of a very strong bark twine—and then use the dogs to drive the boar on to them. Once entangled in the nets, and unable to run, the animal could be speared at our leisure.

Carlo took us to a rocky hilltop, covered with stunted spruce trees and bracken, and indicated a thicket a hundred or so paces away where the boar was believed to have his den. He had the alaunts leashed tightly and Keelie was also tethered by a strong rope, but it was clear the dogs could smell pig. They all strained against their confinement, eager to dash madly into the thicket and confront the beast.

William, Will Scarlet and Carlo spread the long nets in a semicircle, downhill from the hilltop, the way we expected the beast to break, propping them up right with small sticks and twigs: the net was meant to collapse when the pig charged into it. Robin, John and I took up our positions, boar spears grasped in our hands, my heart hammering as if I was about to go into battle.

Carlo, William and Will Scarlet disappeared off to the left, circling round the thicket with the dogs. They would release the hounds from the other side of the hill and follow slowly, cautiously, beating earth with their spear shafts, blowing horns and shouting to each other to make sure that the hog charged away from them and in the direction of the nets.

It was a cold, gray day, the sun was already low in the sky, and our breath frosted into plumes in the still air. Robin, standing twenty yards to my right, looked bored. He was still thin from the poisoning but a dab of color had returned to his cheeks now that he was in the field. He was humming softly under his breath and examining his nails minutely. In the distance we could hear the sound of the dogs, yapping excitedly, but it seemed very far away. Twenty yards beyond Robin, Little John was sitting on a rocky outcrop, sharpening the end of his spear with a spit-smeared stone. Robin wandered over toward John, clearly on the point of saying something to his old friend . . . when, with no warning at all, a giant boar burst out of the undergrowth of the thicket, moving at an incredible speed, a blur of low porcine fury and bunched muscle, heading straight down the hill toward us.

It was huge, far bigger than I had expected and it moved with a silent hurtling savagery that put my heart in my mouth. It was making for the gap between Robin and me, which was now much wider, as Robin had moved closer to John. I gripped my spear tightly; any moment now, I thought, any moment the great pig will hit the nets, become entangled and then we all move in. But it never happened. The great boar charged through the space where the net should have been and didn't slow for an instant. It fixed its mad piggy glare on me, swerved from its line and came barreling straight toward me, three hundred pounds of muscle driven by a manic rage at our threatening intrusion into its domain. All this happened in three heartbeats: from the pig erupting from the undergrowth until he was just a handful of yards from me. And, because of the pig's surprising appearance, I reacted slowly—but just in time: I gripped the shaft hard, leaned forward and I leveled my spear at the charging animal. The huge pig launched itself at me, and as if entirely careless of his own life, he leaped directly on to my wavering spear point. The blade plunged a foot deep into its shoulder, like a sharp knife cutting through a soft curd, and stopped fast at the cross-guard with a huge jolt. The shock, transmitted through the spear shaft, felt like I'd stopped the charge of a rampaging bull. The two-inch-thick spear shaft bent, but did not snap, and my knuckles were white on the shuddering brown wood, my arm and chest muscles creaking under the enormous strain. I was holding him away from me, but incredibly, the beast was moving forward, inch by inch, and pushing me backward with its main strength, its thick forelegs churning the earth, and my own feet sliding in the rocks and shale beneath them. The beast snarled at me in its death-pain, eyes glinting with malice, ropes of saliva swinging from long yellow tusks, which curved upward like twin daggers in the perfect shape to gut a man.

Then it gave a shrugging shake of its brawny shoulders, one immensely powerful writhe and the spear shaft was wrenched out of my hands. The long thick pole was whipped away laterally by the pig's movement and then came crashing back into my shoulder with the force of a swung pick-axe handle. I was knocked sideways by the shock, off my feet, on hands and knees, and then the huge animal was on me. The spear shaft slid past my face and in two bounds the open snout of the great pig was at my chest. I just managed to grab one of its massive tusks with both hands but the strength of the animal, even mortally wounded, was unbelievable. I could smell its foul breath above me, its rank saliva, mingled with blood dripping on my face as I struggled to keep its grunting, slavering snout, and its yellow snapping teeth away from me. The eyes, blue-black and rimmed with red, were inches from my own. It writhed again, the heavy spear shaft smashing against my left forearm, nearly causing me to lose my grip . . . And then a shadow appeared to my left and I heard a high-pitched cry of rage and I felt the impact of a spear thrust deep into the animal's body. It was William, my loyal servant William, with his great spear jammed into the beast's side, and he was trying with only his boyish strength to heave the blade further into the monstrous straining body. The dogs were with me, too, leaping about the massive animal, barking excitedly; Keelie took a hold of its flapping ear and began growling like a demon next to my cheek. Then Robin was there and Little John, too, and there were two more jolting impacts to the beast's body, as they plunged their spears in deeply, and the pig coughed a huge gout of hot blood into my forearms and chest and I saw the rage fade and die in the animal's eyes and, miraculously, all that was left was a colossal weight, and the sound of breathless, hysterical laughter from my so-called friends.

We camped out that night, in a hollow in the rocks, and feasted on roast wild boar. I was not badly hurt, just bruised on shoulder, arm and chest, and a little embarrassed to have so nearly lost a wrestling match with a pig. Little John put a slightly cruder interpretation on it. "God's bulging loins," he said after he had hauled the limp, blood-smeared animal off me, an effort even for someone of his great strength. "I knew you were a horny young devil but I never thought you would get so desperate that you'd fuck a giant pig to death. Bless my sullied soul, what will you young people think of next . . ."

It hurt to laugh—the pig's thick churning forefeet had badly scraped and bruised my ribs, and every muscle above my waist was shrieking in protest—but I did so; I was alive and relatively unhurt, and I thought I detected a brief light of genuine concern in Robin's eye as he helped me to my feet and patted me down briskly to check for broken bones. I thanked William profusely: but for his timely intervention, I said, the beast would have got its tusks into me and I'd be dead. "He lo-lo-looked as if he was going to ea-eat you whole," said William. He seemed, if anything, more shaken by the incident than me.

"What happened to the nets?" Robin asked Carlo. "The pig came straight through them as if they were cobwebs."

The huntsman looked slightly abashed, but shrugged. "Maybe they fall down," he said. "Maybe they not strong enough for him." He shrugged again, and spread his hands, palms up. "Maybe God, He decided to make a hunter's test for this young one," he said and nodded at me. There seemed to be nothing more to say on the subject.

We made a jolly supper-party that night on the hillside; a thousand, thousand glittering stars made a bright canopy above us and, filled with sweet fatty pork seasoned with wild thyme and washed down with a skin of wine that Little John had had the foresight to bring, it felt as if I was back in Sherwood in the happy days at Robin's Caves.

When we had all eaten and drunk our fill, and were dozing happily by the fire wrapped in warm cloaks, Little John stood up slowly, spread his massive arms wide and intoned in a slow, doleful voice: "On earth there's a warrior of curious origin. He was created, gleaming, for the benefit of men. Foe bears him against foe to inflict harm. But women often fetter him, strong as he is. And if men care for him and feed him frequently, he'll faithfully obey them and serve them well. But this warrior will savage anyone who permits him to become too proud. What is his name?"

Little John was famous for his riddles; he had told them in the Caves in Sherwood and in the hall at Kirkton Castle, and we had much enjoyed his skill in describing a common everyday object, but using a clever, often misleading play on words to describe it. This riddle, however, was too easy; I knew the answer immediately but decided to stay silent while the rest pondered John's words.

"Is—is it a dog?" asked William. He had one-eyed Keelie at his feet and he was idly stroking her golden head.

"A good guess," said John. "But not what I had in mind."

"I have it," shouted Will Scarlet excitedly, "the warrior's name is fire." And he was rightly applauded for his perception.

"Your turn to tell one, then, Will," said Little John. And Scarlet furrowed his brow for a few moments. Finally he said: "A chest with only one side, is a seat for a mother; it hides her treasure of gold, but it's just a bite for another."

This too was a simple one, old as the hills, as well—it is an egg. The chest with only one side is the shell; the mother hen sits on the egg, which contains a golden yolk, a fine bite for someone else to eat.

223

I suspected that we all knew the answer—the egg was one of a handful of favorite subjects for riddles—but everyone pretended not to, so that Will Scarlet could enjoy our puzzlement, until finally young William gravely provided the answer. And so it was then his turn. He took a deep breath and gripped his own fist to control his stammer and said: "I am alive but do not speak. An-anyone who wants to can take me captive and cut off my head. They bite my bare white body. I do not ha-harm anyone unless they cut me first. But then I soon make them cry."

This was one I had not heard before. And the riddle was strangely chilling, with its talk of cutting off heads and biting bare white bodies. For a while we all mulled his words but I'll freely admit I had no idea what William could mean. Robin, however, was not so easily defeated: "What makes you cry? In my experience it is usually a woman, but in this case . . . Ah, yes. White body, you can bite into it, but it makes you cry . . . It's an onion!" We all roared out approval and toasted him with the wine. And so it went, riddle after riddle, until lulled by the wine, the meat, and the gentle moaning of the wind in the rocks, sleep claimed each one of us, one by one.

The winter months passed slowly but peacefully in Messina. Each night I slept with Nur in my arms and my command of her language grew—as did hers of French, which was the common language of the army—until we could understand each other in tolerable fashion. One night she told me of her life before we had met—and it was a terrible tale. She came from a small village not far from the coast near the Christian city of Tyre; one day two years ago the village had been raided by Cilician pirates and she had been captured along with many of the young boys and girls of the village. They had been beaten and raped, bound and taken north to the pirates' stronghold near Seleucia. When they arrived there, the boys were cut to make them eunuchs but, to her surprise, she had been treated with a rough kindness. However, when she had tried to run away, an Arabic symbol, a small sort of squiggly backward L had been branded on her ankle with a hot iron, and she had been kept thereafter in a locked harem of twenty or so girls. It was there, at the tender age of thirteen, that she was taught to please men in the many delightful ways that she now used to pleasure me. I felt a stab of guilt that my present joy should have come from such a brutal source—but she reassured me: "Alan," she said, "I have never willingly given myself to a man before now. And if my past pain can make you happy today, then I am glad to have suffered it."

After six months or so in the harem, she was sold to a band of Frankish knights who wore white surcoats with the red Christian cross. I knew that the Templars were involved in the slave trade all around the Mediterranean, although they claimed that they never enslaved Christians, but I was a little shocked and saddened that they had been involved in my beautiful girl's sordid tale. However, as Tuck was often fond of pointing out, God moves in mysterious ways, and it was through the offices of these Knights of the Temple of Solomon that she had come to me. The Templars had sold her on to a merchant in Messina, who traded in incense and silk and spices, and though she had expected to be passed on again, he kept her and a handful of other girls for his personal pleasure. That is where I had found her, in the big ransacked house in the old town. Malbête and his men had broken into the house on that night of havoc, had killed the merchant and his servants outright, but had howled with glee when they saw the quality of his harem. She had watched, speechless, nearly driven mad with terror, as the men-at-arms tied the girls to the whipping posts and raped and tortured them in turn . . .

I stopped Nur's mouth with my hand at this point; I did not want to hear any more.

"Why are men like that?" asked Nur, after a while, in a sad, puzzled tone. "We give them pleasure with our bodies, we serve them food and clean their homes and bear their babies; why should men wish to treat us this way?"

I had no answer, except to say that not all men were the same. "You have suffered so much, my darling, and endured so much cruelty, but now you are safe with me, under my protection and under that of my master Robin, and I will never let anything bad ever happen to you again."

Throughout the winter, Little John and I continued to take turns to spend the days with Robin, restricting the number of people who could get to him, and I began to understand what a complicated business running a small army of four hundred men really was. Each day there were dozens of decisions to be made, punishments and rewards to hand out and rations to be provided for the troops—we had long since eaten all the stores we had brought with us from Yorkshire.

Robin bought vast quantities of corn and barley from merchants in Messina with King Richard's silver and each day our own millers and bakers ground meal and baked hundreds of loaves of bread for distribution. We had brewers, too, who made the ale that was another vital part of the daily fare and that as well had to be served out to the men in exact amounts. Then there were the rations of cheese and meat—fish on Wednesdays and Fridays; fruit and vegetables and dried peas and beans, but all of this was handled very efficiently by Little John and his team of burly quartermasters and I had not much more to do than relay messages from the men to Robin. He would make a decision—over a dispute between two men, or about a request to increase the ale or bread ration, or about which *conroi* or squad of archers would do sentry duty that night, or go foraging for game or firewood—and I would relay his verdict to the captain or vintenar concerned.

I was still no nearer to finding out who the would-be assassin was, but there were no more attacks on my master, and it seemed as if the policy of isolating Robin from the men was paying off. He and I went and made music with the

King on several occasions, sometimes with the other troubadours present, including Ambroise and the odious Bertran de Born, and sometimes just the three of us. I could tell that the King had a real liking for Robin's company and I believe that he was fond of me, too. I had helped him to shine with his verses, to look good in front of an audience at the Christmas feast and, in my experience, this is one of the easiest ways of making any man—prince or pauper—feel warmly toward you.

However, things were not going well for the King with regard to his royal cousin Philip Augustus. The French King had been trying to turn Tancred away from Richard and there had been much whispering, and many secret meetings in which Philip had urged Tancred not to trust Richard. Our King was understandably annoyed with his boyhood friend for this treacherous behavior but he arranged a private meeting with Tancred, gave him lavish gifts and solemn promises, and managed to convince the shaky Sicilian monarch that he meant him no harm. However, there was a much more serious event on the horizon—a genuine cause for resentment on King Philips's side—that threatened to capsize the Great Pilgrimage before it even set sail from Sicily for the Holy Land: the King's impending marriage to sweet Princess Berengaria of Navarre.

In early March, we heard rumors in the camp that the King was bringing a beautiful princess from northern Spain to Sicily with an eye to marrying her. It was a move that many in the army approved: Richard was going into battle for the cause of Christ, it made sense to secure a bride, and perhaps beget an heir, before he risked his life in combat with the Saracens. But the fly in the ointment was that, for more than twenty years, Richard had been betrothed to Alice, the sister of the King of France. Alice was a sad woman: she had been a guest at the English court for so long—since Richard was a little boy, in fact—that she had a certain shop-soiled quality.

When she was a nubile teenager, King Henry, Richard's father, had seduced her to his bed. After a few years he had grown bored with her and abandoned her. And Richard, who was formally betrothed to her, had tactlessly declared that he would rather be damned for all eternity than marry a woman who had been his father's whore.

I could understand Richard's point of view. I should not care to plow the same furrow as my father, but marriage for kings is an act of statecraft and his fastidiousness made things even more difficult with King Philip, who had been urging Richard to proceed with the marriage to Alice. Richard politely demurred and as time went by this became the biggest cause of the ill-feeling between the two monarchs. Now the news was out that Richard was bringing another bride to Sicily, a beautiful Navarrese princess. And King Philip now declared that he was furious at his family's humiliation at the hands of not one, but two Kings of England.

As usual, there was an easy way to mollify the proud French king. Richard sent him a gift of ten thousand marks in gold when his betrothal to Berengaria was publicly announced, and our King had the good sense not to publicly flaunt the fact that his bride-to-be, accompanied by his mother Queen Eleanor of Aquitaine, was en route to Sicily.

However, Philip had still grumpily declared his intention to leave with all his troops for the Holy Land at the end of March so that he would not be present when this affront to his sister's honor arrived in Messina.

King Philip of France and four great ships sailed slowly out of Messina harbor on the last day of the month, to the cheers of Richard's entire army, which had been assembled by direct order of the King to wish their brother warriors of Christ a fair voyage to Outremer. The next day a small but richly appointed ship arrived, discreetly bearing Princess Berengaria of

Navarre, Queen Eleanor of Aquitaine—and my old friend and erstwhile musical mentor Bernard de Sezanne.

I had not seen Bernard for a year and a half, and while I had grown taller and filled out my frame, he had not changed in the slightest except that, as Queen Eleanor's much admired *trouvère,* he was far more richly dressed than when he had been my musical teacher in our outlaw days. In fact, he was something of a popinjay in crimson and green hose and a crimson and gold embroidered tunic. He wore a magnificent velvet hat that looked like a large loaf of Sicilian bread with a long sweeping feather that arced out of the side. Beside him in my drab brownish-green tunic and hose, and travel-worn gray hood, I felt dowdy and pedestrian.

I took him to the Lamb, the tavern in Messina where I regularly met with the other *trouvères.* Having delivered Berengaria safely, Bernard and his mistress Queen Eleanor were leaving Sicily in a day or two, to return to England, and I wanted a chance to talk to him before they left. The tavern provided the two things I knew that Bernard would require for a successful evening: large quantities of wine and a musically appreciative company. Little John was on duty with Robin and so I was at liberty. Bernard and I got to the tavern early, the sun had not yet sunk below the mountains of the west, so I could be sure of some time alone with my friend before the rest of the pack of musicians arrived.

"Well, young Alan," said Bernard, smiling kindly, "you look more like a rough soldier every time I see you. I hope you have not given up the musical life." He was looking at the battered sword and long poniard that hung habitually from two thick leather belts at my waist. I assured him that I had not, and I could not help but boast a little about my popularity with King Richard, and his respect for me as a singer. "So does life in this great swarm of would-be martyrs suit you?" he asked. I allowed that it did, and told him of my newfound prowess with the lance; I was in the middle of a tale of heroic success at charging the quintain when I noticed that his eyes had become dull and glazed, and swiftly ended the story, ordered more wine and changed the subject. "And how are things in England?" I asked.

"They are not good, Alan, to be honest, not good at all," he said, and sighed. His demeanor was sad but I sensed something, perhaps a small amount of joy at being able to deliver bad news. "The country is deeply uneasy with Richard away; each baron is fortifying his castle, the towns are building strong walls. The Welsh are making trouble, too. But the main problem is that little Willie Longchamp, the King's Justiciar, is loathed by absolutely everybody and he can't seem to control his own household, let alone the country. He is an awful little man—no music in him at all—but Richard did make him Justiciar and you would think he would therefore be able to command some respect; but it seems not and his authority is now being seriously challenged by—guess who?—Richard's royal, if not loyal, brother John.

"Our stay-at-home princeling now swanks about the land in a quite preposterous regal style, with his own justicar, his own royal court, a chancellor, royal seals, everything—and his servants talk openly about John being the next King, if Richard were to die while on this pilgrimage. It's quite ridiculous when everybody knows that little Prince Arthur is Richard's acknowledged heir. It's not good, Alan, with the King out of the country, there's no one to keep these ambitious little toads in line . . ." and he broke into a line of poetry:

"As the earth grows dark when the sun departs,
So a kingdom is diminished by the absence of its king."

He took a long swig of wine, and wiped his mouth on his gorgeous crimson sleeve. "And I have worse news," he said, lowering his voice. "I went to see the Countess of Locksley to pick up a letter she wanted me to give to Robin, and I found her in a terrible way. Oh, she's fine in her health and looks, and she keeps up a noble front, but she's very unhappy."

He paused and I realized that he had been waiting to deliver this piece of bad news since he met me at the harbor side.

"Go on," I said neutrally.

"Well, there are these dreadful rumors about her, which are being spread by that snake Ralph Murdac, appalling rumors, the worst kind, and totally untrue, of course, but they worry her and she fears they will reach Robin's ears." He was only just managing to conceal his glee at having such a delicious piece of gossip to impart.

I leaned into him, frowning: "What rumors," I said. I could feel myself growing angry. "What rumors, Bernard?" I said louder in a hard tone of voice. Bernard looked at me. "Don't get upset with *me*, Alan, I'm just the messenger, I'm not the one spreading them; I haven't told a soul. But people *are* talking."

I managed to control my temper. I was very fond of Marie-Anne, the Countess of Locksley. I had even believed myself to be in love with her for a while, and I did not like to have her name sullied by anyone. "What are they saying?" I asked, trying for a more reasonable tone of voice. Bernard was Bernard, after all, my anger would not change him.

"Well, don't get upset, and don't say you heard it from me, but people are saying that . . ." he faltered for a few moments. But I said flatly: "Just tell me, Bernard." And finally, after much wriggling and prevarication, he did.

"They are saying, Alan, and I am sure it is totally untrue, that the Countess was the lover of Ralph Murdac in the summer before last, and that the Countess's son, Hugh, who is acknowledged as the Earl of Locksley's heir, is actually Murdac's flesh and blood." He sat back, having delivered this hammer blow, and watched for my reaction.

I hope I disappointed him: I held my face blank, took a sip of wine and a deep breath. "What a stupid notion," I said dismissively. "Marie-Anne Locksley was Ralph Murdac's lover? Absurd." And I attempted a light chuckle. It came out like a donkey braying in pain.

I was spared from having to develop this rebuttal by the arrival of Ambroise and a couple of the other *trouvères*. I just had time to whisper savagely to Bernard that he must hold his tongue about this matter—he would not, of course—before we were swept up in the whirlwind of vinous merrymaking that always surrounded Ambroise and his friends. While Bernard and the jolly Norman butterball were introducing themselves, swapping bawdy jokes and ordering up more wine—it took less than a quarter of an hour for them to become bosom friends, by the way—I was thinking about my beautiful friend, and Robin's beloved girl, Marie-Anne, the gossip-smirched Countess of Locksley. I had a big problem: despite my play-acting with Bernard, I knew that the kernel of these foul rumors—that Robin's son was in fact Murdac's—was true. And this truth could destroy us all.

CHAPTER TWELVE

I understand, now that I have had children, why blood is so important. When my son Rob died, I felt that quite literally a part of me had passed on as well. My wife and I had raised him with love and care and we had poured all our hopes and dreams in to him. If he had been the son of another man, would I have loved him so much, or felt his death quite so keenly? Perhaps so. But I doubt I would have felt so powerfully that he *was* me, in some strange way, and that his death was my death. Then, of course, in the spring of the Year of Our Lord 1191, when I realized that Marie-Anne's child Hugh was not Robin's son, my first thought was for the shame that Robin must feel. It was bad enough that his wife had been bedded by Sir Ralph Murdac, that in itself would have given cause for many men to disown their wives—that it must have been rape made no difference—but for her to have been impregnated by another man, and a mortal enemy at that, was almost too shameful to contemplate.

There were several reasons why I knew that Hugh must truly be Murdac's son, and why I knew that Robin knew this, too. Firstly, I had noticed the signs of a forced coupling on Marie-Anne's clothing—her dress was torn and bloody—when Robin, Reuben and I had rescued her from Murdac's grasp in Nottingham Castle nearly two years ago. Ralph Murdac had captured her, after the death of King Henry but before Richard had returned to England and taken a firm grip on the throne. Murdac had been hoping, no doubt, to use her as a bargaining tool and as a way of putting pressure on Robin. Secondly, when Robin had killed her captors, he had taken her into his arms and asked if she were hurt; he was in truth asking whether Murdac had dishonored her. I remember her answer clearly. She did not say, "I am unharmed," or "I have not been hurt," but only, "All is well now that you are here." I am sure that if she had been untouched by Murdac she would have said so. The third reason why I knew the child was Murdac's was the coloring of baby Hugh: black hair and pale blue eyes. Despite what Goody had told me about babies changing their looks after birth, it seemed too much of a coincidence that, of all the people in Christendom, the baby should resemble Sir Ralph Murdac so closely. And anyway, the wise women say that immediately after birth, a baby resembles its father, and then later it takes on more of the look of the mother. The fourth point was the previously inexplicable disharmony between Robin and Marie-Anne immediately after the birth. Robin knew the child was not his—and it was my sacred duty to make sure that the rumor was squashed and that my master never found out that I was aware of his ignoble secret.

But, quite apart from Bernard's loose tongue—and Robin would quite readily tear it from his head if he found out that my friend had been spreading this news—Murdac's whisperers would be doing their work in England and there was a real danger that, when Robin returned, he would be a laughingstock. People would assume that he wore the horns of a cuckold, even though the truth was that Marie-Anne had been forced against her will by a monster. Robin would never admit that; he would never admit that he had been unable to protect the woman he loved. And how would this sad business affect the relations between husband and wife? If it became common knowledge, would Robin disinherit Hugh, throw him out of the family? And how would Marie-Anne feel about her baby being universally known as a bastard, a child of rape, a nobody born out of wedlock? She would never admit the truth of that. But could Robin accept a cuckoo in the nest?

As I sat pondering these terrible truths, the party in the tavern was becoming raucous: Ambroise and Bernard were swapping couplets of dirty poetry with each other with great relish, and downing full cups of unwatered wine, and one of the other *trouvères* was already dancing with one of the Sicilian serving women. Leaving them to their revels, I slipped away to find my master.

I found Robin in his chamber in the monastery, reading the letter from Marie-Anne. His face was a cold, emotionless mask and as I entered the room on the pretext of bringing him his evening meal, he gave me a look of such blank metallic savagery that I almost lost my nerve and retreated.

"Your supper, sir," I said quietly. And he merely indicated that I should put it on the table with a wave of his hand. I tore off a piece of the roast chicken with my fingers and took it over to Keelie, who had been watching my movements with great interest from a rush basket in the corner of the room.

"Good news from England, sir?" I asked disingenuously, crouched with my back to Robin, as the one-eyed dog licked the chicken gravy from my hand.

"No," said Robin. And that flat single syllable sounded like a tombstone being dropped on to the grass of a churchyard cemetery. I turned to look at the Earl of Locksley; the letter was lying on the table next to his supper, but he was staring at the stone floor, seemingly in some sort of trance. For ten heartbeats he did not move; I stared at him, he stared at the floor. Then he dragged his gaze up to meet mine and said: "It seems your friend Prince John is causing trouble; wants to be King, I hear." He attempted a smile, but it never reached his gray eyes. I wanted to say something, to comfort him, to tell him that it was all right, that it was not his fault that Murdac had ruined him, that it was not Marie-Anne's fault either. But the gulf between lord and vassal was too wide. "Would you mind leaving me, Alan," said Robin. He sounded unbearably weary. "And tell the men that we will be departing in a week or so for Outremer and so they should prepare themselves. And tell Little John, oh, never mind, I'll tell him in the morning. Good night." As I left, I saw him pick up the letter again and stare sightlessly at the thick vellum pages. I noticed that his hand was trembling slightly.

We left Messina ten days later: seventeen thousand five hundred soldiers and sailors of Richard's grand army crammed into two hundred ships. Mategriffon had been carefully dismantled, piece by piece, and stored in one of the larger busses; the great destriers of the knights, held safely by two stout belly straps, had been lifted and swung out over the harbor by great cranes and lowered into their places in the larger transport vessels; and Berengaria of Navarre, accompanied by Richard's sister Joanna, had been packed into a sumptuous but weatherly cog with all the comforts a mighty king could provide. With these noble ladies traveled one Arab slave girl, now a lady's maid to Princess Berengaria, and to my mind a woman of such perfect beauty that she outshone any mortal woman alive. I had arranged Nur's new position with Robin's help, and a small gift of silver to Berengaria's chamberlain, and I had never seen her so happy. "Alan," she said in her halting French as she kissed me on the dock, "you are a wonderful man, my savior, my *preux chevalier,* and to reward you for being so kind and good, we shall do that thing again that you like so much, you know, with the leather belts and the honey . . ." I shushed her hurriedly and looked around the harbor hoping that nobody had heard. Two yards behind me stood Little John who was organizing the embarkation of our cavalry. He looked as if he had not heard a thing and I breathed a sigh of relief, too soon, of course. The moment Nur had left me to get into a skiff, he came a little closer: "Tell me, Alan, what is the thing you like to do with the belts and the honey?" he asked in a low, confidential tone.

I flushed a deep red. "It's nothing, really," I mumbled, "in fact, I have no idea what she was talking about." My face was burning and I could not look him in the eye. "She's a foreigner; she doesn't understand what she is saying half the time." I tried a nonchalant shrug.

"Really," said Little John. "Well, I'll just ask her then." And before I could stop him, he cupped his hands around his mouth and bellowed across the open water to the skiff that was carrying my beloved to her ship: "Nur, my darling," he yelled in a voice they could have heard across the strait in Italy. "Tell me: what does young Alan like to do in bed with the honey and the belts . . ." Half a dozen people turned around to stare at his booming voice, and I twisted fast as a grayhound and punched him as hard as I could in the belly.

In hindsight, I think the reason John folded up after my blow to his midriff had more to do with the fact that he was helpless with laughter than the strength of my punch. But, as I continued to hit him with my fists, getting in some quite decent blows to his face and body, he did manage to stop laughing long enough to grab me by the scruff of my neck and by my sword belts lift me furious and struggling off my feet and toss me into the dirty water of the harbor.

★ ★ ★

As the *Santa Maria*'s sail flapped and slowly filled, and the crew hauled on a cobweb of ropes to sharp whistles from the master of the vessel, I realized that I was very glad to be leaving Sicily. I had found love there, and happiness, it was true, but the air of surly menace from the defeated Griffons made me constantly uncomfortable—I never went anywhere unarmed—and the feeling of wasting time, while other Christians died for our cause in Outremer, was not a pleasant one. Also there was the problem of the assassin—I still had no idea who it might be, but I hoped that by leaving Sicily we were leaving him—or her—behind us. I felt hopeful and confident, now that we were off again on the great adventure that I had long dreamed of. God would protect Robin, I was sure, now that we were engaged once again on this holy mission. We were heading for the Holy Land, at last, and with His help and guidance, we would soon bring the might of Richard's immense army to bear on the Saracens. In a few months, perhaps, the holy city of Jerusalem would be free again and under good Christian rule . . .

On the third day out of Messina, near dusk, as the sun dipped low behind us and cast a sail-shaped shadow over the inky waves, a great storm came barrelling in from the south. The swell began to rise causing the ship to twist and buck like a wild horse in its forward progress, the wind picked up, rattling the ropes and straining the old canvas sail almost to breaking point, and huge purple-black clouds came scudding across the gray sky—and with them came black rain, a torrent, lashing down like icy whips on the surface of the water. Crouched under a piece of waxed canvas, at the prow of the *Santa Maria*, the world closed in around me. It was like being under a waterfall. The rain drummed madly on the canvas and the ship bucked and rolled beneath my cowering body; it seemed that God had unleashed his fury on the world, a cataclysm to rival Noah's flood. Peering out from under the soaking cloth I could hardly see the next ship from me, a mere fifty yards away. The archers in the body of the *Santa Maria* were taking turns to bail water with their helmets but I could see that it was having little effect; for every capful of water the men threw overboard ten times as a much again and more crashed over the side as the waves pounded alarmingly against our frail craft. Soon we were alone in a roaring maelstrom of water and shrieking wind, with no other ships in sight, carried along at unbelievable speed, dwarfed by mountainous seas, the soldiers and sailors wailing, beseeching God to show us mercy but the sound coming through only in brief snatches between the smashing of the waves against the ship's hull. I crossed myself and prepared as best I could for death, mumbling "Ave Maria" over and over through salt-wet lips, and I begged the Almighty in his infinite mercy to save the life of my beloved Nur, wherever she might be in this watery Hell, and if he had any spare mercy to save the lives of all the men, including mine, aboard this decrepit wooden shell that had been named in honor of the holy mother of His beloved son Jesus Christ.

All night long the storm raged, the ship tossed like a leaf in a hurricane, and I lost any sense of time passing: I crouched in wretchedness, holding tight to a wooden strut, soaking wet and freezing—my canvas shield long snatched away by a howling wrench of wind—and waiting at any moment for the ship to founder and a black wall of water to fall on me and drown my pain. But by God's grace, she did not. And at dawn a weak watery sun rose in the east and I raised my head from its misery and saw that the tempest had miraculously eased. Our brave vessel was scudding along on a brisk westerly wind, still traveling at an alarming speed, but now was shouldering through big green waves with confidence, and causing no more than a fine spray to whip the ship's sides with each impact. We had lost one man overboard, a sailor who had bravely tried to secure a flapping rope and who had been swept to his doom by a freakishly large burst of seawater but, apart from that poor soul, we were relatively unharmed. We all joined together in a prayer of heartfelt thanksgiving, and I realized that I had been deeply wrong to doubt in God's grace, even for a moment. I should have known that he would save us: we were setting out to do his good work, to save the cradle of Christianity itself. We rinsed our mouths with fresh water, stripped our soaking clothes from our bodies, and began to look about for the other ships of the fleet.

Astoundingly, as the clouds cleared overhead and the sea became even calmer, I could see that many of the other ships of the fleet were still afloat, though none were near us. They were scattered over the surface of the moving sea as far as the horizon on all sides, but still swimming bravely. It truly felt as if the hand of God had protected us from the full fury of the Devil. And, best of all, most wonderful of all, on our starboard bow no more than two dozen miles away, I could make out the low gray-green mass of the island of Crete.

We stayed for two days in the old harbor of Heracleon on Crete, recovering our spirits and waiting for the fleet to reassemble. Although we slept on the ships, there was time to visit dry land and bring on board fresh provisions and water— much of our stores had been damaged by water during the storm. I hired a local skiff and visited Robin, Little John and Reuben aboard their ship the *Holy Ghost*, and learned that most of our fighting men were well and we had lost no more than a dozen to the storm, none of whom I knew well. One of our fellows, a seemingly steady Yorkshireman, had run mad during the storm and had tried to attack the master of his ship before throwing himself into the sea. But the majority of our force was intact and bobbing snugly in Heracleon harbor. Despite this news, I was heartsick with worry: twenty-odd ships had disappeared in the storm, among them the richly appointed royal cog carrying Princess Berengaria, Queen Joanna—and my darling Nur.

On the morning of the third day, when it was quite clear that no more ships would join us in Crete, we headed on for Rhodes, which was a good place to gain news situated as it was on a major sea route. I was racked with guilt: I had loved two women who were not of the Christian faith, a Jew and a Muslim, and I wondered if God, as a punishment for consorting with unbelievers, had decided to take both of them from me. I suspected that I was suffering from a touch of sea fever: I had hardly known Ruth, and to say that I truly loved her was a lie. My worry and guilt over Nur, though, was real enough. I remembered every time we had made love, and tortured myself with those exquisite memories. Why had I been so stupid as to send her into service with the Princess? I should have kept her by my side so that I could protect her, as I had promised to do. That was nonsense, of course, and I knew it—how could I protect her from the sea-borne wrath of God?—but that knowledge did not ease my pain.

We spent ten days in Rhodes, waiting for news of the other ships and because the King fell ill with a mysterious malady that kept him abed for a week, vomiting and shuddering with fever. However, looking back I can remember very little about the time there, consumed as I was with worry about Nur. But we did gain some intelligence. Reuben seemed to have made contact with friends of his in the Holy Land, though how, I did not know. It seemed that King Philip was now outside the walls of Acre—along with German and Italian contingents, which had been there some months—and he was preparing to assault the ancient fortified town. In a sort of cruel joke, the besieging Christian army was itself besieged by Saladin's forces: so there was a Muslim garrison in the stronghold of Acre, surrounded by Christians, who were themselves surrounded by Muslims. The situation did not sound very hopeful for our fellow pilgrims.

Finally we heard news of the ships, and it was mostly bad. Several had been sunk by the storm, and many, many men had drowned, but a few ships had been driven before the tempest. And the Princess's cog, the noble ship that contained my precious girl and the royal women, had made it—battered and bruised—to Limassol in Cyprus. My heart skipped in my chest, my head spun: Nur lived!

Cyprus was a rich land. Like Sicily it abounded with fruit trees, olives, grapes and corn, but it was ruled by an evil tyrant, an upstart called Isaac Comnenus, scion of the ruling house of Byzantium, who was now calling himself the Emperor of Cyprus having seized the island by force a few years back with the help of Greek and Armenian mercenaries. King Richard was incensed because the Emperor had imprisoned some of the men from our ships, which had been beached there after the storm, though not the royal ship, thank the Lord, which was anchored unharmed in a small bay to the west of Limassol. The imprisoned men had been ill-treated, despite their status as holy pilgrims, and the Emperor's men had seized the Great Seal of England, which had been carried by Sir Roger Malchiel, one of Richard's most trusted knights, who had drowned when his ship was wrecked on the rocks of Cyprus. The Emperor had invited the royal women to come ashore but, knowing the fate of their fellow pilgrims, imprisonment for ransom, they had refused. The royal ship had two floating consorts, filled with crossbowmen, plus a handful of men-at-arms. When the Emperor had tried to board the three battered ships, his men had been answered with a barrage of crossbow bolts and forced to withdraw. Berengaria was already wildly popular with the men and they would have laid down their lives to protect her from the Tyrant of Cyprus. So it was stalemate: the three ships were too battered to leave the bay and venture into the open sea; and the Emperor could not force the women to come to the land. When the royal ship asked permission to send a party ashore to collect fresh water and provisions, the Emperor flatly refused.

It was a bad mistake on Isaac Comnenus's part. King Richard was not a man to accept an insult to his sister or his future Queen; so, quite casually, it seemed, he decided that we would take the island of Cyprus by force.

"He's gone mad," said Will Scarlet, as we shared a huge bowl of fish soup in a seafront tavern in Rhodes harbor. It was Lent again, and meat had been forbidden to the entire army. "We must go to King Philip's aid at Acre," Will continued, "and help him to take the city; beat Saladin, then on to Jerusalem. We can't go off and conquer what is practically a whole country just because its ruler was rude to us. He should go and get his women, bring them safely back here and we'll all set off for where God intends us to go: the Holy Land."

I understood his outrage. I was as keen as anyone to reach our destination, but I also knew that Richard was not going to take Cyprus just to avenge a slight. "Robin says the island is the key to recovering the Holy Land," I replied blowing on a spoonful of the rich, fragrant soup to cool it. I was pleased that the food was good, since I was paying for it. Will had always been poor, but he was even more so now that he had been reduced to the ranks and was living on a common soldier's wage. What he did not know, and I did, was that he was about to have to get by on even less. Robin had run through the money given to him by King Richard, and was in debt again. Nobody in our division was likely to see wages in the near future, and I did not begrudge Will a bowl of soup: I still had most of the purse of gold that the King had given me.

"Quite apart from the wealth of the island, which is considerable," I continued, "and the fact that Isaac has no genuine claim to be its ruler, if we take and hold Cyprus, we have a base from which we can attack anywhere along the coast of Outremer. If we lose at Acre, which is almost our last toehold in the Levant, we can still come back to regroup in Cyprus. Robin thinks that Richard had always planned to take the island, and that this disrespect shown to his women merely gives him a decent excuse to invade."

"But it could take months," protested Will. "If the local lords back the Emperor we could be in for a long, hard and costly fight."

"Maybe, but Reuben tells me the Cypriot knights do not love Comnenus. With luck, Richard could take the island in one or two battles. If he shows that he's winning, the local lords will quickly come over to our side."

Will still looked unhappy, but I was thinking that it might be very satisfying to meet the man who had denied my Nur fresh water and food, who was, as we sat here eating, torturing her with thirst and hunger. We finished the soup in silence.

The coast of Cyprus lay before us like a naked whore: lush, inviting, but only to be won at a costly price. Below the pretty whitewashed houses of the town of Limassol, which clustered around a large church and winked at us gaily in the spring sunlight, there was a long stretch of yellow beach: fringed with trees, gently rising, smooth, and the perfect place to land shallow boats. Beyond the town were the rich groves of oranges and lemons, stretching away into the distance, and beyond them, field upon field of gnarled olive trees rising up the slope to the mass of low greeny-purple hills beyond.

We had gathered the royal women in the night before and, suitably refreshed and cleaned, Richard summoned them to a feast on the deck; there he had publically vowed that he would avenge their honor, whatever it took. I had missed his speech as I was locked in a passionate embrace with my lovely Nur in a dark corner of the King's great ship, kissing her beautiful face over and over and promising that I would never leave her again. "I always know . . . you will come . . . for me," she said in her halting French. And it wrung my heart. I gathered her up in my arms and kissing her on the lips vowed that from now on I would always keep her from harm; and so we began to make love. Not once in the next half an hour did I think of a similar promise that I had once made to the Jewess Ruth.

When our lust was expended, we lay in each other's arms half drowsing until I was started from her embrace by a call from William, who, breathless with excitement, told me that the envoy had returned from his embassy to the Emperor. I hauled on my braies and hose, and hastily pulled a tunic over my head, smoothed my hair, and went to hear the news on the upper deck, where a great crowd surrounded the King.

I was just in time to hear the herald say ". . . and then, Sire, when I had relayed your formal demands of restitution to him, he merely looked at me as if I had crawled out from under a rock and said, 'Tproupt, sir!' and dismissed me."

"He said what?" asked the King, his handsome face crunched with puzzlement. He had completely recovered from his illness and was clearly fizzing with high spirits.

" 'Tproupt.' I believe he said, " 'Tproupt, sir.' " The herald looked slightly embarrassed. All around him knights were trying out this unfamilar word, it was like a chorus of doves: "Tproupt!" "Tproupt!" "Tproupt!"

"And what is that supposed to mean?" said the King. "Well, never mind. I suppose it's some Griffon insult or other. Tproupt! How extraordinary. So, that's that then: formalities over, now comes the fun part. Gentlemen . . ." And the King began to issue a gushing stream of orders to his men for the assault on the stronghold of Cyprus.

There was scarcely room to breathe in the snake boat. The shallow craft was packed with Robin's men-at-arms; seventeen big warriors in full armor in a vessel designed to take no more than ten. Robin, Little John and Sir James sat in the front, before the mast, and Will Scarlet and myself were crammed in the belly below the square gray sail with a dozen unhorsed cavalrymen. A grizzled sailor perched on the stern and guided us in with one hand on the steering oar.

We were forced to make the initial attack on the beach with only a fraction of our force: a mere three hundred men. But the King had judged that it would be enough, and each commander had been required to choose his best warriors, and leave the rest to watch from the ships. We seventeen in that tiny boat were the cream of Robin's force, and that thought gave me a great deal of pride. King Richard's problem was a lack of small boats. Every snack, skiff, rowing boat and coracle in the fleet had been assembled for the assault; as only boats with a shallow draft capable of landing on the beach could be used. And all were filled with fighting men; knights and men-at-arms in the first wave, followed by a hundred of Robin's archers in the second wave, plus two boatloads of seasick crossbowmen from Aquitaine.

The low sides of the snake boat were dangerously near the waterline, and if it had sunk we would all have drowned immediately due to the weight of armor we wore. But, strangely, I felt no fear. Once again, the presence of the King, two boats along from us, inspired unreasonable courage in my heart. He had that wonderful quality, my King; of course, he was noble and brave beyond measure, but more than this he made all of us feel that, under his command, anything was possible. We were three hundred men attacking a whole island—and one that was well defended.

The Emperor had been busy in the past few days. A huge barricade had been erected on Limassol beach to deny us a landing; it was constructed, it seemed, from anything that came to hand: huge rocks, sheep hurdles, the broken hulls of rowing boats, old planks and dead trees; enormous urns used for storing olive oil, too, were piled up along with every piece of wood in the town: tables, chairs, footstools, doors, even an altar from the church were stacked in a long line across the beach barring our way in a surprisingly efficient and warlike fashion. And behind this formidable barrier stood nearly two thousand men: Greek knights in brightly polished round helmets, dark-faced Armenian mercenaries, Limassol townsmen armed with pikes and crossbows, Cypriot peasants conscripted from the fields wielding no more than makeshift spears and their grandfathers' rusty swords. They had every advantage on their side: the barricade, the numbers, and their homeland to fight for. We were attacking from the sea with a handful of men, weary from travel, far from home and our clothes heavy, soaking wet from the spray. And yet, when I caught sight of King Richard's eager face as he crouched ready to spring ashore in the lead boat, I knew deep in my heart that we would be victorious.

A hundred yards out from the beach, Robin turned to the boats behind us, shouted an order, and the arrows began to fly. The Welsh archers bent their massive yew bows, aimed high and with a sound like a ripping cloth, loosed a cloud of shafts that rose high into the blue sky and fell like the wrath of the Almighty on to the barricades. The first wave of arrows dropped in gray sheets like killing hail: the steel points of the yard-long arrows slamming through mail coats of the knights just as easily as through the homespun tunics of the peasants, punching deep into the defenders' chests and shoulders and backs to inflict horrible wounds; the men behind the barrier cowered under the onslaught, those with shields holding them above their heads, those without suffering catastrophe as the missiles plunged into their defenseless bodies. The wounded staggered away from the barricade, gouting blood, sometimes from more than one wound. The dead were trampled under mail-shod feet as the thick line of men shifted and writhed under the first lash of our shafts. And then the second wave fell on them, arrows clattering on the wooden table legs of the wall, spearing into a rashly upturned face, even

247

puncturing the cheaper kind of helmet, and dropping men all along the barricade by the score. The third wave slammed down upon them, and a fourth. The pitiful cries of the wounded Greeks were heartbreakingly clear on the salty air but I could also hear Little John, clutching his great war axe and keening to himself, a high-pitched drone that sent shivers down my spine, as we raced toward the shore.

The arrows continued to do their grim work of thinning the enemy line. Our Welshmen in the boats behind us now loosing their shafts at will, no longer in waves but in a looser but never ceasing cloud of falling death; and the Aquitainian crossbowmen, finding themselves in range, now added their bolts to the slaughter. Bodies lay draped across the barrier, leaking blood from many holes, and at the ends of the line, I saw the first peasants slipping away, running up the beach back into the fields to escape this barrage of death, their captains shouting after them. But the center—the hard core of well-protected Greek knights around the Emperor and his golden standard—was solid as an iron bar.

King Richard's boat was the first to crunch up the slope of the beach, wedging itself into the sand. And with a shout of "God and Saint Mary!" our sovereign launched himself out of the vessel, staggered slightly as he landed, and then stood tall. As he surveyed the enemy line, a mere thirty paces away, his bright helm, ringed with a golden crown, glittered in the bright light of noon; a crossbow bolt sliced past his face, and he shifted his shield, the two golden lions of his personal device proud on its red background. His huge sword was upright in his right fist and, without so much as a glance to see whether the rest of his men would follow, our King began to run straight up the beach directly toward the makeshift barricade and the Emperor's golden standard, toward the thickest part of the enemy line.

There was no time to watch our noblest knight attack his enemy as our own boat was driving up the sand and I had to

watch my balance as our craft left the smooth water for unyielding dry land. Robin was out first, leaping onto the sand
and immediately sprinting up the slope to support the King,
and I was tumbling after him, with the crossbow bolts whis-
tling around me, just behind Sir James de Brus and Little
John. In five heartbeats we had reached the wall to the right
of King Richard and the squad of hand-picked household
knights that now surrounded him, who were by now trading
savage blows with their Greek opponents across the ramshackle defense. Robin shouted something to Little John that
I didn't catch. The blond giant dropped his great war axe and,
protected by the swords and shields of Sir James and Robin
himself, began pulling at a giant table that was wedged into
the center of the wall. He took a firm grip of a stout round
leg, bent his knees and hauled. There was a great tearing
noise, and the table shifted a few inches; the Greek knights
who had been engaging Robin and Sir James pulled back in
surprise as the whole barricade seemed to tremble; a crossbowman popped up like a vengeful demon in front of Little
John. He put his bow to his shoulder, aimed it at John's
back—so close that he couldn't miss—and stopped. His head
snapped back, a yard of good English ash growing suddenly
from his eye socket, and he fell away behind the barricade.
Our archers had reached dry land. I cut at a bearded face behind the hedge of wood, and forced it to duck away, and then
a man lunged at me across the divide with a spear and I, in
turn, had to dodge rapidly.

To my left, Little John was still hauling at the table leg;
rocking his body back and forward in short explosive heaves.
He gave one final massive pull, the muscles of his great arms
swelling and writhing, the sweat standing out on his forehead, and suddenly the whole table came grinding out of the
barricade in a great rush, like a cow giving birth to its bloody
calf, leaving a small ragged gap in the enemy defenses. John
lost his balance and tumbled into the sand, but dozens of

eager hands began to tear at the enemy bulwark, ripping away chairs, planks and small boulders, and in a matter of moments a great hole had been ripped in the center of the wall—through which our gallant King rushed without a moment's pause or thought for his safety; and we all—Robin, Sir James, myself and a dozen of his bravest knights—came charging after him in a howling phalanx of steel and fury.

I had my sword in my right hand and my poniard in my left; my head was covered with a tightly fitting dome of steel and my body from wrist to knee was protected with a hauberk of fine steel links, and I was determined to bring death to the men of Cyprus who had insulted my Nur. A Greek knight shouted a challenge at me and swung his sword at my head; I ducked and he slammed into me with his shield, but I was ready for this move and rolled my body round his shield to his left away from the sword and hacked at the back of his knees with my own long blade. The blow did not break through his mail leggings but it dropped the knight to his knees, and I dropped my sword, grappled his helmet with my right hand, hauled it back to expose his neck and quick as summer lightning sliced through his throat with my poniard. The blood gushed hotly as I dropped his twitching body, and I immediately knelt to recover my sword—and saved my own life. Another sword slashed through the air above my head, I felt its wind on my neck, and I turned and lunged with my recovered long blade, almost in one movement, catching the attacking man-at-arms neatly in the groin with the tip of my weapon. His armor consisted only of a boiled leather *cuirasse* and a kind of leather kilt and he stumbled away, hands cupped over his cock and balls, the blood leaking through his fingers. We had burst through the line of Cypriots, and I saw to my left King Richard engaged with a mass of knights in rich armor; Robin was beside him, hacking and lunging, fighting like a maniac; and there was Little John, cutting a knight from his horse with a great blow from his axe and a spray of gore.

Another knight attacked me, a decent swordsman, it must be said, and we cut and parried three times, circling each other between blows, but his attention was not on me. He kept looking left and right, seeing to his dismay that his fellows were fleeing the barricade as more and more of our men-at-arms—and scores of Welsh archers who had abandoned their bows to fight with the short swords and axes—boiled through the gap that Little John had torn in their extraordinary defenses. I wasn't concentrating on my opponent fully either, for I, too, was astounded at how quickly the enemy were leaving the field of battle. And I nearly paid dearly for my lack of attention. The knight suddenly stepped in and chopped straight down at me with his long sword, a mighty blow that would have crushed my skull had it landed, and only just in time I blocked with poniard and sword crossed together, my arms almost buckling under the strength and savagery of his attack. Then suddenly, miraculously, his head flew from his shoulders, the square steel helmet with its leaking stump of neck rolling several yards over the ground. The body stayed standing for a few heartbeats and then the legs folded underneath it and it slumped to the bloody ground and I was left standing and facing Sir James de Brus with his bloody sword held double-handed and now extended above his left shoulder in the classic warrior's pose.

"Are you quite well, Alan?" the Scotsman said, looking at me with a puzzled frown. "It's not like you to take so long to dispatch just one man."

"I was distracted, James," I replied. "Look yonder." And I pointed to the edge of the beach with my bloody poniard. The self-proclaimed Emperor of Cyprus was riding for the tree line as fast as his horse would carry him, escaping like the coward he was to the safety of the hills. Behind him followed a shamefaced group of richly caparisoned, well-armored knights, all apparently unwounded, and in the center of the imperial bodyguard, the Emperor's standard of golden embroidered cloth flapped limply in the mild sea breeze.

I had expected some sort of pause after our victory on the beach, perhaps just an hour to tend to our wounds and take a drink of cool water and a bite of bread. But King Richard seemed to be in even more of a hurry than he was before the battle. He grabbed the Earl of Locksley by the shoulder as Robin came up to him on the blood-soaked strand, and said urgently: "There is not a minute to waste; I must have the horses; as quickly as you can, Robert, get me horses for my knights. Get them from anywhere."

Robin turned to me: "You heard him, Alan: horses. Take a squad of men and get up to the town; requisition any steed you can lay your hands on. Quickly."

"Requisition?" I said. I knew what the word meant but I wanted to be clear about what he was ordering me to do. I didn't want to risk being hanged as a thief.

"Oh, for God's sake, Alan, it means steal, take, confiscate. Just go and get the King his horses, as many as you can, any way that you can. You have my permission. And saddles, too, if you can find them. We can't let the Emperor get away."

I rounded up a dozen archers, who were going through the clothing of the dead on the beach and slitting the throats of any enemy wounded they found, and managed to lead them— they were reluctant to follow me away from their pickings—up the beach to the dusty road that led to Limassol.

The town was almost deserted, evidently the people had seen the way the wind was blowing and had fled the place to preserve their lives and possessions, but while there was ample opportunity for plunder, I told the men that I would personally see any man who stole without my permission whipped to bloody rags. I meant it, too.

Limassol was an eerie place without any visible inhabitants, but a pretty town filled with wide sunny squares and cheerful whitewashed houses with blue-painted shutters. In front of many a house was a paved forecourt where vines hung from trellises and provided shade in the summer. And it was behind one of these pleasant dwellings, larger than the rest and with the air of a great man's inn, that we found a corral with a dozen horses. The inn even provided five rather battered saddles and, with my permission, the men helped themselves to some food they found in the kitchen, although I banned them from sampling a barrel of wine that we found already broached in the buttery.

Mounted on the "requisitioned" animals, we found it a speedy business to scour the town for horseflesh and by early evening we had two dozen or so steeds of varying quality—including carthorses, mules and one old mare that looked more than ready for a merciful death—in a loose herd being trotted toward the beach.

The battlefield had changed significantly since the noon fight; the barricade had been totally dismantled and the bay was full of ships, which had come in to land as close as they could for their draft. Skiffs and snacks plied between the big ships and the shore, ferrying provisions, arms, armor and rather seasick-looking horses to the beach. The animals were frightened and confused after the long sea journey, and particularly spooked by the final stage when they had been rowed, one big horse to a tiny rocking boat, from the transport ships to the beach. They were being fed and watered by squires on the sand and walked up and down the beach to regain their nerves and equilibrium.

I delivered my herd to King Richard's grooms and they were added to a large bunch of animals that had been gathered from the surrounding countryside; some, evidently, had been the property of rich knights until recently, their Greek owners having either perished or been captured in the battle.

I dismissed the archers and went to seek further orders from Robin. I found him with the King, and a gathering of leading knights, clerks and members of the King's *familia*.

Sir Robert of Thurnham, the King's High Admiral, was speaking as I joined the group, standing behind Robin on the fringes as befitted my lowly status. The sun was sinking at the far end of the beach, setting the sea on fire, in dazzling hues of red and gold, catching the King's bright locks and seeming to give them an effect almost like a halo. "Sire," said Sir Robert, "our scouts have followed their army and they tell me that the Emperor and his knights are no more than five miles away, and are preparing to spend the night." He cleared his throat, and continued. "But it seems that there are many more of them than we had imagined. The Emperor has been reinforced by knights from the north of the island who arrived too late today to participate in the battle."

"How many are they?" asked the King; he was staring up into the air watching a pair of swallows twist and turn about each other in some elegant avian game.

"Well, sire, the scouts say," Sir Robert swallowed, "more than three thousand men in all, including servants, camp followers and the like. With more men reported to be on the way. When we have disembarked all the men and horses, we shall easily overmatch them, but that cannot be achieved until the end of the week, at the very earliest."

"I will attack them now, tonight, with whatever knights can find a horse and a saddle and have the courage to follow me. I cannot wait until the end of the week. The Emperor will slip away and hide in the mountains if I do not smash him now; and then it will be months before I can take this island. No. I must strike him now."

"But, sire, that is madness," said a senior clerk, a weaselly little fellow called Hugo, whom I knew slightly and heartily disliked. "They are more than three thousand, and we have but fifty horses, look, sire . . ." and he waved his arm toward the corral where less than three score seasick and mismatched animals were being fed with some rather damp, and no doubt salty, hay.

"Sir clerk," said Richard frostily, and I realized with a little peep of wicked pleasure that the King had just been called a madman to his face, "you stick to papers and books, and leave the fighting and the chivalry to us." I stifled a smile to see the clerk put down, but there were more serious matters at hand. The King was attempting a night attack on an army three thousand strong with a tiny force of ill-mounted knights; and the odds against us were sixty to one. Each knight would be facing sixty enemies. Sixty! Perhaps the clerk was right, perhaps the King *was* mad!

CHAPTER THIRTEEN

I counted fifty-two knights when we formed up above the beach in complete darkness, and almost in silence, for there was a somber air about our coming endeavor; all metal accoutrements on the saddles had been muffled with cloth, lest it clink during our advance and give warning to the Emperor's men; the knights spoke in whispers, gravely, as befitted men who were facing death, although I do not believe there was a single coward among them. Priests moved on silent feet through the horsemen, blessing weapons, sprinkling holy water on the knights and murmuring prayers. The most fortunate, including the King and the Earl of Locksley, were mounted on the destriers of captured Griffon knights; the less fortunate on assorted animals, some no better than the cart-horses and mules that I had rounded up from Limassol, or on beasts that had been brought ashore from the ships that evening. I was on Ghost, who had recovered remarkably quickly from his ordeal on the wild ocean, and seemed to relish having his four feet on dry land. I caught sight of Sir Richard Malbête mounted on a thin two-year-old which looked too frail to bear his weight. He caught my look and returned it with his flat feral stare; then, holding my gaze, he ran a finger down the red scar on the side of his face. I smiled at him mockingly, showing my teeth.

At a quiet signal from the King, we moved off in two files, with scouts ahead and to the sides, trying to keep in position and make as little noise as possible as we rode through the orange groves, sniffing a hint of fragrant blossom on the still air. The May night was warm, and a big yellow half-moon gave us enough light to see the man riding in front and beside us; I was feeling nervous, I admit, the ice snake slithering once again in my belly; but I was prepared to trust my King to lead us to victory as he had done so swiftly that morning.

After about an hour, the column came to a halt in an open space behind a low ridge, and with the minimum of fuss those knights with lances, about half of our pathetic force, formed a line in front, and those of us without, including myself, who had not thought to bring more than my usual sword and poniard, and my mace, formed a line behind. The knights in the front rank, each wielding a twelve-foot razor-edged spear, would be the shock troops. They would primarily use the weight of their chargers and the points of their lances to ride over and crush any formation of men that opposed them; the second wave, would mop up behind them, attacking the shattered lines of the enemy with sword and mace. That was the theory.

The King rode between the two lines, addressing us in a low carrying voice. "Gentlemen," he said, "you have all fought with great courage today already, and we have tasted sweet victory. But I ask you now to fight again, to show your prowess once more in our cause. They are many, and we are few; but they have been beaten once and will be beaten again. Now they sleep, warm in their blankets, thinking that we are far away, but we shall show them how this army can fight. Yes, they are many, and we are but a handful, but think how much glory we shall share between us, we few, when victory is ours." The King turned his horse and began to ride back down the lane between the two ranks of horsemen. He caught my eye as he passed and smiled, his eyes gleaming in the moonlight.

"God is with us in this endeavor, and our cause is just," he said, only just audibly. I could see the knights leaning forward in their saddles to hear him. "Now listen close: we will ride straight for the Emperor, and make him our prisoner; nothing else matters. Shout your war cries, call on God's blessing and ride straight for the golden standard; with that in our hands the battle is done, the enemy will melt away like snow in springtime. God be with you all."

And he took his place in the center of the front line.

"Forward," the cry came harshly in the still night, "for God and King Richard." It was louder, far louder than the King's words, and I realized that it was Robin's voice, his battle voice, which could be heard for half a mile, and at the same time two trumpeters began to sound their horns, blasting out the order to charge, ta-ta-taaaa, ta-ta-taaa. It was shocking in the stillness of the orange groves to hear such a tumult, and that was its intention, to cause shock and terror in the enemy; the first line gave a great shout, each man bellowing his war cry, and the line went forward, up the slope of the hill and disappeared over the crest; I shouted "Westbury!" adding my voice to those of my companions, and we in the second line put our spurs to work and followed obediently behind them.

Over the crest of the hill we charged down the slope into a wide grove of olive trees filled with the sleeping enemy. The field was a mass of dark tents and dotted campfires, horses were tethered to the gnarled stunted trees, and dark, blanket-wrapped forms, which leaped to their feet as the first wave of cavalry swept into the camp. The first line thundered into the tents, trumpets squealing, men roaring their challenges, trampling the sleeping forms within and snapping guy ropes with their horses legs. Any man who was upright was quickly speared by a passing knight, the lance abandoned in the body as the horseman rode by, pulling out his long sword to strike at the next man-shaped shadow in the gloom. Our second line came after them, screaming our war cries and bringing our swords to bear on the bewildered enemy.

The whole camp was convulsed in panic as fifty steel-wrapped killers were set loose to rip and slice into the half-awake, half-dressed Cypriots; their cries of terror drowning out our shouts of victory as we slashed and hacked at running shapes in the darkness. We hunted them through the sagging, drunken tents, riding level to a running shape and cutting back and down with the sword before spurring on to seek fresh victims. I was glad that I could not see clearly the results of our handiwork as we cantered between the trees, slicing into white faces with no discrimination at all. I am certain, and I pray that God will forgive me for this grave sin, that at least one or two of my victims were women, but I did not stop to count the cost to the enemy, for in the center of the camp was a ring of torches and in the flickering firelight I could make out a large, striped tent in gaudy green and yellow, and next to that, flaccid in the still air, guarded by two mounted knights, splashed by torchlight, was the golden standard of the Emperor himself.

I put my heels into Ghost and headed for the light. And I was not the only one; there were riders to my left and right, some very familiar, others less so, but we all had the same aim, to converge on the Emperor, and seize him before the whole camp was roused, and mounted, and fully armed—at which point thousands of swords would come to seek our lives.

A dark shape came blundering out of the darkness to my left and I smashed into its head with my mace. Another came

259

straight at me, and I changed Ghost's line slightly with my knees and speared him through the body with my sword. The blade stuck in his ribs and I almost lost my blade; it was only with a wrench that hurt my wrist that I got the blade free of his body before Ghost was past him.

As I approached the Imperial tent, I saw that a fierce fight had broken out around the torch-lit circle; I saw the King cut down one Greek knight with his sword, while fending off another at the same time; Robin was beside him, and Sir James de Brus, each dueling with mounted men; one of the standard bearers was punched from his saddle by a well-aimed lance, driven deep by a knight I did not know and the other man, who was carrying that golden flag, reined in, turned his horse and made a break for the darkness.

I screamed "Westbury!" and leveled my bloody sword, drumming my heels into Ghost's flanks, and the man half turned, saw me and kicked his own horse onward. But another of Richard's knights was there in the darkness before him; I saw no more than a flash of scarlet and blue from the surcoat of the other knight, but the standard bearer turned again, away from this new enemy and galloped back straight at me. He lifted his sword as our horses were nose to nose, and made a great cut at my left shoulder; but I blocked with the steel shaft of the mace and at almost the same time my spearing sword took him straight in the eye.

There was a crack like a snapping twig, and a lightning strike of pain, and I realized my sword was gone, and my right hand was canted at an awful angle. But when I turned to look at my flag-bearing opponent, I saw that he was flopping, stone dead, but still in his saddle, the sword embedded in his skull, as the animal slowed to a trot and then a walk. Wheeling round, tucking my mace into my belt and hugging my broken wrist to my chest, I came up to the dead knight's horse and leaning over plucked the golden standard from its holder on his saddle with my left hand. I threw back my head and screamed, half in triumph and half from the pain that was shooting up my right hand with sickening intensity.

I raised the golden standard high in the sky with my left hand, and screamed again. I was alone on the battlefield, victorious, with the enemy standard, the repository of his honor in my hand; all the Griffons seemed to have fled or found hiding places in the darkness. But then, out of the corner of my eye, I suddenly saw movement. A horse was walking toward me, picking its way through the bodies, and on its back, in a blood-smeared scarlet and sky blue surcoat, was Sir Richard Malbête.

He stopped a dozen paces from me, and cocked his head on one side. We were completely alone in the dark camp, and all that could be heard were a few muffled shouts and screams away in the darkness. "Lost your sword, I see, singing boy," said Sir Richard. And he laughed, a low bubbling sound of sheer malice. "I think you'd better hand over that pretty little flag to me then."

For some strange reason, I thought of Reuben, and the strange foreign words he had spoken in the battle at York.

"Come and get it, you bastard," I said, gritting my teeth against the pain in my wrist. But Sir Richard, it appeared, was not even listening to me, he was leaning over and fiddling with something on the far side of his horse, seemingly hauling on something, a rope or leather strap, I supposed. Then he straightened up and smirked at me. "I shall," he said. And with a great lurch of my stomach, I saw that he was holding a cocked and loaded crossbow in his two hands, and pointing the weapon straight at my body.

He shot, the bolt blurred, and a blow like the kick from a horse smacked into my right side. I was knocked sideways out of the saddle by the force of the quarrel and I was only dimly aware of my shoulders hitting the hard ground before I slipped into a deep darkness.

PART THREE

OUTREMER

CHAPTER FOURTEEN

Dickon's wife Sarah came to see me last night. Her swineherd husband faces the manor court of Westbury tomorrow, if I choose to bring charges against him. If I wished I could even send him to a King's court for the felony of theft. He would receive a grim penalty if found guilty by the King's traveling judges; and his guilt would be easily demonstrated. Half a dozen witnesses have heard him boasting that he stole my piglets, witnesses who are my tenants, men whose families I could throw out into the street if I were displeased with them.

Sarah was shown into my hall by Marie, while I was sitting alone by the fire, long past dusk with a mug of warmed ale in my hand. It was very nearly my bedtime but I threw off my tiredness when I saw her. The tears were streaming down her old face, and she threw herself on the rush-strewn floor in front of me, startling one of my deerhounds from its slumber.

The dog gave her a mournful look and then trotted away to find a more peaceful place to sleep.

Her boots were crusted with snow, and her shawl was white-dusted, too, and I wondered whether we were in for a very hard winter as I waited for her to speak. I called for the hall servants to throw another log on the fire, to bring a stool for Sarah to sit upon and to bring another mug of ale.

Marie showed that she was angry at these small courtesies by banging dishes down hard on the long table as she cleared away the remains of supper. But I ignored her and said: "Get up from the floor, Sarah, and sit. Tell me what it is you want—why do you disturb my peace on this cold night?"

"Oh, sir, it's my old fool Dickon. He is drunk again on Widow Wilkins's strong mead, and cursing you something horrible, and he is . . ." she halted, and I encouraged her to continue. She took a sip of ale. "Oh, sir, he is talking of slitting his own throat. He says you will send him to the King's court and they will hang him . . . and he vows he will not die that way. He says he would rather die by his own hand, like a soldier, and risk eternal damnation, than be hanged as a common felon. I tell him you would not send him to the judges, not for a piglet or two, and that it will just be the manor court and a fine. But he is mad, sir, and he sits in our cottage muttering and swearing foul oaths and drinking yet more and sharpening his knife. Oh, sir, tell me you will not send him to the King's court."

"He stole from me," I said, as coldly as I could manage. "He admits it. Year after year, he took my property and laughed while he robbed me. What would you have me do? There must be justice in Westbury."

She broke down into another fit of violent sobbing that seemed to rack her very soul. And like the soft old fool that I am, I was moved by her tears. "Come, Sarah," I said. "This is no good. Go home now and tell Dickon that he must present himself to me tomorrow morning, sober and clean, and remorseful, and we two men will discuss this matter then."

When the woman had gone, I went over to the big chest where I keep my most precious possessions and, rummaging in the deepest recesses, I found what I was looking for: an ordinary old sword in a battered leather scabbard. I pulled the blade from the scabbard and gazed down at the gray metal, my own tired face reflected back at me. How many men had I slaughtered with this weapon, I wondered? Too many to count, surely. And yet it was an age-old symbol of justice; in the King's hands it signified the power to kill in the name of the law. I made a cut in the air, just as an experiment, and the blade sliced cleanly through the drifting smoke of the hall; my right arm was unaccustomed to the weight of the sword, and my once-broken wrist gave a twinge, but it felt good in my hand. I cut again, and again, my feet moving smoothly in the old patterns, drummed into me by my old friend Sir Richard at Lea, as I lunged and parried, fencing with an imaginary foe.

"What in the world do you think you are doing?" said a sharp voice. It was Marie. "Put that thing away before you do yourself a mischief. You're not twenty years old anymore. Not even twice that!"

For a brief moment, just a heartbeat, the Devil inspired me with a wild urge to strike down my daughter-in-law for those disrespectful words. For a moment, I honestly wanted to turn and hack at her neck and leave her twitching in a pool of blood. I saw myself clearly standing over her corpse, gory blade in hand, my body once again filled with the vigor of battle, the power of youth. And then I regained my senses, God be praised, and I slid the old sword back in its sheath, put it away and sat back down once again by the flickering fire.

Marie came over and draped a thick woolen shawl around my shoulders. "It's cold tonight," she said kindly. But I did not deign to reply. I merely took another sip of my warmed ale. There was honey in it.

A bright strip of luminous yellow hovered in front of my eyes; an angel, perhaps, showing me the path to Heaven? Not an angel. And too painful to look at. It took me a very long while to recognize that it was hot sunlight, spilling onto a white-washed wall. I closed my eyes. When I opened them the yellow strip had moved, and broadened at the base. Gradually I became aware of noises, too: the scurry of sandaled feet on stone; a gentle murmur of conversation; occasionally a cry of pain or the splash of liquid in a bowl. My mouth dry as sun-bleached bone, my tongue rough as a pine log, I closed my eyes again and slept.

This time when I awoke, there was someone leaning over me: dark glossy hair framing a white drawn face with huge sorrowful eyes. The strip of sunlight was now a block of gold on the wall, and I thought: evening. A cool wet cloth was applied to my forehead—it felt wonderful—and a little water was trickled into my mouth. A single word came into my head, a single beautiful, loving syllable: Nur.

She trickled more water between my parched lips, and I swallowed painfully, blinked at her and struggled to sit up, but a small white hand pushed me down with ease.

"Where am I?" said a harsh, croaking voice, which I hardly recognized as my own.

"Shhh, my darling," said Nur. "Drink, don't speak. You are in Akka, in the Hospitallers' quarter, in a dormitory. You have been sick, very sick. But the fever has passed. You are safe now. I am here."

"Acre?" I whispered, and Nur poured a little more water into my mouth. "Don't speak; drink," she said. "Drink and sleep." Her lovely face went away and came back with a clay bowl filled with a bitter liquid. She guided the cool rim to my mouth, supporting my head, which strangely seemed to weigh more than a boulder, and I sipped the rank liquid, and with some difficulty swallowed most of it down. The effort exhausted me, and I let my head flop back onto the pillow and dropped into a bottomless hole.

When I awoke again it was gray morning, Nur was gone. I turned my head and looked left and right: I was in a large, cool stone chamber, in a bed in a row of similar ones, all but one occupied by sleeping men. At the far end of the row of beds, a large, plain wooden cross was fixed to the wall and below it an old man wearing nothing but a chemise sat upright on his cot; he was skeletally thin and almost totally bald; a mere few whisps of white hair covered his pink scalp. He saw that I was awake and smiled and nodded at me but said nothing. I smiled back and then looked away. My head felt clear: Acre, I thought; in the care of the Knights Hospitaller, a monastic order famed for healing the sick and fighting the paynim in the name of Christ. I was safe.

Shards of memory began to roll and tumble through my head; I remembered Sir Richard Malbête; his feral smirk as he shot me with the crossbow. And I recalled a tossing bunk in the belly of a foul-smelling ship, a great pain in my right arm, and a feeling as if my stomach were on fire; and raving, cursing at Reuben as he tended to my wounds, and trying to strike at him. And I remembered a large tent of white canvas on a windy hilltop, and the cries of wounded and dying men around me mingling with the shrieks of seagulls; and Robin's eyes, filled with care, staring down at me and saying: "Don't die on me, Alan, that is a direct order." And I remembered more pain, and the shame of vomiting and voiding myself uncontrollably—and Nur, always there; my sweet angel caring for me as if I was a baby, and washing my loins and limbs, and trying to feed me, and holding me tight when I thrashed in my fever. And most of all I remembered my beloved weeping for me. And how it made me want to die.

I must have slept again, for when I awoke it was full

269

morning and Little John was standing at the foot of my bed, looking about ten-feet tall and as wide as a house, suntanned, bursting with rude health and grinning at me. He was holding up a kite-shaped object; a stout wooden frame around thin, overlapping layers of wooden slats, faced with painted leather, round at the top and tapering to a point at the bottom. It was four-and-a-half-feet long, and nearly two-foot across at its widest; a familiar image of a black and gray wolf's head on a white background snarled at me from the front.

"This," said Little John, rapping the object with his knuckles, "is a shield. It's quite old-fashioned, but they built them to last in the old days. You are supposed to carry one of these when you go into battle. How many times do I have to tell you—all your fancy mincing around with sword and poniard is fine in a one-on-one fight, if you like that sort of thing, but in a proper battle you need a shield."

He began speaking very slowly and loudly to me, as if to a child or an idiot: "If you carry a nice big shield, then nasty people won't find it so easy to shoot you with their nasty crossbows." And he thumped the shield down at the foot of my bed. "I've also brought you another sword, since you seem to have lost yours. God's greasy armpits, you youngsters, next thing I know, you'll be fighting stark bollock naked!"

I wanted to laugh, but my stomach was still paining me, so I merely grinned back at him and said: "You are one to talk: I've seen you rip the shirt from your own back when the battle-fire is burning in you. Anyway, I'm not much good at using a shield . . . don't really have your craven skill at hiding from my enemies behind a piece of wood."

He laughed. "Well, that is easily remedied. When you're on your feet, I will teach you. Somebody has to. It looks like we'll be here for a few weeks, so you'll have plenty of time to get strong. But, I swear on Christ's bones, Alan, if you go into a proper battle again without a shield—I'll damn well shoot you myself!" And he turned and stomped out of the dormitory.

The next day, when Nur had fed me some gruel and washed me from head to toe, Robin came to see me. He was holding a bunch of grapes somewhat awkwardly in his hands, and he seemed not to know what to say or what to do with the fruit. Finally he placed them on the small table beside my head, sat down on the bed and said: "Reuben says you must eat green fruit. Apparently, it is good for ridding the body of evil humors. Green fruit reduces the amount of bile—or is it phlegm?—it reduces something bad anyway."

I thanked him for his gift and again there was a slightly uncomfortable pause. I noticed that he looked tired.

"Well, you seem healthier," he said after a while, "almost human again, in fact." And he smiled, which lifted the lines of worry from his face. I told him that I was feeling much better but terribly weak. "Reuben was certain that you would die," he said, "and I was very worried—worried that I'd have to go to the trouble of finding myself another *trouvère*." He smiled at me again and his silver eyes sparkled with something like their old mischief. "Reuben said that mending your wrist was the easy part," he continued—and I obligingly flexed my right wrist for him, which was stiff, skinny but mobile and had a fresh purple scar running up the forearm—"but the old Jew said the crossbow bolt in the belly would kill you, and when it didn't, he was convinced that the fever you contracted after that would finish you off. I told Reuben, I told him, that you were made of strong stuff and that I didn't believe a single raggedy Griffon crossbowman could put you in your grave but . . ." he tailed off.

"It wasn't a Griffon," I said quietly. "It was Sir Richard Malbête." Robin stared at me for a few moments, his luminous eyes probing mine for the truth.

"Now that is interesting," he said at last. "Sir Richard is very much our *preux chevalier* these days. Since he captured the Emperor's standard in Cyprus, he has become the golden knight in the King's eyes; he can do no wrong. So what really happened?"

I told him, and his mouth opened in surprise. "That fox-faced shit needs killing, if anybody ever did," he muttered when I had finished my tale. "But we have a little problem, Alan, nobody is going to believe you if you claim that Sir Richard, the golden knight, that shining example of chivalry, tried to kill you. You'd better keep that to yourself while we work out how to fix the bastard. Don't go off trying to take him on your own, we'll do it together. But it's not going to be easy; he's with the King a good deal these days, part of his household now . . ."

I had come to a similar conclusion myself. It would not be simple but, easy or hard, I was also determined to kill Malbête one way or another—for my own personal safety, if for no other reason. Although there were more than enough other reasons to put the Beast down: for Ruth, for the Jews of York, for Nur, and those butchered slave girls in Messina . . .

We sat in silence for a while. I took a grape; they were delicious: cool, firm and sweet as honey.

"Robin," I said, slightly hesitantly, "can you tell me what happened; how we got here, how we took Acre. I don't even know what month this is."

He stared at me. "Yes, of course, has nobody told you? Well, it's July; we took Acre a week ago, not without some trouble, but the garrison surrendered in the second week of July, the twelfth day of the month, I think." He paused and looked at me. "I'd better start at the beginning." He reached over and tore off a cluster of grapes and popped them in his mouth. When he had finished chewing, he said: "We found you, and Ghost, in the dawn after the night battle in the olive grove, and we took you down to the beach where a hospital had been set up. The Emperor took to his heels again in the middle of the battle, which was lucky for us, because if he had rallied his troops they would have crushed us like a man stamping on an ant. But he fled, and we won, and your foxy friend Malbête came out of it looking like a hero, the golden standard in his proud right hand. He presented the standard to the King as a wedding present for his marriage to Berengaria in Limassol, a few days after the battle. He's a wily bastard, Malbête; it was exactly the right move to make, and the King was delighted.

"Anyway, we chased the Emperor around the island for a while, but the local barons had turned against him and finally he had to surrender—oh, and you'll like this." He took another grape. "The Emperor gave himself up on the strict condition that King Richard would not bind him in iron chains. Richard agreed, and when Isaac Comnenus came in, Richard had silver chains forged and had him bound in those. He's got a nasty sense of humor, our royal master, very nasty." And he laughed with, I believed, just a touch of bitterness.

"So we had Cyprus, and Richard then set off at last for Outremer, and we ended up here at Acre. The siege was in full swing but going nowhere: the Muslim garrison inside the walls still defied us, and the Christian troops outside were themselves surrounded by Saladin's forces. Of course, King Richard's arrival changed all that. He started building siege engines immediately, great monsters that can knock holes in stone walls, you should see them, Alan, much more formidable than a mangonel. Anyway, we smashed a few holes in the walls, but every time we tried to make an assault, Saladin would attack us from behind. Eventually, after a lot of bloody fighting on two fronts, and when the holes in the walls were big enough, the garrison surrendered—first having received their master's permission, of course. And, as part of the deal, Saladin withdrew as well. We've been lucky, though; I managed to keep our men out of the worst of the fighting . . ." He gave a sour smile. "That is to say we were not invited to join in the bloodiest assaults."

There was a tiny pause. I knew what a great dishonor this

simple statement meant. He straightened his shoulders and looked me in the eye. "The truth is, Alan, I'm not in favor at court, for one reason or another. I believe the King has taken against me and that some members of his circle are whispering against me . . . spreading rumors about my family . . . If I knew who it was I'd slaughter the mealy mouthed sons of whores. But I don't." He looked at his boots for a few moments, and then pulled himself together. "No matter," he said. "On the bright side, we haven't lost too many men, and you are clearly on the mend. But I'm not sure I shall be staying in Outremer all that long, the way things are going. I have a few matters that I need to arrange, and then I may well go home and look to my affairs there."

I couldn't meet his eyes. I knew what these rumors were suggesting. That Marie-Anne had made him a cuckold, and that baby Hugh was not his son.

"We may all have to go home soon. I think the whole expedition may be coming apart at the seams," he continued. "Our gallant King Richard seems to have managed to quarrel with everybody here. King Philip, well, you know how things are between them, and they've got worse. Philip feels that Richard stole his thunder by taking Acre when he couldn't manage it alone. So that's an irritant. But did you know that there are now two men claiming to be the rightful King of Jerusalem? Guy de Lusignan and Conrad of Montferrat—neither has a very good claim, as it happens, only through their women, and as Jerusalem is in Saladin's hands you might think the point moot. But no, it's the cause of another royal quarrel: Philip has declared his support of Conrad of Monferrat, and Richard has taken the side of Guy de Lusignan. So there's more bad blood between them. The word is that Philip is thinking of going back to France anyway. He'll blame his departure on Richard but he just wants to go back so he can snatch some land back in Flanders."

I must have looked puzzled, for Robin went on. "I beg

your pardon, I was forgetting that you wouldn't know. The Count of Flanders died during the siege here, and now that he's dead, Philip has designs on his land, which is directly to the north of his own territory. He'd no doubt like to have a crack at some of Richard's holdings in Normandy, too."

Robin paused for breath. "I haven't told you the worst," he said. "As well as quarreling with Philip and the French, King Richard has alienated the German contingent, too. Have you heard about the fuss over the flags? No? Well, it's just another piece of arrogant stupidity. When we took Acre, Richard and Philip naturally hung their banners over the city, but the Germans, who fought under Leopold, Duke of Austria, felt that they deserved to have their banner up there, too, and they had every right to, in my opinion. They had been fighting and dying here long before Richard arrived. So they hung up Leopold's banner next to Richard's. And Richard was furious—have you ever seen him lose his temper? It's quite a sight. He went storming up to the battlements and person-ally kicked the Duke's banner off the wall and into the ditch below. He said that, as Philip and he were kings, and Leopold was a mere duke, he had no right to fly his flag beside them as if they were equals. Now Leopold is furious with Richard and he, too, is threatening to go home. In a month there will be no Christian army left, at this rate."

I was shocked: it seemed that the Great Pilgrimage, for which we had all traveled so far and suffered so much was fall-ing apart because of petty rivalries, jealousies and stupid quar-rels. We had only just arrived in the Holy Land, and taken only one castle—I had yet to face a single Saracen warrior—and we might soon all be packing up and going back to England.

"What other news? Have there been any more attempts on your life?" I asked him, mainly to change the subject. He looked at me keenly. "As a matter of fact, yes, I believe so," he said. "It's something I wanted to talk to you about. I was walking the perimeter of the city with Owain and some of the men—it was about noon, and sweltering hot, the day after we had taken the place—when an avalanche of rocks began above me: I was wiping the sweat from my eyes and looking up at the sun, or I wouldn't have seen it: first a shower of rocks, then a great boulder the size of a full-grown cow came crashing down. I just managed to jump aside in time. Gave me a shock, I can tell you. A lot of the masonry is loose from the battering we gave the place before we took it, and workmen are doing their best to patch it up, but I thought I saw somebody up there a few moments before the rocks began to fall. It could have been an accident, I suppose. But I don't think so. I don't really think so."

"I was hoping we had left all that behind in Messina," I said. And he nodded agreement.

"But I think I know who it might be," I went on.

He looked at me, surprised. But remained silent for a few moments. "Well then," he said, slightly crossly, "who is it?"

"I'm not certain; and I don't want to give you a name in case I am wrong," I said. "It could cause no end of trouble and bad feeling." Actually, I was worried that Robin might quietly murder the person I had in mind, just as a precaution, and I was not yet fully convinced of his guilt. I did not want any more innocent blood on my conscience.

"Let me make a few inquiries," I said, "and when I'm sure of my man, I'll tell you his name."

"Very well," said Robin, trying hard to be lighthearted. "Play it close if you wish, but if I get murdered because you didn't tell me, my spirit will haunt you till your dying day!" Then he smiled at me and I felt a rush of affection for him. He had a lot resting on his head at that time: a murderer with the face of friend, huge debts unpaid at home and here, a wife who was making him look ridiculous in the eyes of his peers, and a royal master who, on the basis of slanderous lies, had banished him from his inner circle. I wanted to say something comforting to him but I could not find the words. He looked down at his interlinked hands for a moment. "You know, my friend," he said. "I sometimes wish I wasn't an Earl, or the commander of an army, or a holy pilgrim on a sacred mission; I sometimes wish I was just a common outlaw again. If a man maligned me, I killed him; if I wanted something, I took it. Things were somehow simpler . . . and better." And with those words, he left.

Two days later I was able to get out of bed and take some sun for an hour in the stone-flagged courtyard of the Hospitallers' quarter. I had several more visitors to my bed before then, apart from Nur who spent hours of each day with me: my loyal servant William, who actually burst into tears of happiness when he saw me upright and getting stronger; Reuben, who made me piss into a jar before smelling and tasting the urine to determine what I could have told him myself: that I was better—and Will Scarlet.

My boyhood companion looked fit and strong—and happy, and the cause of his happiness was standing beside him in a shapeless green dress, with her white hair as fluffy as a lamb's. It was Elise, the strange Norman woman who claimed to be able to see the future. They were now married.

There was more than fifteen years in age difference between them, and she was half a foot taller, but despite that, I could see that they were well-suited to each other and clearly in love. She fussed over him like a mother hen, it is true, but she seemed to have brought out from his soul some latent strength. His eyes were clear and he held my gaze steadily as he told me their good news.

"Elise predicted that we would be married one day," he said. "She told me on the day that I was whipped in France. And she was right, of course. But I didn't know that I loved her until Messina. At first I told myself it was wrong; that the Devil was tempting me with lustful thoughts about her"—I resisted the urge to smile; there was nothing lust-making about the skinny middle-aged woman before me that I could see—"but then Father Simon told me that if I took her hand in Holy Matrimony, our union would be blessed by God. And so we were wed by him a week ago."

I congratulated him heartily; and indeed I was pleased for both of them. My love for Nur made me want all mankind to have the same happiness. "Of course, we want to have babies as soon as possible," he said. I looked at her white hair, and the wrinkles around her eyes, and murmured, "Of course." But he surprised me by continuing, "So that God can bless our union in this Holy Land, and show us a sign of his divine approval of our match."

It was clear that Will had not become any less religious since he set foot in the land that had given nurture to Our Lord Jesus Christ.

I kissed Elise, too, and just as she and Will were leaving she said: "I know that you don't believe in my prophecies, Alan, but I was right about you, wasn't I? You were not destined to die here in this place; as I told you, you will die in bed, at home, an old man." And then she did a strange thing; she bent down and picked up the old-fashioned wolf's head shield that Little John had left at the bottom of the bed. "But carry this with you at all times; it will save your life," she said solemnly, then she took his hand and they both left. I was struck by the fact that she should echo Little John's advice about the shield, and I vowed that I would learn to use it, and carry it with me whenever I next went into battle.

As the days passed, I grew stronger. Robin had disappeared and when I asked after my master with Owain and Sir James de Brus, neither seemed to know where he had gone. Reuben seemed to have vanished, too. When I questioned Little John, he rather curtly told me to stop worrying, and to stop asking questions; my master's business was his own. But the big man was as good as his word about the shield lessons and came each morning to give me instruction. In truth, it was not difficult, although my tender stomach muscles gave me some trouble to begin with—I now had a short, ugly purple scar to the right of my belly button, where the barber-surgeons had cut out Malbête's quarrel. Wounded belly or no, Little John soon had me skipping about the sunlit courtyard of the Hospitallers' quarter, John striking at me with a yard-long wooden baton, and myself using only the shield to block his powerful blows: high, low, and the tricky ones that aim to come around the edge. At first I was quickly exhausted by the exercise, and even though we practiced in the early morning, the heat soon became unbearable. But as I grew stronger, I was able to enjoy the practice sessions with my huge friend, and endure the discomfort for longer. When John saw that I had mastered the basic moves, he progressed to teaching me more sophisticated maneuvers with the shield: strikes on an opponent with the edge, and how to use the shield to distract your enemy so that he reacted slowly to your sword blow.

One day when we were practicing, I heard a voice call: "Move your feet, Alan, don't forget to move your feet," and turned to see a tall man in a white cloak with a red cross on the breast, long sword at his side, and a wonderfully familiar face grinning at me from behind a huge black beard. It was my old friend Sir Richard at Lea, a Poor Fellow-Soldier of Christ and the Temple of Solomon, and one of the main reasons Robin had embarked on this Great Pilgrimage.

He and a hundred of his fellow Templar knights, perhaps the finest fighting men in Christendom, had come to our rescue in England at the battle of Linden Lea two years ago but only on the condition that Robin brought his men to fight in the Holy Land. And here we were, and here he was.

I was tremendously pleased to see him, and clasped his

right arm with enthusiasm, only wincing slightly as his powerful grip tightened on my recently mended wrist. He greeted Little John warmly and asked after Robin and Tuck, and then he turned and lifted his hand toward a man who had been standing beside him quietly smiling at our reunion: "May I introduce Sir Nicholas de Scras, a good Christian and a fine knight, but one who had the great misfortune to join the wrong order: he's a Hospitaller, may God forgive him."

"Please pardon my friend," said Sir Nicholas, clasping my arm in greeting, although a good deal more gently than Sir Richard had done. "Like many Templars, he has the great misfortune to think that he is amusing."

While the Hospitaller politely greeted Little John, I studied him with interest: he was a man of medium height, iron-gray hair cropped short, slim, fit-looking, with muddy green eyes and dressed in the black robe with the white cross of the Hospitallers. He looked a little too mild mannered to be a warrior, and I wondered if he eschewed battle and preferred to practice the gentler arts that this order of healing knights were famous for. I couldn't have been more wrong. As I watched him, he picked up the shield that I had dropped and examined it closely, testing the strength of the layers of wooden slats with his thumb. "A strange device," he said, at last, turning the snarling wolf's head toward me. "Am I right in thinking that you serve the Earl of Locksley?"

I nodded, and he continued: "And I understand his master of arms is showing you the finer points of combat with a shield?" I nodded again. "Will you permit me to try a turn or two with your formidable friend? I might be able to show you something useful." I merely made a wide sweeping gesture with my arm that suggested that he was free to do as he liked in this quarter of Acre, owned as it was by his order. And Sir Richard and I retired to a stone bench that surrounded the courtyard and sat down to watch the bout.

John looked a little uncertain to be facing an opponent

who seemed so calm and yet who was so much smaller and lighter than him. "Don't worry, Sir Richard, I promise to go easy on him," he yelled jovially over to us on the bench. But, despite his customary bravado, I think he sensed he was facing a master warrior.

"Do your worst, John, he deserves a good thrashing," shouted Sir Richard cheerily, and he sat back on the warm stone to watch the fun. Sir Nicholas merely smiled at John, bowed his head and they began. The two fighters circled for a few moments, and then John attacked, a heavy cut with his sword at Sir Nicholas's shoulder. The Hospitaller merely shrugged it aside with a flip of his shield and immediately counterattacked, with a series of lightning lunges to Little John's face. The big man was forced back, back, ten feet, then twenty, back until he was almost against the stone bench on the other side of the courtyard; and then with the hollows of his knees against the warm yellow stone, he finally roused himself and, snarling at the smaller man, began to batter him with huge cuts at his head and upper body from the left and right in turn. Sir Nicholas blocked and blocked, again and again, using only his shield, gradually allowing himself to be forced back into the center of the courtyard but continually holding his sword poised, his right elbow back, the snake-fast lunge always a potential threat. It seemed he was waiting for John to open up his body for the strike, but how Sir Nicholas survived that mighty battering from Little John without using his sword to protect himself I do not know—however, wherever John's sword struck, there was the shield to deflect the massive blow. He did not use the wooden frame full on to soak up the power of the sword. Instead, Sir Nicholas used the curved outer surface to slide the blows away from his body, and waste John's great strength on the air. And then the knight did something extraordinary: instead of blocking, he ducked a massive swing from Little John, which put the big man off balance, turned sideways, stepped under John's sweeping blade and with the shield tilted the wrong way around—its rounded top down toward his own face, the narrow bottom end pointing upward away from his body—he jabbed up with his elbow and slammed the tapered point up and hard into the side of Little John's head, and immediately dropped the big man in a sprawling heap on the floor. He didn't even look at John, but turned his head and stared directly at me. "Did you see that, Alan?" I gawped at him. He demonstrated the move once more, this time striking at empty air with the tapered point of the shield. Then the knight sheathed his sword, took off the shield, and went to kneel beside the giant on the floor. He wasn't even out of breath. Little John had dropped his sword and, seated on his broad bottom on the stone floor, was swaying slightly and panting heavily. He had a dazed look in his eyes, and his mouth hung open in surprise.

I was no less stunned. I had never seen Little John beaten in a fight, and so quickly; it was almost unthinkable, and yet this slight man, who only came up to Little John's breast, had dropped him in the dust with what seemed the greatest of ease. Sir Nicholas, kneeling beside his victim, examined Little John's head, and called over his shoulder: "Richard, be a good fellow and get one of the servants to bring me a cloth and some water." And then he gently lifted Little John's right eyelid, tilted his head back to catch the sunlight, and began to look deeply into his eye.

Sir Richard at Lea and I retired to the Hospitallers' refectory and ordered a dish of roast fish, stewed peas, bread and wine from one of the brother-sergeants, and while we refreshed ourselves, I asked my friend what he had been doing in the past few weeks since the city had fallen.

"The Grand Master has decided that we will make this place our headquarters until Jerusalem can be recaptured," he said. "So I have been busy arranging our new quarters. But the thing that takes up most of my time is dealing with the damned traders; I tell you, Alan, I've never met such a gaggle of greasy scoundrels in all my life. They're a cowardly lot, always bleating about bandits attacking their camel trains and demanding protection from our busy knights. But then, damned nuisance that it is, protecting pilgrims and travelers from the human predators who roam the desert is one of our sacred duties here in the Holy Land." And he frowned and helped himself to another large piece of fish.

I knew that the Templars, though primarily a religious and military order, had branched out into trade; with their outposts, known as commanderies, all over Christendom, their own huge fleet, and connections up to the highest level, it was natural that they should expand the practice of shipping food and weapons to their own far-flung outposts to include goods that could be sold for a profit. They had even developed a clever system whereby money could be deposited by a merchant in one commanderie in, say, France, where the traveler was given a piece of parchment as a receipt, and on presentation of the parchment at another Templar commanderie hundreds, perhaps even thousands of miles away, he was returned the same amount of money, less a small fee. It made traveling, always a dangerous business for merchants, much safer. The other great advantage the Templars enjoyed was an exemption from all taxes, by order of the Pope. It was often claimed that the Templars, despite their individual vows of poverty, now possessed wealth beyond the wildest dreams of kings and emperors.

"And Saladin hasn't gone away," Sir Richard continued. "He might have lost Acre, but he's still out there in the hills with more than twenty thousand men. He's waiting for us to leave the city, then he'll swoop and we'll have a proper battle, a proper bloody battle, by God. And we need to be ready for that—so when I'm not nurse-maiding merchants, I'm training the new men to fight."

"When will we leave here?" I asked. I was anxious to see Jerusalem, the Holy City, and pray for the forgiveness of my sins at the Church of the Holy Sepulcher, the most sacred site of Jesus's tomb.

"That depends on our royal masters: King Richard is keen to press on south to Jerusalem but Philip is talking openly of going home to France; he claims he is not well, that this damned heat is killing him. The good news is that he and Richard have managed to decide between them who is the rightful King of Jerusalem: they have decreed that it is Guy de Lusignan, but—and this is a nice compromise, Alan—he's only to be king for his lifetime. After his death, Conrad of Montferrat or his heirs will succeed him. At least they've managed to sort that out without more quarreling."

At that moment, I saw Nicholas de Scras approaching our table with William in tow. "I found this young fellow wandering around the hospital, looking for you," said Sir Nicholas with a smile. He seated himself on a bench at the table and helped himself to a piece of fish.

"Sir, the Earl of Locksley has returned and asks that you attend him, if your health permits, at your earliest convenience," said William. The presence of these two imposing knights had made my servant adopt a more formal manner than usual. I pushed myself to my feet, stuffed a last crust in my mouth and made to leave.

"Do not exert yourself too much, Alan," said Sir Nicholas. "The brother-physicians at the hospital say that they are very pleased with your recovery, but you are to take as much rest as possible, d'you hear me?" I nodded, waved farewell and hurried away to attend my errant lord.

CHAPTER FIFTEEN

Robin had commandeered a large building near the main harbor of Acre, in the north of the city, which had formerly belonged to a rich Saracen merchant. It was a splendid house, practically a palace, three stories' high and built of smooth white sandstone, with big cool rooms, large amounts of stabling and a large warehouse attached, in which about half of the men were encamped. The rest of our boys were scattered about the town, finding cheap lodging wherever they could. The merchant who had once owned this magnificent house was now one of the nearly three thousand ragged and almost-starving Muslim prisoners who were now locked in the vast cellars deep below Acre. King Richard was holding them hostage for the agreed ransom from Saladin, two hundred thousand gold pieces, and most miraculously, a genuine piece of the True Cross, the actual cross on which Jesus Christ was crucified, which the Saracen warlord had captured after the disastrous battle of Hattin four years earlier.

"I want you to play for us tomorrow night at a party I'm giving," said Robin when I found him. He was in a luxurious room filled with tall elegant pillars and flapping muslin drapes, which seemed to collect the sea breezes and cool even the hottest day. It was richly appointed with polished cedar-wood furniture, the floor covered with thick carpets and strewn with plump cushions. I almost did not recognize my master when I first saw him: Robin was dressed like a Saracen, in a long loose robe made of some light material, a curved dagger at his waist, his skin seemed to have been darkened with some kind of dye, his head was wrapped in a golden turban, his feet shod with silken slippers. I stared at him but managed to mumble something like: "Of course, sir, it would be a pleasure . . ." before I ran out of politeness.

"Why on earth are you dressed in that ridiculous fashion?" I finally burst out. I could not hold back my curiosity any longer. "And where have you been this past week?"

Robin laughed, and turned a full circle so that I could admire his Oriental finery. He appeared to be totally relaxed, happy and—something else. He had the indefinable air of a man who has just pulled off a great coup. "I thought you might be amused: in these clothes I am the mysterious and powerful merchant prince Rabin al-Hud, wealthy beyond measure, who wishes to enter the frankincense trade, buying the Food of the Gods to sell to the infidels. And I have just paid a delightful visit to some business acquaintances of Reuben's in Gaza. We sailed back from there yesterday."

"Gaza?" I said. He laughed again. I was mystified, but at least I could now understand the fancy getup: as a Christian, there was no way he would be able to mingle with people in Gaza, far to the south, which was in Saracen hands. As I helped Robin to change out of his outlandish rig and into good Christian clothes—green woolen hose, a black tunic and a capacious green hood—he told me what he had been doing in Gaza, and what he planned to do to permanently solve his money troubles.

"Frankincense is a valuable commodity, as I'm sure you know. It is burned at every Mass in every major church in Christendom; so, as you can imagine, we use a lot of it. It is just the dried sap of some scrubby little trees that grow in a place called Al-Yaman, in the far south of the Arabian peninsula, which happens to be Reuben's homeland. Now, the value of the incense increases the further it gets from its homeland. In Al-Yaman, you can buy a pound of frankincense for a few pennies; in England or France, it is worth more than its weight in gold." He stopped speaking while I pulled the black tunic over his head, and then he said: "Jesus, Alan, these clothes are so hot!" and made me bring him a cup of watered wine, before continuing with his lecture.

"For many hundreds of years, since before the birth of Christ himself, frankincense has been transported by camel train along the western coast of the Arabian peninsula, hundreds of dangerous miles through mountain and desert, arid plain and high pass, and for each step the camel takes the frankincense on its back becomes more valuable. Of course, taxes must be paid to the people whose land the camel train passes through, and there are the costs of hiring men to guard the train, and food and water, and supplies for everyone.

"When the Romans came to Egypt, more than a thousand years ago, they hunted down and killed almost all the pirates in the Red Sea. Suddenly it became worthwhile, cheaper, safer, to transport the incense by water. And that is how it is done to this day. The ships' valuable cargos are loaded at Adan, carried up the coast in galleys or felluccas and are offloaded in the Gulf of Aqaba. But they still need camel trains to take the frankincense across the Sinai Desert and up to Gaza. In his youth, Reuben used to work this route, as a guard on the camel trains. He knows the business backward: the people involved, the routes, the timings of the journeys . . ." Robin stopped himself, and a look of uncertainty crossed his face as if he might have said too much. Then he shrugged, and continued. "From great warehouses in Gaza, the frankincense was sold to Christian merchants, who transported it across the sea to Italy, to be distributed to churches all over Christendom. Are you following me?" I inclined my head.

"All that changed when we lost Jerusalem four years ago," Robin went on. "After that, the camel trains couldn't stop in Gaza, as they had before; the buyers were gone. They could no longer meet their Christian merchant friends there and transact their business, as any Christian who showed his nose there would be imprisoned and quite possibly executed by the Saracens. The frankincense trains now have to come further north; more than a hundred, rocky, dry, bandit-infested miles north. Here, to Acre."

I was slightly bemused by this lesson, and I must have looked puzzled, for Robin said, rather crossly: "Don't you understand? Reuben and I went to Gaza to meet these frankincense traders. And we made them an offer. An offer they will find difficult to refuse. We offered to buy their entire frankincense stock and save them the expense and risk of having to camel-train it north through *bandit-infested* desert." It was the second time he had used that particular phrase. "It was Reuben's scheme, and I think it's quite inspired. It's a good deal for them, and for us. Everybody is happy."

"What about these Christian merchants in Acre?" I said. "Won't they be angry that their frankincense is being bought by another merchant? That they are, in fact, being cut out of this trade altogether?"

"I think it is written somewhere," said Robin, with just a little too much self-satisfaction, "that each soul must expect a little disappointment in this life, and he should try to profit by the experience," and with that, the matter was closed.

★　★　★

I was deliberately early for dinner the next day and, finding a convenient corner in the luxurious dining hall, I sat and unobtrusively began to tune my vielle, and to think. My wrist was still not as supple as I would have liked, but it would suffice. I was very curious to see who Robin would be eating with that evening. I guessed Reuben would be a guest, as it was now clear why Reuben was so important for Robin's plans in the Holy Land—plans that had not even the slightest connection with our avowed holy mission to rescue Jerusalem from the Saracens. Reuben was the key to Robin's frankincense ploy because Reuben knew the trade, had worked on the camel trains, knew the right people for Robin to meet: I could now see clearly why Robin had sacrificed Ruth's life in York, and saved Reuben's, but the knowledge gave me no comfort. Robin had allowed a young girl to die to increase his chances of becoming wealthy. It was a chilling realization, but somehow I was not as shocked as I should have been; it was more of a sinking feeling. I felt I was beginning to know the man that Robin truly was—not the shining, noble hero I had wished him to be, but a hard, ruthless man who would do anything to protect himself and further his own cause. I also had the feeling that Robin had some other part of his frankincense plan that he was keeping to himself, and I dared not think what it might be.

I hadn't had time to write any new pieces but Robin had given me to understand that I would just be playing soothing background music to entertain his guest, and possibly to prevent anyone from overhearing what was said. And so I merely ran through a few of Robin's favorites by way of practice and waited for the guests to arrive.

The first to turn up was Reuben, looking lean and tired but in a new and expensively embroidered robe. I was glad that he had arrived first for there was something of great importance that I wanted to discuss with him: we spent a few minutes talking quietly in the music corner, and then, our mutual plans concluded, Reuben wandered away to find a servant and get himself something to drink. The next man to enter the hall was Robin's guest, a thickset man of medium height whom I guessed was an Arab from his dark curly hair and intense eyes, but who wore a Western-style tunic, hose and long seaboots that came up to the top of his thighs. There was a definite salty air about him: the way he rolled slightly as he walked, as if uncomfortable on dry land, to the heavy gold earrings in both ears, and the very businesslike, thick-bladed scimitar that rode on his hip. He ignored me, seated on my stool in the corner, but I was expecting to be invisible that evening. However, the Arab sailor did greet Reuben with a wary friendliness. Then Robin was in the room, accompanied by two archers who I knew slightly, and who were immediately banished to guard the door. He was dressed once again in the long Saracen robe, but was bareheaded and without the dye darkening his skin.

I began to play "My Joy Summons Me," singing softly to accompany myself. And Robin looked over at me and smiled: "Play a little more loudly, Alan, if you would be so good. I don't believe our guest will have heard this very pleasant tune."

Obediently, I began to play and sing with more force, and as a result, try as I might, I could only hear snatches of the conversation during the long meal that followed. Reuben, Robin and the seagoing man, whose name I learned was Aziz, sat on large cushions on the floor around a wide low table. Arab servants entered from time to time with dishes of unusual looking foods—tiny morcels of meat in delicate pastry, dishes of stewed mutton and chicken, bread made with honey and dates and spiced glazed pears—and each time they did the three men broke off their conversation and waited in silence until the serving men had left and they were alone once again.

The first thing I heard, after a long, quiet speech from

Aziz was Robin saying sharply: "Refused my offer? What do you mean they refused? Don't they know a profitable deal when it's handed to them on a plate?" He must have heard a break in the rhythm of the piece I was playing as I strained to listen because he gave me a hard look and then lowered his voice to continue the conversation.

He forgot himself again, perhaps a quarter of an hour later, and I heard him say to Reuben just as I came to the end of a jolly *canso*: ". . . I don't care if they have taken on extra protection, hired more armed men, I can still teach them a damned good lesson. I can still make them fear for their profits this year."

Courses came, were eaten and cleared away; and the servants had just brought in a sherbert—a magnificent dish of mountain snow, lemon juice and sugar, which had my own mouth watering—when I just caught the end of a sentence that Reuben was saying to Aziz. ". . . so you will agree to carry it for us to Messina, at the price we struck before. I take it then that you have no problem with that?"

The meal finally came to an end after a couple of hours. And my newly mended right wrist was stiff and sore by the time the sailor rose to his feet, and bowed courteously to Robin. Whatever business they had been discussing, I got the impression it had been satisfactorily concluded for all parties.

Robin and Reuben also rose and bowed, and as the sailor was leaving, I heard him say, quite clearly, and it was the first time I had heard his voice: "Until the rising of the full moon, then," before he strode out of the dining hall, out of Robin's palace and away into the night.

Two nights later, Reuben and I stood behind a small door in the top room of a half-abandoned tower in the eastern part of Acre, near the royal apartments. It was as dark as a witch's soul, only a dim light seeping in from a small arched window on the other side of the room, and I could only just make out the shape of my friend on the other side of the doorway as he stood with his back to the cool stone, a foot-long, freshly sharpened blade in his hand. I, too, had had my poniard sharpened, but it was sheathed, for although this was work for short blades, I needed both hands free. We had been waiting in silence for more than an hour, ears straining for the sound of footsteps in the corridor outside the door.

Looking at the gray arched shape of the window in the blackness, I imagined that I could make out the faint outline on the sill of the thick rope that we had tied there when we first arrived in this room. It was our escape route; the knotted rope hung out of the window and dangled forty feet down to the stone flags of a small courtyard below, where our two horses were tied to an iron ring fixed to the wall. I was nervous; this was not battle, this was a murder we were planning; a cold-blooded execution. Our intended victim? Sir Richard Malbête, of course: a man who richly deserved to die, but yet . . . Yet, in all honesty, I would have preferred to face him in open battle, rather than cutting him down like a thief in the dark.

Having said all that, having made my excuses, the plan was mine. And the key to it was my servant William. I had hesitated before involving him in a foul deed like this, unsure of whether he would be willing to help me commit murder and, worse, be willing to risk the wrath of Malbête—not to mention the King's fury—if we failed. But when I told him that it was the Beast who had shot me with the crossbow in Cyprus, he was more than eager to help me take my revenge; he actually begged to be a part of it.

The plan rested on the King's new fondness for Malbête, and Malbête's desire to gain favor with his sovereign, and I had devised it when I came across a pile of the gorgeous tabards worn by the royal pages, which were awaiting a wash in the great steam-filled courtyard, draped with dripping sheets, where the serving maids did the royal laundry. I had been to visit Elise in the serving women's quarters, because I had one very important question to ask her concerning Robin's would-be murderer, and having had a satisfactory reply, I just happened to be passing the laundry when the mound of gorgeous red and gold cloth caught my eye. The plan came to me, fully formed, in a flash of inspiration, and after a quick check to see that nobody was watching, I stuffed a tabard inside my tunic—once a thief, always a thief, I muttered to myself—and sauntered away, buzzing with the excitement of a dangerous venture begun.

I had secured Reuben's enthusiastic participation on the night of the secret dinner with the sailor Aziz, and two days later, William, dressed in a gorgeous red tabard embroidered with the lions of England, ventured into the Beast's lair.

Sir Richard Malbête had occupied a small, richly furnished two-story house in the southern side of Acre, near the smaller harbor. It was a house of ill-repute, a brothel. He occupied it with a dozen or so of his men-at-arms, many bearing the marks of battle. They had been at the forefront of the attacks on Acre and had suffered many casualties in the terrible fighting before the city surrendered. They were lounging around the house's central courtyard, drinking wine, fondling the women, a gaggle of sloe-eyed beauties, William told me later, when my servant, dressed as a royal messenger, walked unannounced into their presence. The men-at-arms sat up, straightened their dress, dismissed the women and Sir Richard Malbête was summoned from inside. William said that, despite the hazardous nature of his mission, he had to master an overwhelming urge to laugh when he gave Malbête the message, which purported to come from the King. The message was simple: that the King desired to meet Malbête in this room where Reuben and I now waited after Vespers that same evening. It was a meeting of a discreet nature, said William solemnly, and would Sir Richard be so good as to come alone? Malbête had agreed, and William had left unmolested, and now Reuben and I waited in the dark.

I heard footsteps outside the door, a man's confident tread, and then a soft knock at the door and a voice saying, "Sire?" The door opened and light from a pine torch spilled into the dark room. There was a tall figure in a scarlet and sky blue surcoat looming in the doorway, his face in shadow, and I leaped forward and clamped my arms around his middle, trapping the man's elbows against his body. He dropped the torch in his surprise and, my face buried in his chest, I twisted him out of the lit doorway and round into the darkness of the room. Reuben slammed the door shut. The man gave a short cry of terror and then Reuben was reaching over my back, his knife flashing once as it stabbed into the side of the man's neck, seeking the big pulsing vein there; the victim's body jerked violently as the questing blade cut deeply into the soft skin, and a spray of blood drenched the top of my head and told me that Reuben had found his mark. I kicked the man's legs from under him and released my arms, and he crashed to his knees, bubbling a cry of alarm and clutching his spurting neck. I drew my own poniard, intending to stab the bastard a dozen times, to make sure he was truly dead . . .

Then the door burst open with a shattering crash, and bright light flooded the room. There were armed men spilling into the chamber all in scarlet and blue and I recognized the mocking, red-scarred face of Malbête at the back of the swarm of intruders. Someone swung a sword at me and I stopped the blow with the hilt of my poniard, twisted the blade free and buried it in his belly. He fell and I pulled the dagger free of his entangling guts and stepped back to give myself space.

"Go, Alan, go," shouted Reuben, "the window." A second man lunged at him with a spear and he knocked the shaft aside with his long knife and neatly slid the blade deep on and into the man's armpit, leaving him screaming with pain. Then my friend drew his scimitar, the fine metal coming out of the sheath with a whispering sigh, and he slashed once at another man-at-arms and sliced his face to the bone. I was about to draw my sword, but Reuben shouted again: "Go, Alan, go!" and I hesitated no longer but sheathed my bloody poniard and leaped for the window. I heard a clash of steel behind me, and a shout, and I hurled myself out of the arch, only just catching the rope as I half fell over the lintel, before climbing down the knots as swiftly as I could. I heard more screams and shouts above me, and again the fast clash of blades, and as I reached the bottom I looked up and saw, with relief the thin form of Reuben, ten feet above me on the rope, climbing like a monkey. I saw a head poke out of the window, a dark silhouette, and saw a flash of steel at the ledge. Reuben was nearly with me, he had only ten feet more to climb, when suddenly, sickeningly, he fell, dropping like a hanged man to land with a crack of bone and a hideous scream on the stone-flagged floor of the courtyard. The rope, freshly cut, fell about his body. I had not been idle: I had untethered the horses and with many curses and a good deal of heaving, I managed to get Reuben onto the back of his mount. His left leg was snapped through the shin bone, the bone poking through the skin of his thin leg, and he was moaning, half-delirious in pain, but I got myself onto the back of Ghost and was about to lead Reuben's mount away from that ill-fated place, when I heard a familiar, much-hated voice calling softly from the window above. And stopped dead, in spite of myself.

"O singing boy!" crooned the voice. "O singing boy; did you think I did not expect you to try this?" said Sir Richard Malbête. "Do you take me for a fool?"

I said nothing, but my heart was burning with rage at my own stupidity. Of course, he must have expected this. And I had involved my friends in this disaster.

"Are you there, singing boy?" Malbête called again, and I had to bite back a foul retort. "It seems you have cut up another one of my people, singing boy. I think perhaps I shall now cut up one of yours." He laughed a low, dark, bubbling chuckle. I had heard enough, and I dug my heels into Ghost and led Reuben's slumped and moaning form away from the evil sound of laughter in the dark.

"What the hell did you think you were playing at?" said my master, his silver eyes glinting like a pair of barber's blades. It was later that same night and we were in the Hopsitaller's quarter, where a cowled bone-setter was efficiently splinting Reuben's broken leg. Outwardly, the Earl of Locksley appeared icily calm, but I knew that he was incandescently angry. "You nearly got yourself killed, and, more importantly, you nearly got Reuben killed, and I'm told you even involved your servant William in your childishly stupid scheme."

"All you care about is saving Reuben for your grubby moneymaking plots," I flashed back at him. "Killing Malbête is important! It is a matter of personal honor for me. Not that you'd understand that, you . . . you merchant!"

To my surprise, he merely laughed; a dry hollow chuckle, admittedly, and not a pleasant sound; but it was the sound of human mirth. "You were a snot-nosed little thief when I found you, a cut-purse of no family, no money, no lineage, and now you—hah!—*you* are lecturing me about honor, and calling me a merchant!" He snorted. "You ridiculous, unworldly little puppy; go on—get out of my sight." And I found myself walking away from him; and fighting back a great black wave of self-pity. He was right: I was a snot-nose thief, a cut-purse of no family and no lineage—but I did know about honor.

Reuben's leg was a clean fracture, and though very painful he was well tended in the Hospitallers' dormitory, where I went to see him and to apologize. "Do not concern yourself with it, Alan. We tried to take him; we failed. There will be other opportunities," said my Jewish friend—and I felt better about the whole sorry affair. Robin had not spoken to me since our argument, and I knew I was in disgrace, because even

Little John was distant with me and found some excuse to cancel our shield practice the next morning. As a result I spent much of the next few days making love to Nur in the little house she shared with Elise in the women's quarters, and in the light of what was to happen, I was very glad. I can still remember her perfect face—dark eyes you could drown in, her exquisite little nose, the high cheekbones, her luscious berry lips that begged to be kissed . . . I remember her face so clearly, even now after more than forty years. She was so fragile, so beautiful—it sometimes makes we weep to remember her. I remember her words to me that night, too, when I told her about my spat with Robin: "I know that you always try do the right thing, Alan, always. It is one of the reasons why I love you so very much."

A week or so later, in the searing heat near the middle of August, I was summoned again to see Robin, by William, who found me practicing with sword and shield, alone, in the courtyard of the Hospitallers' quarter. He was accompanied by Keelie, now a glossy, confident fully grown lion-yellow dog who bounded over to greet me and lick my face. King Philip had left Acre at the end of July taking some of his knights with him, but others had remained and were prepared to fight on under King Richard's banner. There was an air of quiet purpose in our army, a sense that we were very soon going to march; and I was determined to prove myself on the field of battle against the Saracens. So despite the crippling heat, and the sweat that drenched me, I practiced my sword and shield patterns every day. There was one fly in the soup: Saladin still had not paid the huge ransom on the three thousand Muslim captives, nor had he returned the True Cross to us—and many said that he had no intention of relinquishing such a wondrous object to his enemies. I secretly thought that the King would have to release the Saracen prisoners before we marched on; we could not possibly guard and feed such a multitude on the road to Jerusalem. It would be a blow to his prestige—but what else could he do?

"The Earl wa-wants you," said William, hauling a slobbering Keelie off me and offering a shy smile of greeting. I had hardly seen him since our disastrous attempt on Malbête's life and even in that short amount of time he seemed to have grown a couple of inches; his face seemed to have changed, too, become less round, the cheekbones more prominent: he must be twelve or thirteen now, I guessed, and it was clear that he was becoming a man. "Something bi-big is going on at headquarters," he said, "everybody is bu-bustling about looking pe-pe-pleased with themselves: people sharpening weapons, packing ba-ba-bags. I think we might all be on the mo-move."

I doubted it; there would have been plenty of rumors if the whole army were to depart Acre. The moon had been waxing in the past few days and, by my amateur calculation, would be full tomorrow night. It was more likely that whatever Robin had arranged with Aziz the sailor would be happening tomorrow.

Robin was curt when I presented myself to him, not a little nervously, that afternoon in the main ground-floor room of his palace by the sea. He was richly dressed in a long silk gown, seated at a table, going through a stack of parchments, checking accounts of some sort. Although I now regretted my outburst of the week before, he looked, in truth, exactly like a merchant. He wasted no time in pleasantries: "Are you fit?" he said. I told him I was. He merely grunted and carried on writing. "When you entered my service, two, two and a half years ago," he said, slightly formally, "you swore that you would be loyal to me until death; do you stand by that oath?"

"I hope I am not an oath-breaker," I said, a little too haughtily.

He finally looked up from his pages and stared at me, his eyes as cold as naked steel in winter. "You might not be

298

an oath-breaker, but you are insolent. What I want to know is: are you obedient?"

It hurt me to be at odds with my master: despite his many faults, he was still a man I respected and liked enormously. In a slightly more conciliatory tone, I said: "I serve you, sir, with all my heart, and in doing my duty, I strive always to be as loyal and obedient as I can."

He finally smiled: "Good," he said. "I need you, Alan, to come with me tomorrow on a . . . on a training exercise. Speak to no one of this, but tomorrow we will be riding out. Be ready, mounted and armed, here at dawn. Oh, and don't wear anything with my badge or blazon on it. You might say that we are to be traveling incognito." And with another brief smile, he looked back down at his papers; I was dismissed.

When I returned to the palace just before dawn the next day—mounted on Ghost, armed with sword and poniard and carrying my old-fashioned shield, with the snarling wolf device painted over with limewash—I was surprised to see Reuben, his leg a massive bundle of splints and bandages, mounted on a horse. He looked pale and had a slightly bemused look on his face, but he greeted me cordially, and I returned his affectionate words with gratitude. "What's going on, Reuben?" I asked. "In the first place, what are you doing on a horse, in your condition? You should be in bed."

"Best to leave the questions till later," advised my dark friend in a slightly slurred voice. "Let us just say that it is necessary that I accompany you. Do not be concerned for my discomfort—I have taken a strong draft of hashish dissolved in poppy juice—and the pain is hardly noticeable. In fact, I feel . . . I feel wonderful." And he giggled a little.

He might be feeling wonderful. But I was not. I had slept badly and awoke feeling dizzy and sweaty, with a slight but persistent headache. But I pushed all thoughts of my bodily weakness aside as we rode out of the high gates of Acre and

299

turned our horses south. We were forty men in our company, roughly half archers and half men-at-arms, and all of us mounted on well-fed and rested horses. As we rode over a makeshift bridge over the trenches that our army had dug while we were besieging Acre, I noticed that almost everybody in the party had a very familiar face, nearly all of them were former outlaws, who had been with Robin for many years. We were an elite group, I presumed, chosen because each man knew and trusted his fellows and had shared hardship and battle with them. There was also a sense of excitement in our band that I had not felt since we left England. We were going to undertake a training exercise, Robin had said, but it felt as if we were riding through Sherwood Forest on some mad escapade that would put silver in our pouches and a blush of shame on the Sheriff's face.

We crossed a shallow river and turned south onto a wide expanse of sand, barely a road at all, that ran along the sea, and I saw that the countryside here could not have been more different to Sherwood: away from the deep blue sea, it was a stark, sun-bleached landscape, sandy and spare and even at that early hour glowering with the threat of a brutally hot day to come. To our left was a rank stretch of marshland and beyond that, five miles or so away, rose a steep wall of green mountains—somewhere in those mountains, a mere morning's ride away, Saladin was waiting with his vast army of Saracens, but I saw none of his famous Turkish cavalrymen that day. However, after half a dozen miles of riding through that blindingly bright sand, the countryside began to bear the marks of Saladin's presence. We passed burned-out farms, charred olive trees and the blackened stubble of whole fields of corn and barley that had been put to the torch. We saw no living thing, save the lizards that stared a proud challenge at us from the rocks on the side of the road before scuttling away at our approach. Saladin had emptied the area of anything that might give comfort to his enemy, and burned anything he could not carry away, and we rode through a grim, blackened wasteland that stank of smoke and fear.

We stopped about midmorning for a drink from the water skins—my headache had grown worse with the ride and now it felt like a tiny man was beating a great drum in my skull—and Robin passed out large black squares of silken cloth. "Tie these over your nose and mouth," he said. "It will stop you from breathing in the dust." We all tied these on and when we had ridden on for a few hundred yards, I did find that it was easier to breathe without choking on a fine mist of dust and powdered cinders from the burned landscape. I also noticed that wearing these kerchiefs over our faces, it was very difficult to identify us. We were now a band of masked men, I realized, riding through enemy territory. For some reason the phrase "bandit-infested" kept echoing around in my skull. And suddenly I knew why. And the realization hit me like a mace to the face. *We* were the bandits, *we* were the predators who infested the countryside; and I then knew what the target for our "training exercise" would be. It was a camel train loaded with frankincense, worth more than its weight in gold.

Robin was not content with merely telling the merchants of Gaza that they were getting a very good deal by selling their incense to him in that southern port; he was going to demonstrate in brutal terms why it was a big mistake *not* to trade with him.

CHAPTER SIXTEEN

As noon approached, Reuben led us off the coastal track and onto a path that led into the foothills. My head was splitting, but we were all suffering in the tremendous heat by that point, the sun beating down on our heads like the open door of a furnace. We all wore thin leather gloves, even in the heat, because to touch a piece of metal that had been so many hours in the sun was to receive a painful burn. Finally we turned off the track onto an even smaller path, fit for no more than goats, and steadily rising. We traveled in single file, and in silence, at Robin's order, heads down, enduring the heat, our universe restricted to the dusty haunches of the horse in front; the only sound the *clop-clop*ping of hoof on stony outcrop, blindly trusting that Reuben would lead us right.

Finally we stopped, long past noon, in a grove of cedar trees, which miraculously contained a small trickling spring.

I watered Ghost and tied him to a bush, stripped off my chain mail hauberk, felt under-tunic and sodden chemise and sponged my body with deliciously cold springwater. I seemed to have no strength at all; my head was pounding, my body felt alternately hot and then very cold. I began to shiver even in the heat of the day. I tried to eat a little, but could not force anything down. Many of the men curled up in the shade of the trees. But I resisted an almost overwhelming urge to sleep.

Little John was idly sharpening his great war axe beside the spring and I sat myself down next to him, hoping to distract myself from my discomforts, and said: "John, what are we really doing here?"

"We are following orders like the loyal soldiers we are," he said, and carried on working the whetstone smoothly along the round edges of his weapon in rhythmic sweeps.

"Seriously, John, please tell me. What are we doing here? What is going to happen?"

"You don't look well, lad. Are you ailing?"

"I'm all right," I lied. "Tell me what is going to happen."

He sighed. "God's greasy bollocks. Don't get all high and mighty, Alan. What we are doing is just the same as what we always used to do in the old days in Sherwood. We are going to stop a train of fat merchants, and relieve them of their wealth. See those scouts up there on the ridge?" I looked over to the slight rise to the east of us; I could make out two human forms lying flat against the dun-colored earth just below the crest. "I see them," I said.

"They are watching for the camel train," said John. "When it comes, we are going to go up that crest, shoot them full of arrows, charge down the other side and kill everybody who resists us. In short, we're going to ambush them. We are going to take their goods—and teach them a lesson." He grinned at me, his old reckless battle-mad grin. "It's what Robin wants; and as his loyal men we are going to carry out his commands. Some people might call it banditry, some might

303

call it highway robbery. I call it a rewarding day's work! Any road, Alan, you cannot speak of this to anyone, ever. Do you understand?"

I stared at him. I knew all the rules of being in Robin's *familia*; and silence was one of the first. I was about to say something about Christ's teachings, right and wrong, good and evil, but suddenly the world seemed to spin, my eyes fluttered, I felt myself falling, falling and everything went dark.

When I came to, I found I was wrapped up like a baby in my cloak and set under a broad cedar tree. Clearly the fever had returned and I found I hardly had the strength to move. I vomited once, copiously, and felt if anything slightly worse. Then I slept again. When I awoke, the sun was hanging low over the sea to the west and I could just make out a faint dust cloud to the south.

A signal was passed to the men and, as silently as they could, the archers strung their bows, and the cavalry mounted their beasts, and they moved into their positions on this side of the crest. Robin insisted that every man wear his black silk kerchief over his face. I had slept for perhaps two hours in the afternoon heat, and while I was not expected to fight because of my sickness, I wanted to see the battle. So I forced myself to my unsteady feet and slowly climbed up the side of the ridge on leaden legs until I was a yard or two from the top. My head was spinning, and my stomach lurching, but I made it, and cast myself down on the hot sand and rock.

Lying down flat just below the crest, I could see the camel train approaching through a haze of dust and heat. There were about forty beasts, ambling along with their peculiar swaying gait; each burdened with two great bundles tied on either side of their humps, and with a man sitting well forward almost on the camel's neck, driving the animal along with a long stick. The camels were tied nose to tail to the animal in front, and beside this long train of beasts of burden rode a single file of cavalry. They were perhaps twenty men, mounted on destriers, big, well-schooled warhorses, the men heavily armed with lance and shield—and wearing, I noticed with a splash of shock, white surcoats with a red cross. They were a detachment of Templar knights. We were going into battle against our friends and allies, the humble knights of Christ, whose solemn duty it was to protect travelers and merchants on the dangerous roads of the Holy Land. I felt a wave of nauseous disorientation that was not entirely due to my fever: I was on the wrong side. These riders were holy knights, doing God's work protecting the weak. My friends and companions were thieves who meant to murder innocent men and steal their goods. My vision blurred, blackened, and I had to drop my head into my arms for a few moments to regain my senses.

When I looked up, the camel train was now a mere fifty paces away. Should I warn them? The Templar knights were riding into a trap. But what of my loyalty to Robin and my friends? Before I could come to a decision, the choice was taken from me. To my far left, I heard Robin shout: "Up!" and twenty bowmen sprang out of the earth on the ridge; pulled arrows from their arrow bags on their hips and nocked them to their bows. "Stand fast . . ." shouted Robin. "Aim at the horsemen, we only want the horsemen . . . And loose!"

There was a noise like a passing flight of birds and the first wave of arrows smashed into the column of Templar knights like a mighty wind rattling a stand of dry reeds: the yard-long ash shafts clattering shields and armor, some of the steel bodkin heads lancing deep into mail-clad torso and thigh, puncturing bellies and lungs. There were yells of pain and gouts of blood; horses hit by accident screamed and cavorted on their hind legs. The camel train, panicking, began to run madly, blindly ahead; coming closer to our position. "Fast . . . and loose," shouted Robin and once again the gray shafts sliced into the white surcoats of the horsemen below us, punching into flesh. Half a dozen saddles were now empty, but these knights were some of the best-trained fighting men in Christendom. There were shouts of command and some sort of order was quickly forged from the chaos of bucking horses and cursing, blood-splattered men. The knights massed in a single line facing the bowmen silhouetted on the ridge and, shields high, lances levelled, they began to gallop toward us—only to be met by another devastating flight of arrows, which emptied another handful of saddles.

By now there were barely ten Templars still in command of their mounts as they came charging toward our ridge in a ragged line, the hooves of the destriers shaking the earth; but the bowmen stood their ground, shooting independently now, but fast and deadly accurate. I saw the leading knight knocked back by an arrow that sunk up to the flight into the center of his chest, and another man go down in a slithering rush of half a ton of dead meat as his horse was hit in the throat by three arrows, one after the other. A third man was pinned through the thigh to his saddle, and then as his horse turned I saw him pinned again through the other thigh in exactly the same place. And then our own cavalry attacked.

Coming from around the side of the ridge, twenty hard horsemen, twelve-foot lances couched, smashed into the side of the ragged, arrow-thinned ranks of the Templar knights. It was the classic cavalry maneuver, known as *à la traverse*. And it ripped the knights apart. The long spears punched through hauberks, the needle points slicing into the flesh beneath; and the Templars died, skewered like spitted hares or cut down by the swinging swords of our cavalrymen as they came round again for a second charge, hacking and snarling at the arrow-stuck knights. One Templar, gore-splashed, his lance gone, sword in his hand, had avoided death on the spearheads of our cavalry and was still charging the line of bowmen on the ridge. He got within twenty feet before a handful of arrows smashed into his chest and stomach simultaneously and tore him, still screaming defiance, from this sinful world.

With tears in my eyes, and a lump of shame in my throat, I saw those brave men die. I managed to get to my feet, I don't know why, there was nothing I could do, and began to move toward my master. As I approached, I heard Robin issuing orders for our horsemen to get after the camel train and stop it before it galloped into the sea, and then I was raving at Robin shouting, "Murderer, murderer," the tears spilling down my cheeks. "You killed them, you fucking killed them all!"

"Not now, Alan," said Robin coolly. "Not now. You are sick, mad with fever, and this is not the time for your childish ranting." And he walked down the other side of the slope with a score of jubilant bowmen following in his wake. I sank to my knees, weighed down with shame and anger—and guilt. How had it come to this? I had wanted to come to the Holy Land to do good, to do God's work; and now I knew I was part of something monstrous and venal, something truly wicked.

I don't know how long I knelt on that ridge, thinking of those noble knights, murdered in a few short moments for one ruthless man's profit—and I believe I may have passed into unconsciousness for a while—but by the time I had roused myself and managed to totter down the ridge to join our men, the camel train had been stopped, and brought back under our control, and Reuben was explaining in Arabic to the drivers that if they agreed to behave themselves and drive the camel train and its precious cargo to a new destination, a small village by the sea called Haifa, where the precious cargo would be loaded onto a ship, they would be rewarded and set free with their camels to return southward. If not . . . he made a short gesture, the flat of his hand moving across his throat in a cutting motion. It did not take them long to decide to agree.

I had been wrong when I accused Robin of killing all the

307

knights. Not all were dead. Three Templars had survived the battle: wounded, bloody, they were now on their knees with their hands tied behind their backs, helmets off, an armed man standing tall behind each of them. But they showed no fear, their eyes seemed to be lit with an inner fire, a certainty about this life and the next; staring proudly, defiantly at their masked captors. One of the knights, I noticed with an awful lurch in my chest, was my old friend Sir Richard at Lea.

"Our ransoms, sir, will be promptly paid by the Grand Master, who is now at Acre . . ." Sir Richard was saying to Robin, as I wobbled unsteadily toward them. The sun was sinking into the blue-gray waters of the Mediterranean, casting long, grotesque shadows in front of the kneeling knights. "There will be no ransom," said Robin heavily, his voice was muffled by the silk kerchief and yet I saw, at once, that Sir Richard recognized it.

"Is that you, Robin of Sherwood, masked like a coward? If it is so, let me see your face," said Sir Richard, trying to struggle to his feet. He was pushed back down by a heavy hand; Little John was standing directly behind him. He turned his head and looked up at the huge, blond masked man looming behind him; but there was no mistaking him from his size. "And I know you are John Nailor, and there"—he jerked a chin at me, and I stopped in my tracks—"that is young Alan Dale!" Sir Richard's handsome face contorted with fury. "Why do you attack us? Why have you killed my men? We are not your enemies, do we not all share in the same mission here in this Holy Land?" He suddenly stopped speaking as Robin pulled down the silk mask; and my master's drawn, tired-looking face was clearly visible in the dying light of the day. He spoke coldly to Sir Richard. "There; now you see me; may it give you a final satisfaction," he said. "We will talk like men, face to face. And I will tell you the truth. I never shared your passion for recovering Jerusalem, I have no quarrel with Saladin nor any Saracen; I would not be here at all were it not for you." He pointed an accusing finger directly at Sir Richard. "I am here not from my own free will but because you forced me to swear an oath to accompany the King to this God-ridden land."

Robin's men, seeing that their master had bared his face, also pulled down their masks. "I care not a jot who holds Jerusalem—Saracen, Jew or Christian," Robin continued, "but because of you and your meddling with my life—and the King's failure to keep his promises of payment—I am now in debt to half the moneylenders of Europe and the Levant. I must have money, and you," Robin paused, shrugged and then said quietly, "you stand in my way. That's all."

Sir Richard stared at my master. "That's all? You have killed twenty good men, decent, noble knights for the sake of a little money. And you say: that's all? God will surely punish you for the foul deeds you did today," he said thickly. "I leave you to your conscience and God's judgment." And then I saw him begin to pray, muttering the familiar words: *Ave Maria, gratia plena, Dominus tecum* . . . under his breath.

"You've seen my face, Sir Richard; I cannot let you live. Go to your God, I truly hope he receives you with open arms. John . . ." And he nodded at Little John, who I saw with horror had a long unsheathed knife in his hand.

Those next few moments are graven on my mind, and will be for all eternity. The blade in John's hand gleamed as it caught a last sunbeam, then his hand slashed quickly from left to right, abruptly cutting off Sir Richard's mumbled prayers. And I seemed to be frozen, a stone statue. I saw Sir Richard fall, in that awful twilight, his hot blood spilling thickly down his neck into the pure white surcoat, and then pooling on the desert sand. And suddenly I was released. I screamed, "No!" and hurled myself toward John, too late, but determined to make my protest. I was screaming incoherently at John, and then I turned, appalled, as the other two knights died also before my eyes, and I turned again and began to shout and swear at Robin like a lunatic; weeping and wailing and shaking my fists and cursing him to the sky as a murderous villain, a man of no honor, a Goddamned cur.

Through my spittle-flecked raving, I heard Robin look past me and say calmly: "Shut him up, John, will you," and something heavy smashed into the back of my skull and I knew no more.

I awoke once again in the sunlit dormitory of the Hospitallers' quarter. But this time there was no Nur, no smooth white hand on my fevered brow, no cool drink of water served by a dark-haired angel. Instead there was William, looking plain and worried, and holding out a cracked earthenware beaker of ale.

I cautiously felt my head; there was a large knot at the back the size of a hen's egg, and an ache like a bar of red-hot iron behind my eyes. My friends had at least carried me back to Acre, it seemed. My body was covered in sweat, and I was freezing cold. I took the beaker of ale, and swallowed it down in one draft. Then I pulled the rough blankets around me and tried to control my shivering.

"Where is Nur?" I asked my anxious-looking servant.

"Oh, sir," he said. "Oh, s-s-sir, I do not know. I have not seen her for three da-da-days, since you rode out with Robin on the exercise. She is not in the women's qu-qu-quarters; Elise has not seen her either. We think she may have run away, gone ho-home to her village."

"I have been here three days? And Nur has been gone that long?" My head was spinning with this news; I could not believe that she would leave me without saying anything. A hideous fear began to creep into my head.

"Yes, sir. You have been ra-raving something awful, sir, about blood and sin and Go-God's judgment. Saying terrible things, sir, about the Ea-Earl."

Even through the fever, and the accursed headache, I

could feel a rising tide of panic, filling my soul with mortal terror for Nur's life. And the name of my terror was Sir Richard Malbête. I tried to suppress the fear that the Beast had laid his foul hands on her, but I could not.

"Where is everybody else?" I asked, for I had noticed that the dormitory was almost empty. There were no Hospitaller brother-knights about either. The place was almost deserted.

"Everyone has gone to se-see the ex-executions," said William.

"The executions?"

"Saladin has failed to hand over the ransom and the Tr-True Cross, and so King Ri-Richard has ordered that all the Saracen prisoners be ex-executed."

"All of them?" I said incredulously. "But there are hundreds, thousands of them. He can't kill them all."

"Sir Richard Malbête has taken on that du-duty, sir," said William, with a perfectly straight face. "They will be ex-executed outside the city walls in fu-full view of everybody, today, sir, at no-noon."

"You'd better help me to get dressed, William."

The battlements of Acre were packed with folk and it was only by way of a good deal of squeezing, jostling and shoving that William and myself found a place to the north of the main gate where we could see what was happening below. On a wide area of sandy plain, beyond the trenches that had been dug during the siege of Acre, were row upon row of Muslim prisoners, each bound tightly and forced to kneel with their heads extended. I found out later from my friend Ambroise—who was writing an account of the scene for his *History of the Holy War*, and who liked to give exact numbers, even if I sometimes suspected that he made them up—that there were two thousand seven hundred prisoners on that plain of death. And they were all to die. The condemned prisoners—men, women and even children—were making a hideous noise, wailing, moaning and chanting the name of their false God, and were hemmed in on three sides by the ranks of our army, so there could be no hope of escape. Far to the south I could see Robin's bowmen in their distinctive green cloaks, and behind them row upon row of our cavalry. I could even make out Robin sitting perfectly still on a horse in front of the first line of archers, only twenty feet from the nearest prisoners. There were occasional jeers, catcalls from the troops in our army, and I could see that a few were making wagers among themselves, but most stood and watched the slaughter like yokels watching a cattle sale at a country fair.

Malbête's men had already begun their grisly task, and they worked in twos: six pairs of men-at-arms, each pair taking a row of prisoners. The first man-at-arms would strip any headgear or any scarves or turbans from the prisoner, then clear the way for the sword blow and then he would hold the victim steady by his hair while the second man-at-arms hacked at his neck until the head was free. It was slow, bloody work and the scarlet and sky blue surcoats of the soldiers soon became a sopping uniform scarlet. Sometimes it took as many as four blows to cut the head from the body, and many a victim lived for many moments after the first slicing blade had chopped into his neck. Of course, the easiest to kill were the children, who were quite often dispatched with a single blow. One pair of executioners was particularly inept, regularly chopping at the neck and missing completely, whacking into backbone or sliding off skull to the laughter of the crowd. Malbête oversaw the whole operation, occasionally striding up to a pair of his men who were making a meal of a victim, his boots sloshing in the puddles of gore, pushing the men-at-arms roughly out of the way and hacking through the wretch's neck with his own long sword to finish the job.

From our vantage point high on the battlements, William

and I could see the whole gruesome display clearly; but the people seemed like dolls, and the whole thing a piece of macabre theater. As I watched, a pair of blood-splashed men finished a row of two hundred victims; they cleaned the red filth from their swords with glistening hands, and calmly began on the first victim in a new row. Hack, hack, a great spurt of gore and the victim falling headless onto his side, neck still pumping blood, the head rolling a little way away, casually stopped by a man-at-arms's boot.

"What has happened to the world?" I said silently to myself. "Have men all run mad? Why does God not stop this? Why do we all not stop this? Am I trapped in some hideous nightmare in a world without mercy, a Godless universe of indiscriminate blood and death?" And yet even while I thought this, a worse idea was crawling out of its slimy pit deep in my skull. "You feel nothing," said a dark maggot's voice in my head. "You see true horror, appalling brutality, blood being shed on a massive scale—hundreds of men, children even, slaughtered in front of your eyes—and you feel not a thing. Are you still human? Have you lost the power to feel anything?"

My head was swimming, and I closed my eyes; images of slaughter were whirling in my brain: Sir Richard at Lea's body falling to the rocky ground, his blood flowing black as tar; the severed heads littering the sand like discarded rotten cabbages in the plain before me; the chop of a blade, a curse, and a gust of laughter from the crowd as the man-at-arms missed his mark. The world spun, turning like a child's toy; I could feel my body beginning to sag, my legs turning to water.

"William," I whispered. "I think I need to go back to the dormitory."

My fever returned that night with all the ferocity of a rabid wolf. And with it came the dead. My dead—the ghosts of all the men whose lives I had taken, all the men I had seen die; and they were many. I screamed in my sleep as images too terrible to bear came crowding into my racked brain. I saw the first man I had ever killed, in a long-ago skirmish in Sherwood Forest, his young face grinning at me, his neck bleeding from my sword cut. He was cutting the throat of my mother while Sir Richard at Lea looked on, totally unconcerned, saying: "She had to die, Alan, she stood in my way." I saw Little John once again take up his great axe and cut the limbs from a brigand strapped to a woodland floor, and Robin, laughing, pushed over a Saracen prisoner with his foot, howling with demonic glee as the head fell off and rolled away, leaving a trail of red in the sand.

I lost the ability to tell if I were awake or asleep: dead men came to my bedside in the dormitory that long night and spoke to me, and I raved and screamed at them, begging them leave me be. Malbête came up to me as I lay there with two servered children's heads, one in each hand like monstrous bloody oranges, and told me I must eat them: "Fruit will cleanse the evil humors from your body," he said, but in Reuben's voice. Then he laughed his deep mocking cackle.

There was a figure in the room; small, dark, dressed head to toe in black cloth, its face totally covered with a black veil. The figure came toward me, holding a single candle: as I shrank back, gibbering in fright, a small white hand came out and felt my forehead: it was cool and perfumed. And I knew with great relief that it was Nur, my lovely Nur had come back to me; my beautiful girl was beside me again. But I could not see her face. I reached out a hand, grasped the black veil and pulled. The veils slipped easily away from her head—and I screamed, screamed and screamed, yelling loud enough to rouse a thousand corpses from their coffins.

Instead of the fresh lovely face of my beloved was a monster, a caricature of the beauty of my girl. The lips had been hacked from the face, exposing teeth splintered to shards and pink gums in a skull's permanent grimace; the hair had been shaved to black stubble; the nose had been sliced away, leaving nothing but a pink, blood-and-snot crusted hole; and those beautiful dark eyes were now red-veined with her suffering. She turned her head away and bent down, fumbling for the veil, which had fallen to the floor, and I saw that her ears, too, had been crudely hacked off, leaving a suspicion of an earlobe just hanging on below small bloody holes in the side of her head.

I gaped at my beloved Nur with astonishment and deep horror; she moved her head toward me, just a fraction, and I swear I could not help but cringe away from her hideousness. She saw me recoil and snatched at the veil with her small white hand, wrapped it around her head, dropped the candle to the floor and ran from the room, leaving me only the whisper of cloth as it brushed the stone in her passing, and a lingering smell of her perfume.

My screams had roused the dormitory and brought me a visit a few moments later from Sir Nicholas de Scras, a lantern in his hand, his cropped gray hair tousled from sleep.

"Your young friend came to see you, then," he said. "I told her she should not visit until you were fully recovered. But I see that she disobeyed me. Did she frighten you?"

"What happened to her? My God, she was so, so beautiful, so perfect . . ."

"She would not tell me who inflicted those grievous wounds but I got the impression it was some of our knights— have you offended anyone recently? She had been raped, too, very brutally, our brother-physicians had to sew up her nether regions." He was entirely matter-of-fact about this most inti-mate of operations. "But there is nothing seriously wrong with her, Alan. She is a healthy girl and her injuries are mainly to her vanity. She should recover in time, with God's mercy— and your loving care, of course."

What the Hospitaller said was no doubt true. But for one who had been so beautiful, what sort of life would she have as

315

a freak: a hideous curiosity that would have children running from her in terror? And what about me? I had sworn that I would always love her: could I love her so brutally stripped as she was of her beauty? I didn't want to think about it.

I felt a white-hot wave of fury for Malbête; for I was certain it was he, or his minions, who had mutilated her. I could hear his words in my head: "It seems you have cut up another one of my people, singing boy. I think perhaps I shall now cut up one of yours." In that moment, I'm ashamed to say that I felt self-pity, too. He had taken away the one truly beautiful thing in my life, and perverted her into a monstrosity. And I felt guilt, too. Most of all, guilt. If I had not tried to kill Malbête in that cack-handed fashion, she would not have been harmed.

More guilt, too, for in my secret heart, I knew I could never truly love Nur looking as she now did.

CHAPTER SEVENTEEN

I awoke the next morning clearheaded but weak—knowing exactly what I must do. It would be humiliating, but I must go to Robin and beg his forgiveness. Without his help and protection I would have no chance of taking the fight to Malbête and revenging the awful hurt done to my poor girl.

There was no sign of Nur in the women's quarters, and Elise told me that she had taken all of her belongings and left at some time during the night. Will Scarlet was with his wife when I spoke to her and they both seemed pleased to see me much recovered from my fever. However, I was shamefully relieved that Nur had fled. I had no idea what I would have said to her. I had promised to love her always, and to protect her, but I knew what the truth was: I could do neither. She was gone, and to be honest, a part of me was glad. Another part of me ached for the beautiful girl who had shared my bed these past few months; the first girl who ever truly owned a piece of my soul.

Elise knew the secrets of my heart, I don't know how. Perhaps it was just ordinary women's insight, maybe her special gift. "I grieve for your love, Alan," she said. "It entered by the eyes, as I said it would, and I see that it has flown the same way. But do not blame yourself, such is the fickle way of men; you cannot love truly, the way a woman loves, with the whole of your heart. But that is how God, in his great wisdom, has made you."

I presented myself to Robin in his harbor-side palace, and went down on one knee before him. I had prepared my speech as I walked there, but when I delivered it to him, I realized that it was not half as eloquent as I had hoped, and not a quarter as sincere. I finished by begging his pardon for the things I had said during the attack on the camel train, and saying that if I had not been out of my head with fever I would never have said them.

"I doubt that very much," said Robin coolly. "I think that fever or no, you meant every word you said. I think that you want me to help you to kill Sir Richard Malbête, and that is why you are here, on your knees, abjectly begging my pardon. But no matter. We shall call it the fever speaking, if you wish. But I tell you now that if you ever speak to me like that again—fevered or well—I shall have you roasted to death for your insolence. Now go and begin gathering your things; we leave tomorrow. This Great Pilgrimage"—there was a hint of a sneer in his voice—"is taking the road to Jerusalem."

I turned to go, but he stopped me, and said in a different, quieter voice: "Alan, I am truly sorry about what happened to Nur." I said nothing for I could feel tears forming behind my eyelids, a knot in my throat. "If there is anything I can do . . ." he said and tailed off.

Then Robin sighed and said: "Alan, you said a while

back that you thought you knew who it was that was trying to kill me. Of your goodness, tell me his name."

I turned back and looked at my master. His silver eyes were boring into mine, willing me to reveal what I knew. I shrugged and wiped my wet face: "I thought it was Will Scarlet, with help from Elise, who is now his wife," I said, looking at the floor and sniffing loudly.

Robin considered it for a while, tapping his chin with a finger. "Yes, I can see it," he said at last. "He resented being punished and demoted, although he deserved it. I humiliated him in front of his men, which was perhaps a mistake. And he has always had open access to my apartments. She loves him, and knows the countryside, the ways of serpents and poisonous plants. Yes, I can see them as my murderers."

"But it is neither Will nor Elise," I said flatly.

Robin stared at me, his eyes glittering dangerously. "Do not make sport with me, Alan. I warn you."

"It cannot be Will or Elise because they were being married at noon on the day after we took Acre, the day that someone showered broken masonry around your head. I asked Elise for the exact day and time of her wedding, and I checked the truth of it with Father Simon, who performed the service. They were in the porch of a church in the southern part of Acre at the time you were attacked, with a dozen witnesses. It cannot be them."

"Very well," said Robin, disappointed. "But you will continue to make enquiries?" I nodded. "If you give me the name of the guilty man, you will have my complete and utter forgiveness for your intemperate words the other day, and I will help you to destroy Malbête as swiftly as you like," he said. It was a good bargain and, as we clasped hands to seal the deal, I was surprised to find that I still felt some warmth toward the man, greedy, Godless, murdering monster that I now knew him to be.

★ ★ ★

The army assembled the next day on the plain outside Acre, where two days before Malbête and his men had taken so many innocent lives. Great barrels of sand had been brought up from the seashore and spread over the worst of the blood, but the stink of slaughter hung in the air like a curse.

Earlier that morning, I had been pleased to run into Ambroise, my tubby *trouvère* friend, as I was hauling my gear to the stables. After an exchange of pleasantries, I asked him what had driven King Richard to make that awful decision to kill all the Saracen prisoners; I was still shocked by my sovereign's actions, and I admit my faith in him as the noblest Christian knight of all had been shaken.

"It wasn't a pretty affair, I know," said Ambroise, "but it was necessary. Quite apart from revenge for all the Christian blood spilled by these people during the siege, all those crossbow bolts fired from the walls into our camp, what was Richard supposed to do with them?"

"He could have waited until the ransom was paid," I said, "and then released them. Saladin has the reputation of a gentleman, a man of his word; he would surely have paid up given enough time. Wouldn't he?"

"Oh, Alan, you are naive sometimes. Yes, they say Saladin is a gentleman, but he is also a soldier, a great general. While Richard held those captives, our King could not move from Acre. And Saladin knew that, which is why he delayed the payment for as long as he could. Richard was, in effect, pinned down here by the prisoners. He could not afford to let them go; they would merely swell the enemy ranks; he couldn't take them with him on the road south to Jerusalem—think of the men required to guard nearly three thousand people on a long dusty march, and feeding and watering them would be an expensive problem, too. No, he couldn't let them go, and he couldn't take them with him. He waited for Saladin to redeem them, but when it became clear that the Saracen

320

lord would not pay up—or part with the piece of True Cross—Richard had no choice but to do what he did."

I shook my head. I was sure that there must have been another way.

"There is one more point to make in this bloody affair," said Ambroise, "no less important. We have captured Acre, but that isn't the last fortress we have to take on the road to the Holy City, not by a long chalk, there's Caesarea, Jaffa, Ascalon . . . and many more before we take Jerusalem. And all those cities are watching very closely how Richard behaves here at Acre. And what have they learned? That Richard follows the rules of warfare: he will accept surrenders, and spare the inhabitants of cities, *as long as the bargain made for their surrender is kept.* But he will have no qualms about slaughtering anyone who stands in his way or who breaks a bargain with him. Those cities have seen what Richard will do, if necessary, and I'll wager his actions here at Acre will make the taking of them a whole lot easier."

I shuddered slightly, as if a goose had stepped on my grave. King Richard's attitude seemed to me to be uncannily similar to Robin's ruthless approach to life and death.

Later that morning, mustered with Robin's cavalry and awaiting orders, I looked down at the brownish, clotted sand as it crunched under my boots, and wondered if all that blood really would make the battles for other cities easier for our men. It seemed unlikely to me: surely if I were defending a city and I knew I was likely to be executed by Richard if I surrendered, I would fight all the harder to defend my walls. But what did I know?

The King had ordered the army into three great divisions, each roughly containing five or six thousand men, for the march south. In the lead division were the King's chosen men, among them Sir Richard Malbête, the knights Templar and Hospitaller, along with the Bretons, the men of Anjou and the Poitevins; in the second division were the English and Norman contingents, who guarded King Richard's personal Dragon Banner, and the Flemings under James of Avesnes; and in the third division came the French and Italians, led by Hugh, Duke of Burgundy, the most senior French noble in the Holy Land. We were to hug the coast, with our fleet shadowing us on the march, the great ships which would haul the heavy equipment and supply us with provisions along the way. Thus, with our right flank guarded by the fleet, we only needed worry about the left.

Before we set off, Robin called all his senior lieutenants and captains together, to give us our orders. "We are heading for Jaffa, which is eighty miles from here and the closest port to Jerusalem," said Robin when his senior men were gathered around him in a loose circle. "It will not be an easy march. We must take Jaffa if we wish to take Jerusalem, and Saladin, of course, aims to stop us." He looked around the circle to make sure everyone was paying attention.

"Our position is to the rear of the central division; cavalry will form up in the center with a screen of infantry, bowmen and spearmen, on the left and right of the horsemen. We stay together, we all march together, I can't emphasize that enough. Any stragglers are likely to be cut up by Saladin's cavalry. So, if you want to live, don't get left behind, is that clear? The infantry's job is to protect the cavalry. At some point during this march we will face Saladin's main army and in order to beat him we must keep our heavy cavalry intact. So I say again: the bowmen and the spearmen are to act as a screen against their light cavalry, and their job is to protect our heavy cavalry at all costs. Sir James de Brus has more experience of our enemy, so I think it would be helpful to hear his views. Sir James . . ."

The Scotsman scowled and cleared his throat. "According to the few reports we have, Saladin fields some twenty to thirty thousand men, mostly light cavalry, but he also has two thousand fine Nubian swordsmen from Egypt, and a few thousand superior Berber cavalry—lancers, for the most part. In numbers alone, his force overmatches ours but his main arm, the Turkish light cavalry, is weaker, man to man, than our own horsemen. They are fast, much faster than our destriers, but only lightly armored, and they use a short bow that can be shot from the back of a horse; secondary weapons are the curved sword or scimitar, the light lance and the mace. One on one, our knights will always beat one of their horsemen, but that's not how they fight. They don't stand and slug it out against single enemies."

Someone muttered: "Cowardly scoundrels," and Sir James stopped and glowered round the circle of hard men. "These men are no cowards," he said. "Their *tactic*," and he gave special weight to the word, "is to ride in close to the enemy, loose their arrows, kill as many as they can, and ride away again before they can be challenged. That way their enemy gets hurt but they don't. It is not cowardice, just good, plain common sense. But they have another tactic, too, when facing Christian knights, which is to harass the enemy with their arrows, and try to provoke a charge. When our knights attack, the Turks disperse in all directions, and the heavy charge suddenly finds itself with no target. It's like a big man trying to punch a swarm of wasps. Our knights become separated from each other, the force of the charge has been dissipated and the individual knights, scattered all over the field, can then be surrounded and slain by a dozen lighter, faster cavalrymen."

Robin took over the briefing once again: "So we do not charge them. Our cavalry does not charge until we can be sure of landing a heavy blow on their main force and smashing it. And so when they attack us, the infantry must soak up the punishment. The archers, of course, will take our revenge at a distance; but the spearmen must stand firm and take what they have to give us." Here Robin gave a wintry smile. "It is not all bad news for the foot men," he went on, "they will be divided into two companies, each taking a turn to defend the cavalry for one day on the left flank, the flank nearest the enemy; on the second day they will march between the cavalry and the sea, on the right, and enjoy a delightful stroll with hardly any danger at all. Anyone lucky enough to be wounded gets to ride in one of our nice comfortable ships." The men laughed, more as a release of tension than because the jest was a particularly good one.

"Is everybody clear?" said Robin. "If so . . ."

"What if we are directly attacked? Surely we can charge then," asked a dim-witted cavalry veteran named Mick.

Robin sighed. "They will feint at you often, but your job as a horseman is simply to march, march, march southward to Jaffa; try to understand this, Mick. The enemy wants you to charge him because he is faster than you and so you cannot catch him, and it will break up our formations. Once our cohesion is broken, and the men are scattered, the enemy has us at his mercy. So what will we do, Mick?"

"Ah, oh, I suppose we should march, march, march all the way to Jaffa," said Mick, slightly embarrassed. There was more laughter, in which I was glad to see Mick joined.

"Good man," said Robin.

It was truly a wondrous sight: like a gigantic glittering snake, nearly a mile long, the Christian army set out from Acre, pennants flying, clarions crying, the hot sun reflecting shards of light from thousands of mail coats, shields, buckles and spear points. We left behind a strong garrison; most of the young women we had accumulated in our travels, including Richard's new bride Queen Berengaria and his sister Queen Joanna, and two or three thousand or so sick and wounded. I wondered what had become of Nur, whether I would ever see her again—whether I wanted to—and then pushed that thought away: this was not a time for self-pity.

King Richard, splendid in his finest gilt-chased armor, a golden crown on the brow of his steel conical helmet, rode up and down the line all that first day with a company of knights, exhorting the commanders to keep their companies close together and not allow any to lag behind. He seemed to be brimming with energy, now that we were finally setting off toward our destination, and his strong voice could be heard in snatches up and down the column, over the immense tumult of nearly eighteen thousand men on the move.

We marched in the rear part of the second division, myself riding Ghost at a walk in a double column with eighty-two surviving mounted men-at-arms, led by Robin and Sir James de Brus. Like all the other troopers, I carried shield and lance, and wore an open-face helmet, knee-length hauberk and felt under-tunic beneath the mail, despite the blistering heat. We were plagued by huge clouds of flies that buzzed and crawled over our faces, drinking the sweat and as we were forever slapping and brushing at them, we must have looked like an army of lunatics, twitching and flapping and sweating as we ambled along in the harsh morning sunshine.

To my left walked Little John's company, a mixture of archers and spearmen. To my right, past the other line of cavalry troopers, marched Owain's men on the seaward side. We had one hundred and sixty-one archers fit for duty and eighty-five spearmen—I knew this because Robin had asked me to make an accurate tally before we left. Some of our men had died en route to Outremer, some perished in the siege, and some were sick with fever and had to be left at Acre, but ours was still a formidable force. The archers and spearmen had been divided between two companies: one commanded by Owain, and the other by Little John. If attacked, the spearmen were to form a shield wall and stand firm, and behind them the archers were to shoot down the foe. We cavalry-men were not to take any offensive action, unless absolutely necessary: as Robin had hammered home to us, our job was to march, march, march—and stay together.

Behind us came a small force of belligerent Flemings, and then the French knights of the third division. They were the rear guard, and also had charge of protecting the baggage train: forty lumbering ox-carts, several strings of packhorses, and three dozen mules. Most of the baggage was onboard the galleys of the fleet, which could just be seen, keeping pace with us out on the calm blue water to our left, wet oars dip-ping and flashing like freshly caught mackerel in the sunlight.

By midmorning it was already evident that the column had problems. The gap between our second division and the Frenchmen of the third seemed to grow larger with every step. And we were reluctant to slow our pace because it would mean losing touch with the Norman knights in front of us. So we stuck rigidly to our pace and the space between our com-pany and the French grew wider. At one point, King Richard came thundering past with a tail of sweating household knights, and I could hear him shouting angrily at the French com-mander, Hugh, Duke of Burgundy, telling him in no uncertain terms to keep up. I could not hear the Duke's reply, but the harangue seemed to have no effect at all as the hole in the marching column continued to grow. At noon, having covered no more than five miles, we stopped for a meal and a much-needed drink of lukewarm water from our skins. It was then that I noticed, for the first time, the enemy scouts.

Three hundred yards to my left, riding along the top of a small sandy ridge, was a line of cavalry: small, lean men on small, wiry ponies, their heads wrapped in black turbans, from which the crown of a steel helmet with a cruel-looking spike emerged. I could see the shape of their short bows, pro-truding from a leather carrier behind the saddle. They looked an evil crew, their dark bearded faces seemingly marked with malice and a lust to spill Christian blood. Despite the heat, I shivered.

As we resumed our march, the enemy cavalry kept pace with us, hour after hour, walking their beasts, and coming no closer. Occasionally one rider would peel off from the column, and gallop away to the northeast to make a report to the main body of the Saracen host, which was out of sight somewhere in the hills. By midafternoon, I noticed that the line of Saracen scouts had thickened considerably. Instead of a single row of walking ponies, there were now a thick column of men and horses, three or four deep. And behind the enemy column I could see more horsemen coming to join them. I looked behind me: the gap between our division and the ranks of the French cavalry had opened even wider. There was now a good quarter of a mile of empty space between us.

"Should we stop and wait for the French?" I asked Robin. I knew what he would say before I even finished the question.

"We have our orders," said Robin tersely.

I twisted in the saddle and looked behind me again. The third division was composed of a little more than a thousand mounted knights, mostly French but also with a few hundred renowned Italian noblemen from Pisa, Ravanna and Verona. They were accompanied by more than five thousand spearmen and crossbowmen, unhorsed men-at-arms, servants, muleteers, ox-cart drivers and assorted hangers-on. Despite King Richard's clear orders, they even seemed to have brought along all their women. In the vanguard of the division, in two glittering ranks, rode five hundred French knights, splendid in bright surcoats and riding under gaily fluttering pennants. Behind them trundled the ox-carts and the mule trains, guarded on either side by the footmen: tall spearmen in leather armor and skilled Italian crossbowmen, their bows over their shoulders, singing as they marched. In the rear was another double row of knights. The formation was a good one, designed as it was for the defense of the supplies in the wagons, or it would have been but for the yawning space between the third division and the rest of the army. There seemed to be no sense of urgency, but I could see that the real problem was the ox-carts, which moved along too slowly. Even moving at a walking pace, the double row of knights at the front was constantly having to rein in and wait for the big wagons to catch up to them. And every time they did this, the space in our column gaped a little wider.

"Alan," said Robin, "ride up to the King and inform him of the situation; tell him we are in grave danger of leaving the French behind, and that we must slow the march. Go on, quickly. I don't like the look of those Saracen horsemen."

I guided Ghost between two of Little John's walking spearmen and put my spurs into her sides. As I galloped up the left-hand side of the army, I looked over to the East and I could see what Robin was concerned about. A river of horsemen, hundreds, perhaps thousands of them, was spilling out into the coastal plain roughly opposite Robin's force— but they were heading toward the gap in the column. If they got between the main body of our army and the French they could surround the wagon train and cut it up at their leisure. I put my head down and raced Ghost as fast as I could toward the royal standard, a rippling splash of wind-tossed gold and red that fluttered half a mile ahead; and, in what seemed like only a few moments, breathless, sweating like a slave, I was calling out to the household knights to let me pass and, suddenly, I was in the presence of the King. He looked older than when I had last seen him this close, on the beach in Cyprus, and more careworn, and I knew I was about to add to his worries.

"Greetings, sire, from the Earl of Locksley, and he says that the French and the baggage-train are being left behind and we must slow the march or abandon them. Also, it looks as if a large body of Saracen horse is on the verge of getting between us and that same division."

"Are they, by God! William, Roger, Hugh, you three come with me; the rest of you keep the column going. Blondel," I smiled with pleasure at the King's use of his personal nickname for me, "how many cavalry does Locksley have, about four score, isn't it?" I nodded in agreement. "Right, let's go and see if they are any good."

As we cantered back down the column, the King, his three bravest knights and myself all riding abreast, I saw that we were already too late. Three or four hundred Saracens in loose formation were galloping their scrubby little horses straight at the leading knights of the French division. All had their short bows in their hands, and as we watched, they let fly a cloud of arrows, which sailed high, came down, and rattled against the knights' shields and chain mail coats. Without slowing their horses, the Saracens plucked fresh arrows from quivers on their saddles, nocked and loosed again, and again, and again. I was astounded, their rate of fire was faster even than our own Sherwood bowmen, and they were accomplishing this from the back of a galloping horse! Just as the Saracens must surely smash into the ranks of the French knights, who had levelled their lances, and were trotting forward ready to receive them, the Saracens swerved away from the line of knights, rode swiftly along the face of the division shooting another shower of arrows, skewering horses and men at close range, and then curved away back the way they had come, turning in their saddles to give the French one last parting volley from their short bows. It was an amazing display, and I doubted if anyone in our army could match their skill on the back of a galloping horse.

As they rode away from the knights, I noticed something strange: although many of the Frenchmen were stuck with arrows, some even had three or four shafts jutting from their mail, there were only a handful of empty saddles: far too few for the volume of arrows loosed at them. And then it dawned: the arrows might come thick and fast, but they had little power to penetrate proper armor, unless the horsemen were close. Certainly their weapons did not have the immense power of a Christian war bow, which could smash an arrow head through the interlocking steel rings of a hauberk, through the felt padding underneath and on deep into the body of a knight.

The King was now very close to Robin's men, and we were still a good half mile from the French division, but I swear I heard the roar that the French knights gave as they dug their spurs into their horses' flanks and began to enthusiastically pursue the fleeing Saracen cavalry.

The King shouted: "No, you fools, no!" And we pulled up, panting, next to Robin and his marching men, as five hundred of the finest knights in France galloped madly across the field in front of us, the giant destriers bearing heavy, fully armored knights, chasing the bouncy little ponies that skipped away into broken scrubland to the east. The knights charged in a compact mass, but on reaching the broken ground they split up into knots of twos and threes chasing after Saracens like a pack of terriers dropped into a rat-infested barn. And worse than this—no sooner had the knights charged than another smaller force of Saracens, perhaps two hundred or so warriors, emerged from behind a low ridge and headed straight for the now-unguarded, open face of the wagon train. With stunning speed, they charged straight through the gaggle of crossbowmen who had hastily assembled to bar their way, cutting down men with their scimitars and shouldering the footmen aside with their ponies, and began slaughtering the unarmed drivers of the ox-carts with their blades, and leaning low in the saddle to hamstring the draft beasts. Within a dozen heartbeats, the whole baggage train had been brought to a standstill. The French knights at the other end of the third division were too far away to help, and although a handful of unhorsed men-at-arms and spearmen fought valiantly, they were no match for fast-moving men on horseback. In front of our eyes, the Saracens butchered the foot soldiers, slicing unprotected into faces and warding hands with their cruel curved swords, and began to loot the wagon train. It was sheer carnage, footmen reeling back, blood jetting from terrible face wounds, others simply running to the rear, oxen bellowing in pain, drivers trying to hide beneath the heavy carts to escape the fury of the marauders—and the Saracens, almost unchallenged, helping themselves to goods, clothes, valuables, food and trotting away at their leisure with their plunder hanging heavy from their saddles.

We had not been idle, however. Robin's cavalry force of eighty tough, well-trained men had turned around and formed up in two ranks, lances raised, and at the King's command of "Advance!" we trotted toward the bloody chaos of the French division.

The men advanced in perfectly straight lines. At a command from Sir James, the lances of the first rank came down in unison and forty horsemen leaped forward as one man. The first line covered the ground to the wagon train in ten heartbeats and crashed into the handful of Saracens who had been particularly greedy or just tardy in making their getaway. Moments later the second line followed them in. Sir James de Brus's hours and hours of patient training had showed their worth. The lines of mail-clad riders surged forward like a rake through long grass, and the long spears plunged deep into the disordered enemy, skewering them in the saddle, and hurling their punctured corpses to the ground. However, only a few dozen raiders were caught by our sharp lances; most had seen our approach and were galloping eastward, heads turned back to watch us, as fast as their laden horses could carry them.

And then, having swept the enemy away from the wagons, and taken as many as we could on our spear points, we did the proper thing. We halted the charge with exemplary control a few hundred yards past the strewn wreckage of the lead ox-cart, and returned to the safety of the division. I had killed no one; in fact, I never came within twenty feet of a Saracen; but order had been restored to the wagon train in a short space of time, and the marauders had been seen off.

"Neatly done, Locksley," called the King to Robin. "Very neatly done." And my master bowed gravely in the saddle at his sovereign, but I thought I caught a flicker of intense relief crossing his face, as brief as summer lightning.

"Blondel," my King was calling to me.

"Sire?"

"Get back up to the head of the column. Go and tell Guy de Lusignan to rein up—I beg your pardon, I mean kindly request His Highness the King of Jerusalem to halt the march at my request. We will camp here today and try and get this mess sorted out. Off you go. Quickly now."

And so I went.

The French knights drifted into the camp very late that afternoon in ones and twos, exhausted, thirsty, on lame, sweat-lathered horses. Their charge had had no impact on the enemy, as they had not been able to bring their lances to bear on them. They had achieved nothing; and lost more than half their number in the bloody spread-out skirmish that followed. After the charge had petered out, the knights found themselves scattered, alone, in unfamiliar territory, and they had been swiftly surrounded by swarms of Saracens, who appeared as if from nowhere; their horses were promptly killed beneath them, stuck with dozens of arrows, and then the unfortunate noblemen were either taken prisoner, or briskly slaughtered by enemies who outnumbered them ten to one. No more than two hundred of the knights who charged so boldly that afternoon made it back into the camp that evening, and many of those bore grievous wounds that would ultimately bring them face to face with their Maker before long.

I got all this from Will Scarlet, who watched some of the surviving French knights come limping in, and had spoken to their sergeants. Will had done well in our brief charge against the looters of the wagon train. He had killed a man with his lance, goring him through the waist above the hip as the Saracen was trying to escape with two great sacks of grain, which were so large that they had significantly slowed his horse. Will was excited at having, as he put it, "struck a proud blow for Christ," and I was pleased for him. I could not remember why I had ever suspected him of being Robin's potential murderer. Looking at his honest face, with his cheerful gap-toothed grin, as he told me yet again about how he had directed the lance-head for the killing strike, I realized that he was a true friend, and a good man to have by my side when we were so far from home in an enemy land. I felt a wave of sheer misery when I thought of England; I longed for the cool air of Yorkshire, for Kirkton; I longed to see my friends Tuck, Marie-Anne and Goody again; for a brief self-indulgent moment, I wished for nothing more than to be home once more.

The next day we stayed where we were, within a morning's brisk ride of Acre, but we saw nothing of the enemy save for a few lone scouts on the skyline. The King had decided to reorder the divisions, much to the shame of the French. From now on, Richard decreed, the knights Hospitaller and Templar would take turns in guarding the baggage in the wagon train. It was the position of maximum danger and, correspondingly, the most honor, and he was relieving the French of that duty. It was a slap in the face for Hugh of Burgundy, of course, but Richard was angry that his orders had been disobeyed on the first day of the march and he wanted to punish the Duke.

The King also realized that, in the heat of late summer— it was by now the end of August—we could not march in the middle of the day and so he ordered that the next day we all rise in the dead of night, so as to be ready to march at break of day. And that is how we proceeded from then onward: stumbling out of our blankets while the moon was still high; saddling horses by sense of touch, shuffling into our positions in the dark and moving off as the first pink streaks stained the eastern sky above the mountains. We halted each day before noon, made camp, and fed and watered the horses, before collapsing exhausted in any shade we could find to sleep away the afternoon.

Even traveling only during the morning, it was a very hard march; the problem for me was not so much my chain mail hauberk, which was heavy enough, but the thick felt undergarment that I needed to wear beneath the mail to serve as padding and give me sufficient protection against the arrows of the Saracens. It was almost unbearably hot to wear, and yet I dared not take it off while we were on the road, for we were under threat every day.

We were attacked somewhere along the column almost constantly, small harassing raids on a place where the enemy perceived there to be a weakness. A couple of hundred Saracens would swoop in, riding like the wind, swing past our marching line, shooting arrow after arrow into our ranks and then gallop away, still firing their short bows as they retreated. It was humiliating, rather than truly dangerous, at least to the mounted men-at-arms.

Unless shot from very close, the arrows would not penetrate through our mail and felt under-jackets, but stuck in the metal rings leaving us looking, after a prolonged cavalry attack, like human hedge pigs. Each arrow strike was no harder than a slap from a man's hand but it was still unnerving and painful to feel a weapon strike your body, even if little damage was done. The real danger was to the archers—who built themselves makeshift shields from old wicker baskets or empty wooden boxes and who wore as much extra padding as they could in the searing heat—and to the horses: clad only in a cloth trapper, these brave animals were especially vulnerable to the arrows. Although they penetrated only a hand's breadth into the animal's muscles, half a dozen arrows could drive a horse mad with pain, and several animals went berserk during the march, killing men of our own side by kicking and biting like demons, until they were put out of their misery by a brave knight with a sword or, more often, a crossbow bolt or arrow from a few yards away.

Robin's company fared better than most. The Saracens soon learned that if they came too close to our ranks, and the great Wolf's Head banner that we marched under, they would lose scores of their men from the sharp arrows of our bowmen. In fact, we were seriously attacked only three times over the next ten days as we marched through that heat-blistered terrain.

We marched past Caesarea, which had been razed to the ground by Saladin, and did not even pause for a drink at this once-proud Biblical city; but we did not lack for supplies, even though the baggage train was attacked on an almost daily basis. In the early evening, food, supplies and sometimes great barrels of freshwater and ale were brought ashore from the galleys of the fleet. And, on the whole, we ate well in the cool of the dusk. One evening, the King asked me and several of the other *trouvères* to come to his fireside and sing, but, while we pretended some jollity, drank his wine and made verses together, it was an uncomfortable meal. Sir Richard Malbête was there and he spent the whole meal staring at me across the fire with his feral, splintered eyes, but saying nothing. I imagined that I could see the mutilated face of Nur hovering above his shoulder, and it put me off my versifying. The King had received a spear thrust in his side during one attack on the column, not a serious wound, but enough to give him pain when he moved too quickly, and he was not in the best of form as a musician. And, on top of all that, it felt somehow wrong to be singing witty ditties about fair ladies and their elegant games of love when we were in the middle of a desert, with the cries of the wounded breaking the night, and with a vast army of pagans somewhere out there in the darkness who would be trying to kill us in the morning.

One evening, William came to me, bearing a message from Robin. My master had been distant with me since the raid on the caravan, despite the fact that we were now officially reconciled. And I was not unhappy with that state of affairs.

"The Earl wants you to come to his te-tent, as quickly as possible," said William.

I found Robin in his pavilion, seated on an empty box with a drawn sword in his hand.

"What is it, sir?" I asked as I entered. Robin jerked his chin at the bed, a simple pallet with a rough wool blanket on it. "Pull back the blanket, carefully. It's not a snake this time," he said. The hairs on the back of my neck bristled. And very cautiously I peeled back the woolen covering. Then I stepped back with a gasp of disgust: a huge, mottled brown furry ball as big as my hand was lying in the center of the bed, and then, very slowly, it moved one of its many greasy legs.

"What is it?" asked Robin. He used the flattest, dullest tone possible, the one he used when he was feeling some strong emotion but wished to disguise it.

"I think it is a spider, but I have never seen one so big," I said. "Reuben would know." Suddenly, Robin moved, he stood up, lifted his sword and lunged all in one smooth action, stabbing the great hairy beast through the center of its body, the blade splitting the canvas of the pallet. The legs writhed as the animal was impaled on Robin's blade, and biting back my deep disgust, I could see yellow pus seeping from its death wound.

Reuben was summoned and he hobbled into the tent on a pair of crutches. His broken leg, it seemed, was healing well, and he had suffered no ill effects from his horseback jaunt with

Robin on the day of the frankincense raid. "It's a tarantula spider," he said. "Give you a nasty bite but not fatal. And it was in your bed? Again?" He sounded incredulous.

Robin waved us out of the tent, he wanted to sleep, he said, but Reuben stopped me just outside. Taking my arm he led me out of earshot and said: "I understand that you have had a falling-out with Robin." I made some meaningless grunt by way of reply. "He is a hard man, certainly; ruthless, and he can be cold as the grave, but you must try to put yourself in his shoes. He carries the weight of many lives on his shoulders, and he does not complain: his men, his wife Marie-Anne, and their little son, you, and even myself—we all are beholden to Robin. And he does the things he does, even the terrible things, to succor us all."

I said nothing. I knew Robin's philosophy well: he would do anything to protect those inside his *familia*, his friends, loved ones and retainers, and all the men and women who served him. But anyone outside that charmed circle was nothing to him; enemies, strangers, even comrades of the Cross did not exist as real people for him. They were to be used, lied to, tricked, ignored, even killed if it served his aims.

"I am a Jew," said Reuben, "I understand about family, and about protecting your own. And I know why Robin does what he does. And I can respect that. He is a great man, truly he is. And that is why"—he stopped for a few moments—"that is why, if you know who the person is, within our camp, who wished to harm Robin in these foul and underhand ways, you must tell me now."

He looked at me, his dark eyes catching a hint of fire-light, and waited for me to speak. I wondered if he knew that Robin had abandoned his daughter to death in York, and how that would change his opinion of the "great man." Perhaps he had not seen, as I had, Robin make that awful decision. I guessed not. But something stopped me from telling him the truth about Ruth's death. Instead I said, slowly and clearly: "I do not have any idea who it is who wishes to kill Robin."

I was lying. I was almost certain who the guilty person was. I just did not know *why* he wanted my master dead. And a part of me was not sure anymore that I wanted to stop him.

CHAPTER EIGHTEEN

Saladin had picked his battlefield well: a wide, gently rising plain of short springy turf, which might have been designed by God for horsemen to exercise on. Naturally, he took the higher ground, to the east, farthest from the sea. As we marched out of a deeply wooded area to the north, and onto the wide plain of Arsuf, as this place was known, I saw the whole Saracen host arrayed against us: a great, moving smear of black and brown and white, almost a mile long. It was difficult not to be awed by their numbers. Rank upon rank of Turkish cavalry on their small wiry ponies, green and black flags flying above them, helmets shining in the clear air, thousands of warriors in neat rows, bows in their saddle holders, their horses' heads down cropping the grass. In the center of the line were the huge Berber horses, their riders' heads draped with white cloth against the heat, long, sharp lances gleaming in the morning sunshine. Here and there were regiments of footmen, with big swords and small round shields. These were strange seminaked dark men from the far south of Egypt, I had been told, well-muscled brutes, with faces and skins the color of aged oak, and brilliant teeth. It was rumored that they could leap over a horse with a single bound, that they felt no pain, and drank their enemies' blood from cups made out of skulls.

The scouts had reported the presence of the Saracen army before we debouched from the forest, and Richard had issued clear orders to the whole army. We were to stay together, all the divisions tightly connected, the rows of men so close together that an apple thrown into the ranks would not hit the ground, and wait for them to attack us. We were to hold fast, we were not to attack until the King gave the signal. He repeated this point many times. We were to endure their assault until the time was ripe, and then on the King's signal, we would charge: two trumpet blasts from the first division, two from the second, and two from the third. Robin has issued extra arrows to our bowmen, some of the last of the ones we had brought from England. Then he checked that everybody understood the King's orders.

As we filed out from the forest that early morning in September, the King was in the vanguard with his military household and two hundred white-clad knights of the Order of the Temple of Solomon. They were followed by the warriors from the wide Angevin lands and Aquitaine; the Normans came next, and we English, and I gazed up at the great red and green Dragon banner of Wessex that Robin's men had been personally charged with protecting by the King that dawn. It was strange to see a great Saxon symbol in all this Norman pageantry, but our men were proud to have been chosen as its guardians, and walked all the taller to be marching under the flag that our people had fought so bravely under since the time of King Alfred.

Behind us came the Flemish under James of Avenses, a great hero to his men, and then the French knights, who had recovered some of their bounce since the disastrous first day of the march and looked eager for a fight, and last of all came the Hospitallers, two hundred and thirty warriors, as skilled in war as they were in mending men's broken bodies, riding close to the precious baggage train. This time no mistakes were made and the ox-wagons, the sides of the great brown beasts trickling with blood from the urging of sharp goads, were hard on the heels of the French. I could have thrown an apple, had I been so inclined, and hit the cheerful face of my clever and kindly friend Sir Nicholas de Scras, who was riding in the front rank of the Hospitallers. Instead, I waved a friendly hand, and received a salute in return.

When the whole army had emerged onto the plain, nearly twenty thousand men, the King gave the signal for a halt when the vanguard approached a shallow, marshy river that ran directly across our path and down to the sea. The trumpets rang out and a message was passed from commander to commander down the line. We all had turned left to face the vast enemy, who were now less than a mile away, the spearmen and archers on the right of our march, the seaward side, the west, pushing through the horses to form up in front of our cavalry ranks facing east. We were a great, fat line of men and horses and beasts of burden. Our right flank, in the south, the King's division, was anchored on the river. The left, the Hospitallers and the baggage, received some protection from the woods. A mile away, the enemy sat still on the higher ground to the east, making no advance, content, it seemed, to allow us to make our formations, although I could see units of horsemen and their dust in the far distance moving laterally behind their front lines. For a quarter of an hour nothing happened. There was just the rustle and chink of our men sorting out their weapons and equipment, and the murmur of soldiers talking quietly with their neighbors. "Now what?"

said a loud voice from in front of me: Little John, of course. "Now," said Robin in his carrying battle voice. "Now, we wait. Stand down, but don't leave your positions. We wait for them to make the first move."

And wait we did, for an hour or more, as the sun rose over the hills to the east and began to burn the joy out of the day. We stood or sat on our horses, all in our full battle gear, sweat trickling down our ribs, staring at the ranks of the enemy in the distance, and trying to guess their numbers, and keep our fears at bay. Saladin had been reinforced, I had been told by Ambroise, and his force was now in excess of thirty thousand strong. It was a daunting thought: we had some fourteen thousand footmen, wielding spears, bows, swords and crossbows—but only about four thousand knights. We were heavily outnumbered and every man in the line knew it.

Priests moved along the front of the line reciting prayers and sprinkling Holy Water on the troops who knelt to receive the blessings of the holy fathers. Father Simon was working his way through our ranks, blessing weapons and assuring the men that God and all the saints were on our side and would come to our aid. "And any man who dies in this struggle can be assured of a place at the right hand of the Father in everlasting bliss," he said. I hoped it was true, that God would welcome all our dead into Heaven, for I felt that my death was close. Once again, the ice-snake of fear slithered in my belly—I had always been lucky in battle, perhaps this day my luck would run out. I mumbled the *Pater Noster* under my breath, hoping that the words that Christ himself had taught us would give me courage and strength.

"God's great bleeding arse-grapes, what's the matter with these people. Are they shy? Don't they want to fight? What are they doing up there, lined up so pretty and brave if they don't want a nice battle? Christ on a crutch, this is beginning to get very dull." Little John's blasphemous words shocked me back into reality. And strangely they gave me comfort, too. I had fought beside these men before and triumphed. I could not seriously imagine anyone killing Little John, or Robin for that matter. I looked to my right and saw the Earl of Locksley sitting on his horse, as cool and unconcerned as if he were on a picnic. He was humming under his breath, as I knew he often did before battle; his helmet rested on the pommel of his saddle, a slight smile was playing over his face and he was idly twisting a long eagle's feather in his fingers, admiring the play of sunlight on the tawny colors. He must have sensed me looking at him for he suddenly glanced over at me, and half-smiled. I looked away quickly, ashamed that he had caught me staring at him. *Remember: his hands are stained by the innocent blood of Sir Richard at Lea,* I thought, furious with myself.

A messenger came riding down the line, a *trouvère* whom I knew slightly; I noticed that he stopped and conferred with the commanders of each division in turn, and soon the word was out. We would move on; there would be no battle today. My cowardly heart gave a leap of joy. I had a reprieve. If the Saracens did not want to fight, well, we would just keep on marching down to Jaffa, which was now less than fifteen miles away. As the news spread, the whole column seemed to rise and shake itself like a large, long-bodied dog, a fierce wolfhound perhaps, getting up after a snooze by the fire. A flurry of activity ran all the way down the line, orders were shouted, those cavalrymen who had dismounted, pulled themselves back up into the saddle, the foot men who had been seated got up, shouldered their arms, and the whole pack of us prepared to march. Trumpets blared, whistles blew, junior officers shouted at their men and the whole massive column began to lumber off the field, away from the enemy, the first units splashing through the wide shallow river to the south of the plain. There would be no battle; we were on our way to Jaffa.

Just at that moment the enemy drums began to sound; a deep booming noise that vibrated the chest, and put a shiver into a man's legs. Alien pipes shrieked, cymbals clashed, and brass gongs sounded. I could hear a faint cheer, and there was a ripple of movement in the enemy lines. And for a moment, the whole Christian army seemed to pause. It felt as if I had been sitting in a small room with another person, a stranger, neither of us speaking, and just as I had got up and decided to leave this churlish companion, he had suddenly addressed me. We were wrong-footed, slightly confused by the enemy's timing. And while we hesitated, and their drums boomed, and their clarions blared, a huge mass of Turkish cavalry on the right flank of the enemy, opposite the Hospitallers of the third division, broke away from their line and began to move slowly toward us. We had moved only about a quarter of a mile, perhaps less, when the enemy began to advance, but no one gave the order to halt, and so some of our men carried on marching and some stopped. Suddenly, disastrously, there were gaps appearing all along the column between those who had decided to march and those who had stopped to face the enemy. Men cursed and stumbled, knocking into the men in front; others were buffeted by men from behind. King's messengers, heralds and *trouvères* charged up and down the line bellowing that we were to halt, and close up the gaps in the lines again; urgent trumpets reinforced this message. And into this mess, an army, strung out on the march, trying to change its mind, charged a thousand highly trained Turkish cavalrymen, bows in their hands, pagan wickedness in their hearts.

The enemy riders made straight for our extreme left flank: the baggage train guarded by the Hospitallers. Like a wheeling flock of sparrows, but with the noise and thunder of a mountain avalanche, they swooped in drums booming in unison, like the heartbeat of a giant, coming closer and closer to the slowly moving wagons. A thousand bowstrings twanged as one, a thousand shafts were loosed forming a black smudge in the pale blue sky, and they descended like a thousand tiny thunderbolts onto the Hospitallers, foot and horse, clattering against arms and armor like a child drawing a stick along the palings of a wooden garden fence; another volley swept up into the air, but lower this time, and smashed into our rear guard, and then the horsemen swung away, turning their ponies as neatly as dancers, and loosing one last volley as they raced away back to their lines. The attack had taken no more time than a *Pater Noster*, but the effect on us was devastation. The shafts had slammed into the ranks of the footmen guarding the baggage train, spitting Christian limbs and dropping good men in bloody twitching heaps. It seemed the Turks had learned from their previous failures to pierce our mail and this time they had held their fire until the horses were merely dozens of yards away from the Christian lines. The spearmen of the third division had stood firm; meeting the blizzard of arrows with their teeth gritted and their shields high, and many died for their bravery, pierced with a handful of shafts at the same time; others took horrific wounds to face or neck. A few crossbows answered the arrow storm with a return fire of wicked black quarrels; and when the Turks pulled back, I was glad to see that they left a trail of bodies in their wake.

I saw a knight in the black habit of a Hospitaller, racing his horse up the rear, seaward side of the line toward the King's division. "That'll be them asking for permission to charge," said Sir James de Brus.

"They won't get it," was Robin's laconic reply.

And then the second wave of Turkish cavalry began their charge. While the first wave had been attacking the Hospitallers, a second formation as large as the first had moved forward and, as the first unit sped away from the baggage train, firing backward from their retreating saddles, another thousand screaming light cavalrymen thundered in their comrades' hoofprints to bring a storm of death to the battered black knights and their beleaguered foot soldiers. Some Hospitallers led their horses to safety behind the lines and took their place, afoot, long lance in hand, in the thinning line of spearmen. And still the drums boomed, pipes squealed, cymbals clashed, and the Turkish arrows thrummed through the air; I could hear the screams of the wounded and the war cries of the knights and footmen above the hellish din—and then I had to tear my eyes away from the valiant defense on the left for, suddenly, we had our own problems. A large force of Saracen light cavalry—some hundreds of them—had peeled from the main body of the enemy and was trotting directly toward Robin's men. The battle was now coming to us.

"Shield wall," bellowed Little John. And eighty burly spearmen moved with smooth precision into a formation they had practiced a hundred times. They formed a line, standing shoulder to shoulder, fifty paces long, their big round shields overlapping and held tightly together, long spear shafts resting in the dip between adjoining shields, and creating a barricade of wood, muscle and steel; a wall of heavy wood with an impenetrable hedge of spearheads protruding frontwards. If it held firm, no horse would willingly charge that barrier—for the animal to launch itself on those spears would be suicide.

Behind our wall of spearmen stood a double line of archers in dark green tunics, bows strung, short swords in their belts, their arrows stuck point first into the turf in front of them. And behind the archers, twenty yards behind, was the mass of our cavalry, with myself next to Robin and Sir James de Brus in the front line, ready to deliver my master's orders or relay his messages anywhere on the field.

Screaming like the demons of Hell, the wiry horsemen raced toward us. At a hundred and fifty paces they pulled back their bow cords, nocked their arrows and prepared to darken the sky with their shafts—but we were much quicker off the mark. Owain the master bowman shouted a command and with a noise like an old oak tree creaking in a gale, a hundred and sixty archers pulled back their bowstrings to their ears and loosed a wave of gray death over our shield

346

wall directly into the surging tide of charging Turks. The arrows smashed into the front rank of the enemy horsemen like a gigantic swinging sword, cutting down the entire forward line, hurling men from their saddles and plunging steel arrowheads six-inches deep into the chests and throats of the charging ponies. The animals tumbled forward, veered to the side or tried to rear away from the pain, throwing the whole mass of horsemen behind them into confusion. Our bows creaked and the arrows whirred again, and another swarm of needle-pointed death thrummed into the enemy formation. The horses behind the first rank crashed into their dead or dying leaders; delicate equine legs snapped like twigs under the impetus as half-ton charging animals, maddened with pain, barged into one another; men cartwheeled out of their saddles, limbs spread, weapons flying, and landed with a sickening thump on the dry ground; and another volley of arrows scythed into the press of the enemy punching into the third and fourth ranks and creating yet more carnage. A few hardy souls, still a-horse, nimbly picked their way through the dead and dying men and animals, and tried to continue the charge, but they were soon cut down by the archers, firing at will and picking their targets. The whole charge had come to nothing, destroyed by a few hundred yard-lengths of ash, hurled by a long stick and a piece of hempen string. I could see that the rearmost ranks of the enemy were pulling their mounts around and heading back to their lines. Riderless horses trotted aimlessly across the field, an unhorsed man, his black turban unwound in a long black trail of cloth to reveal a shiny spiked helmet, was cursing and rubbing his bruised body. He shook his sword at us in rage and then, as an arrow thumped into a horse carcass beside him, he backed away, and, looking fearfully over his shoulder, he started to run back up the hill to safety. The archers let him live, and they cheered themselves lustily for having broken the charge—but halfway through the celebrations, the cries died in their throats, for only seventy yards away, coming round the side of the wreckage of the Turkish squadrons, which had screened their advance, and coming on at a canter in perfect order, was the brigade of Berber lancers. Five hundred men advanced, wrapped in fine-mesh steel mail and loose white robes, each armed with two short, light, throwing javelins and one long stabbing spear, on big fresh horses. And they were coming for our blood. We just had time for one ragged volley of arrows from the archers and these elite and savage horsemen were upon us.

The Berber charge came at us obliquely, from the right, avoiding the tangle of broken men and maimed, kicking horses that strewed the ground directly in front of our lines; they came from the right, and their charge was preceded by a lethal shower of javelins, which fell like a dark killing sleet on our thin line of footmen. The yard-and-a-half-long weapons rose in an elegant arc and sank into the bodies of the archers and spearmen, dropping them in a shambles of flailing arms and spurting gore; I saw one bowman taken straight through the neck by the slim throwing spear, another man sat on the earth looking bemused and holding tight with both hands to the javelin that grew from the center of his blood-darkened belly. Little John was bellowing for the shield wall to close up, close up, when a second flight of javelins crashed into the shields of our men. On the back of Ghost, I raised my own shield, and tucked my left shoulder behind it.

The throwing spears were much heavier than the few arrows that the Turkish horsemen had managed to loose at us. As they crashed into the heavy round shields, the spearmen were often sent reeling back, the line breached until the man could regain his footing and press back into his appointed slot. Stuck with a javelin, a shield became unwieldy, unbalanced, difficult to use with any skill. I saw one spearman killed instantly by a javelin to the face, and at the same time his shield-mate on the right stopped two missiles with his wooden round and, unsupported on the left, the double blow threw him off balance. He staggered back leaving a two-man hole in the shield wall—through which a brave Berber lancer immediately spurred his horse. He stabbed at an archer who scrambled away just in time, and screaming a high ululating challenge—it sounded like a child shrieking "la-la-la-la-la"—to the line of our cavalry now facing him, he spurred forward.

Sir James de Brus was the first to react, he kicked his horse and it leaped a few yards forward eagerly toward the Berber. Using his shield to bat aside the savage lance thrust from his opponent, Sir James deftly jabbed forward and jammed the point of his spear up under the Berber knight's chin and hard into his brain. The man fell back pouring blood from the wide gash in his neck and Sir James calmly pulled his bloody point free of the man's lolling head, tipping the body from the saddle, and walked his horse forward to fill the gap in the shield wall with its bulk. Elsewhere in the line, under the deadly shower of javelins, holes had appeared, but Little John seemed to be everywhere, his height and long reach allowing him to wield his great double-headed war axe with devastating efficiency against the mounted foe. He pushed and pulled spearmen back into the line, bawled at them to close up, and when a Berber threatened to breach the wall, he snapped lances with an axe blow, and cut down any horses and riders within reach like some insane forester, swinging the great weapon as if it were no heavier than a hatchet. And our archers had not been idle: they knew that their lives depended on keeping the Berbers beyond the shield wall, where the white-robed horsemen now milled about looking for a gap in the line and hurling their slim missiles with terrible accuracy. Between dodging javelins, and avoiding lance thrusts, the bowmen kept up a steady stream of arrows hissing at the enemy horsemen. Sometimes shooting at a range of as little as a dozen feet, the archers' shafts frequently passed straight through the bodies of the Berbers, sometimes even striking men or animals on the other side. Arrows and javelins flickered through the bright air, and the horseman directly behind me suddenly gave a great cry and fell back in the saddle with a javelin in his shoulder. I turned and saw that it was Will Scarlet. His face was white, his eyes staring, blood streaming down his hauberk, and he slipped from the saddle without a word. I gritted my teeth and turned back to face the front. We had strict orders not to break rank, even to help our wounded. Another javelin whistled over my head; I snuggled deeper into the lee of the shield, hardly daring to look beyond it . . .

And suddenly it was over. The surviving Berbers rode away leaving the dead and wounded piled in a low, stinking writhing mound in front of our line. We had held on by the skin of our teeth; and Ghost and I had not moved a hoof in the whole course of that desperate fight.

As the surviving archers drew their short swords, and ran out beyond the shield wall to cut the throats of the wounded Berbers and Turks, and loot the clothing of the dead, I looked back to where Will Scarlet had been. His place was now filled by another cavalryman and I could see behind the lines that Father Simon was tending to my redheaded friend by the mound of personal baggage. Will was not the only casualty by any means; in fact I could see scores of our men, mainly archers and spearmen, lying or sitting behind the lines, and waiting to receive the attention of Reuben, who was hobbling about from man to man, trying to save those he could. William and the other servants were scurrying about taking water to the worst hurt, and bringing bandages to Reuben. I looked away from that scene of blood and pain and glanced right at Robin. His face was devoid of expression, save for a grim tensing of the muscles around his mouth.

I looked past my master and could see that we were not the only ones who had faced the fury of the Saracen cavalry. At least two other parts of the line were under attack by units

350

of the Turkish horsemen. Even though we had just faced an attack such as these, and many of our friends had suffered and died in it, I still found it an impressive sight to watch. The horsemen were superb, galloping in with enormous skill, loosing their arrows in great clouds on the part of the line they were challenging, and then, right in the face of the enemy, turning their horses about with their knees and galloping away, still keeping their enemies under attack as they retreated. They were inviting our men to charge, to break their ranks, and come out into the field to be slaughtered. By and large, their casualties were very low: we had few archers in the army, the majority being with Robin, and so the only damage they suffered was from a few well aimed crossbow bolts as they thundered into range and swiftly out of it.

"They are merely probing for weakness all the way up and down the line," said Robin to me. I was shocked: probing? I felt we had survived a major attack. I was also slightly surprised that Robin should address me, as our relations were still frosty, but then I realized that with Sir James de Brus out of position, he was just making a remark to the next man in the line. "And I think they may have found a weak spot," Robin continued. And he pointed past me to the left where the gentle Hospitallers were once again being menaced by another horde of enemy horsemen, which was trotting purposefully toward the extreme left of our line.

"Ride to the King, will you, Alan, and tell him that we in the center are firm, but the left is about to take another battering. Ask if he has any orders for us."

I turned my horse around and threaded my way through the wounded to the seaward side of the army. As I came clear of our pain-racked men, I twisted my head to look north behind me and saw that Robin was right: the Hospitallers were once again being mauled by massed formations of mounted bowmen. Ignoring the deep humming of the Turkish bows and the screams of wounded knights and horses behind me,

I galloped south toward the King's division to relay Robin's warning. It was glorious to be moving in that terrible heat, to feel the wind on my face, and smell the tang of salt in the air from the sea which was no more than a couple of hundred yards to my right. As I reached the group of knights that surrounded the King, ignoring a menacing glare from Sir Richard Malbête, I saw that a great argument was already in progress. My friend Sir Nicholas de Scras was gesturing passionately with his hands. "My lord," he said, "I implore you, the Hospitallers must charge—and soon. We cannot take much more of this; the Turks' arrows have nearly wiped out our footmen, and the horses," he swallowed painfully, "the horses are being slaughtered from under us, and we do nothing. We must charge—else there will be no mounted force left to charge with."

"Tell the Grand Master that you must stand, like the rest of us; we must all endure until the time is right."

"But, Sire, men will say that we are cowards, that we fear to attack the enemy because—"

Richard turned on him savagely. "Hold you tongue, sir. I am in command. And we will attack on my orders. Not before. By God's legs, be damned to your Grand Master and his talk of cowardice . . ."

A household knight was plucking at King Richard's sleeve. "Sire, look!" he said, pointing down the line to the far end. We all turned our heads to look.

Nearly a mile away, a perfect line of black-clad horsemen stepped delicately out of the shambles of the shattered third division. They held their lances vertically, a pale fence of spears, sunlight winking from the points, and they walked their horses slowly forward. You could clearly see the white crosses of the Hospitaller Order of Saint John of Jerusalem on the black trappers of their horses. We were all stunned into silence; I hardly dared to breathe. Then a second line of black knights emerged behind the first.

"So they are going to charge anyway, without permission," muttered one of the King's noble companions.

Ahead of the Hospitallers was a large crowd of Turkish horsemen, many had dismounted to have a more stable platform from which to shoot their arrows at the foe, others were forming up for another charge at the wavering Christian lines. They seemed as surprised as we that the Hospitallers had emerged from between the wagons of baggage train that they had defended for so long. A few loosed arrows at the black ranks of horsemen, but they had no visible effect. Then the Hospitallers smoothly, silently, like some great cat, moved on to the attack. The first rank of knights, perhaps seventy men, broke into a trot, the mail-clad bodies rising and falling in the saddles in unison, then the canter. The lances came down to the horizontal position; the first line moved up to gallop. The Turkish enemy were still hastily mounting their ponies, desperately loosing a final arrow and scrambling to get out of the way when the first black rank of knights smashed into them. Men died screaming on the Hospitallers' long spears, the weight of the heavy horses easily punching the steel spear-heads through the light armor of the Turkish cavalry, the colossal impact of the charge splintering the mass of horsemen into tiny shards of individual Saracens fleeing for their lives. Few survived, as the first line swept through them like a roaring wind, and then the second line, the Hospitaller sergeants, came boiling into the fray, swords swinging, maces crushing skulls, more than sixty angry black-clad servants of Christ taking their revenge for the humiliations they had suffered all morning from the stinging arrows of these men. Behind them came a great mass of the remaining French knights, their boldly colored surcoats gaudy in comparison with the somber black of the first two lines of charging men. The whole of the cavalry of the third division, all those that still had horses to sit upon, charged. Some three hundred knights, the cream of our army, galloped forward to the attack—in total disregard of King Richard's orders. The French horsemen, screaming their war cries, piled into the great mass of enemy cavalry, slaughtering any Turks they could find with glorious abandon, blades swinging, gore splashing, their big warhorses biting and kicking out at the behest of their blood-crazed Christian masters.

"Sire," said one of the household knights, breaking the spell of stunned silence. "He is moving at last, look, I believe Saladin is committing his reserves to the battle." And he pointed at the enemy lines, where large masses of men, some thousands, it seemed, were moving forward on the left against the Hospitaller knights—who were still engaged in a furious mêlée, hacking at the surviving Turks with their great swords, carving men and horses into red ruin.

"Well, that's it, then. Saladin has weakened his center. We must seize the moment," said King Richard. He looked at me. "Blondel," he said, "pass the word to Locksley. He is to move up in support of the third division; pull the Hospitallers' chestnuts out of the fire, if he can, and then attack the enemy's right flank—that's on *our* left. Is that clear? He can take James of Avesnes and the Flemings with him. We will all attack now, all along the line. That is the order. Trumpeter!"

As I turned my horse to deliver the King's message, my heart was beating hard with excitement. Out of the corner of my eye, I saw him point directly at Sir Nicholas de Scras. "You, sir," he thundered, "you, sir, can tell your Grand Master that I will have words with him after this day is done, if he survives!" And then the King turned and began to shout for his best lance and his new gauntlets.

I raced back to Robin's men, but I could see the news of the order to advance had outstripped me. All along the line the horsemen were moving forward. I rejoined the line of Robin's cavalry, taking my place beside my master. "The orders are to support the Hospitallers, sir, and then to attack the enemy's right wing," I said to Robin. "The Flemings are to ride with us. It is a general attack, sir, all along the line." And, for no reason that I can easily explain, except that I must have been infected with the King's battle-madness, I grinned at him.

"Yes, it is, Alan; yes, it is. And about time, too." And he gave me a wide, easy smile.

CHAPTER NINETEEN

We advanced in a single line, riding out beyond the tidemark of dead men and horses in front of our position, and we angled our charge toward the northeast, where the scattered Hospitaller knights, having cut their opponents to bloody shreds, were hastily trying to re-form in the face of a body of heavy Berber cavalry two hundred strong that was bearing down on them from Saladin's right wing. As we approached at a trot, with the Flemings hard on our heels, two hundred yards ahead the Berbers launched a shower of javelins and then hurled themselves at the bunched Hospitallers in a furious rush of galloping horse, snarling white-clad warrior and lunging spear. But, tired though they were from their previous fight, the Christian knights were masters of this kind of war: they met charge with charge, and lance with lance; and the two forces, smashed into each other with a crash of splintering wood and the squeal of steel grating on steel.

I looked over my right shoulder to the south and saw that the whole first division, King Guy de Lusignan's knights, the Angevins, Poitevins and Richard's knights from Aquitaine, with the Templars in their distinctive white surcoats on the furthest right flank—more than a thousand heavily armed soldiers of Christ—were charging in a great mass eastward, along the line of the marshy river, toward the center-left of the Saracen lines.

I looked over my left shoulder and directly behind us were the rest of the English cavalry and the King's grim Norman knights two hundred and fifty yards to our rear. But they had not moved from their position in the center of our former line—and I wondered why, when the whole of the rest of our forces had charged. Had not the order been for a general attack? Richard, his golden crown flashing in the afternoon sunlight, was riding up and down in front of the English and Norman knights—some of the best and most renowned fighters in his army—and he was clearly speaking to them, though the words were lost at that distance. They were lined up in the order of the charge, but not a horse stirred in that hot blazing sunshine. Why did they not advance, why were they holding back?

But there was no time for further speculation. Sir James de Brus shouted an order, a trumpet blew, and suddenly we were flying toward the enemy, Ghost galloping smoothly between my knees, my shield tight on my left arm, right arm holding the lance steady. The Berber cavalry were spread over a wide area, those still living exchanging cuts, scimitar against sword, with the Hospitaller and French knights, their horses whirling and stamping, men cursing and screaming in pain, as Christian and Muslim knights fought out their individual duels. Our line of horses crashed into the mêlée at a gallop, one moment we could see a vicious cavalry battle taking place before our eyes, the next we were in among them.

In front of me, I saw a white-robed warrior slash with his scimitar at a helmet-less French knight, catching him with a cruel blow across the face and flaying the skin from the Christian's cheek with a spray of bright blood. I lined up Ghost with my knees, gripped the spear shaft more tightly between my elbow and side, dug in my heels and surged forward to plunge the point of my lance with all my might deep into the small of the man's back. The shock of the blow was immense, as if I'd stabbed the point at a gallop into an oak tree; the spear shaft was ripped from my hand, I felt a twinge in my broken wrist, and then I was past my enemy, and looking over my shoulder to see what damage I had caused. He was still in the saddle, and I hauled out my sword, turned Ghost, and galloped back to challenge him again. But he was clearly no longer a threat, the white robe crimson with blood from waist to knee, the long lance waggling from the center of his back, I guessed that the point had plunged right through him and out of his belly pinning him to the high pommel of his saddle and keeping his body upright. His eyes were wide with unimaginable pain, his open mouth was working soundlessly in the agony of his death, and, purely as a mercy, I hacked into his throat with my sword as I passed him by, to send him onward more swiftly.

In a few moments, the Berbers were all dead or gone from the field and I heard the brassy song of our trumpets sounding the recall. Looking around the field, I saw that many of the dead wore the black robes with the white cross of the Hospitallers—touchingly their horses seemed the most loyal of beasts, many standing beside their dead masters, and nuzzling at them, urging the corpse to rise—but that there were still three score or so of the black-clad Christian warriors alive, and several dozen French knights, and they, like our men, were trotting over to the great white banner with the snarling wolf's head, which was our rallying point.

Our own horsemen had not suffered too badly in that desperate fight, and I could see at least seventy of Sir James's men joining Robin and the Scottish knight by the flag. We formed up again but this time in two ranks; those who still had their lances, or who had thought to pick up discarded ones from the field, were placed in the front rank. The rest of us would follow the front rank in with our swords. From my position in the second rank, I looked forward over the heads of the lance-men and at the ranks of the enemy's right wing a mere four hundred yards away. Immediately in front of us was a thick line of foot soldiers hundreds strong, each holding a long sword and a small round shield; their chests were bare, their loins wrapped in brilliant white cloth, their faces were grim as they awaited our attack—and their skins were as dark as midnight. These were the fearsome warriors from Egypt—the mighty leapers, the drinkers of human blood. Behind them was another mass of Turkish cavalry, bows already in their hands. I shivered as I looked on the enemy host that we were shortly to charge, the sword hilt was sweaty in my hand, and I found I was gripping my shield tighter to my left shoulder.

Another trumpet blast and we were moving forward, sword in my sweaty fist, shield strapped tightly to my left fore-arm. The arrows from the horse archers began to fall on us, rattling against my shield and helmet as I crouched under their lash. I tried to ignore the stinging rain of deadly shafts and concentrate on keeping Ghost in line with the rest of the *conroi*. And we did not have to endure for long. We rose to the canter, then the gallop, and then we were upon them. The front rank spearing into the lines of dark-skinned men hurling them backward, we in the second rank followed hard on their heels. A huge half-naked black man rushed at me from my left, he howled some dreadful pagan war cry and then leaped at me, springing high in the air, higher than I sat on Ghost and he swung his long blade at my head in the same movement.

More by luck than skill, I caught it on the top of my shield and deflected it in a hissing flash over my head, and my own sword lanced out and took him in his muscular belly. He fell away, off my sword, screaming and spraying blood from his wound. But two of his fellows were running at me, one from the left again, and more dangerously, one from the right. I heard Robin shouting: "On, on, take the cavalry, take the cavalry," from somewhere close by but I was too busy to heed him. Instead of leaping at me, the dark man on my left crouched and swung his long gray blade in an upward strike at Ghost's belly, hoping to eviscerate my faithful beast, but I dropped the pointed end of my shield, and parried his low blow before swinging overhand across my body with the sword, clipping his shield, which was held above his head, with my blade's edge and driving it past to chop into the gap between his neck and shoulder, slicing deep and dropping him with a nearly severed head. For a few moments my blade stuck in his collarbone, and I had to twist and tug to free it as his hot blood pissed up my face and right arm. I was off balance, having leaned far out of the saddle to my left-hand side to strike the blow, and out of the corner of my eye I could see the other dark man, just yards away, bringing back his arm for a massive strike at my twisted waist.

The world seemed to slow, I could feel every heartbeat as if it were the boom of a mournful funeral drum. I knew what would happen next, I could not swing my sword round in time to parry his blow, and his long, heavy blade would arc into my side, smash through the chain mail, and cut deep into the side of my belly. I was a dead man.

And then a miracle occurred. There was a rumble of hoofbeats, a big horse thundered past; a long spear took the Nubian full in the chest, lifted him off his feet and hurled him away, naked body crumpling to the turf with his arm still raised, sword cocked and ready for the blow that would have killed me.

The horseman reined in a dozen yards away. He pulled out his sword and raised it in salute and grinned at me: it was Robin. I straightened in the saddle and lifted my own blade in return. "Come on, Alan," he said, "no more slacking. We can't hang around here, we have to push the cavalry off that ridge." And he gestured over his shoulder to where a huge mass of Turkish horsemen was milling about uncertainly on a low rise between us and the center of Saladin's vast army. "And on your best behavior, too, Alan," Robin continued, "the King will be watching." And he grinned at me again. He cupped one hand around his mouth and bellowed: "On me, form on me," in his brass battle voice. "Trumpeter, sound re-form."

At the mention of the King, I turned and looked back at our lines, and saw a wonderful sight: the King, his golden ringed helmet marking him out of the crowd, was advancing at speed up the center of the field. And behind him were a thousand fresh knights from England and Normandy. Their armor gleamed, lance points glittered, pennants fluttered gaily in the air, and their big horses shook the ground with the thunder of their hooves. They were headed straight for the center of the enemy line. In a flashing moment, I saw why Richard had delayed his advance. He had let our men bleed the strength from the center, sucking regiments to the right flank to face us, and the left where the Templars and Angevins were still engaged in a furious mêlée. With the center thinned by attacks on either side, Richard was now about to strike it a powerful hammer blow. Would he succeed? It was too soon to say: Saladin still commanded a mighty host, and if Richard was pushed back, and Saladin counterattacked, every man in the whole Christian army would be fleeing for his life by nightfall.

Our cavalry, Robin's men, the Flemings and what was left of the Hospitallers and French, were scattered all over the field. The brave Nubian footmen had died where they stood, cut down in droves by our horsemen. But the half-naked tribesmen had exacted a dreadful price for their deaths: scarcely a hundred mounted men were able to answer Robin's call. I offered up a quick prayer for Richard's success, and ours, and added a humble request that my life would be spared, too. And them we were off again: no neat lines this time, just the big, jostling crowd of Christian horsemen that Robin had gathered, bloodied swords drawn, grinning like wolves with the wild joy of battle and galloping madly up the hill any old how to savage the crowd of Turkish light cavalry at the ridge.

I will not say the Turks were cowards; they had faced these same blood-hungry men three times already that day and been mauled in each encounter. It was in their nature as light cavalry not to stand and face the heavy horse of Christendom, but to sting and run, regroup and return, to harass and kill from afar. But nevertheless, when a hundred exhausted, gore-flecked knights rampaged into their front ranks, swords swinging, shouting "St. George," and "The Holy Sepulcre" and one lone voice hoarsely crying "Westbury!"—the Turks fled, turning their neat little ponies and riding east as fast as they could. The dust boiled around them and thousands of fine horsemen showed their backs and galloped from the field.

It was the beginning of the end for Saladin that day. Richard's knights had smashed into the center and the King and his men were busily chopping their way through the Sultan's elite guards toward the man Richard most wanted to duel with face to face. But it was not to be. Under the combined assaults on the left, right and center, the great Muslim warlord ordered the retreat, and with a pig-squeal of trumpets and a cacophony of cymbals, leaving the regiments of his loyal bodyguard to cover the withdrawal, he quit the field in a cloud of churning dust.

We were too exhausted to pursue him. And I merely watched with a drooping head, my whole body aching with fatigue, as Richard's men smashed the last formations of the enemy in a series of lightning charges. The day was won, and praise God, I had lived through it.

Many of our men had not. Sir James de Brus was dead. I came across his body as I was riding slowly back toward our lines. He had been hacked into several pieces by the Nubians, half a dozen of whom lay dead or dying about his shattered corpse. His horse had been eviscerated and stood by his remains, whimpering, with great fat purple-green entrails hanging around its blood-splashed hooves. I put it swiftly out of its misery with a deep cut through the neck from my poniard and marked the position of Sir James's body by means of his upright sword thrust into the turf. I meant to return later and arrange for a proper burial for my friend, but the sun was low in the sky and I had no way of carrying the pieces of him back to our lines with dignity. I could feel the blood drying on my face in great scabs and when I looked at my hands it seemed that I was wearing a pair of red gloves, so thickly were they slathered in gore. More than anything, while it was still light, I wanted to go down to the sea and wash some of the battle-filth from my body. Then I wanted to rest for a month.

I returned to our lines to find that my friend Will Scarlet, too, had died of his wounds. I felt a deep welling up of sadness in my chest as I looked down at his body; the blue eyes staring sightlessly upward to Heaven, where I prayed he would now be warmly welcomed for his part in our venture. So many dead on this pilgrimage to Jerusalem; so much blood spilled in the name of Jesus Christ: I thought of the Jews of York who killed their own children and taken their own lives rather than be slaughtered by blood-drunk Christians who believed they were doing God's will; I thought of dead Ruth, whose deep eyes and womanly figure had so captivated me for a day or so, and which I now could no longer remember with any clarity. I remembered Sir James de Brus and the terrible scowl that he used to conceal a kindly heart, and poor dead Will, now lying at my feet, who had wanted to be liked by his men, and who had found a strange kind of happiness with Elise. And most of all I thought of Nur—of the shining beauty she once wore effortlessly, like a golden halo, and the poor mutilated monster that she had become—and all because of me.

The tears were streaming down the sides of my nose when my servant William came to me with a piece of bread, a hunk of pork and a bottle of spring water. "Are you hu-hurt, sir?" he asked, looking at the blood that caked my hauberk, face and limbs with deep concern.

"I am well, thank you, William," I said, sniffing, "but I must wash before I can eat. Let us go down to the sea."

And so we took the narrow path that led away from the army, down the steep red-earthed cliffs and toward the blue water in a sheltered bay away from prying eyes. I could only move stiffly down that winding path, but Keelie gambled about us like the puppy she had so recently been, happy to be alive and curious about every scent that wafted past her black nose. I wondered at her energy—I myself could hardly move and I gave William my shield to carry for suddenly I found the weight of it almost unbearable. At the sandy edge of the wide Mediterranean, I stripped to the flesh and leaving William and Keelie to guard my weapons and clothes, naked as the day I was born, I waded out through the gentle wavelets and plunged into the cool embrace of the sea. I did not travel far out from the beach for my swimming skill was poor, but with the water only chest deep, I frolicked in the comforting swell like a dolphin, washing the gore from me in the last warmth of the sun, which hung like a great bronze shield far out to the west over the dark blue waters.

Coming to the surface and looking back at the shore no more than forty yards away, I noticed something odd. I moved in toward the beach to see more clearly what was happening.

There were two figures, men-at-arms, standing beside the mound of my clothes, and one stunted shape that appeared to be a dwarf beside them. I noted the color of the surcoats, as I splashed forward through knee-high water, and my heart sank down into my bowels. They were scarlet and sky blue—and then I saw that the tall man standing slightly ahead of the other had a lock of white hair in an otherwise russet head. It was Sir Richard Malbête.

"Come out of the water, singing boy," said Malbête. "Come closer and we shall have a pleasant little sing-song on the beach." His deep voice was rich with black mirth. I stayed where I was on the edge of the water, twenty yards away; standing naked, dripping, with my hands cupping my private parts. Sir Richard Malbête did not move: he stood there, one hand on his sword hilt, and stared at me with his feral brown eyes. The man-at-arms moved over the dwarflike figure, and pulled a long knife from his belt. I saw that it was William, bound hand and foot, with a red mark on the side of his head where somebody had hit him. He was bound tightly in a crouching position, but he looked more furious than frightened when the man-at-arms put the knife to his throat. Beside the boy was the corpse of Keelie, her golden yellow head smashed open by some savage blow. I could feel a deep current of rage begin to flow in my heart, black and strong, at the death of that happy dog.

"Come to me, singing boy," crooned Malbête in his deep tones, "or your servant will surely die."

I had no choice: it was a matter of loyalty. William had been a good and faithful servant to me and I could not save myself by running away and condemn him to death, even if it meant my own doom. And I did not want to run away; I was willing to crush Malbête with my bare hands if necessary or die trying. So I began to walk, very slowly toward the two men. I stopped, just out of sword-reach, by the mound

365

of my clothes. Malbête showed his big yellow teeth. "This is going to be a great pleasure," he said in his deep, slow voice, "one that I've looked forward to for a long while. I came to this strand only looking for a quiet place to bathe, and look what I found!" And very slowly he pulled the sword from its sheath, the metal grating against the scabbard lip and setting my teeth on edge. He grinned at me horribly and took a pace forward.

Then I said: "Sir Richard, surely, you would not kill a naked man? Might I have permission to dress myself first like a decent Christian?" I was trying to sound as humble as possible; and discretely eyeing the area around the mound of my clothes at the same time. The other man-at-arms spoke then. Standing up beside William, he hauled out a heavy tangle of sandy leather belts from behind his body, from which hung my poniard and my sword. Dangling them from his fist, he said: "Was this what you were seeking, sir?" and he barked out a laugh. His calling me "sir" was in some ways worse than being called "singing boy." Disappointment showed in my face and Malbête began roaring with laughter. "By all means, dress yourself, singing boy. I am in no hurry. I like to take my time over my little pleasures." With his left hand he gestured magnanimously toward the pile of my gear.

I bent slowly toward the ground, keeping my eyes on Malbête, my hand reaching down, fingers extending, groping through the sand, feeling my way—and snatched up a fist-sized rock from the beach that I had been eyeing since I had left the water's edge. Spinning fast, I whipped my arm forward and I hurled the stone as hard as I could toward Sir Richard's face. I have said before that I am a good shot, and I have boasted that I am quick in battle, but at that moment I was as fast as I have ever been. The stone hurtled from my fist and streaked toward Malbête's head, half a pound of flying sea-smoothed rock aimed directly at his nose—and, just in time, he ducked. But God was with me that day—for the rock whirred over Malbête's head and smashed into the mouth of the man-at-arms who had just moved directly behind him. It landed with stunning force. The man-at-arms dropped like a sack of meal to the sand, and Malbête curled away from me, keeping low, darting incredulous glances at the unconscious man-at-arms, and just giving me enough time to grab my shield. Then Sir Richard lashed out with his long blade and, with a flat *crack,* I managed to block it directly with the face of the shield.

I took a step toward the fallen man-at-arms, trying for my weapons, which lay in a tangle at his side, but Malbête was too canny to let me near him. He stepped forward and slashed at my head, and then my right side in quick succession. I stopped his cuts with the shield, and backed away. I was suddenly conscious that I was totally naked and armed only with an old-fashioned shield. Sir Richard had regained his equilibrium. He swung quickly at my bare shins and laughed as I skipped out of the way of his blade. "This is going to be more fun than I had imagined," he rumbled, and I saw that he really meant it. He was enjoying the fact that the odds had moved a little in my favor, but it was clear that he still had no doubts at all that he could kill me easily. He slashed at me again, and seemed delighted when I stumbled. I was still trying to edge round toward my weapons, but every time I moved that way, he warded me off with a few well-aimed sword blows and I had to skip and dodge and block to stay alive. I stared at him, panting, over the rim of my shield; hating him with my whole heart and soul. I felt that dark current of rage move again, and this time it began to bubble up inside me, erupting in my brain as a black fighting fury—I knew I could not be killed by this man. I knew I would kill him—for Nur's sake, for Ruth's sake, for Reuben's sake, for my own sake. This day his soul would be traveling to Hell.

He must have seen something in my face, for he stopped laughing, and muttered, "Well, that's enough jesting, time to end it," and he stepped forward striking right and left in a welter of powerful blows that would have carved me into ruin had they landed. I blocked and parried, and waited for the swing that I wanted—a backhand blow that opened his body at the end of the strike, and when I saw it coming, instead of defending myself with the shield, I ducked his swing, lifted my left elbow and lunged toward him. He was already coming forward, and the tapered point of the shield smashed hard up under his chin, straight into his Adam's apple, with the full force of my weight behind it. The cartilage in his voice box exploded with a glutinous *pop*, the wind pipe collapsed and his feral eyes flew wide as he dropped to his knees in front of me, both hands clutching at his crushed throat, unable to breathe or comprehend what had happened. I leaped a yard past him and swung the edge of the shield back and down in a vicious arc, crashing the hard frame into the back of his neck like a wooden axe. There was a sound of cracking bone, his head flipped backward and he flopped to the ground, his feet drumming on the sand, his head canted to the side in an unnatural angle that could only mean one thing.

I spared no time to look at him but rushed up to the stunned man-at-arms, ripped my sword from its sandy sheath, which lay beneath his body, and sliced through his throat in almost one jerky movement.

"Oh, Alan," said William, "that was bra-bra-bravely done indeed. I have never seen a more knightly dis-display of prowess." As I stood there, trying to control my ragged breathing, watching the man's blood drain into the sand, naked but armed with a bloody sword and battered shield, I had never felt less like a knight in all my life; in truth I felt like a fighting man from the mists of time, one of those blue-painted warriors who defied the red-cloaked Romans, before the Normans and their horse-knights even existed. And then the moment was gone. My heart began to calm, and I gave William a grin, and lifted my sword in salute.

"Will you un–untie me pl–please, Alan," said William. And I took a step toward him—and then stopped suddenly. I looked at him again with fresh eyes. There was something about the way he was bound that struck a distant chord of memory with me. His knees were bound to his chest, his hands tied to his feet, in front of his knees. He looked like a bird ready for roasting at a Christmas feast. And then I knew; I had suspected for some time, but now I was certain. I knew that William was Robin's would-be murderer. And I knew why he had been trying to kill Robin for all these long months.

CHAPTER TWENTY

I stared at William for a few heartbeats, sitting trussed as he was on the sandy beach. Then I laid down my sword and shield in the sand, pulled on my braies and chemise. Though the sun was sinking, I felt too hot and bruised to dress fully—I would have liked another swim but there was no time. However, I swiftly recovered my sword belt and strapped it around my waist before I went to kneel beside my faithful servant William.

For a few moments, I merely stared at him, making sure in my own mind that he was the one. William looked puzzled; then he said: "Of your go-goodness, master, will you not cu-cut me free? My bonds are pa-paining me."

"Tell me your name first." I said.

He frowned at me. "But, sir, as you well know, my name is Wi-William."

"Tell me your full name; tell me the name of your father," I said coldly, thinking of snakes, and poison, and falling rocks and giant spiders.

He stared back at me, his expression slowly changing. His normally helpful mien—a servant's look; humble, cheerful, honest—changed and became hard, bleak and stonelike. He said nothing but stared at me with ancient pain-burned eyes glowing in an adolescent's downy face.

"Your name is William Peveril," I said. It was not a question. "Your father was Sir John Peveril—and Robert Odo, now Earl of Locksley, had him mutilated, humiliated, destroyed as a man before your very eyes."

He still said nothing. As I stared at him my mind went back three years to a time when I was not much older than William himself. I remembered a wooded glade in Sherwood at dawn, a big man strapped to the forest floor, the wet crunch of Little John's axe as he hacked three of his limbs off at Robin's command, leaving only his left arm. And the boy, a ten-year-old lad whom we thought harmless and tied up like a Christmas goose but left alive to spread the tale; the same boy who now was tied up before me on the beach and staring at me with bleak, vengeful eyes.

"Speak!" I shouted at him. "You have nothing to gain by silence. Tell me that it was you who put vermin in Robin's bed, and poison in his food and wine; admit it was you who pushed masonry on to his head at Acre . . ."

"Why do you care?" hissed William. "You hate him, too. I have heard you raving in your fever that he is a murderer, a thief, a Godless brute. He took my father's manhood and left him a mewling beggar, unable to care for himself, unable even to shit with dignity."

I noticed that his stammer had completely disappeared.

"There was no one else," he went on still in that hate-filled tone, so unlike his ordinary voice, "so I cared for him: changing his pus-filled dressings, clearing away the shit from his arse, begging, stealing food for him—and each day resenting him a little more. For a full year he lived, a half man, a despised cripple, until he found the courage to end his miserable life with his own dagger. I hate Robert Odo for what he took from my father, and for taking my father from me. But I know that you hate him as much as I do. He is evil and you know it. Cut me free and we will kill him together, you and I, cut me free and we will rid the world of a piece of rancid filth . . ." And he burst into a fury of racking sobs, a thin slime bubbling in his nostrils, tears streaming down his cheeks.

"Tell me first, William, tell me how you came to be among us. Was this murder always in your heart? Had you planned this from the day we first met in Nottingham?" He nodded. I was awed by his commitment to this vengeance. And not a little frightened. The stammer, the humility, the good-fellowship, it was all a fraud, all a means to his lethal end. "When my father had ended his own misery, I made a holy vow. I swore before the Virgin that I would kill the monstrous Earl of Locksley or die in the attempt."

"But I trusted you with my life!" I said. "Would you have cut my throat, too, while I slept?"

"Not you, sir, never you. You were kind to me." He sniffed wetly. "But I would gladly have killed the monster and crept away in the night, perhaps to join a monastery as a servant and spend the rest of my days repenting."

"And what about the boar?" I said coldly. "That came near enough to killing me in Sicily."

"I am truly sorry for that, sir," sobbed William. "I fixed the nets to fall but then the Earl-monster moved his position. I did not mean to hurt you, sir, on my life, I did not!"

I could still hardly believe that my biddable servant had planned this, my cheerful William, who had served me so faithfully for so many miles, had had this dark murderous secret, and had kept it hidden, so well, for so long.

"If I let you go now, will you promise to forgo vengeance

on my master Robert of Locksley," I said formally, half dreading the answer. "Will you swear on our Lord Jesus Christ, and in the name of the Virgin, and all the saints, to leave off your attempts to kill my master, and to leave our company and never return?"

"Never!" His eyes flashed at me. "I will never stop trying to slay that monster; I will hunt him down to the ends of the earth to have my vengeance; he must die a death worthy of his malignity . . ." I saw that flecks of spittle had formed at the corners of William's mouth and, foreseeing his fate, he began to struggle against the ropes that bound him.

I moved behind him, drew my poniard and, may God have mercy on my soul, I cut his throat as quickly as I could. When he stopped struggling, and I let his blood-slick body topple over on to the sand, I fell back myself as if I had been the one to suffer a death wound and I stared upward toward Heaven where God and his angels resided. But I could see nothing of the Divine. Night had fallen, and clouds covered the stars, and as I stared up into the darkness, lying boneless among the three fresh corpses I had made, I felt my own eyes fill with tears at the pity of life. As my tears welled, I thought about vengeance and feuds, of murder and holy warfare, and of loyalty and love. I pondered my loyalty to my master, which, despite his many grievous sins, had just now been put to the ultimate test; and of a boy's love of his father that became twisted into something hideous. I had killed William because it was necessary. It was necessary for Robin's safety, because the boy would not renounce vengeance, and I was, I discovered in that moment, and despite every evil thing my master had done, still Robin's loyal man. But, there is sometimes more than one truth, and sometimes, when I have taken more than my usual quantity of wine, I believe that I killed William because of Nur.

I had not been loyal to her. After she had been mutilated by Malbête, I had screamed in horror when faced by her deformity—and she had fled. But, in fleeing, she was acknowledging that I could not love her, looking as she did. And it was true. So it follows that I had not truly loved her, for love surely transcends mere physical beauty, and, worse, I had not had the strength to be loyal to her either. And so I killed William, in some strange way, for Nur's sake. Because I had proved disloyal to her, whom I claimed I loved, I wanted to prove that I could be loyal to Robin, whom I claimed I did not love.

On that dark beach I wept for William, and for me, and for Nur and Robin, and all of us poor sinners here on Earth, and at that very moment it began lightly to rain, and it seemed that the whole dark universe had joined in my silent weeping.

Finally, I roused myself. The blood-clotted poniard was still in my right hand. As I looked at it, I thought about all it represented. A gift from a kind man, who had been butchered before me at the command of my master; a tool that had been used to end the life of a young boy, cruelly wronged, in the name of loyalty to my master. I could hardly bear to look at it, and so I pulled back my arm and hurled it spinning in the dark air to splash, unseen, somewhere in the forgiving ocean.

I stripped naked again and dragged the bodies as far out into the sea as I could, Keelie's corpse, too, and left them to sink and sleep forever with the fishes, and then I washed myself once again from head to toe, scrubbing my body raw with the fine sand in the shallows. Next I dried, dressed and armed myself and walked wearily up the narrow cliff path back to the army.

I found my master in his tent, with Reuben kneeling before him tending to a wound in his thigh. He lifted his chin to me in acknowledgment when I entered and said: "Arrow wound: it's not that serious, Reuben tells me." He waved his hand toward a tray that held a flagon of wine and several cups. I helped myself to a drink and sat on a cedar wood chest while Reuben finished wrapping a clean white bandage around Robin's upper leg.

"So what is troubling you?" asked Robin, a little distantly. He sounded slightly irritated that I should have barged in on him. "I thought you would be carousing with the rest of them. Celebrating our glorious victory."

"I've killed Malbête," I said bluntly. "On the beach. I broke his neck with my shield."

"Good for you," said Robin. "So you did not need my help after all." He seemed indifferent, and then I saw that Reuben had given him something powerful for the pain. But the Jew looked up at me, a dozen questions in his dark eyes.

"And I killed my servant William, too. I slit his throat from ear to ear. Also on the beach."

That made them quiet, both staring at me as if I were a madman. "He was the one who was trying to kill you," I said tiredly. More than anything I wanted to get to my blankets and sleep. The wine was loosening my grip on the world. I poured myself another cup. "He was a Peveril. He was the boy we left alive when you punished Sir John three years ago. He's been trying to get at you more or less ever since."

Both Reuben and Robin were stunned into silence. Then Reuben spoke: "That kindhearted young servant boy?"

I stood up, finished my wine and looked directly at Robin. "So, my lord, you no longer have anything to fear from those quarters." And I turned my back on them and, ignoring the babble of questions that followed me, I stalked out of the tent and went in search of my bedroll.

Three days later we reached Jaffa. Saladin had razed the wall of the city and most of the inhabitants had fled before Richard's victorious army. In fact, the town was in such poor repair, little more than a vast pile of rubble, that we were forced to camp in an olive grove outside the city. Ambroise had been right: Richard's barbaric treatment of the Saracen prisoners at Acre had echoed across the Holy Land, and townsfolk would rather abandon their homes to his army than suffer siege from the victor of the Battle of Arsuf.

Ambroise pointed out exactly how clever he was when we shared a jug of local wine and a plate of figs under a striped awning near the royal encampment. "He's very fond of you, you know," said Ambroise, leaning forward like a conspirator. "The King, I mean. He thinks your music is refreshingly rustic. And he has asked me to approach you on his behalf." I was bemused. What could this mean? "Um, he knows, of course, that you serve the Earl of Locksley, and have done since, since . . ." Ambroise could not think of a polite way to say "since he was an outlaw" and so he just took a big sip of his wine. "Well, he knows, of course, that you are bound to the Earl, but certain people have been saying that you are not too happy with your place there; that there have been . . . *words* . . . between you and your master. And his Royal Highness wonders whether you would not prefer, or rather whether you might not consider joining his household, as a *trouvère*. As I say, he is fond of you, and he admires your music, and he knows that you fought well at Arsuf."

I was struck dumb. The King of England wanted me to join his household? Me, a former cut-purse, as Robin had so rightly called me—a snot-nose thief from Nottingham? I had been asked to join the King's company of nobles and friends. I could not think of anything to say. Ambroise, politely pretending that he could not detect my delighted confusion, went blithely on: "He would, of course, knight you himself. He does that with all the members of his inner circle. And there would be lands and a substantial stipend, in gold . . ."

It was too much to take in, and I mumbled something about thinking about it. But I could not sit still while Ambroise chatted about other things, watching me carefully out of the side of his eye, I contemplated my glittering future as a member of the Royal *familia*. I would be Sir Alan Dale; Sir

Alan of Westbury; Alan, the Knight of Westbury . . . the thought made me feel drunk.

When I left Ambroise, I was walking on air. I tottered through the olive groves, beaming like a fool, the horrors of the past few weeks forgotten, and feeling a sense of deep benevolence to all mankind. There was only one strange thing to mar the night. I had the strongest feeling that I was being followed. As I strolled along, jaunty as Robin Redbreast, out of the corner of my eye I could see a small, dark figure trailing me. But each time I turned to look, it was gone. As I walked along the course of a dry stone wall, I suddenly turned and looked and I'm sure I could make out the shape of a woman, dressed all in black, from head to toe in the Arab-style, fifty paces behind me. I shouted: "Nur!" and rushed back to the spot where the figure had stood, but there was no one there. I was staring at a shadowy field of olive trees with no trace of a soul anywhere to be seen. Was it my imagination, fueled by Ambroise's wine? Was she a figment of a young man's guilty conscience? Or had she really been there? A shiver crawled down my spine.

But when I got back to the Sherwood men's camping area, grizzled Owain brought me back to solid reality and told me that Robin wanted to see me. Still feeling uneasy about my vision of the dark Arab woman, I walked over to his tent and, announcing myself, went in.

Inside, Reuben, Little John and Robin were gathered around a map on a scroll on a small table. All the men bore the marks of battle: Robin's wounded leg was bandaged with a fresh cloth, I could see. Reuben was hobbling around, his broken leg still splinted, and even Little John had a long, crudely stitched cut on his forehead.

I stood in front of the three of them and waited for Robin to notice me. They all stood straight, Robin released the map, which rolled up with a crisp snap, and he turned to me. Without any further delay he said: "We're going home, Alan. At

377

least I am, and so are John, Owain and most of the men. Reuben's going to Gaza, for good. He is going to represent my interests there in the, uh, frankincense trade. But I have some family business that needs my urgent attention at Kirkton. My wife—and my *son*—need me there."

He put a special emphasis on the word "son" as if making a definite statement. I knew what he was saying, and it lifted my heart. He would stand by Marie-Anne and baby Hugh, he would be loyal to them, despite the disgrace and shame that others felt were his due, he was going home to be with his family, and by doing so he was declaring that, blood or no blood, they *were* his family, their honor was his honor, and he would fight to the last to defend it.

"So I'm going home," Robin repeated. "The King is content to let me go; wants me to do him a small service in England and to keep an eye on his brother John, who is being a nuisance, apparently. The official excuse for my departure is my wound," and he tapped his bandaged leg, "but the thing is, I have done what I set out to do here; King Richard has won his battle; and it's time to quit this God-cursed place and get back to the green dales of home. My question is—are you going to come with me?"

I was completely taken aback. He had never asked me whether I would follow him before. It had always been taken for granted. I moved my mouth soundlessly a couple of times and then Reuben said kindly: "We have heard that the King has offered you a position in his household; and we know that you have not been happy with Robin since . . ."

I was even more surprised that Reuben's intelligence was so good. I had only been told about the King's golden offer a mere hour before. But then Ambroise had never been particularly closemouthed about anything.

"If you wish to leave me and join the King, with great regret, I will release you from my service—and give you my blessing," said Robin. And he gave me a sad smile, his eyes glowing with a silvery light.

I swallowed. On the one hand, a knighthood, a well-paid post as musician to the most noble monarch in Christendom, the chance to complete our task here, to free Jerusalem, the holiest city in the world, from the clutches of the Saracens; and, on the other hand, continued service to a man who seemed to have no concept of proper morality, who obeyed no civilized laws, and who would happily murder innocent Christian men, women and children for his own profit.

There was absolutely no question in my mind as to what I would do.

"Long ago," I said, my tongue thick in my mouth, "I swore an oath to you, sir; I swore that I would be loyal until death. I have spilled much blood for that oath, too much blood—but I shall never break it. Let us go home."

And Robin smiled.

EPILOGUE

When Dickon came to see me the next morning at the hall in Westbury, I had seated myself in a high wooden chair, with my naked sword across my knees. He looked very old standing there in front of me: his thin face had a yellowish tinge from drink, what little hair he had left was milk-white; the empty sleeve adding to his forlorn air.

I sat there in silence for a long while, just glaring at him, while he shuffled his feet and began to look more and more uncomfortable. Then he spoke: "You called for me to see you, sir," he said in a wavering, frightened voice.

I let his words hang in the air for a few moments and then said: "Tell me, Dickon, how did you lose your arm?"

He was taken aback by my question. "But, sir, you know full well yourself," he said. "You were there with me at Arsuf.

You know that I lost it to one of those dirty heathens with a great big curvy sword. Surely you remember!"

I did remember. I remembered Dickon as a bright-eyed young archer, not much older than me, a rare Englishman in those ranks of tough Welsh boys. I remember him taking his wound, a scimitar cut, in the fight with the Berber horsemen, and his cheerfulness afterward, in spite of the pain, when I visited the wounded the day after the battle and brought food and water to them.

"You served with Robin Hood, then; before he was made Earl, in Sherwood?" I said.

"Yes, sir, as did you." Dickon was now completely confused. I could see that he was wondering whether old age had stolen my mind.

"What would Robin Hood do to an outlaw who stole from him?" I asked quietly. And suddenly, all the blood drained from Dickon's face as he was transported back more than forty years to the wild days in the forest when my master ruled his men by naked terror.

"I was trained by Robin—he taught me much about crime and its suitable punishment," I said, my voice as menacing as I could make it. Then I stood up, hefted my sword and walked over to Dickon. He fell to his knees, trying to beg for mercy but his mouth was too dry to allow him to speak. I put the sword tip against the stringy bicep of his one remaining arm, resting the sharp point gently against it.

"Believe me when I say this to you, Dickon," I continued. The poor man kept glancing down at the sword and then up again to my face. "If you steal from me again, if you take from me so much as a crust of dry bread, I will hack off that one remaining arm and feed it to my pigs. Do you hear me?"

Dickon nodded. He was actually trembling with fear.

"But, like our old master Robin, I do not care much for courts of law, and so I will not prosecute you in the manor court, nor the King's court for the theft of my piglets; but I

382

will fine you a shilling to recompense me for my loss. This is my judgment as the lord of this manor, and this is also the agreement between us as former comrades. Do you swear to abide by it?"

He licked his lips and croaked: "I swear it."

"Very well then, you may go." And I watched him lurch to his feet and stumble out of the hall door.

I knew that Marie would be angry that I had let him off with a small fine; and Osric would be very puzzled. But, my master Robin, although now rotting in his grave, would have approved. Dickon had fought bravely with me in the Holy Land; he had suffered with me there, and for forty years after he took his wound he had faithfully tended my pigs here at Westbury, year in, year out, rain or shine. I would never have seen him hanged for a piglet or two; and neither would Robin.

It is simply a matter of loyalty.

HISTORICAL NOTE

The idea that Robin Hood should become a crusader might seem a perverse one, but it made perfect sense to me that an illustrious nobleman, a powerful member of the Anglo-Norman fighting caste, should be involved in one of the greatest bellicose movements of his times—willingly or otherwise. England was gripped by a frenzy of religious fervor before and after King Richard's departure on the Great Pilgrimage, as the Third Crusade was referred to then, and tens of thousands of knights from the Pennines to the Pyrenees, from Brittany to Bavaria, were prepared to risk their lives, their wealth and the security of their families to take part in what must have seemed to them a great and holy adventure. I think it would have been a little bizarre if my fictional Earl of Locksley had not taken part in some way.

It was this religious hysteria that was the main cause of

the shameful and sickening events in York of mid-March 1190. A crowd of armed townsmen, whipped up by a mysterious white-robed monk preaching hatred of the Jews, besieged about a hundred and fifty Jewish men, women and children, who had fled to the King's Tower of York Castle (now called Clifford's Tower) for sanctuary.

After several days of siege fighting, when it became clear that they could not safely surrender to Sir John Marshal, the sheriff of Yorkshire, the Jews, led by Josce of York and Rabbi Yomtob, chose death at their own hands on Saturday March 16th rather than the prospect of being torn apart by a mob of blood-drunk Christians. For an academic but deeply moving account of this appalling event, read *The Jews of Medieval York and the Massacre of March 1190* by R. B. Dobson (University of York).

The faith-crazed townsmen of York were led by, among others, a knight called Sir Richard Malebisse. And while my fictional villain Sir Richard Malbête is obviously based on him, it is important to be clear that they are not the same person. Malebisse was not killed during the Third Crusade and, although disgraced in 1190 by the massacre in York, he returned to prominence after Richard's death in the reign of King John. He is recorded as being given a license to build a castle in Yorkshire in 1199, and dying in 1209 or 1210. I believe there are several of his descendants still around today.

There is no evidence, of course, for the presence of two Christian warriors among the courageous Jewish martyrs of York—or, rather, one Christian and Robin Hood—but it is the novelist's prerogative to place his fictional heroes at the center of any historical catastrophe and have them emerge more or less unscathed.

The real events of the Third Crusade occurred pretty much as I have described them in this book—I took John Gillingham's magisterial *Richard I* (Yale University Press) as the source for most of my information. In the summer of 1190, the main part of Richard's army met up with the French at Véze-lay. They then marched down to Marseilles, sailed to Sicily and over-wintered in Messina, where the crusaders, led by King Richard, and responding to a good deal of provocation from the locals, sacked the town and looted it thoroughly. Relations between Kings Richard and Philip slowly began to deteriorate during that long winter of inactivity, and when King Philip departed for the Holy Land on 30th March, just a day before King Richard's bride Berengaria arrived in Messina, the two monarchs thoroughly distrusted each other. Richard's huge army followed the French ten days later but while Philip was at Acre by 20th April, Richard's fleet was scattered by a great storm near Crete and the ships of his royal women ended up, badly damaged, anchored off Cyprus, where they were denied freshwater and food by the upstart Emperor Isaac Comnenos.

Richard attacked Limassol much as described and drove the Emperor off the beach, smashing through a hastily assembled makeshift barricade with only a few hundred men behind him—the King's small contingent of Welsh archers playing a significant role in the victory. The success of the surprise attack in the olive groves that same night by the ill-mounted Christian knights sealed the Emperor's fate. And he was indeed bound in silver—rather than iron—chains when he finally surrendered to King Richard on 31st May 1191.

After a siege that had lasted nearly two years, Acre fell to the crusaders on 12th July 1191, a month after Richard's triumphant arrival. And while the weary Christian besiegers welcomed Richard's appearance, and the massive reinforcements he brought with him, the King of England's notions of diplomacy often left much to be desired. He alienated the German contingent by kicking their Duke's banner off the ramparts and he further strained relations between himself and King Philip by supporting a rival candidate for the role of King of Jerusalem. When the French and Germans quit the Holy Land, Richard was left weaker—but, importantly, in sole command of the remaining Christian forces.

Richard really did order the cold-blooded execution of 2,700 Muslim prisoners of war—an atrocity that was chronicled by the Norman *trouvère* Ambroise in his *History of the Holy War* (translated from the Latin by Marianne Ailes; published by The Boydell Press)—before leaving Acre and marching south down the Mediterranean coast toward Jaffa (near modern-day Tel Aviv) to threaten Jerusalem. In order to stop his march south, Saladin was forced to confront Richard about fifteen miles north of Jaffa near a small village called Arsuf.

The Battle of Arsuf, on September 7th 1191, was hailed as a victory for King Richard and his armored knights—but it was not a decisive one. Saladin received a mauling that day and withdrew his forces but, in the next weeks and months, he was reinforced by troops from all over the Near East until his army was soon once again at its former strength. But the battle did have a deep impact on the fate of the Third Crusade: as a result of his defeat, Saladin vowed never again to permit his light Turkish cavalry to face the might of the heavy Christian knights in a pitched battle. And this proved to be a war-winning strategy: instead of challenging the knights head-on, and losing again, the great Muslim leader opted for a policy of constant harassment, avoiding a major clash of arms. He let time and distance from home do his work for him. Over the next year, Richard's forces were whittled away in skirmishes and minor sieges, and by death from disease, until it was clear both to the King and to his wily opponent (whom he never actually met) that, while the crusaders just might, with a huge effort, manage to capture Jerusalem, they would be too weak to hold it for long in a hostile environment. They would soon be forced to relinquish the Holy City to the Muslims and all the blood spilled in capturing it would be for nothing. A year after the Battle of Arsuf, after many months of negotiations, a three-year truce was finally agreed upon. Under the agreement, the crusaders were allowed to keep a crucial toehold on the coast of Outremer and Christians were permitted to visit the holy places in Jerusalem and pray there unmolested. Richard, having at least something to show for the Crusade's massive expenditure of treasure and lives, was now free to leave the Holy Land, which he did on October 9th 1192.

What happened to King Richard on the fateful journey home, and the further adventures of Robin, Little John, Alan and their friends, will be told in the next book in the series.

Angus Donald
Kent, January 2010

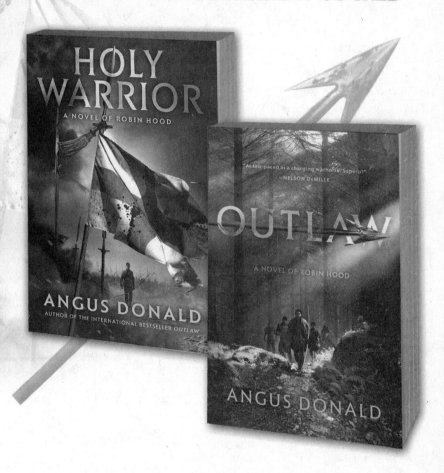